Gettysburg, 1913

The Complete Novel of the Great Reunion

by

Alan Simon

Alan Simon

Gettysburg, 1913: The Complete Novel of the Great Reunion

First Print Publication 2015
First Edition

ISBN: 978-0-9857547-7-8

Originally published as a three-part serialized eBook novel:
Part I (2012)
Part II (2013)
Part III (2014)

PERMISSIONS
Cover photograph credit: United States Library of Congress
Photograph provided by Victoria Heilshorn Studio Historical Art & Imagery – www.victoriaheilshorn.com

Also by Alan Simon

<u>An American Family's Wartime Saga</u>
The First Christmas of the War (2010)
Thanksgiving, 1942 (2012)
The First Christmas After the War (2015)
The First Winter of the New War (coming soon)

Unfinished Business (2010)

Clemente: Memories of a Once-Young Fan – Four Birthdays, Three World Series, Two Holiday Steelers Games, and One Bar Mitzvah (2012 – Nonfiction Memoir)

Visit www.alansimonbooks.com for new releases and book extras

To be notified by email about future books: info@alansimonbooks.com

Visit Alan Simon's blog about the real-life Great Reunion: gettysburg1913.wordpress.com

"But, in a larger sense, we cannot dedicate –
we cannot consecrate – we cannot hallow this
ground. The brave men, living and dead, who
struggled here, have consecrated it far above
our poor power to add or detract."

- President Abraham Lincoln, Gettysburg, November 19,
1863

———

"Whom do I command? The ghostly hosts who fought
upon these battlefields long ago and are gone? These
gallant gentlemen stricken in years whose fighting days are
over, their glory won?"

- President Woodrow Wilson, Gettysburg, July 4, 1913

———

"Surely never before in the world's history
have so great a number of men so advanced in
years been assembled under field conditions."

- Lieutenant Colonel A.E. Bradley, U.S. Army
Chief Surgeon, October 24, 1913

Prologue

May 1, 1912

In his dream, Doctor Samuel Chambers was no longer in the present day of 1912 but rather in the long-ago year of 1863. July the third, specifically. He was seated in a grassy meadow near the borough of Gettysburg, Pennsylvania, across from a lovely young woman. Both of them were dressed in the attire of the day; a wicker picnic basket rested between them.

The woods of Seminary Ridge were half a mile distant in one direction; Cemetery Ridge was one half mile away in the other. Samuel's attention shifted between watching the sweetly smiling woman unpack the basket – boiled eggs, roast turkey and bread, cherry pie, iced lemonade – and looking in one direction and then the other, thinking about the more than ten thousand Confederates massed on Seminary Ridge and thousands more Yankees awaiting their assault over on Cemetery Ridge.

The time was fifteen minutes past twelve noon. The temperature was close to ninety degrees and the mid-day stickiness enveloped Samuel with perspiration underneath the bright sunshine; the woman also. Neither seemed to mind, though, nor did either one give much thought to the soldiers massed on either side of them. Samuel had learned enough about the Battle of Gettysburg in the course of his responsibilities for next year's Great Reunion that he knew within the hour the Confederate artillery would open fire against the Yankees, a barrage that would last for more than one hour. Somewhere around two o'clock more than twelve thousand Confederates would begin their march into history, many of them treading right over the ground where Samuel and this woman were beginning to enjoy their picnic. For now, though, the air was still and the ground untrampled. Carnage and death would come soon enough; tranquility was the sentiment of the moment.

Samuel turned his attention back to the young woman, gazing intently at her smiling face that was partly shadowed by her bonnet. My Lord, he thought to himself; she's beautiful! Even more pleasing to Samuel was that in the world of his dreams this woman was rapidly falling in love with him, and would soon fill the void in that part of his life.

Dream-time passed in a flash as it so often does. The first boom of Rebel cannon shattered the stillness. Neither Samuel nor the woman showed any concern; they both remained seated on the grass, smiling lovingly at one another as another boom came, and then another.

Samuel wondered even as he continued to gaze at her: who was she?

Chapter 1

May 10, 1912

"Pop?"

Chester Morrison had almost dozed off; the sound of his son's voice snapped the aging man fully awake. His tired eyes squinted at the nearly empty tumbler of Old Charter clutched tightly in his right hand and resting on his lap, and then up at his son. Even wearing his spectacles his son's face was blurry; unfocused. Ah, the continuing ravages of my advancing years, Chester thought to himself for perhaps the fifth or sixth time this very evening, much as he did every evening after the workday had ended.

Seeing his father jolt, Jonathan Morrison continued.

"Did you see this?" he said as he leaned forward from his spot on the sofa opposite his father's easy chair, his left arm extended, hand clutching this evening's edition of *The Philadelphia Evening Telegraph*. He remained stationary as his father seemed to take an extra second or two to react and reach for the newspaper. Almost identical to the older man's own thoughts a brief moment earlier, the younger man fretted that the accumulating passage of time was increasingly taking a toll on his father as the age of 70 approached.

Chester took the paper from his son and squinted again as he scanned for whatever it might be that his son apparently wanted him to read. Jonathan was just about to lean even further forward to point out the specific editorial when the old man's eyes landed on the column.

"The Gettysburg Celebration"

The decision of the United Confederate Veterans at their Reunion, to accept the invitation extended through the Grand Army of the Republic, to attend the celebration of the fiftieth anniversary of the battle of Gettysburg on the noted field in July, 1913, is what would be expected of the chivalrous men who upheld the cause of the South in the crucible era.

Upon finishing that lengthy first sentence of the editorial, Chester Morrison raised his head from the *Telegraph* and looked at his son who was peering intently back at his father, studying the old man's face as he read. Chester's gaze remained locked on his son, as if wary – perhaps even afraid – to resume reading the editorial. Finally, he lowered his head again but instead of picking up where he had left off his eyes lit upon a passage farther down the page.

They are passing away very rapidly, those actors in the great drama, both

North and South. For forty-nine years the grass has covered with its beautiful green those long rows of impressive mounds, beneath which the Northern and Southern soldiers have slept after giving their 'last full measure of devotion' to the cause which each believed to be right. Their comrades, the venerable men of today, both North and South, owe it to the memory of those long-departed to avail themselves of the occasion offered next July a year to revisit the scene of that mighty struggle.

Chester Morrison's eyes scanned the rest of the editorial but he only half-absorbed the remaining words. His thoughts had taken flight, instantly traversing some 120 miles of southeastern Pennsylvania villages and farmland and coming to rest in that small borough just north of the Maryland state line. Not unexpectedly, Chester's thoughts negotiated time as well as space, as if they were being carried along by the time machine from Mr. Wells' sensationally popular story. The images, one after another, that clocked before him were no longer of the present day.

The Mind's Eye.

*　　*　　*

Chester Morrison was a Titan of Industry. He had been instrumental in steering Baldwin Locomotive through lean years as well as bountiful ones. He had fearlessly rallied the company after the Panic of 1893 to help lead the industrial giant to new heights of prosperity as the railroad industry embarked on its next wave of expansion with the conclusion of the 19th century and the beginning of the next. Then, when the Panic of 1907 came but this time Baldwin's fortunes began to erode along with those of the railroad industry as a whole, Chester Morrison steeled himself and his comrades to make the unpleasant but necessary cutbacks to keep the company viable. The old man had been ready to retire, his sixty-second year having arrived, but instead he faithfully went into his office each morning at precisely 8:30 and worked until long into the evening, steadfastly and valiantly confronting and then vanquishing one problem after another.

The Panic eventually passed and even though the company had had to adjust to a new reality with its fortunes and aspirations nicked here and there, Chester Morrison began to prepare for his delayed retirement from the firm, his intention being to travel much of the world by ocean liner and luxury railway car with his wife Sadie. For several years they planned to be among the wealthy elite who would cross the Atlantic on the maiden voyage of that behemoth liner being built over in Belfast, and as the date in early 1912 grew closer they finalized arrangements to cross the Atlantic in mid-November of 1911 on the RMS Mauretania; spend Christmas, the New Year holiday, and the winter in London and Paris; and finally travel back to America on the Titanic when it set sail.

Sadie's sudden death from influenza in October of 1911, less than a month before their Europe-bound voyage would have begun, was devastating to Chester Morrison but he faced this tragedy with the same resolve and steadfastness with which he had faced Baldwin Locomotive's difficulties in business: like a man, accepting what the fates had cast his way and bravely looking forward, not backwards. After the terrible news of the Titanic's tragic sinking less than one month prior to this very evening, Chester thought to himself with absolute certainty that if his beloved Sadie hadn't passed away and if they had indeed been on that ship when it had collided with that iceberg, he would have courageously faced the end of his days in those last fateful moments just as Guggenheim and Astor, two men Morrison knew in passing from business dealings, were alleged to have done…hopefully after seeing Sadie safely onto one of the lifeboats so she would be spared the icy grave.

In the months that followed his wife's passing, Chester Morrison relinquished thoughts of imminent retirement from Baldwin Locomotive. Workdays filled with planning for the company's future interwoven with the mundane routine of modern business life helped dull the sensation of his loss. Plus the presence of his eldest son Jonathan, now 46 years of age and senior-most among Baldwin's next generation of leaders, as his lieutenant and chief confidant throughout each workday helped both men cope with the absence of Sadie Morrison that they were still getting used to.

During those same months Chester Morrison also began spending nearly every evening at his eldest son's stately Main Line residence, a mile away from his own manor. It was his daughter-in-law Anna – Jonathan's wife – who had suggested that Chester begin staying through the night with them a few days before the first Christmas without Sadie arrived and to continue to do so through the New Year. None of the three of them could recall how the arrangement had become permanent but by the time April of 1912 came around, Chester had sold the house where he and Sadie had raised Jonathan, his four brothers and three sisters as well, to one of those "new money" industrialists who had quickly become wealthy from manufacturing chassis parts for the motorized passenger automobiles that everyone wanted these days.

Since then, before retiring most evenings Chester and his son Jonathan spent a final hour playing a game of chess, conversation about the looming presidential election interwoven with move and counter-move. Both men favored the reelection of President Taft but feared the near-certain reemergence of former President Roosevelt as a Progressive candidate would divide the Republicans enough to hand the election to Woodrow Wilson, the unpredictable Governor from neighboring New Jersey. What a Wilson Presidency would mean for Baldwin Locomotive neither could say with certainty, but both sensed that more days of fearlessly navigating through adversity lay ahead.

The tenth chime coming from the hallway grandfather clock signaled Jonathan that his father's just-concluded move would be the last of the evening, and after saying goodnight to the old man he headed up the stairs to join Anna in their bedroom, leaving his father alone in the drawing room with his thoughts. A moment later Chester refilled his tumbler of Old Charter once more, staring at the bottle as he did. "Ask any Colonel" the bourbon maker's slogan went and the allusion to a military rank suddenly and unwillingly dragged the old man's thoughts back to the time and place he had deliberately tried to shut out for the past hour. Chester Morrison had indeed been a Colonel once, having attained that rank two months before that climactic day at Appomattox Courthouse that brought those terrible years of war to an end. Twenty-two months earlier, however, he had been a green private, about to face battle for the first time...

Ask any Colonel. Chester Morrison contemplated that slogan, its words, though he didn't need to give the underlying sentiment much thought. One could indeed ask any Colonel – Colonel Chester Morrison of the Army of the Potomac, perhaps – and the answer would undoubtedly be that no amount of Old Charter bourbon could burn away the terror of those three horrific days at the beginning of July, 1863.

That night Chester Morrison succumbed to dream after dream; nightmare after nightmare. He was back with the 69th Pennsylvania, frantically repelling the furious Confederate attack on Cemetery Ridge on the second of July and then even greater fury and horror the following day as Pickett and the other Rebel generals made their famous, fateful charge; two days of battle in which more than half of the 69th's men became casualties. Nightmare after nightmare; attack after attack; long-buried memories of actual events during those terrible days intermingling with inventions of Chester Morrison's vivid imagination to the point where in any given dream sequence that night, Chester knew not whether he would survive miraculously unscathed as he had in reality or instead fall in searing agony from a Minie ball or after being run through by a Rebel bayonet.

Chester Morrison – Titan of Industry, for years stoically courageous in the face of industrial adversity as well as personal tragedy – awoke in the dark sometime around 3:00 in the morning, weeping as a baby might, and forced himself to remain awake until the approaching light of dawn offered the safe harbor free from falling back into another unwilling, helpless journey of the mind back to those fateful and horrific days that had long since been cordoned off with other troubling or terrifying memories from his past.

For nearly fifty years, even in the midst and immediate aftermath of other battles during that terrible war against once and future countrymen, no terror had come close to scarring the mind of Chester Morrison as those first three days of July, 1963 had done. As memories of the war faded with the passing years and his ever-increasing responsibilities at the service of Baldwin Locomotive became uppermost in his thoughts, Chester Morrison had been able to think about and even share a smattering of tales from later clashes with the Rebels he had experienced as he advanced through the ranks of the 69th: Spotsylvania, Petersburg, Appomattox.

But he never spoke of Gettysburg. Not to fellow businessmen; not to Sadie, nor to Jonathan nor Wilbur nor Mildred nor any of his other children. Not to his grandsons when they eagerly asked him about that long-ago war that Grandpa had fought in. (Other than one time; a hesitant, quiet "Yes, I was there" response once to Jonathan's oldest boy years earlier when asked if he had been at Gettysburg during those fateful days before the youngster had been shooed away, an apologetic look on Jonathan's face as he did so.)

That morning as he groggily carried his coffee onto the front porch of his son's Main Line home, the first glints of light to the east foretelling dawn's imminent arrival, the aging man thought about what he had seen in yesterday's *Evening Telegraph*; specifically, the one passage that read "Their comrades, the venerable men of today, both North and South, owe it to the memory of those long-departed to avail themselves of the occasion offered next July a year to revisit the scene of that mighty struggle."

A glorious springtime sun slowly eased its way into the eastern sky as Chester Morrison reflected. Why was he feeling as he did? The Blue and Gray sides had met at

Gettysburg before, including a commemoration of the 25ᵗʰ anniversary of the battle back in 1888. On two additional occasions – a year earlier in '87 and then only several years ago, in 1906 – veterans of the Philadelphia Brigade, of which Morrison's own 69ᵗʰ Pennsylvania was part, had come together on the old battlefield with former enemies who long before had served directly under General Pickett.

He hadn't attended a single one of these commemorations but neither had Chester Morrison found himself shivering and weeping when learning of those earlier occasions. And given his stature among the elite of Pennsylvania businessmen, Morrison had certainly been aware of the intent of this upcoming grand event for several years now. Chester Morrison had certainly felt a few shivers when learning of the idea for a massive Great Reunion that would be attended by perhaps tens of thousands, but had been so intently focused on rescuing Baldwin Locomotive in the immediate aftermath of the Panic of 1907 that he simply refused to give the memory of those terrifying long-ago days or the ideas of a commemorative reunion more than a second or two of consideration whenever they tried to force their way into his conscious thought.

Then there had been the preparation for his retirement and the subsequent voyages with Sadie that, alas, were not to be, but in the meantime were uppermost in his thoughts, crowding out memories of Gettysburg and the prospects of that 50ᵗʰ anniversary commemoration that was slowly unfolding. And then Sadie's sudden passing and the months that followed; and then the sudden sinking of the ocean liner they were to have been on, news that stunned the world…

When his son Jonathan handed him the *Evening Telegraph* hours earlier, though, and when Chester Morrison drank in the words from that column, all of his past defenses against the reliving of that terror suddenly crumbled away. And as the sun continued its ascent this fine May morning, the old man could only conclude that not having his beloved wife to lean on for that "last full measure" of strength had allowed the terrible memories to finally breach the walls of his defenses. And so the knowledge came to Chester Morrison – husband and father, Titan of Industry, long-ago soldier – that his steadfast courage over the years had been due at least in part to his devoted Sadie being unfailingly by his side.

But now he felt better; cleansed; at peace, even. It was as if finally allowing that terrifying concoction of memory and horrific fantasy to envelop his mind, nightmare after nightmare, had also convinced himself that that particular horror was indeed nearly half a century in the past, never to be relived. Perhaps it was time, Chester Morrison thought as he rose to stroll back into the house to prepare for the day's work, to comply with the urgings of the *Evening Telegraph* and others that when "next July a year" arrived a pilgrimage to the old battlefield to "revisit the scene of that mighty struggle" might well be his duty.

Chapter 2

January 7, 1913

Samuel Chambers was worried.

He looked again at the dispatch from Governor Tener's office he had received earlier that day, his eyes again focusing on the two sentences it contained:

"We now expect more than 40,000 veterans to attend the commemoration, and perhaps as many as 50,000. Hospital and aid facilities shall be adjusted accordingly."

Forty thousand, maybe even fifty thousand old men outdoors for days under what could well be a blazing July sun and temperatures in the 90s! That would be a fine way to commemorate the 50th anniversary of the battle, Chambers thought; to have hundreds, maybe even thousands of old men survive for fifty years after that horrible war only to die from exposure to Pennsylvania's suffocating mid-summer heat and humidity!

Chambers glanced at the window nearest to the wingback chair in which he sat, his eyes drawn to the swirling snow and the frigid temperatures outside. For a brief moment Chambers felt foolish fretting about soaring summertime temperatures and stifling humidity. Samuel felt a sudden, shivering chill at the thought of walking even the four and a half blocks from The Union League to his brownstone through what was shaping up to be the first nasty snowfall of the new year, and made a mental note to ask the doorman to hail him a carriage a half hour before he planned to depart.

But frigid cold and blustery snowfall was the here and now; relentless heat and humidity and blazing sunshine was highly probable, perhaps even inevitable, less than six months from now since Gettysburg's summertime weather was often as oppressive as Philadelphia's.

Why couldn't the commemoration have been set to another season of the year? Back in '06 the Philadelphia Brigade and Pickett's Division had come together on the old battlefield but had done so in early September, after the worst of summer had passed. Many of those men who were still alive would also attend this Grand Reunion but were closing in on yet another decade of age, and they would be joined by tens of thousands of others who were also far closer to the grave than the cradle. While there was certainly historical symmetry in having these men come together exactly fifty years after the three days in which that famed battle had occurred, Chambers couldn't shake the feeling that the quest for historical symmetry would come at a terrible cost.

He wasn't the only one who felt trepidation about what might happen if the worst of south-central Pennsylvania's summertime weather insisted on appearing, but Samuel Chambers had special cause for his perpetual anxiety. He was the man assigned by the Commonwealth of Pennsylvania's Commissioner of Health to be responsible for coordinating the field hospital facilities, doctors, Red Cross nurses, additional hospital facilities…all of it fell to Chambers personally to have in working order.

It wasn't only the 40,000 or more elderly Civil War veterans who would be exposed to the elements, either. Thousands of visitors from all over were expected to flood the tiny borough for the festivities, bringing the total of people who might potentially need medical care to over 100,000!

What a folly, Chambers thought to himself yet again as he eyed the snifter in his left hand, empty now save for a small pooling of Hennessey resting at the bottom, and contemplated another. Most evenings at the Union League, no matter the season, were spent as this one was: sipping Hennessey or, on occasion, a vintage port (1873 W. & J. Graham being his preference) and conversing with other Philadelphia gentlemen about important matters of commerce or society just read in a freshly inked *Evening Telegraph*, or the events of one another's professions that held relevance for other members of the Club.

His worries also drew his attention to this very building itself and the irony that he, like several other members in good standing of the Union League, were among the handful of men on whose shoulders the success or failure of this majestic event had been placed. The stately French Renaissance-style building had originally been scheduled to open in March of 1865 with President Lincoln himself present, but the delay of barely two months had of course allowed the assassin's bullet to intervene in the days following the end of that terrible war. To Samuel Chambers, this building – not to mention the Union League itself – emitted a broad-sweeping, immutable aura of what remained of the United States during that conflict given the League's founding in 1862 as a vehicle to fervently support the efforts of the President, the Northern States, and the Union Army to reunite the divided nation…which of course was the outcome of the war and the years of Reconstruction that followed.

Samuel's father Edwin Chambers, among the elite of Philadelphia's medical establishment, was a long-time acquaintance of General Henry Shippen Huidekoper, the city's former Postmaster who had not only served with the 150th Pennsylvania Infantry at Gettysburg but who was twice wounded in that battle. His wounds on that first day of the clash with Lee's forces were so severe that he eventually had to have his right arm amputated. Nonetheless, Huidekoper had remained in command of his regiment even after suffering his wounds and had been awarded the Medal of Honor for his bravery.

Back in 1908, sensing the approaching 50th anniversary of that titanic, tide-turning struggle, Huidekoper suggested to Pennsylvania's Governor Edwin Stuart that a reunion of Blue and Gray far greater than any prior one, at Gettysburg or elsewhere, be held. The commemoration of the Battle of Gettysburg would be the central focus but veterans from both sides would be invited, whether or not they had fought during those three days in early July of 1863. Stuart, in turn, presented the idea to Pennsylvania's General Assembly early the following year and was rewarded with the creation of the *Fiftieth Anniversary of the Battle of Gettysburg Commission*. With four years to plan this magnificent, monumental event like none before in American history – perhaps like none before in the history of the world – the men charged with this task under the leadership of Governor Stuart and then his successor Governor Tener began mustering forces from all corners of Pennsylvania to bring General Huidekoper's vision to fruition.

Acquaintances were tapped and favors called in by many who themselves wanted to be part of the planning effort or who, like Samuel Chambers' father, saw the opportunity to rub shoulders with Pennsylvania's elite as steppingstones for their sons towards influence and position for years to come. Chambers' father contacted the aging General who in turn put young Samuel in touch with Governor Stuart's office…who in turn referred him to the Commonwealth's Department of Health.

Samuel Chambers' own stature as one of Philadelphia's new cadre of skilled and respected surgeons made him the ideal candidate for a key role in helping to establish and then operate the medical facilities that would be so necessary for the Great Reunion. After all, plans called for these aging veterans to be housed in tents not unlike those many had occupied fifty years earlier! Samuel became the trusted confidante of Doctor Malcolm Waterston, the contemporary of Samuel's father who was in command of the forces establishing the field hospitals and other facilities. By the time April of 1912 had come around with but a year and a quarter left until the occasion, Samuel Chambers was officially second in command to Waterston.

When Waterston died suddenly the previous October, there was little question that despite his tender age of thirty the logical successor to take command of the medical preparations was young Samuel Chambers himself with less than nine months remaining until the Great Reunion.

Initially petrified at his new responsibilities, the young doctor mustered his strength during the remaining months of 1912 and by the time the new year had arrived Chambers found himself fully immersed in both sweeping panorama and minute detail of the medical preparations; his nervousness had subsided, at least for a short while. The collection of field hospitals, comfort stations, aid stations, and other facilities originally put in place by his predecessor Doctor Waterston and which would be completed after spring arrived several months from now had mostly put his mind at ease, worries about soaring temperatures and humidity notwithstanding.

But with this dispatch from the Governor's office, the uneasiness from back in October upon learning of Waterston's passing and his own ascent into that man's role had now suddenly returned in full force. He decided he would indeed require another Hennessey while his mind went to work recalculating so much of what Samuel Chambers thought had been settled, but which apparently needed to be reconsidered and replanned with even greater care than before.

Chapter 3

January 24, 1913

"So what do you think?"

Edgar Sullivan glanced across the table at his brother, but said nothing in reply. He simply rocked back in his chair, looked again at the cards in his hand – the two black aces being the ones he focused on, of course – and then at the nearly empty glass of rye whiskey. As he did nearly every time he drank Old Overholt (which was most days) he thought of Doc Holliday, dead 25 years now. Holliday drank his share of Old Overholt and had introduced Edgar and his younger brother Johnny to the drink during those long-ago days down in Tombstone.

"Well?" Johnny Sullivan was growing impatient with his brother's silence, and the irritation in his voice was apparent to the other three men gathered at the poker table in the lobby of the Windsor Hotel in the downtown section of Tucson, Arizona.

"You asking about that Gettysburg thing again?" Gerald McLoughlin asked the younger Sullivan brother, who in turn shot back an exasperated look.

"You know I am," Johnny growled before looking back at his older brother. "Ain't I been asking about that all morning? If we're gonna go we gotta let the train folks know so we can get our places and it won't cost us nothin'."

Still no response from the elder Sullivan who instead took his last swig of Old Overholt and contemplated a refill, even though noon was still more than an hour away.

Talk of Gettysburg; remembrances of the war; flashbacks to those days in Tombstone when fisticuffs or even gunplay might be but a flash away at any moment…a man looking at 75 years of age in less than three weeks surely didn't need these thoughts and images rattling around his head if he wanted to ease his way towards that final reckoning with days filled with the peace and quiet of rye whiskey and poker and little else.

Sensing his younger brother was about to badger him yet again, Edgar Sullivan looked over to Sean Connolly, another of the Irishmen gathered for their ritual morning poker game, and asked:

"What would you do? Would you travel all the way back across the country on a train for three or four days and then spend the better part of a week with a bunch of Johnny Rebs who tried to kill you fifty years ago?"

Sensing that Edgar was trying to pull him into the middle of a simmering feud between the two Sullivan brothers, Connolly hesitated before attempting an answer. To his immense relief Johnny Sullivan interrupted Sean Connolly just as he was beginning to stammer out a response.

"He doesn't know anythin' 'bout this," Johnny Sullivan growled to his brother. "He wasn't even born when the war was goin' on; wasn't born for, what, another two years after the end, right?"

He looked over at Connolly, who nodded. Sean Connolly was indeed the youngest of the five men, just now 45 years old. A hardware merchant with his store two blocks down the street from the Windsor, Connolly fell in with these fellow Irishmen – all five had been born in this country shortly after their respective parents had crossed the ocean, escaping one famine or another – and was enthralled by the tales they told. Both of the Sullivans had been associates of the Earp brothers down in Tombstone and told tales of the tense days leading up to O.K. Corral and the aftermath of that gunfight that, as time marched on, was becoming something of legend for those who longed for the now-gone days of the Old West. And the story went – at least according to both brothers – that if it they hadn't been up here in Tucson that fateful day in 1881 escorting a Kinnear & Company stagecoach and its bags of coins and paper money, they both instead would have been in that lot near the O.K. Corral, guns drawn alongside the Earps and Doc Holliday as they faced off against the Clantons and McLaurys. As it was, both of the Sullivans rode with Wyatt Earp on his Vendetta Ride a few months later hunting down those who had murdered one of his brothers and shot another, and they told many stories of their days with mustachioed lawman of legend. The day back in 1910 that Edgar Sullivan brought with him a just-received letter from Wyatt Earp himself, written in the days soon after Earp moved to Los Angeles and suggesting that the Sullivan brothers pay him a visit, was one that Sean Connolly would never forget.

During the war both of the Sullivans had served in the Union Army in General John Buford's famed cavalry division, specifically in the 8th Regiment Illinois Cavalry; not just at Gettysburg but also earlier at Antietam and Fredericksburg. It had been that Illinois connection that put them into the confidence of the Earps even before they moved down to Tombstone. Up in Prescott in 1878 they began regularly playing cards with Virgil Earp, the town's constable and a veteran of the 83rd Illinois Infantry during the war, and the war veterans from the same home state took a shine to one another. Both Sullivans began assisting Earp with escorting stagecoaches and other lawman matters, and a year later when Virgil headed down to Tombstone to join his brothers Wyatt and James in that silver boomtown, the Sullivans weren't far behind.

Johnny Sullivan in particular – in the past frequently joined by his seven-years-senior brother Edgar, though not so much in recent years – filled a great many hour of card-playing by telling one tale after another of the now-vanished times of the Old West to Sean Connolly, Gerald McLoughlin, Patrick O'Connor, and whomever else might be sitting with them on a given day. Slightly less than a year earlier Arizona had ceased being a United States Territory and had become the 48th and final state on the continent, and it seemed to most of these men that achieving statehood had also been the final death knell of the Arizona Territory days of the Earps and Doc Holliday; feared gunfighters such as Johnny Ringo; and Indians such as Geronimo, dead almost four years now, or his long-gone Apache predecessor Cochise. A new era was upon them all, one that was now hallmarked by mechanical automobiles, telephones, and moving picture shows rather than stagecoaches, silver boomtowns and saloons (and saloon girls). The turn of the century thirteen years earlier might have been the start of this metamorphosis, or perhaps the point at which the transition from old to new accelerated, but Arizona's statehood in February of 1912 seemed to be the definitive moment that signified the old days were indeed gone forever.

It was the stories of the Civil War and, in particular, those three days at Gettysburg told by the Sullivans – Johnny mostly – that captivated the imagination of Sean Connolly. They had ridden into the borough on June 30th with Buford's First Division when the General realized that untold thousands of Confederates were converging on the area, and in response urgently began to prepare the Union defenses as they awaited reinforcements. Thus the Sullivan brothers were among the first participants in that epic battle, in place from the moment the first shots were fired...

"Fine, we'll go," Edgar Sullivan said suddenly, raising his eyes from his cards to gaze across at his brother. Connolly, O'Connor, and McLoughlin all looked over in unison at the elder Sullivan, expecting him to follow up his acquiescence with more words, but none were forthcoming. In unison again seven or eight seconds later they all turned their heads towards Johnny Sullivan, who looked at each of them in turn and then at his older brother. But Johnny was also silent, simply nodding his head a couple of times with what the other men took as gratitude for his brother agreeing to something that he so obviously did not want to do.

Looking back over his left shoulder and catching the eye of the bartender, Johnny Sullivan called out, "Another Old Overholt for my brother!" as he contemplated the favorite rye whiskey of not only their old acquaintance Doc Holliday but also Abraham Lincoln himself, who long ago had felt compelled to make the journey to Gettysburg much as the Sullivans would soon do.

* * *

"Are you sure going is a good idea?" Mabel Tomlinson asked her husband Ned, her eyes involuntarily traveling from the elderly man's face to the pinned, empty left pant leg she had observed perhaps ten thousand times over the past fifty years. Though phrased as a question, the old soldier knew for a fact his wife was clearly stating her opinion in opposition to his intentions.

"Why not?" came the reply in Ned Tomlinson's raspy voice, that ever-present cough infiltrating even a two-word answer. "I haven't missed one yet…"

"But you were there seven years ago," his wife interrupted. "Isn't that enough? Isn't it time to put that war to rest once and for all?"

Her husband was about to reply but the old woman wasn't to be deterred.

"You keep going to your meetings down at the UCV hall, that's fine," she continued. "But you're not…" – she hesitated for a moment, before deciding she had to continue – "…well enough to travel all the way up to Pennsylvania and live in a tent for three or four days!" She couldn't help it now, surrendering to the irritation with her husband's insistence for months now that he would indeed join his fellow United Confederate Veterans comrades from Norfolk on this trek back to the battlefield that had hallmarked each one's life. Every time she had broached the subject the stubborn old man had dismissed his wife's concerns for his health and well being as the poppycock of a nagging wife who simply couldn't understand what might drive a man to return to a place that held such significance in his life despite the horrors that had occurred there. Whatever fragments might still remain of Ned Tomlinson's left leg were plowed into the ground somewhere on that battlefield; his very soul, it seemed, was still held captive by that field of battle and what had occurred there during those three days…especially on the final day as he mustered his courage for that march across three quarters of a mile of open field into the volley of rifle and artillery fire along with more than 12,000 of his Confederate brothers in arms.

One of thousands of Rebels taken prisoner, many of them wounded as Corporal Ned Tomlinson had been, he had been taken to the Yankee prison at Fort Delaware, where he remained for almost two more years until Lee's surrender. The Yankee surgeon in the field hospital at Gettysburg had done a fair enough job finishing off the amputation of his left leg that the artillery shell had begun, and by the time disease after disease ran through the ranks of the Fort Delaware prisoners and guards alike, Ned Tomlinson was strong enough to stave off scurvy, smallpox, typhoid fever, malaria, and the other ills that took their toll on those within the grounds of the Fort – even the Yankee guards.

On his long journey home to Norfolk, Tomlinson encountered hundreds of now-former Rebels who had also fought at Gettysburg, many of them also survivors of Pickett's Charge. Some had made it through that final day of battle miraculously unscathed, or wounded only lightly and able to continue fighting for the Confederate cause in later battles of the war. Others had been more severely wounded but were able to recover from their wounds and rejoin The Cause later in '63 or '64. Ned Tomlinson felt an overpowering sense of camaraderie with these veterans, perhaps even more so than those with whom he had gone into battle at Gettysburg. Many who had previously been friends and comrades of Corporal Tomlinson and who began marching into history at 2:00 that fateful afternoon of July 3rd had been killed before the sun set that day. Many of the other survivors of Gettysburg who joined Ned in the Yankee prison at Fort Delaware had died before the end of the war from one disease or another. But these other survivors whom Ned Tomlinson encountered during his journey back home told much the same tale that Ned did, especially those who wound up in some other Yankee prison fort war after some other battle later in the war.

Many were missing limbs or carried disfigured faces. All had marched into hell and had somehow survived with their lives.

Ned began going to meetings of former Confederates in Norfolk almost immediately after returning home to what remained of his small farm. He attended the 25th anniversary commemoration at Gettysburg back in '88 along with both of the reunions of Pickett's Division and the Yankee's Philadelphia Brigade. When the United Confederate Veterans formed a national organization in 1889, Ned was among the first to join and attended many of the national reunions beginning with Chattanooga in 1890, then New Orleans and Birmingham and…

Mabel's continued protest interrupted his thoughts.

"They say it's going to be more than ninety degrees there the whole time," she began but then he interrupted her.

"Well it was close to ninety when we made the charge, and we walked a whole lot farther that afternoon than we will during the commemoration…"

"You were fifty years younger!" Mabel interrupted back, now becoming irritated at her husband's irrational stubbornness. She almost added "You also had both your legs when you started out on that fool's errand, marching straight into the Yankee guns!" but knew she would get nowhere with such an utterance.

Ned Tomlinson just shook his head and turned away from his wife, looking out to the snow-dusted fields where, in three months time, he would plant his next crop of cotton. (In recent years, every April or May as he planted Ned Tomlinson found himself wondering – though he never shared these thoughts with Mabel – if this would be the last year he would do so before the Good Lord called him home.) They were standing on the back porch of their aging but still immaculate-looking clapboard home as they discussed the merits, or lack thereof, of Ned Tomlinson attending the commemoration at Gettysburg. Though he would never acknowledge as such to Mabel, he knew her fears for his ability to withstand days of oppressive summer Pennsylvania heat were valid. Norfolk summers annually took their toll on him, and every crop season he felt a little bit weaker and moved a little bit slower than the year before. If he left aside the purpose of spending those upcoming days in Gettysburg, the idea of spending more than half a week exposed to the elements by day and then sheltered only by a tent at night was indeed foolish. Lined up by the hundreds for meals from a field kitchen; using field latrines for bodily necessities…

Yet beyond the discomfort and even hazards Ned Tomlinson felt an overpowering sense that this particular commemoration and reunion would eclipse any of the others he had previously attended, including the earlier three at Gettysburg. Only days earlier General Walker, the present national commander of the UCV, communicated to the many local UCV chapters the organization's acceptance of the formal invitation to the commemoration, his communiqué bearing the words:

> Your commander feels that the time has come, when, by invitation of our one-time foes, we can united with them in celebrating that permanent peace, which we pray may forever bless this our great and glorious country. Not the country for which we fought, but that which has arisen from the ashes of that great

revolution and the country in which
we have our homes and firesides and
that country which we will teach our
children ever to love, maintain, and
be proud of.

General Walker's words in his communiqué followed his
statement that both the Chief Justice of the Supreme Court
and the President of the United States would participate in
ceremonies laying the cornerstone of a peace memorial,
and Ned Tomlinson was enveloped by an overwhelmingly
strong sense of obligation to be there to witness these
events in person.

He looked back from his flurry-covered fields towards
his wife – like Ned himself, Mabel was now seventy years
of age, grayed and stooped, yet still carrying the spryness of
someone who has worked hard for a lifetime and built up a
reserve of vigor as energy for her advanced years – and
uttered more quietly and tenderly than Ned would
normally say to her:

"Just this one last time; I need to go there, and I
promise I will take care of myself."

Knowing that her husband's mind was made up, Mabel
Tomlinson offered only a quick nod of surrender before
turning and walking wordlessly back into the house they
had shared for nearly 47 years since her marriage in the
springtime of '66 to the former Confederate infantryman
who, despite missing his left leg, was everything she had
wanted in a husband.

*   *   *

Philip Roberdeau eased himself into the wicker chair on the front porch of his Dumaine Street home in the New Orleans French Quarter. The day was chilly, a hair below the fifty degree mark, but the fresh air and mid-winter crispness felt invigorating to the 73-year old man. One of the benefits of living in New Orleans, he had always thought, was the generally mild winter temperatures, which more than made up for the oppressive heat and humidity during the summer.

He carefully unfolded the brittle old newspaper page he had carried out of the house with him. It had now been more than two years since he last had gazed upon the fading newsprint because in recent years he took care not to handle the piece of paper too frequently, lest it crumble away just as the event it described had done.

IT'S AGAIN A TENTED FIELD: SICKLES AND LONGSTREET AT GETTYSBURG, the headline read, datelined July 1st, 1888. Even though it was a Yankee paper – *The New York Times* – that had printed the story, Roberdeau treasured this single article more than any other he had clipped and saved from any other newspaper, including the *Times-Picayune* that he read daily to learn of hometown New Orleans occurrences.

Sunday, July 1st, 1888: exactly 25 years to the day after the beginning of the Battle of Gettysburg. Some long-forgotten *Times* reporter had been posted to Gettysburg for the 25th anniversary commemoration and filed his story that described how the famed Confederate General James Longstreet had met with and warmly greeted one of the Yankee generals who had been on the opposing side during that famed battle.

Back in '88 General Longstreet had still been alive and not only attended the commemoration, he had been its star attraction. Roberdeau had been among the three hundred or so former Confederates who had attended and personally witnessed Longstreet's meeting with General Sickles of New York, watching the old Confederate general spot the Yankee and, after offering his war-casualty right hand to Sickles, wrap his arm around his former adversary in a gesture of friendship. This moment had been faithfully reported in the article.

What wasn't reported in the article – and there was no reason it should have been – was that a moment earlier Longstreet had been engaged in conversation with Philip himself. The two men, after recognizing each other, had been reminiscing not only those days at Gettysburg but also how Roberdeau had been at Longstreet's side in New Orleans during the Battle of Liberty Place more than two decades later when the old General, then the Adjutant General of the State Militia, had been shot, captured by the Crescent City White League, and held prisoner with Philip and several others until – irony of ironies – they were rescued days later by Yankee troops.

The memories began materializing right in front of Philip's tired eyes; marching in a precise cadence, one behind another, as if those memories were personified as young and energetic West Point cadets as Philip himself had once been.

Philip Roberdeau of Louisiana had been a First Classman – a Senior, half a year away from graduation and commissioning – at the United States Military Academy on November 6, 1860, the day Abraham Lincoln was elected President of the United States. By the beginning of February, 1861, Roberdeau had withdrawn from West Point and was headed back home to New Orleans on the same steamship as P. G. T. Beauregard, his former West Point Superintendent (for all of five days before the

Southerner Beauregard had been dismissed amidst the drumbeat of impending civil war) who was soon to achieve fame at Fort Sumter, Manassas, and Shiloh. For his part, Roberdeau's West Point experience, despite being cut short because of secession, gained him an appointment as a First Lieutenant in Beauregard's new Confederate Army of the Potomac where he saw action against the Yankees at First Manassas.

When General Beauregard became second in command of The Army of the Mississippi in early 1862, Philip Roberdeau remained with Beauregard's now-former army —renamed as the First Corps of the Army of Northern Virginia and now under the command of Lieutenant General Longstreet. For the next two years, Roberdeau engaged in one clash with the Union forces after another as a member of the Louisiana Tigers, rising to become a Lieutenant Colonel serving under Lieutenant General Jubal Early. Early, always quick to temper and seemingly eager to find fault in his subordinates, never seemed to turn his fury on Roberdeau and Philip soon found himself a trusted aide to General Lee's so-called "Bad Old Man" in matters involving the Louisiana Tigers. At Gettysburg, The Tigers and Roberdeau fought on Cemetery Hill, a clash in which Roberdeau sustained the Minie ball wound that would cause the limp in his left leg that he would carry with him for the rest of his life.

Beauregard. Longstreet. Early. Only Longstreet had been at the gathering back in '88, but the other two generals had still been alive then even though they elected not to attend. But all were gone now, joining the many other eminent Confederate generals with a link to Gettysburg who had passed on before them: Lee, Stuart, Pickett, Armistead, Pettigrew, Hood, Hill, Wright...

Indeed, only Evander Law, who had taken over for the wounded John Bell Hood during the attacks on Little Round Top and Devil's Den on the second day of Gettysburg, was still alive out of more than fifty Confederate generals who engaged the Yankees during those three days. Perhaps General Law might attend; no word had come forth from the United Confederate Veterans or any party if that would be so.

Philip Roberdeau had already decided that he would make his way to that small Pennsylvania borough five months hence as he had two and a half decades earlier, and no doubt encounter and exchange memories with scores of former soldiers he had not seen for 25 or even 50 years. And not just fellow Confederates; Yankees too. But in many ways, even though this upcoming commemoration would be far more momentous than the one 25 years ago, he couldn't help but feel that the day had already come and gone for a meaningful reunion, at least from a Confederate's point of view.

Because it seemed to Philip as if this time a play was being cast with no lead actors; only supporting players.

Chapter 4

February 14, 1913

"You look especially lovely this evening," First Lieutenant Terrence Sterling II was saying, but his voice sounded slightly muffled, a bit "off," to his wife Louisa. At first she thought it might be because of the din in the background at the Carlisle Barracks Officers' Club – after all this was Saint Valentine's Day, and the Club would be even more crowded than on the typical Friday night as scores of Army officers squired their wives – but curiously the entire Officers' Club was deserted save the Sterlings.

"Thank you," she tried to reply but was surprised when no sound at all emitted from her lips even though she found herself forming and then speaking the words. Louisa began to feel an immense sense of frustration; she urgently wanted to express her gratitude for her husband's appreciation for how she looked this night, especially after…after…after something, but she couldn't quite grasp what that "something" was…

"After supper I'm going away," he was now saying as he lovingly touched her left shoulder, but Louisa already knew that. In fact she knew that he had actually already gone away, and that…

"Mother?" a young boy's voice was accompanied by a light jostling of her left shoulder. Louisa found herself struggling to shut out this latest voice and the sensation of the touch; she so much wanted to remain alongside her husband…

No use. The vivid dream crumbled away and her eyes slowly opened, heartbreaking reality washing in along with the dawn of first light this chilly morning.

"Yes, Randall?" she asked her eight-year old son. "What is it?"

"I don't feel well," he said. "I don't think I should go to school today."

Louisa Sterling blinked several times, fighting the urge to swim back down into the dream where she was once again with Terrence rather than acknowledge the power of her motherly instincts to immediately care for her son, presuming his complaints of not feeling well were genuine. Most likely the boy really didn't feel well; he had learned by now that attempting to fool his mother, who was also a skilled nurse, with a concocted illness of some sort was an exercise in futility.

So much for the world of dreams in which Terrence Sterling was still alive. Louisa raised herself up on her right elbow and reached with her left hand towards her son's forehead in a single time-tested motion. A few seconds of pressing the back of her hand against the boy's forehead and she confirmed to her own satisfaction that the boy had a moderate fever. Two minutes later, the mercury of the glass thermometer settling at a hair above 101 degrees provided the precision she needed.

As always, even the slightest hint of a fever in her son caused an immediate sense of worry that far exceeded what a nurse such as Louisa Sterling would ordinarily feel. Fevers in an eight-year old boy, especially at the apex of the winter chill here in Gettysburg, were a commonplace occurrence. But the memory of her husband Terrence clocking a fever that initially measured at the very same 101 her son now had but which quickly spiked upwards to 104 and stayed there until he died from typhoid fever meant that when it came to Randall Sterling, Louisa would take no chances.

She marched her son off to his bedroom with a full ice bag and instructions to alternate between pressing the bag tightly against his forehead for five minutes and then his chest for another five, and then back to his forehead. The boy settled into his bed, Louisa bustled about the kitchen preparing a breakfast of soft-boiled eggs and toast for him along with a cup of tea for the sore throat she knew was brewing.

As she shuffled from one task to another, Louisa thought about the vision of her late husband in her dream. It suddenly occurred to her that he had been wearing West Point gray rather than the Army Officer's dress uniform he would have been wearing had those fleeting moments been genuine, as Louisa heartbreakingly wished were so.

Cadet Terrence Sterling II, United States Military Academy, Class of 1903. So many times over the past six years her mind would buffer the pain of losing her husband by transporting Louisa back to happier days, as if trying to convince herself that she had been fortunate to have had even a brief number of years with Terrence rather than to have not experienced that love at all. She often thought about the mixer on an unseasonably warm Saturday evening in early March of 1902 when she had first took notice of Cadet Sterling. Her escort for the evening, Cadet Ulysses S. Grant III, had gone to get a glass of punch for Louisa when she had looked across the room and noticed the lanky cadet with the disarming smile look in her direction at the very same instant...

"Mother?" The faint voice from the upstairs bedroom interrupted her thoughts, bringing her back to the present once again.

"Coming," she called loudly enough for Randall to hear her as she swiftly scooped the soft-boiled eggs onto the toasted bread that was already on the boy's breakfast plate, and then headed upstairs with the breakfast and the tea.

Once in Randall's room she placed the food on the top of the stand next to his bed and then walked to the hallway closet to retrieve the household bed tray. She returned to the room and proceeded to get her son all set to eat his breakfast propped up in his bed. She watched him eat the first few bites of his eggs and toast and satisfied with what she observed – an appetite healthy enough to assuage further worries that this ailment was anything more serious than a simple childhood cold – she left the boy to finish his meal while she headed downstairs.

She then bundled up against the gray Gettysburg morning chill and walked next door to ask Patricia Fredericks if she could come stay with Randall for the day while Louisa went to work at Gettysburg Hospital, and after arrangements were made she hurried back home to ready herself for another day of work. Despite her conscious thoughts ever-shifting between those last fragments of worry about her son's health and the rush to get out the door and to work at the hospital, yet another part of Louisa's mind insisted on time-traveling back to happier days.

*　　*　　*

Louisa May Talbot had been born in Germantown, Pennsylvania on July 3, 1883; exactly 20 years after the climactic final day of the Battle of Gettysburg. Her mother, Rebecca Talbot, was a voracious reader of the works of Germantown's most noted native daughter, the authoress Louisa May Alcott; by the time she had turned twenty Rebecca had read *Little Women* and *Little Men* half a dozen times each. Before completing the works that would bring her fame Louisa May Alcott had briefly served as a nurse in the Union Hospital in Georgetown during the Civil War, and in fact had personally cared for Rebecca Talbot's father as he recovered from his wounds received at Second Manassas.

Blessed with the arrival of her first child in the form of a daughter, Rebecca convinced her husband Randolph, a prominent Germantown physician sought out by patients of means from all over Philadelphia, that this newly arrived baby girl must without question be named after her own favorite writer, nursing caregiver to her own father, and former Germantown resident. Randolph Talbot had simply shrugged and agreed to his wife's wishes, not that he had any strong feelings one way or another.

Louisa had performed well in her schooling and so when the turn of the century arrived along with the girl's seventeenth birthday, Randolph Talbot arranged for his daughter's admission to Vassar. Louisa had originally wished to attend Bryn Mawr, much closer to home, but her father had been insistent that his daughter see a bit more of the world – or at least the northeastern part of the United States – before finding her husband and starting a family. Given the proximity of Vassar to Yale and the proclivity of Yale men for Vassar girls, the hopes of Randolph Talbot – and his wife as well – were that Louisa would win the affections of a young Yalie of vaunted family stock who would be the perfect match for their little girl.

During her first year and a half at Vassar, Louisa dutifully followed the roadmap laid out by her parents. She had shown an unnaturally keen proclivity for her studies and found herself with a voracious appetite not only for literature – in particular, the works of the authoress for whom she had been named – but also the sciences. More important to her parents, though, she was escorted along with any number of other Vassar girls two or three weekends each month to dances and social occasions in New Haven and had been introduced to her fair share of young Yale men of impeccable breeding and family name.

One Thursday afternoon in mid-February of 1902, however, her friends Alice Pendergast and Mildred Breville came skipping excitedly into Louisa's dormitory room.

"We're going to go to a Saint Valentine's Day dance at West Point Friday night!" Alice exclaimed excitedly. "You must come with us!"

Louisa looked up from the biology book she was engrossed in.

"West Point?" she replied. "I thought we were going to the dance at Yale this weekend?" Louisa's thoughts immediately shifted to the memory of a moonlit walk two weekends earlier through the winter chill with a Yalie named Richard Gentry II; a walk that had ended in a sweet kiss as they parted for the evening with promises of seeing each other again as soon as possible.

"We were," Mildred answered, "except there is a posting in the Commons that all Vassar girls are invited to a big Saint Valentine's Day dance at West Point because those poor boys are all by themselves, and they really need girls to dance with…"

"Think about all those handsome boys in those gray uniforms," Alice interrupted. "Think about the fact that they don't get to see girls very often…"

The two interlopers immediately broke out in unison into a fit of lusty giggles as they contemplated the notion of swarms of girl-hungry West Point boys surrounding them, dancing with them one after another…

Louisa thought for a moment. She had so much been looking forward to seeing Richard Gentry again, but she was a bit irked that the sweet letter she had written to him a day after that moonlight walk and had posted the next day was yet to be answered. Maybe a little bit of mystery, a little bit of standoffishness, was called for.

"Well, why not," Louisa answered. "I always wanted to meet one of those West Point boys to see what they were like."

"*One* of them?" Mildred gasped, and this time all three of the girls dissolved into a fit of giggly girlishness.

*   *   *

"Louisa May Talbot, may I introduce you to Cadet Ulysses S. Grant III."

The dance hostess – the matronly wife of an Army Colonel who was on the West Point faculty – dutifully flitted about among the clusters of girls and the crowds of cadets and making introductions as she saw necessary, doing her best to break through shyness and hesitancy since time marched steadily on this evening. The musical ensemble had been playing for nearly half an hour, yet surprisingly very few cadets had yet mustered the courage to approach a Vassar girl and ask for a dance. So far, only a few First Class cadets – West Point vernacular for seniors – who were all but engaged to their sweethearts had graced the dance floor. Thus the duty of each hostess was to drag the boys to the girls and vice versa.

The cadet noticed the look come to the Vassar girl's face and he spoke before she could even ask the question.

"My grandfather," he acknowledged the question that he knew was about to be uttered.

Recovering from her surprise – my Lord, she had just been introduced to the grandson of the great General and former President! – Louisa Talbot began to talk with the young man as they strolled over to pour a glass of punch for her. Grant was a Second Classman, a Junior; a member of next year's Class of 1903 should he finish West Point's incredibly tough curriculum…which seemed to be all but a given, since later in the evening Louisa learned that young Grant was ranked sixth overall in his class. He seemed pleasant enough and though they each danced with others throughout the evening, they agreed by the end of the night that Louisa would be Cadet Grant's date for an upcoming social three weeks later, this time on a Saturday evening.

Back at Vassar Louisa tried to downplay this encounter but Alice, Mildred, and several of the other Vassar girls who had gone to West Point that evening made sure that by the end of the next school week nearly everyone at the college – in fact, nearly everyone in the entire town of Poughkeepsie! – knew that Louisa May Talbot had not only danced several times and chatted at length with Ulysses S. Grant III, but was headed back to West Point in three more weeks as the young man's date.

"Maybe he will introduce you to his grandfather!" Mildred's roommate Frances Breville exclaimed when she encountered Louisa along with Alice in the courtyard in front of the Main Building that Friday after classes had been completed for the week.

"Uh, he's dead, Frances," Louisa said.

A shocked look suddenly came to Frances Breville's face.

"Oh my God! You just met him!" she exclaimed.

Louisa looked over at her friend Alice and then back at Frances.

"Not the grandson," she answered, trying not to laugh at poor Frances. "I mean his grandfather; you know, the President."

Frances appeared not to follow.

"President Grant," she repeated. "General Grant? He died a long time ago, almost twenty years ago, I think. That's who I meant."

Louisa and Alice managed to turn the corner on the way back to their dormitory before giving way to spasms of laughter at their friend's flightiness.

* * *

The social on Saturday evening, March 8, 1902 started as a pleasant occasion for Louisa Talbot, though Cadet Grant seemed a bit distant that evening. Their conversations were cordial yet superficial; their dances together seemed a bit strained, as if young Ulysses was making an effort not to hold the girl too tightly or too intimately, unlike most cadets who seized the day when it comes to a modicum of female contact intruding on their all-male world at West Point – once breaking through their initial shyness at any given mixer, that is.

About an hour into the evening, Ulysses Grant III having wandered off to talk with three of his friends and leaving his date alone for a spell, another cadet sauntered over to Louisa as she stood alone.

"I see my friend and classmate Grant has abandoned his lovely date," the cadet brashly said, as if his friend's mere absence of the moment had granted this interloper permission to move in.

Louisa smiled politely, but not too warmly.

"I believe Ulysses is talking with several of his friends and I expect he shall return shortly," she replied.

"Ah," the cadet nodded. "Then during his brief absence please allow me to introduce myself. I am Douglas MacArthur, also a Second Classman as your date is." He paused for a split second. "Though I should add that while Mister Grant is currently sixth in our class, I am first."

He paused, as if waiting for his proclamation to instantly flame the fires of affection in this Vassar girl.

"Tell me, Douglas," Louisa replied, "was your father also a General and President?" She felt the need to put this brash young man in his place.

"Not President," Douglas answered quickly and confidently, "at least not yet. But my father *is* a General, and almost as famous as Grant's grandfather." Not seeing any sense of recognition on the young girl's face, he continued.

"Major General Arthur MacArthur?" Still nothing. "A hero during the Civil War while a First Lieutenant? He was awarded the Medal of Honor for his heroics at the Battle of Missionary Ridge?"

Louisa recognized neither the name nor the tale, nor knew of that specific Civil War battle; but she did respect heroics in battle from her own upbringing and her own grandfather's reticent tales of that same war.

"I'm pleased to make your acquaintance, Douglas MacArthur," she said with a touch more warmth – just a touch, though – than in her previous utterance.

"As I am yours," the cadet replied just as Ulysses S. Grant III reappeared at his date's side.

"I see you've met my friend Douglas," Grant said to Louisa, an interesting combination of pique and amusement tingeing his words. "I'm sure Douglas has told you about our competitions these past three years to finish at the top of this next class. After all, as Douglas tells it, his father is the equal of my grandfather as a General, and indeed may someday also be President..."

The two West Pointers bantered back and forth; good-naturedly, Louisa thought, though it was easy to see that there was an intense competition between the two of them. She sipped at her punch as she listened to the two of them for nearly five full minutes. At a point when the conversation seemed to be on the verge of getting a bit terse she abruptly handed her glass to Ulysses and asked,

"Would you go get me another glass of punch, please?"

Ulysses looked at her for a moment, then at his friend MacArthur, and for a moment thought that this Vassar girl was throwing him over on the spot in favor of the other cadet. But then Louisa added,

"You could go along with Ulysses, Douglas."

Dismissed, Douglas MacArthur curtly smiled, gave a slight bow, but then headed in the opposite direction of Ulysses S. Grant III as they both left the presence of Louisa May Talbot.

It was a brief moment later that she first spotted Cadet Terrence Sterling across the room, at the very same instant he gazed upon his future wife for the first time.

Chapter 5

March 17, 1913

John K. Tener, the Governor of Pennsylvania, felt overwhelmed.

Today was Saint Patrick's Day, and for a man born in County Tyrone in Ireland this was a day of significance that came close to rivaling Easter and Christmas Day. Tener sighed as he reached for a towel to wipe the remaining blotches of shaving cream from his face with his left hand while simultaneously placing his shaving brush in a soaking cup with his right hand. These simple acts hallmarked what had become of most hours of Tener's days, especially during the past year: the necessity of doing two things in unison that he might have otherwise accomplished one after another, simply because of the immutable finiteness of clock and calendar.

Finishing his morning business in the bath that adjoined their bedroom at Keystone Hall, the Governor's Mansion on Front Street along the banks of the Susquehanna, Tener began dressing as he ran through his schedule this day in his mind. A Saint Patrick's Day Proclamation in the assembly room outside his office at precisely nine that morning; his usual Monday morning meetings with his confidantes to review pertinent matters of the Commonwealth that required the Governor's attention; and then a walking tour of the neighborhood near the Capitol Building down towards the Susquehanna, with stops at each of the six Irish pubs along the route where he would join the patrons in a toast to Saint Patrick and his day.

This afternoon would take a different tone, Tener thought, and he made a mental note not to partake too liberally with his fellow celebrants before heading back to his office for important business. Beginning at two o'clock and lasting most likely for at least three hours was a meeting with Colonel James M. Schoonmaker, the chairman of the Commonwealth's commission charged with the success of the upcoming 50th anniversary reunion at Gettysburg (and also Tener's acquaintance and ally from the Governor's days as a Pittsburgh businessman).

Tener's thoughts shifted towards the upcoming commemorative reunion, now less than four months away. His predecessor in the Governor's seat, Edwin Stuart, had been the original proponent of this grandiose gathering at the urging of General Huidekoper of Philadelphia. The initial planning for the reunion had occurred under Stuart's administration, but only for a short period of time. When 1910 came about Tener was asked by the state's Republican establishment to step in and run for the Governor's office in the aftermath of a scandal of epic proportions about the millions of dollars in cost overruns of the Commonwealth's new Capitol Building. Tener, a Pittsburgh banker and former major league baseball player, defeated his two opponents in the general election that November to keep the governorship in the hands of the Republicans.

Tener set about doing his best to not only restore credibility to the Commonwealth's governmental institutions but also provide greater investment from the state's coffers in public education, women's suffrage, and road construction for the seemingly endless supply of automobiles that almost everyone could now afford. He also inherited the executive leadership of the *Fiftieth Anniversary of the Battle of Gettysburg Commission* with the event scheduled to commence less than two and a half years after Tener's inauguration in January of 1911. The new Governor then asked Schoonmaker, the Pittsburgh-area coal and coke magnate and vice president of the Pennsylvania & Lake Erie Railroad who did business (and also socialized) with Andrew Carnegie and Henry Clay Frick – and who also had won the Medal of Honor for his heroic actions during the Civil War at the Third Battle of Winchester in 1864 – to head up the Commission for the duration of its monumental planning effort.

Schoonmaker and William Granville, the President of Pennsylvania College that not only adjoined the Gettysburg battlefield but whose facilities would be instrumental to the success of this reunion, were scheduled in the Governor's office that afternoon to brief Tener on what was getting close to the final hour-by-hour itinerary for the commemoration. Also on the agenda to discuss was the dithering of the new President of the United States, Woodrow Wilson – now two weeks in office this very day – as to whether he would accept the Commission's invitation to speak on July 4th at the height of the commemoration. Privately, Tener could easily understand how the man who until only weeks earlier had been his neighboring Governor to the east in New Jersey would be hesitant to deliver the first Presidential address at Gettysburg since Lincoln's magnificent oration only four and a half months after the battle itself. But if Wilson were to accept the invitation as was hoped, significant preparations needed to be made beyond simple adjustment of agenda, speaking positions, and the like. Perhaps soon, after settling into his new role as Chief Executive, he would reply in the affirmative to his former fellow Governor.

"You appear to be lost in thought," the voice came from behind the Governor as he paused in the upper hallway at the top of the main staircase of Keystone Hall, seeming as if he was in need of specific direction to head downstairs to partake in a quick morning meal before beginning his morning walk to the Capitol building.

Turning to face his wife Harriet, Tener smiled.

"Ah," he replied. "Just thinking of what's coming my way on this Saint Patrick's Monday." The Governor's wife at first thought her husband would continue espousing his thoughts, perhaps share the list of his meetings and tasks with her, but he didn't say anything else before she spoke again.

"Perhaps a few pints of stout on your mid-day rounds would help ease the mind?" Harriet Tener said mischievously. "You could sit and imbibe for the remainder of the afternoon with both Republican and Democrat Assemblymen alike, and the reporters from both the *Patriot* and the *Telegraph* would then write flattering portrayals of how your marvelous leadership has forged new bonds of cooperation for the benefit of all throughout the Commonwealth."

Tener chuckled.

"A wonderful idea," he joshed. "Then I would not only be known as the Governor who once played baseball and was born in Ireland, but the one who also spends his afternoons in a state of public drunkenness and leads other politicians in his state astray in the same way. My notoriety would be sealed for all time!"

The Governor and his wife embraced quickly and then walked down the mansion's staircase together towards the kitchen where the staff had already prepared and laid out the couple's breakfast.

*   *   *

Half an hour later, accompanied by his bodyguard as he strolled the streets of downtown Harrisburg to the Capitol Building, John K. Tener's thoughts wandered back to the tentative plans for the new President to deliver an address at Gettysburg on July 4th...an address that would be attended by perhaps one hundred thousand people! Tener knew Woodrow Wilson well enough given that the two had been neighboring Governors, and for a moment he couldn't help but imagine that it was John K. Tener himself, not Wilson, who was now President of the United States and who would travel from Washington to deliver that address. Having been born in Ireland near the end of July of 1863, barely three weeks after the climactic third day of the Battle of Gettysburg, the Presidency was of course an office forever unattainable to the Pennsylvania Governor, but in the theater of Tener's mind that limitation was suspended for a few moments. (Ironically, Tener had been born in the same County Tyrone from which President Wilson's paternal grandparents had come to the United States many years earlier, in the first decade of the 1800s.)

Tener saw himself standing upright – all six feet and four inches of his height, ironically the exact same height as Lincoln and a characteristic that had given him a commanding presence on the pitching mound during his baseball days as well as later in business and politics – on an elevated podium, addressing a near-endless sea of Civil War veterans and spectators alike on a bright July 4th afternoon; words yet to be written but which, like those of the 16th President spoken at that very location fifty years earlier, would be revered for generations to come. (And unlike when Lincoln delivered that famous address, Tener's actual voice making his own masterful speech would be preserved for all time on one of Edison's wax cylinder recorders, available to be heard over and over again long into the future.)

As a baseball pitcher for Baltimore, Pittsburgh, and – most significantly – the Chicago White Stockings, one of the best teams of that era and which had evolved into today's Chicago Cubs, he had pitched before throngs that had sometimes reached 10,000 people, occasionally more. But perhaps 100,000 souls, veteran and spectator, gathered on an occasion such as the one that would soon take place in Gettysburg! Would Wilson be up to the challenge?

The new Chief Executive had been a college president at Princeton before becoming New Jersey's Governor and would have held the Presidency for only four months by the time the Great Reunion commenced. More worrisome was his family's leanings – and perhaps those of Wilson himself, albeit it as a youngster in Virginia – towards the Confederacy during the war. Tener clearly recalled the evening slightly more than a year and a half earlier that the two men, along with the Governors of New York and Ohio, had adjourned to the Union League in downtown Philadelphia to share brandy and cigars following a day-long summit to discuss common concerns. Wilson, undoubtedly aware of the League's founding in support of the Union during the Civil War, still proceeded to describe in awe-filled terms how as a boy he had once stood next to Robert E. Lee himself and how that memory was one of the most cherished of his entire life. While Lee was still respected even these many years later as an accomplished West Point-educated general despite his eventual leadership of the Confederate Army, any utterance such as that one to the crowds gathered at Gettysburg – the very site that turned the tide of the war against Lee's forces – would likely not be well-received. Hopefully, should he accept the invitation to speak, the new President had enough sense to carefully mask any such sentiments…

"Governor?"

The sound of his bodyguard's voice interrupted Tener's daydreaming.

"Will you be needing me on Good Friday? If not my wife would like me to attend Mass with her in the morning."

Good Friday! Only four days hence, Tener suddenly remembered, which of course meant that the Holy Day of Easter was but six days away, the earliest date in the year since long ago in 1856, before the Governor himself had even been born. Even more to do in the days immediately ahead this week, he thought, though responsibilities to prepare the family for Easter would fall to his wife Harriet while he attended to the business of managing the affairs of the Commonwealth.

"No, Patrick," Tener replied. "I'll be attending Mass myself and I would expect that no one would intend me any mischief or harm on Good Friday. So you can be a good Irish Catholic and accompany Katie and your children." The Governor made it a point to know the names of the wives and children of members of his staff and his bodyguards. In a case such as Patrick O'Carroll, however, a native of Dublin who already had nine children, recitation of each child's name in his response would have seemed forced…not to mention have taken a fair bit of time to accomplish. Still, should the occasion call for it, Tener could ask about any of his bodyguard's children by each one's good Irish name; a skill any good politician should strive to possess, he reasoned.

Tener's thoughts drifted back to this year's early Easter Sunday and his week's workload which now must be accomplished during four days rather than five because of Good Friday. As the two men turned the corner onto 3rd Street, the Capitol Building now in sight, Tener audibly sighed as he contemplated his condensed workweek.

*   *   *

"I must first report to you that General Wagner has informed me of his resignation," James Schoonmaker began as soon as he, Tener, and Pennsylvania College President Granville were seated in the Governor's office.

Tener looked at his former business acquaintance with surprise. General Louis Wagner had occupied the post of Treasurer of the 50th Anniversary Commission since its inception in 1909. To resign now, only months before the event itself, came as a surprise to the Governor. The men speculated about Wagner's reason for a few moments — none had been offered — before Tener said to Schoonmaker,

"What about Samuel Todd as a replacement?"

Schoonmaker nodded even as the Governor was speaking the man's name, indicating he was thinking the same. Samuel C. Todd, another business and ally of Tener's from the Governor's business base in Charleroi, just outside Pittsburgh by thirty miles or so, would be the perfect replacement for the old general...and perhaps just in time as well, since the bulk of the appropriations for the commemoration were about to be released by the

Commonwealth. To date only $60,000 had been spent but six times that amount - $165,000 for transportation costs and another $195,000 for general expenditures – was about to be made available from Pennsylvania along with hundreds of thousands more from the Federal government and from the other states; more than one million dollars in total that needed to be carefully dispersed and managed. Todd would likely prove himself even more competent than his predecessor, and the two men agreed that their business ally would be invited to immediately join the Commission as the new Treasurer.

The discussion then shifted to medical and hospital preparations that were proceeding under the leadership of Doctor Samuel Chambers of Philadelphia.

"Is he proving capable?" Tener asked Schoonmaker, recalling that Chambers had only been in this position since the previous October when his predecessor Waterston had died suddenly.

"More than capable, John," was Schoonmaker's response. "He's a very young man, only thirty years of age, but he shows a talent for organization equivalent to that of many of our own business colleagues."

Schoonmaker proceeded to relate to the Governor what he had learned from Chambers the previous week when the two men had met in Gettysburg along with Granville, and the college president offered his own thoughts not only about Doctor Chambers' abilities but about the preparations themselves.

"We have arranged for a number of comfort stations set up throughout the borough, Governor, along with a relief station to be located at the Tuberculosis Dispensary," Granville recited from memory before looking briefly at a sheet of paper in front of him on the table. "We will have eleven aid stations in the camp proper along with one field hospital and three regimental hospitals. Thirteen Red Cross nurses will be assigned to each of the hospitals…"

Granville proceeded to recite more of the statistics from his sheet of paper but Tener's attention was divided between listening to this recitation and some back-of-mind calculations, trying to determine if indeed young Doctor Chambers had prudently allowed for adequate care should a worst-case situation occur when the thousands of old Veterans encountered the worst that Gettysburg might offer in early July weather.

"I shall confer personally with Doctor Chambers next Tuesday," Tener declared when Granville had finished. "With so many aging veterans gathered together under the watch of the Commonwealth during those days, we must leave nothing to chance. The sun and temperatures during those days might be in God's hands, but the preparations are in ours."

"You'll arrange for that, James?" he continued, and Schoonmaker, the aging Civil War hero himself, nodded to his friend the Governor.

"Of course," he replied before the meeting's discussion shifted to how they might best approach President Wilson and encourage his attendance at this monumental event. Shortly before the meeting's scheduled five o'clock conclusion an assistant eased into Tener's office after knocking and informed the Governor that there was an important long distance telephone call for him, a call that had originated in Philadelphia. Tener immediately presumed the call had something to do with the Gettysburg Great Reunion or state business but before agreeing to accept the call asked the assistant for the name of the caller.

"It's Mister William Baker," came the reply and Tener simply shook his head upon hearing the name of the President of the Philadelphia Phillies of the National Baseball League. Baker had approached Tener several months earlier with the idea of the Governor and former baseball player becoming the President of the National League. Tener, amused at first at the offer ("Do you not think I have enough to do most days as Governor?" had been his affable reply to Baker), actually found himself intrigued at the prospect even though he would be holding this lofty position at the same time he was also serving as the Commonwealth's Governor, at least for a while. Still, with the Gettysburg commemoration requiring a significant amount of his time and attention, he had gotten Baker to agree to wait until after the commemoration was concluded – and this coming baseball season as well – and the two men would revisit the idea sometime this coming autumn of 1913.

"Please inform Mister Baker than I am meeting with Colonel Schoonmaker and President Granville at the moment and will speak with him tomorrow," Tener said to his assistant. Apparently Baker was not one to accept "not now; perhaps in a few months" for an answer. Still, the president of a baseball club would have to accept that the concerns of his profession must be secondary to those of a different and loftier President as Tener and his colleagues resumed their discussion of Woodrow Wilson and the Great Reunion.

Chapter 6

March 20, 1913

   Devin McAteer shuffled past the open front door of his son's home onto the front porch, a cup of hot tea in his left hand and the letter from his cousin Seamus McAteer in his right hand. He had already skimmed the letter that had arrived fifteen minutes earlier in the afternoon post delivery, the last one before tomorrow's Good Friday ushered in the Easter weekend as well as the spring season, and after making himself a cup of tea wanted to read it more carefully. A slight chill, winter's last gasp, had descended upon the late afternoon in Pittsburgh, but the old man could barely feel it; his mind was preoccupied with what he had gleaned from his cousin's response to Devin's own letter from two weeks earlier.

   Settled into the slickly varnished rocker his son Kerwin had bought two years earlier for his father's sixty-fifth birthday, he began to read.

Thursday, March the Thirteenth, 1913

Dear Cousin Devin,

I am now in receipt of your letter of this past Thursday, March the Sixth, in which you stated your reasons for declining my request that we join in the commemoration this July at

Gettysburg. I wish to respond to your objections by once again declaring my reasons that I believe not attending this event will be a mistake in judgment you will come to regret.

The substance of your argument is that you are not a veteran of the Battle of Gettysburg, and in fact were on those very days fighting instead at the Battle of Vicksburg more than one thousand miles distant, as I was. And therefore you believe that you would be an intruder of sorts at Gettysburg this July since you had not personally participated in that particular battle fifty years ago.

I shortly shall relate my own thoughts and feelings to you and hope that since you and I share not only blood as cousins but also as fellow combatants who saw many battles side by side in that long-ago war, you will come to believe as I do.

Further, I have carefully read the invitation sent by the GAR and other correspondence related to the commemoration, and the authors of those posts have made it clear that the Gettysburg Commemoration is being held in honor of all veterans of that war, not just those who fought in that particular battle. They have but one objective: to have this particular commemoration be the grandest of all reunions and commemorations and forever be looked back upon as the high watermark of healing for that war; and by including those of us who fought elsewhere they might better achieve their aims. I have discussed the matter with other members of the Grand Army of the Republic here in Luzerne County, most of them veterans of Gettysburg, and all are unanimous in agreement that we are not only welcome at this event but are in fact obligated to attend if health and other matters permit us to do so.

I do understand your reluctance. We both volunteered in the 45th Pennsylvania in 1862 with expectations that we would be defending our state from the Rebel invaders who were so close by. And indeed, Lee's Army did invade Pennsylvania and caused havoc at York, Carlisle, and Hanover; in towns and boroughs all the way up to the Susquehanna. But then, after three days of ferocious battle at Gettysburg they found themselves hurled back, never to return. But where were we? Not at Gettysburg; instead the 45th was with General Grant's Army of the Tennessee besieging and then conquering Vicksburg, the climax of our battle ironically coming but one day after the decisive conclusion at Gettysburg.

I look back on those days, however, and think that others who served in the Army of the Potomac and who fought at Gettysburg suffered much the same difficulties as we did in Vicksburg; faced the same terrors. We are all brothers in arms — even those who will be attending the commemoration wearing gray rather than blue — and we are all closer to the grave than the cradle at this point in our lives. I fear that to miss the events of this coming July will leave an unfillable hole in each man who is able to attend but chooses not to do so. I would hate that come 1914 or 1915 or, if God smiles on you and blesses you with a long life, come 1920 and beyond one of the great sorrows of the remaining years of your life is that you chose not to come to Gettysburg in July of 1913 for the grandest commemoration and gathering of veterans from our war that was ever held.

I should also add, on a personal note, that with both you and I at our advanced age, and for years now living in vastly different parts of our great and large state of Pennsylvania, that we know not when we shall have the opportunity to see each other again before the Good Lord calls one or both of us home. I desire this commemoration to serve two purposes then: a grand one to reunite with long-forgotten comrades from our war, and a personal one where we can be assured of seeing each other at least once more.

I beg of you to reconsider the invitation and await your letter informing me of your decision.

Your cousin,

Seamus

Sighing, Devin neatly refolded the letter and took a sip of his cooling tea before slipping the letter back into the envelope. Even as he was absorbing his cousin's plea, he couldn't help but also think that for a coal miner from Pittston, Pennsylvania Seamus McAteer wrote especially eloquently, no doubt because for fifty years now he had had his nose buried in one book or another when he wasn't mining for coal or fighting in a Civil War battle. Even back as far as the siege of Vicksburg Seamus found every possible spare moment to read a few pages of Emerson, Thoreau, or Hawthorne. He had carried his prized books with him all the way from Harrisburg to Mississippi and back again to later battlefields following triumph at Vicksburg. After the war, when Seamus decided not to return to Pittsburgh with his cousin and instead made his way to the northeastern Pennsylvania coal fields, his passion for reading continued. Obviously, Devin thought as he did whenever he would read one of his cousin's many letters over the years, absorbing the writing of great authors had also shaped Seamus McAteer's own wordcraft.

Beyond his admiration for his cousin's artistry with words, though, Devin found himself contemplating the old man's pleadings that the retired steelworker from Pittsburgh reconsider his refusal to attend the commemoration in Gettysburg. Unlike his cousin Seamus, Devin McAteer's war did not end with Lee's surrender at Appomattox in April of 1865. Devin, by then brevetted to the rank of Captain – a rank he was able to retain even after the cessation of major battle – decided to remain in the Union Army and was posted to New Orleans, Louisiana for another decade as part of the nation's Reconstruction effort.

Though his prolonged tour of duty was mostly without the frequent danger of the war years until the Confederacy capitulated, the occasional skirmish with Louisiana's Knights of the White Camelia and their brethren in the Ku Klux Klan kept Devin and his troops in a tense state much of the time. The Presidential election of 1868, with General Grant running as the Republican Party's nominee, was a particularly tense time as the Knights did their best to intimidate Blacks from voting through threats and violence following the state election in March of that year. Then, in September of 1874, the Crescent City White League rebelled against the Reconstruction state government and took control of the State House, the armory, and downtown New Orleans until Federal troops – including Captain Devin McAteer – entered the city and quelled the uprising. McAteer's company rescued several Louisiana militiamen who had been taken prisoner by the Crescent City White League including, much to his surprise, the famous former Confederate General James Longstreet.

In 1875, with Reconstruction nearing its end, Devin did something he had sworn he would never do: return home to Pittsburgh. As terrible as the War years had been, from

Vicksburg to Spotsylvania to Cold Harbor, and as tense as Reconstruction days in the South were, nothing related to the horror that had occurred in Pittsburgh only weeks after Devin ran away from home at the age of sixteen with his cousin Seamus to join the 45th Pennsylvania Regiment.

For more than a year prior Devin had found work at the Allegheny Arsenal, a munitions facility along the banks of the Allegheny River that manufactured cartridges for Union rifles. He left behind his schooling days when the war began with the blessing of his father and mother, who saw the opportunity for young Devin – as well as Aileen and Ryanne, two of his five sisters – to earn small amounts of money each day to help support the McAteer clan. At first, the excitement of working in an actual war materiel facility thrilled the teenage boy, but soon the repetitious work became more than he could bear. Conspiring with his cousin Seamus, six months older than Devin himself and also looking for adventure, the two hopped a railcar one day in late August of 1862 and jumped off when the train arrived in the Capitol city of Harrisburg, where they promptly signed on with the 45th Pennsylvania Regiment of the Union Army and awaited further orders.

This rash decision, one that no doubt caused his parents great anguish when they learned of it, saved Devin McAteer's life.

On the afternoon of September 17th of 1862, the main laboratory of the Arsenal exploded into flames and by the time the fire was extinguished 78 workers, many of them young women and teenage boys who, like Devin, were responsible for the handiwork in cartridge manufacturing, had died from the flames. Among the 78 dead were Aileen and Ryanne McAteer. Had Devin not surrendered to his impulses and accompanied his cousin to Harrisburg, the

McAteer family would have lost one more member that terrible afternoon.

These remembrances flashed through Devin's thoughts as quickly as a lightning flash during a mid-summer Pittsburgh thunderstorm as he sat on his son's porch reflecting on his cousin's letter. In some ways his life had been blessed. He was wounded only once during the war – at Spotsylvania Court House, a minor nick on his left thigh from a Minie ball but one that still caused him a touch of difficulty walking nearly five decades later – and he had not perished along with his two sisters in the fire at the Arsenal. He had survived three ambushes by the Knights of the White Camelia and two others by the Ku Klux Klan during the Reconstruction years in the south. He survived the Battle of Liberty Place unharmed. And then after spending sixteen years toiling near the blast furnaces of Carnegie's Edgar Thomson Works, perilous work that claimed many lives over the years and maimed thousands more, he switched to the Homestead Works just in time for the watershed strike of 1892 and the violent clashes with the Pinkerton guards that became known as the Battle of Homestead; a landmark occasion along the timelines of both the United States' labor movement and the steel industry. Again, Devin McAteer survived without any major harm, though his occasional severe headaches to this very day were a frequent reminder of a lead pipe wielded by a Pinkerton guard that did find its way to a glancing blow against Devin's skull.

After selling Carnegie Steel to J. P. Morgan, the old Scotsman Carnegie went to work on his legacy – and likely his conscience as well – by establishing pensions for Homestead Works steelworkers, and by 1911 and upon reaching the age of 65 years, Devin McAteer left behind a lifetime of hard work and frequent danger for what he hoped would be the better part of a decade until that final reckoning.

"Would you be ready for your dinner soon?" The voice of his wife Noreen interrupted his thoughts. Devin had met and married her late in his life; in 1876, just shy of his own thirtieth birthday and more than a year after returning to Pittsburgh from New Orleans. Having spent his formative courting years in the Union Army in Louisiana, when most southern women would just as soon spit on a Yankee occupier as give him a favorable glance, Devin McAteer postponed the idea of marriage until he eventually left his Army years behind him and returned to Pittsburgh. He always felt himself fortunate to have found a young lovely girl such as Noreen – only 22 herself when she agreed to marry him – so far along in his own life, and did his best to treat her well. As a laborer for Carnegie Steel there was only so much Devin McAteer could provide his wife in the way of material goods, yet he always tried to have a kind word and an attentive ear for her.

"Yes, I suppose so," he replied, wincing slightly as he eased his way up from his rocker, thinking again as he did almost every night that while he was grateful for the hospitality and comfort of their son Kerwin and his wife Kaitleen for allowing Devin and Noreen to move in with them, he wished that he still had his old house not far from the Homestead Works. Alas, Carnegie's pension might provide a small stipend to someone who toiled in the old Scotsman's mills for years, but the amount was hardly enough to support the rent of their old home and even modest living expenses. And so Devin and Noreen packed up a few of their belongings, sold what they could, and moved in with Kerwin and his family, only a few miles downriver.

"What did Seamus write you?" Noreen asked her husband, eyeing the letter in his hand. "Is he still trying to change your mind about traveling to Gettysburg?"

Devin nodded as he followed his wife in the front door.

Not hearing anything further from her husband, she paused and turned back to him.

"Well?"

The old man just shrugged.

"I'll think about it," he said quietly.

Chapter 7

March 25, 1913

Samuel Chambers could feel the perspiration break out underneath his coat, vest, and shirt, and did his best to will himself to fight the sense of overwhelming heat – and a growing sense of nausea – he felt as he waited to be ushered into the Governor's office. The spring day was definitely a warm one, that was certain; south-central Pennsylvania had been blessed with a glorious start to the spring season, beginning on Good Friday and growing slightly warmer each day.

Still, Samuel knew that the heat was but a small part of the cause for the outbreak of nervous perspiration overtaking him at this moment. Colonel Schoonmaker had informed him one week earlier that the doctor's presence had been ordered in Harrisburg on this day for the purpose of relating to Governor Tener himself the detailed preparations for the care and well-being of those attending the Gettysburg commemoration. The Governor evidently shared the doctor's concerns about what excessive heat might bring, and wanted to personally discuss the matter. Chambers' own worries about illnesses and death caused by excessive heat had been alleviated slightly as a result of his own exhausting work in organizing and staffing a network of aid stations and hospitals in the encampment itself and also in the borough of Gettysburg. Still, almost nightly he endured at least one nightmare in which Gettysburg, circa July of 1913, looked much like the Gettysburg of fifty years earlier...or most any other Civil War battlefield. An endless sea of prone bodies, though due to having succumbed to the ravages of weather rather than Minie ball or bayonet or cannon fire. Still, acre upon acre of casualties…

"Please come with me," the male voice interrupted Samuel's thoughts. The moment was here. He felt a fresh burst of perspiration overtake his torso as he rose and followed the attendant into Governor Tener's office.

"Doctor Chambers," the exceptionally tall man said as he rose from behind a stately oak desk and strode towards the door, exuding confidence and control with each of his few steps.

"Governor," Samuel replied, extending his sweaty hand to clasp the one offered by the Governor who seemed not to take notice of the clamminess as they shook hands.

"Please sit," Governor Tener motioned towards a kelly green wingback chair opposite the identical looking one into which he was easing himself.

The two men made small talk for a few moments about their respective Easter Sundays. Samuel sensed that the Governor felt a tad ill at ease when, after asking Samuel if he had attended Easter Mass with his wife and children, the doctor had replied that he was in fact unmarried and had instead attended the Easter service with his parents.

"A bit too much time studying and doctoring to settle down and find a wife, I presume?" was the Governor's eventual response.

Samuel hesitated for a moment.

"I was engaged for several years while completing medical school," he said, wondering even as he uttered the words why in the name of Heaven he was speaking these words to the Governor.

"She decided to marry an automobile man from Packard Motors in Philadelphia instead." He paused for a moment, contemplating if he should continue.

"They both perished in the railroad collision near Ligonier last July, though."

Tener nodded, instantly recalling the terrible collision of a passenger train with a coal hauler in Westmoreland County the day after the Fourth of July celebrations; a fiery accident that had taken more than twenty lives. He had personally visited the site a few days later as part of his responsibility to maintain safety and order within the Commonwealth or, when failings occurred that cost lives of its citizens, to do his best to ensure those failings were not repeated.

"I'm sorry to hear that," he replied, then seemed to puzzle over what to say next. "I expect that since she had married someone else it wasn't quite the same as losing your own wife, but I'm sure you felt sorrow upon learning that news."

"I did," Samuel quietly affirmed.

"Well," Governor Tener offered, "I'm sure a bright young doctor such as yourself will soon find a wife. I myself was the grand old age of 26 when I met Mrs. Tener. I married her during my final year playing with the Chicago White Stockings…"

By the time Tener had finished his tale of meeting his future wife, and had thrown in a few anecdotes about his days playing professional baseball back when the sport had barely begun, Samuel Chambers felt totally at ease and even took notice that he had stopped perspiring. The conversation swung around to Samuel's plans for hospitals and aid stations, doctors and nurses, and overall care of the veterans and other visitors who would be attending the

Gettysburg commemoration. More than two hours passed as Samuel related what had been done already and what was planned. The Governor asked questions that Samuel answered with increasing confidence as the meeting progressed. Tener offered a few ideas that Samuel thought were very valuable and acknowledged to the Governor that he would indeed fold them into the remaining planning.

"I'd like you to remain in Gettysburg for the final three and a quarter months until the commemoration begins," the Governor proclaimed near the end of the meeting, locking eyes with Chambers as he did. A directive; not a suggestion.

"I know many of your colleagues with whom you consult on matters of the reunion are back in Philadelphia but by the second or third week of April I would like all concerned to be fully working from Gettysburg in the interest and spirit of expediency and accuracy. You especially will be coordinating with the Army surgeons, the Red Cross nurses, President Granville of Pennsylvania College..." Tener went on to list several more individuals by name or affiliation but his message was perfectly clear to Samuel: he was to return to Philadelphia, pack his belongings, and by the beginning of the next week have settled in Gettysburg as a temporary resident might do.

"Who knows," Governor Tener said as both men rose at the conclusion of their meeting and he placed a lanky arm around the young doctor's shoulder as he escorted him to the door, "one of those nurses from the Red Cross or a Gettysburg hospital might perhaps turn out to be your future wife, and you'll be exceptionally glad that you had the opportunity to spend your time in Gettysburg for several months courting her."

Samuel nodded and as he shook hands in parting with the Governor, simply said:

"Perhaps."

Chapter 8

April 4, 1913

"Mother?"

Louisa Sterling looked up from her knitting at the sound of her son's voice.

"Yes, Randall?"

"Can I help the Boy Scouts with the war reunion?"

Louisa smiled at her son.

"You're too young," she said softly. "You have to be ten years old to be a Boy Scout and you're only eight."

"But I'll be nine a little bit after the war reunion," the boy retorted, obviously having prepared this counter-argument in advance.

"I'm sorry…" Louisa began but her response was cut off by the continuation of her son's plea.

"All they are going to do is help give directions to people, and run errands, and help out at the hospitals, and…"

"I know what they're going to do," Louisa interrupted. "We have a number of Boy Scouts who will be helping me, and the other nurses at the hospital by Cemetery Hill, and…"

It was Randall's turn once again to interrupt.

"But I can do that!" he said, his voice taking on that tone common to so many eight-year olds as they plead to be allowed to do something they've been told is out of the question.

"You can certainly help out at the hospital," Louisa said. "There will be lots of boys and girls other than the Boy Scouts who will be helping during the entire time. You can meet those old soldiers and they can tell you stories about what it was like back then, and…"

The watering in her son's eyes caused Louisa to pause.

"I want to wear a uniform, not just help," Randall Sterling said quietly. "I want to wear a uniform like Father used to."

*   *   *

Louisa May Talbot had become Louisa Sterling on June 20, 1903, nine days after Terrence Sterling's graduation from West Point and commissioning as a Second Lieutenant in the United States Army. Terrence Sterling II had graduated fourth in his class – two places ahead of Ulysses S. Grant III but, alas, still behind Douglas MacArthur who had indeed finished first as he had predicted to Louisa more than a year earlier on that same night she first met Terrence.

The two of them had become engaged on Christmas Day of 1902 after seeing each other frequently during the nine preceding months following their first unanticipated, breath-taking shared glance that March night. At first Louisa's parents – her father in particular – were none too pleased about her enchantment with the young cadet and when Terrence asked Randolph Talbot during the Thanksgiving break of 1902 for permission to ask his daughter to marry, Randolph was inclined to send young

Terrence away with an answer of "no." As it was, he dallied for most of December as he investigated young Sterling's background before grudgingly giving his approval. The boy seemed to come from a good Baltimore family and while Randolph Talbot wasn't enamored with the thought of his daughter following an Army husband to locations far away such as Texas or Oklahoma – or perhaps even a frontier post way out in Arizona Territory – she seemed genuinely fond of the young future officer. She could do worse, Randolph finally convinced himself and he let young Terrence know that indeed he could propose to Louisa on Christmas Day, provided he did so in their home in Germantown.

"Fond" hardly described how Louisa felt about Terrence Sterling. Like most of her friends Louisa's affections frequently shifted among various boys, and during the previous several years while at Vassar several Yalies had, at one time or another, had their name doodled on one of Louisa's lesson books preceded by "Mrs." Indeed, for three brief weeks in early 1902 there had been the occasional scribble of "Mrs. Ulysses S. Grant III" and even one "President and Mrs. Ulysses S. Grant III" after she had agreed to attend that fateful dance with the grandson of the former President and famous general.

Those had all been mere infatuations, Louisa now realized. What she felt for Terrence Sterling as she anxiously awaited the proposal of marriage that she was confident was coming could only be pure love.

Like many of his just-graduated classmates (though neither Lieutenant Grant nor Lieutenant MacArthur), Terrence found himself married only days after his graduation and commission. As was customary for the top graduates in any West Point class, he was commissioned into the Army Corps of Engineers and fortuitously found himself posted to Carlisle Barracks in south-central Pennsylvania, only hours away from Louisa's girlhood home in the Philadelphia area and also from his own family home in Baltimore. Time would eventually take them farther away, he knew, but at least for the near term they could be near Louisa's family and his own when their first child or two or three would arrive.

The first of the Sterling brood – young Randall – was born in August of 1904. The birth was a difficult one for Louisa and as one year passed and then another and then another, she had yet to again become pregnant with child. Possibly the Sterling household might only be blessed with one child; that was a distinct possibility, both Terrence and Louisa realized. Still, both joyously embraced life with their only (thus far) son.

In late August of 1909, nearing the end of an exceptionally hot summer in southern-central Pennsylvania, Terrence Sterling developed a moderate fever of 101 degrees. He stabilized over the next week, though he never really felt better as his days become hallmarked with a nagging cough and a perpetually aching head. Initially Louisa nursed him at home, but by early September his condition had worsened and he was admitted to the Post hospital at Carlisle Barracks. He never recovered and died from typhoid fever on September fifth of that year.

Not too long afterwards, ironically, was the initiation of a program to inoculate the entire United States Army against typhoid fever. The vaccine had been developed by an Army physician – Doctor Frederick Russell – in 1909, shortly after Terrence Sterling's death, and had proven so effective that the Army undertook its immunization efforts by 1911. Alas, for Terrence Sterling – and the wife and child he left behind – these wonderful accomplishments came too late.

Louisa allowed herself several months to grieve this terrible loss before summoning every ounce of strength she could muster to decide what she should now do. Uppermost in her mind was caring for her five-year old son Randall, now fatherless. Thinking about the matter, Louisa felt a calling of sorts to help those who were ill do their best to recover. She had lost the battle trying to nurse her beloved husband back to health; perhaps she could save some other poor young wife the tragic grief she was now feeling.

Harkening back to her affinity for the sciences while at Vassar, Louisa decided to learn the nursing profession and was accepted as a student at the Carlisle Hospital. Louisa also decided that she would not only become a nurse but remain as close to Carlisle Barracks – and the grave of her late husband – as possible, so when she was unable to find a position in Carlisle upon completing her studies she then secured one less than 30 miles away, in Gettysburg.

Her parents were not pleased at all with their daughter's intentions. They made their wishes very clear that they would prefer she bring young Randall to live with them in Germantown. Though unspoken, her mother's wishes – Louisa's father's as well – were that the young woman would overcome her grief, find a new husband (perhaps from among the young doctors in Philadelphia with whom Randolph Talbot frequently worked or socialized, especially now that Louisa was a nurse), and begin a new chapter in her life.

Louisa was not to be dissuaded from her decision, and eventually her parents acquiesced to their daughter's wishes on the condition that she visit them in Germantown as frequently as she could manage.

*   *   *

Also not to be dissuaded was Randall Sterling in the matter of the Gettysburg commemoration. He pestered his mother with annoying regularity that she find some way for him to participate with the Boy Scouts in the upcoming festivities at the Gettysburg Battlefield. He had been old enough when his father had died to realize that Terrence Sterling was a soldier, and all the hubbub about the upcoming commemoration and the gathering of tens of thousands of aging former soldiers on the battlefield where they had once fought had captivated the boy's imagination and fostered some sort of connection back to images of his departed father in an Army uniform.

Worn down, Louisa Sterling promised her son that she would look into the matter as she turned her attention to the upcoming review the following Monday by the Philadelphia doctor in charge of the Commonwealth's medical and comfort facilities for the event.

*   *   *

The large lecture room at Pennsylvania College seated close to 350 people and every seat was occupied by a doctor, nurse, or aid worker. Close to another 100 people stood along both side walls of the cavernous room and along the back. This heretofore unusual mandatory gathering of every available medical staff member would be but the first of many over the next three months, each one occurring at the insistence of Doctor Samuel Chambers of Philadelphia, very soon to be a temporary resident of the borough of Gettysburg. With the eyes of Governor Tener, the Pennsylvania Assembly, Colonel Schoonmaker and the entire *Fiftieth Anniversary of the Battle of Gettysburg Commission*, the United States Congress' own committee devoted to the reunion, and reporters from countless newspapers all focused on this event, Samuel Chambers was leaving nothing to chance when it came to whatever was within his realm of authority.

The purpose of this initial meeting was to not only introduce himself to anyone present whom he had not already met – and many he already had become acquainted with during his travels thus far to Gettysburg, of course – but to hear for himself the state of preparation of each and every field hospital and aid station. While the plans that Samuel himself had either drawn up or, if accomplished by others, reviewed and approved appeared adequate, the doctor was savvy enough to realize that simply because figures and details had been committed to ink and paper he had no guarantee that adequate progress on the facilities and measures themselves was being made. The very last thing Samuel wanted to happen was that dozens or hundreds of old soldiers would be overtaken by the summertime July heat and be assisted to comfort stations or hospitals only to have those places short on staff, beds, and supplies. The images from scores of photographs taken after significant Civil War battles continued to play with regularity in the theater of Samuel's mind. One impression in particular – a sea of Confederate wounded lying prone in a grass field in front of Smith's Barn following Antietam, most of the men covered by makeshift small tents as they awaited medical attention that was hours away, if it would ever arrive at all – was particularly seared in his mind. He was determined to do everything within his power to prevent any such scenes from being reprised in the present day of 1913, no matter the reason.

Beginning with the field hospital, Chambers began his inquisition as to the protocol for admitting, diagnosing, and then treating incoming patients. He sporadically asked any one of the doctors and nurses whose hospital or aid station was in his sights at a given moment about specific assignments; about what one would do in a given situation, such as being swarmed by dozens or even hundreds of incoming heat-stricken patients all at once.

Seated in the center of the second row was Louisa Sterling. She paid close attention to what this Doctor Chambers of Philadelphia was saying and took meticulous notes in a lesson book not unlike the ones she had carried more than a decade earlier at Vassar. By half past one o'clock in the afternoon, the day far from over, Samuel suggested that the attendees adjourn to the College's mess hall in the next building for a brief mid-day meal before resuming for the remainder of the afternoon and continuing into the early evening hours. Samuel stayed behind for a few moments to speak with President Granville of Pennsylvania College, who made it a point to attend this particular meeting since he knew of Governor Tener's intense personal interest in the medical preparations.

Neither of the men noticed the attractive nurse standing a dozen yards away, watching both of them intently to detect the moment their conversation was concluded and she might then beg a word with President Granville. Her eyes were mostly locked on the bespectacled, portly gray-haired man with whom she was waiting to speak, but once or twice she minutely shifted the focus of her vision to the thirtyish doctor who had spent the morning addressing the room. He had a slightly familiar look about him, and she realized that in some ways he resembled her beloved Terrence. Both were on the tallish side, about five feet ten inches, and slender yet not too thin. Terrence had had a soldier's lean muscular body, and though Doctor Chambers was wearing a woolen suit jacket over his vest, she could almost see her husband's body superimposed on this man as well. Chambers' hair was lighter than Terrence's had been (it was, in fact, her husband's jet black hair that had caught her attention a split second before she had noticed his face when she first saw him across the room at that West Point mixer); mid-brown with, Louisa could notice even from a distant, the first flecks of gray making their appearance. The doctor's face was pleasantly attractive, yet weary; no doubt due to his workload for the upcoming commemoration and the accompanying pressures of responsibility.

She forced her attention back to the older college president, waiting to speak to him about her son's fervent wishes to be allowed to join the uniformed Boy Scouts if only for the momentous commemoration. No doubt President Granville had much more weighty matters on his mind, but she had promised Randall…

Seeing both men nod simultaneously and begin to turn towards the lecture room's door – towards Louisa – she began to walk towards them, stopping several feet in front of but off to the side of these gentlemen; she didn't want to come across as overly aggressive, as if she were trying to block their progress by halting directly in their pathway.

"President Granville?" She waited until he acknowledged her with raised eyebrows above his glasses and a distracted "Hmmm?"

"May I speak to you for a brief moment about a matter related to the commemoration that is very important to my son?"

The college president was in a pleasant enough mood; responses from those who had spoken thus far during the morning session had been satisfactory, and he saw no reason to deny this pretty nurse's request to speak with him.

"I'll meet up with you in a short moment," Granville said to Samuel Chambers as the doctor continued walking as the college president turned his attention to Louisa Sterling. She cast a quick glance at the doctor as he passed by her, catching his eye and nodding politely and deferentially as she would to any doctor…but with a small quick smile on her face.

Louisa May Sterling began to describe to the President of Pennsylvania College what her son so urgently wished for, and why. She was unaware that as he walked away behind her, Doctor Samuel Chambers was looking back over his left shoulder at Louisa in much the same way that West Point Second Classman Terrence Sterling II had done one fateful March evening more than a decade earlier.

Chapter 9

May 17, 1913

Truth be told, Angus Findlay was more worried about angry encounters with other former Confederates than his long-ago Union foes, and was strongly considering reversing his intention to attend the Gettysburg commemoration.

He had heard the sentiment expressed hundreds of times over the years, the words more or less the same:

"If ol' Jeb Stuart hadn't been a moseyin' around the countryside and instead had showed up any old time before the battle was half over, we'd a likely won at Gettysburg and then won the whole war!"

Whenever anyone found out that Angus Findlay had once been Captain Angus Findlay, Army of Northern Virginia, Cavalry Command, *aide-de-camp* to Major General J.E.B. Stuart himself during the campaign that culminated with the Battle of Gettysburg, the old sentiments about "if only ol' Jeb Stuart hadda done…" invariably came out. Ironically, in the years immediately after the war Angus Findlay – by then a former Confederate Cavalry Colonel – heard these utterances only rarely; Virginians in those days were more preoccupied with comprehending and surviving the Yankee-imposed Reconstruction than engaging in speculation about how a different outcome to the war might have come about. And since by the late 1860s Angus Findlay had become a notable figure in Virginia politics, doing his best to keep the Republican scalawags at bay and helping Richmond and the rest of the state rebuild, those who obtained an audience with him almost always had more pressing and relevant matters than rehashing what-ifs courtesy of the Lost Cause movement and the alleged shortcomings of "Ol' Jeb Stuart at Gettysburg."

After Reconstruction had ended, however, the South clawing its way back to some sense of normalcy with the Yankee occupiers now departed, young and old alike often fell to rehashing crucial moments from the war at which, if they were to be believed, the Confederates would likely have emerged victorious in both a given battle and the war itself. One of the more pervasive suppositions was based on the arrival of J.E.B. Stuart's Cavalry at Gettysburg not on the first day of engagement with the Army of the Potomac but rather on the afternoon of July 2nd, halfway through the three-day battle. Allegedly rebuked by General Lee himself for tardiness, Stuart and his men – Angus Findlay included – set out to redeem themselves. As almost anyone living in the former Confederacy during the last half of the 19th century could recite, Stuart's cavalry was ordered to engage the Yankees from the rear as part of a coordinated attack to disrupt the Union defenses against the forces of Pickett and the other Rebel generals marching straight at them from the opposite direction across open ground. Alas, the Yankee cavalry units commanded by General Gregg and General Custer repulsed Stuart, Findlay, and their fellow horsemen; Pickett's Charge failed to accomplish its aims; and the dreams of the Confederacy began to die.

Sometimes the "if only…" discussions were genteel, but oftentimes not, especially if whiskey was present at the discussion. J.E.B. Stuart was long gone, and often it seemed partway into an increasingly angry confrontation that Angus Findlay, the General's former aide, was thought to have been personally responsible for the failings of the former hero of the Confederacy and thus the downfall of their short-lived, self-declared nation.

Angus steered clear of Blue & Gray reunions – and even "Gray only" gatherings, such as the many United Confederate Veterans regular meetings and annual conventions one could find all around the South, year after year – and learned to deflect questions that might arise in the course of daily life about where he had been during the war and just what role he had played. Instead, he would deftly steer questioners to matters of rebuilding the South, still an ordeal in some parts of the old Confederacy even decades after the war had ended.

If he were to attend this upcoming Gettysburg commemoration, however, sidestepping discussions about General Stuart, or conjectures about what might have happened if only the General had arrived earlier, would be difficult if not impossible. No doubt Angus would encounter former members of Stuart's cavalry he hadn't seen in close to fifty years…not to mention survivors of Pickett's Charge who may very well boil over in anger at anyone with a linkage to Stuart's forces who suddenly became a reminder of the slaughter they had endured. Could he bear these encounters? At eighty-five years of age now, stooped over with his once-forceful gait subdued to a shuffle, he imagined himself powerless to fend off the blow of a fist or an angry cane wielded by a more vibrant – yet unreasonably angry and perhaps intoxicated – former Johnny Reb; maybe one no longer in his right mind and now unable to distinguish right from wrong. He had survived Gettysburg once; perhaps tempting fate a second time was not a wise move for the old Virginia politician.

He would think it over; there was still a little time to make his decision. He wished he could consult his beloved Charlotte, but she was gone for more than a decade now.

All four of his sons had gone west to Denver and California; he supposed he could telegraph them, but short bursts of half-sentences across the telegraph wire just didn't seem to be the means to solicit thoughtful advice on such a weighty matter. He could ask the opinions of his two daughters who were still alive (two other daughters had gone to their graves shortly after their mother) and who lived nearby in Richmond, but what would women know about this particular decision? Maybe he should ask the opinion of their husbands, his sons-in-law...

A light, pleasant rain began to fall and Angus Findlay looked back from his small tobacco patch that he dutifully tended to each year towards his old house a hundred yards distant, and thought about shuffling his way back to get under cover. But the rain was more of a mist and seemed to bring a sense of serenity to his troubled thoughts. No doubt his Charlotte, if she were still alive, would be calling as loudly as she could for Angus Findlay to come back to the house before he caught his death from the rainfall and the cold that would of course follow.

Maybe, though, death was not quite the unwelcome visitor for the lonely eighty-five year old man, and he turned back away from the house towards his tobacco as the gentle rainfall continued.

Chapter 10

June 28, 1913

John K. Tener, the Governor of Pennsylvania, had had enough of Woodrow Wilson and his administration down in Washington.

Receiving word this very day, on the very eve of opening the Gettysburg encampment, that Wilson would now be attending and speaking at the commemoration July 4th; that was irritating enough. Handbills had been published on April 4th announcing the President's appearance at the event, as had been decided during the preceding weeks. Shortly afterwards, however, the President withdrew his intention to appear and speak, meaning not only that the promise of the nation's Chief Executive gracing the event would now be an unfulfilled one, but also that the schedule for the morning of July 4th no longer contained any all-encompassing climactic event...nor any other events, for that matter. For weeks, the commission had spent many hours attempting to fill the void for that day.

But now came word that Wilson had changed his mind yet again and would be coming to Gettysburg to speak as his predecessor Lincoln had done half a century earlier. Another wrinkle in the plans, however: Wilson would arrive in Gettysburg mere moments before his appearance; transit to the encampment grounds to speak; and then immediately depart. Nothing more.

The fortunate part of this last-minute change, the Governor thought to himself, is that because of Wilson's dithering there was still an entire morning open for the President as had been originally planned, meaning that no other events needed to be switched around or cancelled despite the many hours already expended trying to fill that gap in the schedule for the commemoration. And with the President only at the commemoration for such a short period of time, security and protection concerns at the encampment for the President would be minimal. While it would have been a sight for the ages for the new Chief Executive to mingle with thousands of old warriors in food serving lines meal after meal, or along the boardwalked streets of the battlefield, or for him to share coffee and memories with old men wearing both blue and gray outside one of the thousands of sleeping tents night after night, the itinerary as it now stood seemed to be the best possible outcome…Wilson's last-minute change of mind notwithstanding.

This problem now at its apparently satisfactory conclusion (presuming the President didn't change his decision yet again in the next days, Tener realized; but there was nothing he could personally do to prevent that from happening so why worry, he thought), the Governor turned his thoughts to a much more critical problem…one that appeared to have been finally resolved at 6:00 this very Saturday morning.

Only eight days earlier, Wilson's new Secretary of War, Lindley Garrison, had sent a telegram to the Gettysburg Reunion Commission coldly declaring that because "the number expected at the Camp and the number required to be taken care of at the Camp will be fifty thousand instead of forty thousand" – as reported to Garrison by the Army's quartermaster in charge of equipping the encampment – "it is absolutely impossible from the funds available to take care of any more than the forty thousand. If you have arranged that ten thousand in addition attend, you must provide the funds to take care of them."

Garrison's telegram – received that Friday evening, just in time to cause a crisis among the Commission and the Commonwealth's government as a whole that entire weekend – concluded with this dismissive statement:

> "If you have committed yourself to the entertainment of more than the forty thousand initially estimated, you must make it perfectly plain to all those over the forty thousand that the responsibility is entirely yours and that you will provide for them. So far as I am concerned, I have as stated to you above, no facilities nor any prospect of getting any, which enables to do more than take care of the forty thousand who up to this time have been the expected number. LINDLEY M. GARRISON, Secretary of War"

Tener felt his blood begin to boil as he recalled not so much the telegram nor even the message itself – government appropriations were always a tricky business, as he well knew himself – but the condescending tone and the "perfectly plain" directive that Garrison and the War

Department had no intention of working with the Commission or Tener's Pennsylvania government to find some sort of solution during these final days before the commemoration began. Tener felt as he had on occasion during his professional baseball days, wanting to argue nose to nose with an unreasonable umpire; perhaps angrily kicking the dirt surrounding home plate all over Garrison's suit as he might an umpire's. As it was, Garrison was scheduled to speak on the opening day of the event immediately before Tener, and the Governor grimaced at the thought of sharing the stage with a man who could send such a telegram and cause such controversy in such a seemingly nonchalant manner.

There was an element of truth in the core of what the War Secretary had written, Tener acknowledged. In mid-May as the fourth and final meeting of the representatives from the states to the Committee was conducted, the estimated attendance by veterans had settled in at 43,000; with expected attrition that put the planned attendance right around 40,000. However, almost week by week, the estimate crept upwards until it was now just under 55,000! But clearly, despite the factual nature of Garrison's telegram, it was the cold-blooded, compassionless tone and disregard for the unified body of these aging veterans that angered Tener. After all, the additional sum needed was a mere $35,000…a drop in the bucket to the War Department!

As it was, Governor Tener swung into action, meeting the next day – a Saturday – with the leadership of the Pennsylvania Assembly to plan for appropriating the additional funds that the War Department was refusing to provide. One wrinkle in the plan, though: the Pennsylvania Constitution provided that every proposed bill must be read in its full length on three different days in each House of the Pennsylvania Assembly, meaning the earliest the desired wording could be added to the General Appropriations Bill was this Thursday June 26th...only three days before the encampment would officially open, and even as the earliest veterans were arriving. What a race against clock and calendar!

Then, as so often happens in governmental matters, a deadlock between Pennsylvania's Senate and House occurred on Thursday morning and by the time the conflict had been resolved and the bill voted upon, it was now 6:00 on Saturday morning of June 28th. Upon word of the bill's passage, however, work at the encampment resumed, this time at a fevered pitch.

Tener and the Commission had also cleverly tried to head off the work stoppage ordered by the Secretary of War by rallying forces from states all across the country through a series of telegrams to the GAR, UCV, the Associated Press, and the governments of the other states, all sent that Monday June 23rd in parallel with the Assembly beginning its work on the problem. The message of each telegram was to please make sure that your veterans know that Pennsylvania has introduced legislation to procure the additional funds that the War Department will not provide, and that we will absolutely provide for each and every one who makes the solemn journey to Gettysburg, or who might already be on his way; no one will be denied, and that cancelling trips was not necessary. And at the same time, Tener tried to get the War Department to rescind its work stoppage in light of the upcoming appropriations, given that with less than a week remaining time was of the essence.

Alas, no. Garrison's department was silent for three days and then brusquely replied on Thursday, the days ticking down, that regardless of Pennsylvania's intentions no supplies would be sent nor would any work resume "until State so appropriates."

But it was all resolved now, Tener breathed a large sigh of relief this Saturday evening as he prepared to journey to Gettysburg himself. Woodrow Wilson appeared once and for all to have made up his mind, and would now be attending and speaking in the slot originally allocated to him. The additional appropriations, painful as they were to come by, had been finalized and work on the encampment had resumed earlier this very day. Veterans had begun to arrive…though there were now indications from the railroad companies that far more than the anticipated 6,000 arrivals for Sunday the 29th would occur; perhaps double, or even triple that number would be on hand by sundown tomorrow!

John K. Tener allowed himself a touch of self-congratulations at having commandingly navigated through these several last-minute crises and complications on the very eve of what was promising to be an event for the ages. As he lowered himself into the chair in his personal office in the Governor's Mansion to draft a few more paragraphs of his own speech at the commemoration (fighting the impulse to include a biting commentary about the events of the preceding week thanks to Garrison's telegram immediately following that man's own speech; perhaps declaring "if it had been left to this man who just preceded me in speaking, thousands of you might have been turned away!"), he thought to himself that maybe some good would come out of this clash with the War Department over a small amount of money and what seemed to be an afterthought on the part of President Wilson with regards to his attendance at the grand commemoration, now that both matters had been favorably resolved. Namely, that veterans of the nation's future wars might be treated more respectfully and less dismissively, especially after very many years had passed and those future soldiers would be in the twilight of their years, by a government more appreciative of their sacrifices than this particular administration seemed to be.

Chapter 11

June 29, 1913

"Pop?"

Chester Morrison had dozed off again in the passenger seat of Jonathan's Pierce-Arrow Model 36; the sound of his son's voice snapped the aging man awake.

"We're almost there," Jonathan shot a quick glance towards his father before turning his eyes back towards the road. "About another five miles."

Not receiving any response, Jonathan looked back at his father and noticed the confused look on Chester Morrison's face.

"Gettysburg?" Jonathan continued, thinking perhaps he had to remind his father where they were headed.

"I know," his father quietly replied. In fact, Chester Morrison had been dreaming of another arrival in Gettysburg; this one fifty years earlier, and on foot rather than riding in his son's luxurious motorcar.

Father and son had made small talk during much of the four-hour journey from Philadelphia; except, that is, when Chester Morrison frequently dozed off for a few moments here and there before once again awakening. Each time he briefly slept during the trip, he dreamt not about the Battle of Gettysburg itself but rather some particular event from the days leading up to the moment the proverbial hellfire and damnation began raining down on the men of the 69th. Curiously, several of his dreams were vivid recollections of particular moments having to do with receiving his soldier's pay. Slipping into the world of dreams when Jonathan's motor car was somewhere around Lancaster, Chester omnisciently watched himself – more precisely, his eighteen-year old self, a newly volunteered Private – reading the General Orders document that had been issued by the War Department's Adjutant General's Office and which detailed how various advance payments and bounties would be paid during either the next three years or for the duration of the war. Upon waking Chester recalled, for the first time in many years, the $50 bounty he had received upon completing two years' service in the Army of the Potomac…a near-fortune to the poor Irish boy he had been then before the war ended and he began his climb through the ranks at Baldwin Locomotive.

In another dream he saw himself lined up with other long-forgotten faces from the 69th in a farmer's field in Uniontown, Maryland, on the afternoon of June 30th, 1863 – fifty years ago tomorrow – waiting to receive two months of eagerly anticipated back pay, not realizing that two days later they would all be fighting for their very lives and solder's pay would be the farthest thing from his mind for the next several days.

Finally, during this most recent slumber from which Jonathan awoke his father as they approached Gettysburg, Chester had been dreaming of the all-day march from Uniontown to Gettysburg and their arrival at dusk on July 1st, near the end of that first day's fighting. Upon awakening and regaining his wits, it seemed to Chester Morrison as he recalled fragments of his dreams over the past four hours that his mind was forcing away thoughts of

Cemetery Ridge and Pickett's Charge but sensing the need for his dreams to be filled by some matter or another related to Gettysburg, instead took him down the memory lane of long-ago paydays and marches from one encampment spot to another before his first encounter in major battle with the Army of Northern Virginia. There had been fleeting skirmishes with the Rebels along the way from the time Chester had joined the 69th, but nothing like what he was about to face the day after the calendar turned over into the second half of 1863…

Jonathan again looked over towards his father, his mind frantically searching for some other diversionary topic to broach, but with the borough and the battlefield only mere miles away now he saw the futility of idle chatter as a tactic to distract his father from what he was about to encounter. If they were at home instead of in a moving automobile Jonathan could bring out the chessboard, or perhaps put one of the new Edison disc records on the phonograph and listen to music. Alas, wheeling along in his Pierce-Arrow, neither was possible.

His father broke the silence.

"I imagine with all the Irishmen of the 69th there, one of us will break into *Abie Sings an Irish Song*, no?"

Jonathan smiled. The new Irving Berlin song had become one of his father's favorites during the past month since its publication, and most nights as father and son played chess or relaxed with evening's edition of *The Philadelphia Evening Telegraph* that particular Edison disc made it onto the phonograph at least two or three times during the course of the evening. To Jonathan's surprise Chester Morrison began to sing aloud as the Pierce-Arrow moved along the York Road into the borough, headed towards the final turns towards the encampment.

In an Irish neighborhood,
Abie kept a clothing store;
But business wasn't good.
No one came into the store and Abe wondered why
But soon winked his eye
Then bought up ev'ry Irish song that he could buy;
In an hour and a half
Someone taught him how to sing the Irish songs,
Somehow he learned them all with ease;
Them Irish melodies
He knows them all by heart and now...

Jonathan couldn't resist joining his father in the chorus as they motored past store fronts and well-kept houses.

When an Irishman looks in the window,
Abie sings an Irish song;
When a suit of clothes he sells,
He turns around and yells
"By Killarney's lakes and dells!"
Any time an Irish customer comes in the place
Thinking that it's owned by someone of the Irish race;
If he looks at Abie with a doubt upon his face
Abie sings an Irish song...

Father and son eased right into the second verse as the buildings of the borough slid behind them.

Ev'ry morning Abie goes
Through the store a-singing
"Where the River Shannon flows"...

Then they both saw it.

Slipping past a rise on the Emmitsburg Road, headed slightly southwest, the acres upon acres of tents came into view all at once. Jonathan heard his father gasp slightly but by the time he looked to his right the old man had composed himself and seemed to have narrowed his eyes, intently staring at the vision rising up in front of his son's motor car.

"An amazing sight," Chester Morrison solemnly declared, and Jonathan was struck by the forceful calm his father had commanded into his tones.

And what they gazed upon was indeed amazing. On the grounds of that long-ago battlefield stood some 5,000 sleeping tents, one after another; close to 300 acres of encampment grounds in all. Jonathan instantly became concerned again about the thought of his father, nearing seventy years of age, sleeping along with seven other old men in one of those tents for the next five nights. Was he physically up to the challenge after a life of Main Line comfort? True, his father was a hard worker by day but to the best of Jonathan's knowledge, since the end of the war Chester Morrison had not slept anywhere but under the shelter of a house or rented room.

Jonathan slowed the Pierce-Arrow to a crawl behind the slowly moving line of other motor cars along the Emmitsburg Road, headed towards the camp. Even though most of the Blue and Gray veterans would be arriving by railroad, there would be an abundance of old soldiers coming from locations around the Commonwealth of Pennsylvania, and many of them would, like Chester Morrison, be accompanied by a son or perhaps even a grandson and arriving by automobile instead. Even some of the former Confederates coming from northern Virginia would likewise be doing the same. The result, then, was this slowly creeping line of automobiles – mostly Tin Lizzies but a few of the more luxurious vehicles such as Jonathan's Model 36 interspersed among the Model T's – that Jonathan and Chester now joined.

Almost half an hour passed until they reached the area just outside the encampment that had been set aside for the parking of automobiles as well as horse-drawn carriages. Jonathan wheeled his Pierce-Arrow in between a Schacht Roadster and what appeared to be a brand new Pope Hartford 33. Where he parked looked to be about a quarter mile from where a large concentration of men gathered. Most of the crowd appeared to be made up of old veterans but there were also a number of relative youngsters such as Jonathan who were accompanying fathers, grandfathers, and uncles.

Jonathan came around to let his father out of the passenger side of the motor car but Chester had already done so himself. Jonathan instead retrieved his father's two travel bags from the automobile's rear seat and carried both of them as the two men began to walk towards where they thought the registration area was. Jonathan, of course, was not staying on the encampment grounds; in a tent or otherwise. The commission responsible for the gathering had made it abundantly clear in each of their mailings and all other printed materials that only invited veterans of the Civil War would be housed on the encampment grounds. Anyone else, such as Jonathan Morrison, who was accompanying one of the veterans must do the same as someone who was coming to Gettysburg as a spectator to witness the historic festivities: secure a room in one of the local boarding houses or hotels.

As one would have expected, rooms in or just outside the Borough were quickly secured and those who had dawdled found themselves forced to find hotel or boarding house space as far away as York to the east or Harrisburg to the north; even Frederick, Maryland, nearly forty miles to the south, was about to be inundated by travelers because of The Great Reunion.

Thanks to his stature in the Pennsylvania business community, though, and also because he had acted promptly when his father made the decision to come to Gettysburg, Jonathan Morrison was able to secure a room at the Hotel Gettysburg in town and thus could be nearby his father throughout the commemoration rather than dozens of miles away. After getting Chester Morrison registered and helping him to wherever it was that he would be assigned for sleeping quarters, Jonathan would check himself into the hotel and then return later in the day to walk around the grounds with his father.

After another fifteen minutes Chester and Jonathan made their way to the front of one of the registration lines. A man in civilian clothes was seated next to others dressed in the same manner, all behind a long table filled with stacks of cards. Nearby several Army soldiers milled about; some observing the goings-on, others engaged in conversation with one or more of the just-arriving old men.

After offering his name and state credentials, the man behind the table handed Chester Morrison a two-sided identification tag, each side bearing the phrase "To be Carried in Your Pocket During the Gettysburg Reunion" along the bottom. On the front side were spaces for Chester to fill in his name, address, age, height, and weight; the reverse side ominously bore the words "In case of SICKNESS or ACCIDENT please communicate with…"

in the middle along with space underneath for someone's name to be filled in. Chester reached into his suit jacket pocket, retrieved his fountain pen, and scribbled his personal information on the front and Jonathan's information – including the fact that he would be located at the Hotel Gettysburg during the reunion – on the back.

Chester handed the tag back to the man behind the table who took a quick look at both sides and then pleasantly said,

"Welcome to Gettysburg, Mister Morrison. Would you like someone to help you find your way to the Pennsylvania delegation area? When you arrive there they will direct you to the tent you've been assigned and will issue you your mess kit, show you where the latrines are, point out the postal office and the Western Union temporary office…"

The man continued on for nearly a minute longer, regurgitating the words that he no doubt had spoken dozens or even hundreds of times already this day and would speak again hundreds of times more. When he had finished (or at least appeared to have finished), Chester replied, nodding to Jonathan as he did,

"My son is with me. If you just point me towards the Pennsylvania delegation he can walk with me there." He looked around at the ever-growing crowd that seemed as if it had swelled markedly even while Chester and Jonathan had been waiting in line.

"It appears as if your guides are needed for those who are arriving by themselves, so I don't want to take up the efforts of any one of them if they are needed for these many other men."

"That's very thoughtful of you, sir," the man behind the table replied. "We had been expecting around six thousand of you to arrive today, but it appears that more than twenty thousand will actually arrive. So we are struggling to keep up with everything, especially since it's getting so blazing hot!"

The man wiped the beads of perspiration from his brow as he spoke, and Chester was forced to acknowledge that indeed, this day seemed especially hot. As all would learn soon enough, Sunday the twenty-ninth of June, 1913 was a day that the thermometer in Gettysburg would eclipse one hundred degrees, and many of these old men would succumb to the heat and humidity throughout the day and require medical attention.

"Don't forget to make sure you receive a mess kit," the man said as Chester and Jonathan prepared to step aside for the person in line behind them. "Our first meal will be supper tonight, and from that point on we will serve three meals each day up through breakfast on July the sixth, if you will be staying with us that long."

"Thank you," Chester replied, and father and son headed in the direction the man had pointed them to. As might be expected, the number of veterans from Pennsylvania eclipsed that of any other state – more than 21,000 of all those attending – and thus the area set aside in the Great Camp for the Pennsylvania delegation was by far the largest. The commission had made the assignments within the encampment area for the various states based on the ever-shifting counts of expected attendees, but within each of those areas the states themselves assigned the attendees to their respective tents as registrations arrived. It wouldn't be until he made his way to the Pennsylvania registration area, further within the Great Camp, that Chester Morrison would find out which specific tent it would be where he would spend the remaining nights of the encampment.

* * *

"There are fifty-five pay telephones around the grounds," the man behind the registration desk was saying to Devin McAteer.

"I hope you saw in the registration information that you needed to notify anybody who will be sending you mail or a telegram that they need to add 'Veteran in the Pennsylvania Delegation' after your name so you can be easily found."

"I did," Devin answered.

"That's good," the man nodded. "And if you need to send a telegram yourself just ask any of the Boy Scouts to direct you to the temporary Western Union facility."

The man leaned forward, lowering his voice for reasons of propriety.

"You will find ninety latrines throughout the camp," he said. "We have seating for 3,500 at any one time."

Devin just nodded. Whatever facilities had been arranged were just fine with him. For years, even after the war and his continued service during Reconstruction, he had toiled in Carnegie's mills with sanitary facilities as limited and as primitive as those he had been forced to endure while in the Army. A few days of field conditions was fine with him; he would be returning home to Pittsburgh and the comforts of Kerwin's home soon enough.

His identification tag filled out and in hand, Devin picked up his travel luggage but had only taken a dozen steps before he saw a familiar face.

"Hello, Devin," Seamus McAteer said as he walked directly towards his cousin. The retired coal miner looked a touch older than the last time he and Devin had seen one another – six years earlier – but for the most part appeared to be hale and healthy.

"Seamus," Devin said, lowering the suitcase in his right hand to the ground and then extending his hand towards his cousin.

Instead of clasping hands, Seamus dropped both of his bags when he reached Devin and embraced his cousin. In response Devin lowered his other bag and completed the hug with both of his own arms.

"It's insufferably hot today," Seamus said. "Far worse than the past three days have been." Seamus McAteer had been in Gettysburg since the 26th, attending the three-day annual encampment of the Pennsylvania Grand Army of the Republic that immediately preceded the Great Reunion's own encampment. Seamus had been active in the Luzerne County GAR for years, and almost without fail attended both county and state-wide meetings and encampments. Devin, on the other hand, steered away from any sort of veterans' organizations; almost as if his extended Army time through Reconstruction had given him enough of anything to do with soldiering to last for a lifetime.

"How is Noreen?" Seamus asked.

"She is well," Devin answered. "And Helen?" referring to Seamus' wife.

"She is also well," Seamus replied. The exchanged inquiries about each other's children, their children's spouses, their grandchildren; each one's remaining brothers and sisters; neighbors known to the other; most anyone.

Seamus looked his cousin squarely in the eye.

"I'm so very grateful that you decided to attend," he told Devin.

Devin McAteer shrugged.

"It was your last letter that did it, you know," he replied.

"I figured as much," Seamus allowed a sheepish grin to come to his lined face. He looked around the grounds where the two of them were standing.

"You've never been to Gettysburg at all, have you?" he asked.

Devin shook his head.

"No, never."

"I've been here four times prior," Seamus nodded. "Each time for a Pennsylvania GAR encampment."

He looked around some more before continuing.

"But nothing I've ever seen here, or anywhere else, matches the magnitude before our eyes at this very moment."

"I imagine so," Devin replied.

Both cousins turned to watch two Boy Scouts approaching, one of whom appeared to be especially young.

"May we help you sirs locate your part of the encampment grounds?" the older one asked.

"I believe so," Seamus answered.

"To what state's delegation do you belong, then?"

"Pennsylvania," Seamus replied.

The Boy Scout looked over at Devin, who responded with,

"I as well; Pennsylvania."

"That's fine, sirs, we can escort both of you together. If you will follow me…"

The two Boy Scouts began walking in the direction of the sleeping tents.

"What is your name?" Seamus McAteer asked the older Scout.

"Christopher Reynolds, from Frederick, Maryland," came the reply. Seamus was just about to ask the younger Scout – who had yet to speak a word – the same question when the small boy spoke up.

"My name is Randall Sterling, from here in Gettysburg," he said.

"Well, it's my pleasure to meet you, Master Sterling. And you also, Master Reynolds," Seamus said. "My name is Seamus McAteer, from Luzerne County, and this other gentleman here is my cousin from Pittsburgh, Devin McAteer."

Devin wordlessly tipped the edge of his hat in greeting towards the two Boy Scouts.

"My father was in the Army," the younger Scout said.

"But he died."

The two cousins looked at each other.

"I'm very sorry to hear that," Devin McAteer offered. "I'm sure your father was a brave man."

"I think he was," young Randall Sterling replied. "I don't remember him very well but I wanted to be a Boy

Scout for this reunion so I could wear a uniform like he used to."

The older scout looked up at Devin McAteer, and then over at Seamus. In hushed tones he said,

"He's been telling that to everyone we've taken into camp."

"Well," Seamus replied, "I'm sure he misses his father, so being at this momentous gathering is probably something he very much wanted to do."

"We're here," the older Scout suddenly said. And indeed, the quartet had arrived at the crowded registration and assignment area for the Pennsylvania veterans. The two Boy Scouts bid the old veterans farewell – for the time being – and together walked back to the main registration area of the encampment area.

After another half hour of waiting in the scorching sunshine, making small talk with other men in line – no one either of the McAteers had once known, though; so far all the other Pennsylvanians in line were veterans of Gettysburg – the McAteers made their way to the table. They conferred with the assignment staff and were each handed a small slip of paper bearing the number of a particular sleeping tent along with their mess kits. As expected and per each one's prior request, the tent numbers were the same.

The McAteers each grabbed their travel bags again and followed the verbal directions the man at the table had given them: four rows over to the right of where they stood; another right to begin walking along one of the avenues between tents on both sides; and then down about eight tents on their left.

Two minutes later, each of the McAteers huffing and freely perspiring, they verified that they were in front of the correct tent and walked inside, immediately grateful to be out from under the broiling sun. A solitary man was seated on one of the sleeping cots, slightly hunched forward, his mess kit resting in his hands. He appeared to be deep in thought but as soon as the McAteers entered and he noticed that he was no longer alone, he stood and walked towards them.

"Hello," Devin McAteer said, lowering both of his travel bags and extending his right hand. "I'm Devin McAteer, from Pittsburgh, and this is my cousin Seamus McAteer from up in Luzerne County."

The man stopped in front of them, shaking Devin's hand first and then Seamus'.

"It's a pleasure to meet both of you; it appears we will be sharing accommodations for the next few days," the man said. "I am Chester Morrison, from Philadelphia."

Chapter 12

June 30, 1913

"So what do you think?"

Edgar Sullivan looked over to his brother Johnny in response to the younger Sullivan's question as they both shuffled towards the entrance to the Great Tent. The sole event in that enormous venue this day before the official opening of the commemoration was to be a reunion of the survivors of General Buford's cavalry in attendance along with – surprisingly – the veterans of Joe Wheeler's Confederate cavalry who were in attendance. Even though Wheeler's men had fought in the South's Army of Tennessee rather than Lee's Army of Northern Virginia, and had not been participants in the affairs at Gettysburg, the organizers felt that starting off right away with a joint Blue-Gray event of some sort would set the tone of chivalrous, reconciliatory brotherhood for the entire event. And since horsemen of cavalry units often were chivalry personified, matching Buford's and Wheeler's survivors seemed to be an appropriate beginning to the commemoration. Some on the commission felt that J.E.B. Stuart's cavalry would have been a better selection for the Confederate side of this gathering considering that Stuart's forces had fought at Gettysburg, but for whatever reason the organizers selected the survivors among Wheeler's men who had trekked to Pennsylvania, and the event would be conducted that way.

"Well?" Johnny asked after it became apparent that his older brother did not intend to respond. He was growing irritable at Edgar's demeanor, more withdrawn than usual, ever since they had arrived at the railroad depot in Tucson five days earlier.

It had started on the platform when an elderly man dressed in a baggy, worn dark gray business suit, apparently also on his way eastward on this very train, tipped his faded gray Confederate cavalry hat in greeting as both Sullivans walked past him. Edgar had slowed slightly, locked eyes with him, and snarled "Howdy there, Reb!" in as surly of a voice as he could muster. The old Confederate appeared to pay no mind to Edgar Sullivan's "greeting" but Johnny Sullivan was horrified. Would the entire train trip to Gettysburg be like this? The entire time at the commemoration?

Only ten men would attend The Great Reunion traveling from the new state of Arizona (which both brothers still referred to without fail as "Arizona Territory" despite last year's statehood). Seven of them, including both of the Sullivans, were Union veterans and they were joined by three Confederates. Nine of the ten – all but one of the Yankees – would be traveling together by train courtesy of nearly one thousand dollars worth of tickets paid for by Dwight B. Heard, the Arizona cattle baron and new publisher of *The Arizona Republican* since purchasing the newspaper last year. The Sullivans and this elderly Confederate – Clyde Hodges by name, long ago a member of the 17th Georgia Infantry that had fought at Gettysburg – were traveling together from Tucson to Phoenix where they would join up with the other six. Three of those men (two Yankees, one Rebel) were from Phoenix while the others would be coming from farther reaches of the vast new state.

Edgar and Johnny sat by themselves for the journey to Phoenix, apart from Hodges, saying little other than a few comments here and there about the desolate desert scenery as it slipped past the window next to their train seats. This first leg of their journey ended soon enough and on the platform at the Phoenix depot, Mister Heard gathered together all nine of his passengers for the flashbulbs of one of his *Arizona Republican* photographers and the script pads of two of his reporters. Perfunctory introductions were made among the nine and then a half hour was set aside before departure for interviews of the attendees by *Republican* newsmen. Upon learning of Edgar and Johnny Sullivan's past association with the Earps, Tombstone, and that corner of long-ago Arizona history, one of the reporters began intensively questioning the brothers until Edgar snarled "Enough, already!" and stomped off.

The first four hours of the journey from Phoenix was a repeat of the train ride from Tucson. Johnny sat with Edgar apart from any of the other travelers, though on several occasions he rose from the seat next to his sullen brother and went over to talk to the other Civil War veterans. Finally, somewhere just past the New Mexico state line, Johnny turned to his brooding older brother and said:

"If this is the way you're going to be the entire time, I wish you had just stayed back in Tucson, playing poker and drinking your Old Overholt. I aim to have a good time and I ain't gonna let you spoil it for me."

A few moments of silence followed, and then Edgar turned to look at Johnny.

"So I was thinking when that Johnny Reb, what's his name, Clark Hodge?"

"Hodges," Johnny corrected. "Clyde Hodges."

"Yeah, Clyde Hodges. Anyway, I was thinking when he was walking towards us that suppose fifty years ago he was with Harry Heth's Rebels who ran right into us and started the whole fight. And suppose…"

"He wasn't," Johnny interrupted. He said he was with the 17th Georgia, and I think that they…"

"Yeah, I know what he said," Edgar snapped at his brother. "That ain't the point. I'm just saying suppose he was with Heth. And if it ain't him then you know damn well we'll run into more than one feller that was. Now can I finish what I was saying?"

More than anything Johnny Sullivan was surprised and intrigued that his brother seemed to be on some sort of introspective journey of thought. He simply nodded for Edgar to continue.

"So anyway, like I was saying, suppose this Hodges feller was one of the Rebs we ran up against on July the first. And suppose at one point there he had *me* in his gunsights, and fired a shot at me but missed. It just don't feel right makin' pleasantries with someone who might well have killed me and just pretending that it didn't happen."

He paused for a moment, looked out the window at a mass of pines, then looked back at his brother.

"You understanding at all what I'm saying here?"

Johnny thought for a moment then responded.

"Yeah, I get it, but ain't that the whole point of this thing? That once and for all we and the Rebs who are still alive all these years later put all of this behind us? It don't matter who tried to kill who, or who shot who, or anything like that. Hell, I'm willing to bet that somewhere on those grounds there's gonna be one of us or one of them who lost a leg or an arm, and he's gonna be talking with someone from the other side and by golly, they're gonna figure out that it was that other feller who done that."

Johnny paused, looked out the window himself, and then back at his brother to continue.

"But you know what? It wasn't personal. Gettysburg was a whole battle with, what, almost a hundred thousand of us and about seventy or eighty thousand of them. That's a whole lot of soldiers in uniform all shooting at each other all around one battlefield. It wasn't like down in Tombstone where the Cowboys were gunnin' for Wyatt and Virgil and Doc in particular, or afterwards when we were all hell bent on huntin' down every last one of them who we knew by name and by face and then killing each one of them dead when we found 'em. Gettysburg was different. Hell, every battle we were in during the war was different."

He paused again.

"Hell, it just ain't personal and I just ain't gonna give much thought to wondering if some Reb I walk by or start talking to in a chow line maybe might have taken a shot at me fifty years ago. If that bothered me, I wouldn't be going."

Edgar shrugged.

"Maybe you're right," he nodded towards his younger brother. "I can't help the way I feel, but maybe as this whole thing gets going I'll think about it the way that you do."

You better, Johnny Sullivan thought to himself, but didn't say anything.

* * *

The days of the train ride passed uneventfully. Edgar Sullivan warmed up slightly to his fellow travelers, even Clyde Hodges and the other two Confederate veterans. There was some exchange of tales of the three days at Gettysburg, but for the most part the nine men danced around that subject and instead talked about other battles they had been in during the war; and even more about what each had done after the war was over. As might have been expected, the mention of Tombstone and the Earps back at the Phoenix depot had the effect of immediately making Edgar and Johnny Sullivan the center of discussion for much of the journey.

The train rolled past Pittsburgh somewhere around 2:00 in the morning on June 30th; only hours to go, Edgar Sullivan thought as he gazed out the window, his brother snoring away next to him. Sleep was impossible this final night on the train, and he continued to second-guess his decision to make this journey.

During the journey, nearly every moment that he wasn't reluctantly engaged in discussion with his brother and the other men, Edgar found himself thinking about his late wife Katie. She has passed back in '99, and reflecting on the more than dozen years since losing her Edgar admitted to himself that his general mood and happiness had deteriorated markedly since she had died. Their three children were all still in Tucson and Edgar regularly rotated Sunday dinner among each of them and their families; that gave him some sense of remembrance for the thirty years he had had with Katie. She had followed him from Paris, Illinois, where he had met her two years after coming home from the war and where they had married, all the way west to Prescott then down to Tombstone and then finally up to Tucson by the time the '90s had rolled around.

They had less than ten years together in Tucson after the restlessness and tensions of the Prescott and Tombstone years had been left behind for good. They had been a good ten years, Edgar reckoned. But then they were gone when she was taken by acute phthisis, the same disease that had taken his friend Doc Holliday.

Edgar looked over at his snoring brother. Johnny had been married briefly after the war, but his wife – Laurabelle – wanted no part of the brothers' trek westward to Arizona Territory, and she stayed behind in the state capitol of Springfield and obtained a divorce. Johnny mostly went with saloon girls after that and more than a few times in a drunken moment told his older brother how much he envied Edgar's marriage to Katie and the children brought forth from that union.

Now, though, Edgar's marriage was no more because of his wife's passing while Johnny still occasionally paid a visit to one of the houses just outside downtown Tucson, even though the age of seventy was creeping up on him. Johnny hadn't had the thirty years of marriage that his older brother had had, but neither did he have to bear the more than thirteen years (and counting) of painful loss that followed. Who was better off? All Edgar knew was that compared against himself, his younger brother generally had a more tempered outlook on life; drank less; and generally got into fewer verbal confrontations these days. So maybe, just maybe, the pain of living for more than a decade after losing a love meant that he might have been better off in the long run living as Johnny had.

Edgar Sullivan shook these morose thoughts from his head. Only hours more to go, he again thought to himself as he watched the wilderness of Pennsylvania pass by for the first time since Buford's cavalry rode into Pennsylvania at the very end of June of 1863.

*   *   *

The Sullivans and their Arizona comrades disembarked at the Gettysburg depot and headed en masse to receive their credentials for the commemoration. One sleeping tent would accommodate all ten of them. For the most part, each of the twelve-man tents blanketing the encampment grounds would house only eight men to give these old veterans some stretching-out room, but all ten of the Arizona attendees would bunk down together. Which also meant that unlike many states' delegations, Yankee and Rebel would share the same tent for the duration of the encampment.

After waiting in line for nearly an hour – my Lord, the heat and humidity are unbearable, both Johnny and Edgar thought to themselves as they waited; even worse than blazing Arizona! – and upon completing their registrations, the brothers headed for their assigned tent along with three of the other Arizonans while the others decided to explore the grounds. Johnny and Edgar had barely enough time to stow their travel bags before heading in the direction of the Great Tent and the gathering of many of the surviving members of those who first encountered the Rebels and set in motion the three days of conflagration.

*   *   *

"So what do you think?" Johnny Sullivan asked his brother again. This time Edgar shrugged in response.

"I suppose we go in now, that's what I think," the older Sullivan replied, actually smiling a bit as he did. And inside the Great Tent the brothers went.

Immediately upon entering a broadly smiling, glad-handing old man, his portly figure overstuffed into what seemed to be a surprisingly pristine Union Army blue uniform, came strolling briskly towards the Sullivans.

"Howdy boys!" the man said, his right hand already extended. "Hiram Phillips is the name. You boys are Union, right?"

Neither of the Sullivans was wearing any clothing that indicated which side of the war they had been on. Both were dressed in light gray suits of clothing; each wore a pale green bow tie, and upon each head was a brimmed straw hat.

"We were with Buford," Johnny Sullivan replied, extending his own right hand. "I'm Johnny Sullivan," he said then nodded to his right. "And this is my brother Edgar Sullivan."

Hiram Phillips narrowed his eyes for a moment, appearing to be deep in thought. The broad smile disappeared from his face as he pondered, and then suddenly reappeared.

"No, I don't expect that I know you fellows. What regiment were you with?"

"8th Illinois," Johnny answered.

"Ah," Phillips said, "that explains it. "I was with the 9th New York, in the Second Brigade. The 8th Illinois was with the First Brigade as I recall, right?"

Johnny Sullivan had to search his memory. While he certainly recalled the number of the specific Illinois regiment he and his brother had joined and had ridden with, so very many years had passed that he couldn't quite recall exactly which Brigade in Buford's Division the 8th Illinois had been part of. But what this man Hiram Phillips was saying seemed to trigger a long-buried memory.

"I suppose so," Johnny continued. "But I reckon that I don't fully recall, it's been so long."

"Ain't that the truth," Hiram Phillips responded, his smile broadening even more – if that were possible. "It's been a whole lot of time that's gone by since those days. You fellows ever get back here to Gettysburg since then? You come to the 25th reunion back in '88?"

Johnny shook his head, and was just about to answer when Edgar finally spoke up.

"Nah, we ain't never been back in Pennsylvania since we rode south," he said.

Hiram nodded, apparently glad that this other Sullivan fellow finally decided to join the conversation.

"So where did you boys come from? You still in Illinois?"

Johnny's turn to reply.

"From out in Arizona Territory," he answered. "Tucson, if you ever heard of that." He decided that no matter where the conversation went, for now he would leave Tombstone out of the dialogue. Even he was getting tired of talking about those days.

"Arizona, huh?" Hiram said. "I never been out there myself, even though I did go all the way to San Francisco once back in the '90s."

The banter continued for another couple of minutes, Edgar actually joining in the conversation here and there.

Finally Hiram Phillips looked at Edgar first and then Johnny and said,

"Well, I'm gonna try to search out some of the fellows from the 9th New York; gonna see if I recognize any of them or if any of them remember me."

Johnny nodded.

"I'll be seeing you boys around the grounds, I expect," Hiram continued.

"I expect we will," Johnny agreed and the three men shook hands in parting as Hiram walked back to the center area of the Great Tent, in search for some of his own long-ago comrades.

The Sullivans wandered around the Great Tent together for some fifteen minutes, scanning faces. Fifty years had passed but Johnny in particular felt sure that he would recognize the features of at least some of those they had once ridden and fought alongside. More than 500 men had ridden with the 8th Illinois Cavalry into Gettysburg; at least some of them should still be alive and among this gathering of old men.

Johnny and Edgar were still wandering when a young Army second lieutenant strode up to the brothers. Both brothers took notice of the young officer as he made his way towards them, and both immediately had the same thought as they watched his strides: a West Pointer, for certain.

"Am I able to be of assistance to you gentlemen?" the lieutenant asked.

"We're just seeing if anyone from our regiment is in the crowd," Johnny replied.

"And what regiment might that be? I may have already spoken with someone from your regiment and I could then direct you to him." The lieutenant's manner of speech dripped with military precision.

"8th Illinois," Johnny said.

"Ah," the Lieutenant responded and his face took on the same appearance of concentration that Hiram Phillips' had a short while earlier. He turned his head to look behind him, scanning the faces.

"I believe I've spoken with two gentleman thus far who indicated to me that they were with the 8th Illinois Cavalry," he said. "But I do not see them at the moment. If you would like I can accompany you around the Tent to help you locate them."

"That would be fine," Johnny replied and the three of them began walking towards the concentration of old veterans near the center of the tent.

The lieutenant, marching between the two brothers, Johnny on his left and Edgar to his right, looked in the direction of Edgar who thus far hadn't said anything in the presence of the young man.

"I am a cavalry officer myself," he offered.

Edgar looked at him.

"That right?"

"Yes, sir," the lieutenant affirmed. "I graduated from West Point in the class of '09" – upon mention of The Point the two brothers each leaned slightly forward and shot brief "we were right about that" glances at one another as the officer continued speaking – "and was commissioned directly into the cavalry."

He held out his right hand to Edgar as he continued walking.

"Second Lieutenant George Patton, United States Army Cavalry," he offered.

Edgar offered his own right hand, though he slowed his pace slightly as he did.

"Edgar Sullivan," he said.

"Johnny Sullivan," came the sound from the lieutenant's left and after shaking Edgar's hand he turned to shake Johnny's as well.

"I have a personal interest in this commemoration," Lieutenant Patton said as the three of them continued walking forward. "My great uncle, Lieutenant Colonel Waller Patton, was mortally wounded during Pickett's Charge. He died weeks later at the field hospital at Pennsylvania College; he never made it back home alive to Virginia."

Edgar's pace slowed to a crawl.

"I'm sorry to hear that," he said, thinking perhaps that this lieutenant was curious as to whether the two old men whom he was accompanying at this very moment had had anything to do with his great uncle's death; thinking also of the uneasiness he had confided to his brother during the early portion of their train travel to this commemoration. "We had been pulled away from the field by then," he continued, "so we..."

"Oh, no," Lieutenant Patton interrupted. "I'm not implying that either of you two might have been personally responsible for shooting my great uncle. I was merely commenting that for my family, Gettysburg is a revered field of battle. Even though I am from Virginia and my family fought on the Confederate side, I am personally a member of the United States Army Cavalry as you men once were, and we likewise share a bond because of this common call to duty on behalf of our country."

The men walked in silence for another minute, closing in on the crowd at the Tent's center.

"I believe I see one of the men who may be a veteran of your 8th Illinois," Lieutenant Patton pointed, and the three men continued walking forward.

As they came closer, both Edgar and Johnny Sullivan believed that the old man they each thought this young lieutenant was pointing at was indeed someone they recognized from long ago, and they each prepared himself for what they expected would be the first of many handshakes with someone they had once known but hadn't seen for nearly five decades.

Chapter 13

June 30, 1913

Samuel Chambers was worried.

Another hour and a half of blazing sunshine remained in this cloudless, season-lengthened day, and even though the temperature had ticked down two degrees since its apex at 6:00, the air was as heavily sticky as it had been all day; and the stifling weather continued to take its toll on these old men. Many of these old veterans had wandered around the encampment grounds for hours without shelter because of an apparent shortage of sleeping tents, and several hours earlier Samuel had overhead Governor Tener angrily demand that Major Normoyle, the Army's Quartermaster in charge of facilities and supplies at the encampment, "move heaven and earth to secure more tents by nightfall no matter what the Secretary says or writes!"

The thought of hundreds of these old men traveling hundreds or even thousands of miles to this magnificent event only to be left to their own devices because of a shortage of sleeping facilities saddened Samuel, and only moments before he had gazed upon a group of men leaving the encampment grounds, travel baggage in hand, apparently headed back to the Gettysburg train platform. Still, he shook these thoughts and images from his head. His primary concern of the moment upon which he needed to focus was the mounting count of victims of the day's relentless heat and humidity; a count that was now over two hundred.

So far, four old men had expired: two yesterday, and two so far today. Truth be told, the count of fatalities was far below the level that Samuel feared it would be by this point, and for that matter he had privately expected many times more than the 220 or 230 overall victims of the heat that were currently under the treatment of the medical staff at this point. So on the one hand, as the minutes of the final day of June, 1913 ticked away, the toll wasn't nearly as severe as it might have been. Yet Samuel knew that at any moment a dozen more of those aging men currently resting in one of the treatment beds could slip away, so vigilance was the order of the moment.

"Doctor! Over here!"

Samuel had been on his way across the grounds to seek out Lieutenant Colonel Bradley, the officer placed in charge of the overall medical facilities for the reunion only weeks earlier by authority of the Army. Bradley seemed to be a reasonable man and recognized that the preparations that had been made under Samuel Chambers and his predecessor Malcolm Waterston were well-planned and well-executed, and therefore a heavy hand on behalf of the United States Army's Medical Corps was unnecessary. Still, Bradley insisted on being informed throughout the day as to the shifting counts of patients under care after they fell victim to the day's heat (or for any other reason, including more than two dozen men admitted to the hospital after over-indulging in alcohol throughout the day, and one old Confederate who had been diagnosed with malaria).

Samuel rushed over to the nurse who had called for help. She was kneeling over an old gentleman dressed in a dark suit of clothes that could have been worn by a veteran from either side, yet the gray cavalry hat resting next to his head indicated what side of the war he had been on. Samuel drank in the entirety of the scene as he arrived and knelt on the other side of the prone man. This old Confederate was 80 if he was a day; probably 85, Samuel reckoned.

"He collapsed just as I was walking by," the nurse said to Samuel but without raising her head; she remained looking at the victim as she maintained a firm grip on the glass thermometer she had placed in his mouth, watching for the first signs of convulsion to prevent him from crushing the glass and mercury while the device was still placed in his mouth.

Seeing that the man was still conscious, Samuel asked him even as he was fitting the stethoscope device in his ears,

"What's your name, soldier?"

The man's response was only a groan. After waiting a few more seconds, Samuel asked the man's name again. In a moment he would reach inside the old man's suit pockets, one after another, and find his identification card to learn exactly who he was. For now, it was important to see if the man's thoughts were still lucid and if he could muster enough strength to respond to the physician's question.

"Findlay," the man croaked a weak response.

"Findlay?" Samuel repeated. "Is that your first name or your last name?" he continued the questioning.

"Angus Findlay," the man responded, this time more quickly and in a firmer voice.

"How old are you, Mister Findlay?" Samuel asked his final question before he would listen to the man's heartbeat through his stethoscope device.

"Eighty-five," came the reply. This time the man's eyes opened for a moment and he looked at the physician whose questions he was answering, and then over at the nurse kneeling on his other side. A crowd began to gather around the three of them as others took notice of one of their comrades in distress.

Samuel was just about to ask the old Yankees and Confederates beginning to gather to please give them some room when the nurse spoke up.

"Could you gentlemen please leave us some room here? We want to keep the air moving while we attend to your comrade." She had looked upwards and scanned the concerned faces as she spoke.

Upon hearing the nurse's voice, Samuel Chambers lifted his own head and for the first time since he had rushed over to the scene a few moments earlier, he gazed upon the nurse's face. She looked familiar and even while concentrating on the sounds of Mister Angus Findlay's heartbeat, he searched his memory for why that might be so. No doubt he recognized her from one of his many review sessions in the Pennsylvania College lecture room, or from making one of his dozens of inspection visits as the commencement of this magnificent event grew closer. Still, there was something especially familiar about this particular nurse; he just couldn't recall why or how at this moment.

Samuel concentrated on the sounds emanating from the stethoscope's earpieces and was concerned by what he heard. The man's heartbeat sounded erratic. He was just about to ask the nurse if she had gauged the man's body temperature when she held out the glass thermometer in Samuel's direction. The very fact that she didn't speak the temperature and instead wanted Samuel to see for himself was an ominous sign.

Samuel saw the mercury resting on the one hundred and four degree mark and knew that they had to act fast.

"Please secure an ambulance car." His words to the nurse were spoken in firm tones yet not barked as an order as many physicians might do. Her reply of "Yes, doctor" as she rose was equally firm and professional. For the moment, the two of them, physician and nurse, had but a single purpose: to get this prone eight-five year old Confederate to the closest field hospital and save his life.

The ambulance came. Angus Findlay was quickly placed inside by the orderlies and the vehicle sped off, the driver carefully looking out for old veterans wandering here and there as the day before the official beginning of the event grew closer to its end. The nurse went along with Mister Findlay, and she had promised Samuel that she would personally see to the ice bath and the intravenous treatment that would be needed to bring Mister Findlay's temperature back into safe territory.

The remaining hour or so of daylight slid by as Samuel rushed to and fro. He finally located Lieutenant Colonel Bradley shortly after 8:30, and spent the next half hour with the Army surgeon conferring over the day's medical events and making minor adjustments in the protocol for the next day's events based on what had happened throughout this day. Both men were thankful that the number of deaths – thus far – was still only four, though each realized that before midnight came the count might rise suddenly and significantly.

His day far from over, Samuel Chambers made his way back to the field hospital on the encampment grounds to see for himself how the scores of admitted old veterans were bearing up. He hoped that with the arrival of twilight, and with the temperature now nearly ten degrees below its high mark of the late afternoon hours, that those factors along with the ice baths and intravenous treatments being seen to by the nurses of the Gettysburg hospitals and the Red Cross will have started to have their intended effect and the number of critical cases will now be on the decline…at least until tomorrow.

Within fifteen minutes Samuel's hopeful aspirations had been largely realized. Most of the ailing men were now sitting up in their beds; more than a few asked Samuel if he might intercede with the nurses and allow them to rejoin their fellow veterans for the remainder of the night, assuring Doctor Chambers that indeed the worst had passed.

Samuel gently but firmly declined each request, assuring each man that he could depart the field hospital at the arrival of tomorrow's dawn but for the remainder of this night he was safest remaining exactly where he was at the moment. More than once, Samuel added conspiratorially to a former Yankee or Rebel while nodding in the direction of whichever nurse was also at the man's bedside,

"Why would you want to leave now? Stay for the night and watch this pretty nurse take care of you."

The clock's hands showed a tick or two past 9:30 when Samuel Chambers made his way to the bedside of Angus Findlay, who was also sitting upright, a deck of cards splayed across his bed tray.

"You seem to be feeling much better, Mister Findlay," Samuel said, recalling the man's name with ease. He looked towards the nurse on the other side of Findlay. Not quite sure why he felt a slight tightness in his own chest, he recognized the nurse as the same one who had summoned his assistance several hours before after she had come upon the stricken Confederate.

"How is Mister Findlay doing?" he asked the nurse, ready to step away from the bed if the nurse minutely nodded her head to the side indicating that she didn't wish to discuss the old man's condition where he could overhear.

To Samuel's relief she immediately replied.

"He's doing much better, Doctor. His temperature dropped to one hundred point five degrees by an hour ago and it's stayed down. The ice bath worked very quickly on him…"

"That's wonderful," Samuel interrupted. Looking at Angus, he said,

"I think tomorrow you can rejoin your comrades if you feel like doing so."

Angus Findlay nodded, but didn't say anything before looking back at his playing cards.

"Where are you from?" Samuel asked. For whatever reason, he suddenly felt a strong urge to learn a bit more about this particular man.

"Virginia," Angus replied. The tenor of his voice was much stronger than it had been hours earlier when he had croaked out his name to Samuel and this nurse; indeed, it was a voice much stronger than one might expect from an 85-year old man.

"Richmond," Angus then added for a bit more precision to his answer.

"Were you at Gettysburg?" Samuel continued his questioning.

The man nodded.

"Cavalry," he added.

Samuel was about to ask yet another question when Angus Findlay added,

"I served under General Stuart. I was his *aide-de-camp* during the campaign."

Immediately recognizing the name of the famed Confederate cavalry general, Samuel looked at the man with new intensity, but seemed to be at a loss for words. What should he ask Angus Findlay; what was J.E.B. Stuart, the man himself, like? Were you there when General Lee allegedly rebuked Stuart for arriving late to Gettysburg – and was that the way it actually happened? Were you present at Yellow Tavern when Stuart was mortally wounded? Did you actually witness the fatal shot?

Instead, Samuel asked Angus Findlay about what he had done after the war, and for the next twenty minutes Samuel listened, enthralled, as the former Colonel told the physician about his role in the political machinations in Virginia during the first years of Reconstruction. Samuel thought to himself more than once that he was listening to history personified...a feeling that he would experience again and again in the days ahead now that tens of thousands of Civil War veterans had arrived and the Great Reunion was about to formally get underway tomorrow.

The clock had already struck ten when the nurse who had been attending Angus Findlay returned and reported to Samuel that not a single patient in the ward had regressed and only a handful were still in imminent danger with elevated fevers. Samuel nodded, and then asked her,

"When is your workday over?"

The nurse hesitated for a moment.

"It was supposed to end at 8:00," she replied uneasily, not wanting to make it sound that she was complaining that she had remained caring for these many patients for two additional hours beyond when she had been supposed to leave.

"Well," Samuel replied, "I think it's fine for you to go home for the night. Everything seems to be progressing satisfactorily here." He nodded in the direction of the many other nurses and doctors who were still present, checking and rechecking one patient after another.

"I think I myself am going to leave for the night, it has been an exceptionally long day," Samuel added.

The nurse nodded.

"Thank you, doctor," she replied and then turned away from Chambers but began to walk towards one corner of the ward rather than directly towards the double doors. For the first time Samuel noticed a small boy wearing a Boy Scout uniform slumped on a wooden stool, propped up against the wall, sleeping. He watched as the nurse headed in the direction of the boy and then knelt down, gently touching his left cheek that was facing outward from the wall. It took a moment but the boy's eyes finally opened and even from a distance of twenty five yards Samuel could tell the boy was intensely disoriented.

He watched the nurse say something to the boy – above the subdued din in the ward he could make out the words "we can go home now" and then "I'm sorry" – and then observed her hoist the boy into her arms before turning towards the doors.

Samuel heard himself call out "Nurse?" as he began walking in their direction. She didn't seem to hear him so he repeated, "Nurse?" a bit louder. This time she halted and turned back in the direction of the sound. The look on her face told Samuel that she thought for certain this doctor was going to intercede with her departure; that some urgent medical matter had just surfaced within the past minute since she had left his company.

"There's nothing I need," Samuel said quickly, trying to put the nurse's mind at ease, that he had no intention of stopping her.

She noticed him looking at the boy.

"My son," she answered the unspoken question, then smiled lightly. "He's had a very long day too."

Samuel noticed that the boy seemed exceptionally young; younger than any of the other Boy Scouts he had seen in passing on the encampment grounds over the past week as preparations for the commemoration went into their final stages.

As if reading this doctor's mind, the nurse replied in hushed tones.

"He is actually too young to be a Boy Scout but I was able to secure a special request by President Granville for him to participate."

She halted abruptly, as if deciding at the last second to check her words.

"What's his name?" Samuel asked.

"Randall," she replied. "Randall Sterling."

Samuel waited for what he hoped would be said next, but the words were not forthcoming so he asked the question.

"And your name?"

"Louisa," she replied. "Louisa May Sterling."

"And I'm Doctor Samuel Chambers," he replied. She nodded even as he spoke.

"I know, Doctor Chambers," she replied. "I've sat in many of your preparatory sessions during the past two months."

Of course she had, Samuel realized to himself. He didn't rebuke himself too much for declaring the obvious, though; common courtesy called for an introduction by name in response to the woman's.

"I hope your husband hasn't had to wait for two hours while you've been caring for these brave old men," Samuel said, noticing the woman wince slightly, a split second after he uttered the word "husband."

She paused for a moment, as if thinking about how exactly she should word her reply.

"My husband is no longer alive," she answered in lowered tones, looking at Randall's face as he rested in her arms, more asleep than awake. "It's just Randall and me."

Samuel was immediately enveloped by an unsettled feeling unlike any he had felt in a long while.

"I'm so sorry," he quickly replied. "I...I just assumed..."

"It's alright," Louisa Sterling interrupted him, smiling sadly. "It's been more than three years now, almost four."

Nothing further. The two of them stood across from one another, the uncomfortable silence hanging over them.

"Well, I should let you go home now," Samuel broke the silence. Louisa nodded and smiled again as she turned towards the door. A thought suddenly came to Samuel.

"Do you have an automobile nearby?" he asked her. She turned back towards him, shaking her head.

"No, we'll walk home," she said.

"Do you live far from here?" Samuel asked.

"I don't mean to be forward," he quickly added. "I just realized that if you hadn't stayed here two extra hours you and your son would have walked home in daylight, not blackness."

"I live near the southwest portion of the town," she answered. "It's about two miles from here."

Samuel immediately felt even worse, thinking about this young widow and her very young son walking for miles. It would be perhaps a quarter hour before eleven, maybe even eleven o'clock, before they arrived home! And perhaps she might have to carry the boy most or all the way, too!

A thought came to Samuel.

"Nurse Sterling, I don't mean to be forward but I feel terrible that you and your son must walk all that distance alone this late at night simply because of your commitment to the care of these old veterans under this terrible heat they've endured. I would offer to drive you, but not only do I not have an automobile I also do not know how to drive. I could accompany you though, since I do need to walk that way myself and then beyond to Pennsylvania College where I am staying."

Louisa Sterling appeared to contemplate the words of Samuel Chambers for a moment before answering.

"I thank you for your kindness, Doctor Chambers. To be honest with you, I have been feeling a bit of trepidation at the idea of walking through the darkness this evening. Ordinarily in town I walk about throughout the day, but since we are here on the outskirts of the town these encampment grounds are unfamiliar to me, and I would feel better with an escort for Randall and myself."

"It's settled then," Samuel replied, wondering why he felt his heart leap just a little bit at the nurse's words. He felt himself minutely shake his head, as if trying to shake away any thoughts of…well, he just wasn't certain exactly what.

"Randall," Louisa called softly to her son lightly dozing in her arms, "we are getting ready to go home now. Would you like me to carry you?"

The boy almost seemed to take offense to his mother's words. He suddenly became fully awake and retorted, almost indignantly,

"I can walk by myself!"

Samuel thought perhaps young Randall, dressed in his Boy Scout uniform, would feel ashamed to be seen carried by his mother as he passed through the older Scouts on the encampment grounds.

"Fine," Louisa Sterling replied, easing her son to the ground. Samuel thought that she would no doubt be relieved not having to carry her son more than a mile in her arms.

They exited the field hospital and walked out into the encampment area. By now the temperature was in the low 80s and most of the humidity had left the air. A light breeze had developed and the night's coolness felt refreshing flowing over Samuel's sticky skin; Louisa's also. Even through the blackness each could see the outlines of acres and acres of tents. Each was struck by the thought of the ancient warriors, each now in the twilight of his years, resting or sleeping inside each of the tents at this very moment. Many of the veterans were wandering the grounds even at this hour, and until the threesome had departed the encampment area they walked in silence, absorbing the living history they were passing through.

Upon reaching the edge of the Emmitsburg Road that would lead them directly into the borough of Gettysburg, it was Samuel Chambers who broke the silence.

"How do you like being with the Boy Scouts?" he asked young Randall Sterling who seemed to have found a renewed energy despite the late hour.

"I enjoy it very much," came the reply, followed by:

"I'm not really a Boy Scout, though. I'm too young. You have to be ten years old to be a Boy Scout and I'm only eight years old. But I wanted to be a Boy Scout for the reunion so I could wear a uniform like my father used to."

Upon hearing these words, Samuel looked up from young Randall to the boy's mother.

"My late husband was an Army officer," she explained. "I had told Randall that he was too young to wear a Boy Scout uniform but for months he asked me over and over again, and I begged a favor from President Granville to intercede and see if Randall could be temporarily assigned to one of the Boy Scout posts that was helping with the commemoration. He was kind enough to do so."

Samuel nodded. Lowering his voice, though he knew young Randall could still hear him, he asked,

"Did your husband die in the Spanish War?" Even as he was speaking the words, though, he knew the answer would be "no." The war with Spain had happened fifteen years ago, back in '98. Clearly if Louisa Sterling's husband had been killed in battle on San Juan Hill or elsewhere in that war, there was no way he could have left behind a son who was only eight years old! Samuel cursed himself for

not thinking more clearly before asking such a personal question. But Louisa didn't seem to take offense at all.

"No, he died from typhoid back in '09," she replied.

Samuel had seen enough cases of typhoid since he had been practicing medicine.

"I'm so sorry," he replied.

"He was a West Pointer," Louisa continued, almost rambling. "He graduated fourth in his class which meant he was commissioned into the Corps of Engineers, and we lived in Carlisle until he passed away."

"Is that where you are from? Carlisle?" he asked.

"No," she shook her head. "I'm from Germantown, in Philadelphia."

"I'm from Philadelphia also!" Samuel answered.

She nodded.

"I know, you mentioned that at the beginning of your first gathering."

Samuel cursed himself again for answering too impulsively. He wondered if he sounded foolish to this woman. He certainly sounded foolish to himself.

"My father is a physician in Germantown," she continued. "Doctor Randolph Talbot."

The name stopped Samuel Chambers in his tracks.

"I know your father!" he exclaimed. "In fact, my father and he know each other very well, and have for years!"

The mention of "my father" by Doctor Chambers seemed to spark a memory in Louisa Sterling.

"Would your father be Doctor Edwin Chambers?" Samuel was nodding even as she spoke.

"My Lord, yes," he answered, and he could feel himself smiling almost as a village idiot might. "In fact, it is through my father's association with your father that I know Doctor Talbot...I mean, your father."

Now Louisa Sterling joined Samuel with a broad smile coming to her own face.

"That is quite a coincidence," she said.

"Yes it is," Samuel agreed. "We are each from the Philadelphia region, and we are each in the medical profession, and our fathers have known each other for many years."

"Quite a coincidence," Samuel continued, repeating Louisa Sterling's words.

"So your name before you were married was Louisa Talbot," he said, more to himself than to the woman walking on the other side of her son as the lights of the borough became brighter ahead of them.

"Louisa *May* Talbot," she amplified, and told Samuel Chambers the story of how her mother had named her after the famous authoress.

The conversation continued as they walked along the darkened county road towards the borough. Randall Sterling walked in silence between them, almost as if he didn't want to interrupt as his mother and this doctor bantered back and forth about matters of the city of Philadelphia; their shared profession; the Great Reunion; and other topics. Upon reaching the intersection of the Emmitsburg Road and Long Lane, barely more than a quarter mile from Louisa Sterling's small house, Samuel felt a sudden rush of sadness that their conversation would soon be coming to an end. The time was nearing eleven o'clock but he felt as if they could converse for hours longer, perhaps through the first hours of July 1st.

He wondered if she felt the same.

He hoped she did.

*   *   *

Upon reaching the Sterling house, Samuel looked at his watch. Eleven minutes after eleven o'clock, exactly. As he halted and watched Louisa Sterling and her son walk up the four steps onto the front porch, he fervently wished there were some way he could remain in her company despite the late hour. An impossibility, of course, but that didn't make him want it any less.

"Thank you very much, Doctor Chambers," she said as she reached her front door, unlocking it to let Randall inside the house as she lingered for a moment. Samuel remained below at the foot of the porch steps.

"I'm very grateful to you for escorting us home," she continued.

"My pleasure," Samuel replied, not caring now if the tone of his reply sounded too familiar; too personal.

She smiled at him.

"I hope to see you tomorrow on the encampment grounds," Louisa May Sterling said to Samuel Chambers.

"Though I very much hope it will be under less trying circumstances than with Mister Findlay," she added.

Samuel barely heard the second part of what she said. His mind was already churning the words "I hope to see you tomorrow" over and over.

Chapter 14

July 1, 1913

The conjured events that occurred during Samuel Chambers' dream shortly after falling asleep as the clock ticked past one o'clock in the morning on the first day of July, a dream he could recall with unusual clarity when he awoke after being asleep less than one half hour, should have caused him tremendous anxiety as they unfolded in that imaginary realm. They didn't, though.

In his dream The Great Reunion had gone horribly wrong, and the blame could be justly and fully laid at the feet of Doctor Samuel Chambers. He had been responsible for…well, for something he was supposed to have ensured had been accomplished before the reading of the Gettysburg Address, a monumental occasion that in the dream occurred on the opening day of the splendid event rather than one day later as in reality. What that "something" was supposed to have been Samuel wasn't quite certain as he as he lay in bed reflecting, but whatever it was he had failed miserably because instead he had been intent on courting Louisa Sterling. In the backstory to this night's dream he had spent nearly his entire time in Gettysburg for months in her drawing room or squiring her about the borough or otherwise gazing lovingly at her for hours on end, instead of carrying out his responsibilities.

In the dream nobody knew who fired that first shot or from which encampment the offender had come, but by the time President Lincoln – it had been Lincoln himself reading the Address in the present day of 1913 in this curious dream – had come to the phrase "...engaged in a great civil war" as he reprised his famous oration from half a century earlier, old men dressed in blue and gray were shooting at one another; killing one another. Somewhere in the distance in that dream the boom of cannon could be heard. Samuel Chambers calmly watched the events unfold under a blistering sun (even in the dream Samuel absorbed the suffering heat and humidity that was expected for the first days of July) as he lounged in a rocking chair next to Louisa Sterling on her front porch sipping an ice-filled glass of lemonade. Another oddity: in the dream Louisa's house sat squarely in the midst of the battlefield itself rather than at the edge of the borough more than two miles away, so both Samuel and Louisa were granted a keen vantage point from which to observe the unanticipated unfolding carnage.

The imagery in his mind then instantly shifted to Governor Tener's office in Harrisburg where Samuel calmly listened to the blame-filled diatribe spill from not only the Governor but also an enraged President Woodrow Wilson. When the Governor and the President paused, their cause was taken up by President Lincoln himself and then by General Lee – both seemingly flesh and blood rather than ghostly apparitions as one might have expected from the present-day attendance by these long-dead luminaries – and then followed by an ensemble cast of bearded General Officers in both blue and gray, another dozen or so of these men adding to Samuel's denunciation. The message from all of these men was the same: Samuel Chambers, through gross dereliction of his responsibilities (whatever they were to have been; even at this point in the dream Samuel was still unclear exactly what he had neglected to accomplish), was single-handedly responsible for the outbreak of hostilities on the battlefield of Gettysburg this morning of July 1st, 1913, causing an occasion of healing to suddenly turn into a day of bloodshed and tragedy.

In the dream Samuel listened calmly to these illustrious men scream his failings to him, and he patiently waited until the last man – General Pickett, Samuel thought the gray-clad officer might have been – had finished and Governor Tener dismissed Samuel from his office. Samuel then calmly turned, exited the office, smiling as he briskly made his ways through the hallways of the Capitol because he knew Louisa Sterling was anxiously waiting for him just outside and they were about to take a picnic together on a glorious, bright summer's early afternoon.

Exiting the front of the Capitol Building Samuel immediately spotted Louisa, who smiled back at him. The pitched battle of Aging Blue versus Ancient Gray had apparently spilled over from the Gettysburg battlefield many miles north to downtown Harrisburg, because all around Louisa anonymous armed old men wearing one color or the other were shuffling about, croaking out meaningless jumbled orders to no one in particular and occasionally pausing to fire their rifles. Looking to his left Samuel observed a cluster of old men wearing Yankee blue huffing as they struggled to shove a cannon into a new firing position up a sharply angled slope of green lawn in front of the Capitol Building.

Samuel observed all of this and then looked back at Louisa, still smiling, a wicker picnic basket clutched in her hands in front of her. She seemed to radiate a glow of some sorts, and the Madonna-like vision brought great joy to Samuel Chambers as he strolled towards her, the fighting surrounding the two of them fading to a gauzy background just as his dream itself faded to translucency before surrendering to his moonlit room at Pennsylvania College.

Samuel Chambers lay in bed for nearly two full hours before sleep came again, reflecting on his dream, inserting wishful events of his own choosing into his mind's reenactments. Alas, there was no reprise of his dream that night, nor another similar one that was hallmarked by his growing infatuation with Louisa May Sterling.

July 1, 1913
Veterans' Day

Alan Simon

"The honor falls to me, as chairman of the
Pennsylvania State Commission, of presiding at
the opening exercises of a celebration
unparalleled in the history of the world."
- Opening ceremony remarks by Colonel James M.
Schoonmaker, Gettysburg, July 1, 1913

―――――

"We meet on this occasion to participate in a
ceremony that stands unmatched in all recorded
time."
- Opening ceremony remarks by Pennsylvania
Governor John K. Tener, Gettysburg, July 1,
1913

―――――

"You may search the world's history in vain for
such a spectacle...This is a day to thank God for,
and remember. And any American is dull of soul
and unworthy of citizenship if he does not feel his
heart glow and his thoughts turn to Gettysburg
with thanksgiving."
- *The Columbus Citizen*, July 1, 1913

Chapter 15

3:20 A.M.

Devin McAteer finally acknowledged that trying to sleep was but an exercise in futility. He rose on his right elbow and looked over at his cousin Seamus, still sound asleep as he had been since well before midnight. Again, Devin thought about gently waking his cousin and, after they would quietly exit the sleeping tent, talking through what remained of the morning darkness until the sun began to illuminate the sky to the east of the encampment grounds. Mere moments after the five o'clock hour arrived the first tiny streaks of yellows and oranges and reds would insist on their presence being acknowledged by anyone gazing towards the eastern sky. An hour and forty-five minutes until then; the cousins could use that time to continue catching up with each other's lives.

Once more, though, Devin McAteer abandoned the idea as a selfish one. Let Seamus sleep, he again convincingly told himself. Yesterday had been an event-filled day from the moment he had stepped onto the train in Pittsburgh, through his arrival at the encampment and then so quickly encountering Seamus. And then, for the remainder of that blazing hot afternoon and into the evening, the many handshakes and brief conversations with other old men, Blue and Gray alike.

So far neither Devin nor Seamus had encountered another veteran whom either had known in those long-ago days in the 45th Pennsylvania. No doubt others from the 45th were present, but given that more than 20,000 of those gathered on the grounds – not quite half of the overall contingent of old veterans, but by golly pretty close to half – were from Pennsylvania, plenty of the Commonwealth's veterans were in attendance whom neither of the McAteers had yet to meet, many of them not even yet arrived at the Jubilee. Before long, a familiar name – if not necessarily a familiar face – would surely be encountered.

No; if Seamus is able to sleep, he should remain asleep. Once daylight broke, this first day of July would be every bit as event-filled and exhausting as yesterday had been. Devin envied his cousin's rest, and was worried about his own ability to make it through the entire bustling day, and under another scorching sun, without having slept at all.

Devin shifted into a seated position on his cot and stiffly leaned forward, reaching underneath the cot until his increasingly gnarled right hand brushed against one of his boots. He clasped that one – his right boot – and pulled it out from under the cot, wincing as he straightened up. As with most mornings, he paused for a moment, his head slightly dropped and his lips pursed, as he mustered the strength to ignore these morning pains until he got moving and the stiffness and achiness would subside – mostly – for the rest of the day.

He repeated the ritual to locate his left boot and after both boots were on his feet he rose, using his left hand to help himself stand. Careful, old man, he told himself; this is a cot you're rising from, not your much heavier bedframe at home…so be careful not to brace yourself too hard against the lighter frame and send the cot flying and yourself as well.

For a brief instant Devin felt unsteady on his feet, a bit more than usual in the immediate aftermath of getting out of bed, but he instantly attributed that feeling not so much to his 67 years of age but more to having not slept plus being in unfamiliar surroundings out here in the encampment grounds south of the town of Gettysburg. The uneasy feeling of instability passed as quickly as it had arrived, and after taking one final look at Seamus – of course secretly hoping Seamus would awaken at that moment and then wish to accompany Devin outside – he walked the seven or eight paces towards the sleeping tent's flap and slipped out into the still-cool early morning darkness.

Devin McAteer's senses immediately insisted on noting the difference between the temperature as it now was as compared to the oppressive, deadly heat of the previous day. Rumors had swept the encampment grounds as night had been falling that dozens of old veterans had fatally succumbed to the blazing sun and stifling humidity that the final day of June, 1913, had insisted on inflicting upon these men. However, within the hour the rumors had been squelched by the circulating doctors and nurses and people from the Pennsylvania College who were helping to coordinate the Jubilee's activities.

It was true, the veterans learned, that two of their comrades had indeed passed, and as midnight arrived word circulated to many of those still awake that yet another had fallen; a man in the New York delegation. But thus far it was only those three, not the many dozens that had been murmured about. Dozens, indeed more than two hundred, had in fact been admitted to one field hospital or another after falling ill but almost all had survived and indeed, many had already been released to rejoin their states' delegations. No doubt more would pass before the occasion's conclusion, but so far – unlike fifty years earlier – the Angel of Death had not decided to visit the fields surrounding the borough of Gettysburg and carry away his bounty.

"You can't sleep either?"

The voice coming from his left startled Devin McAteer so severely that for an instant he felt that the shock of the sudden sound directed at him might well cause a recurrence of the heart problems he had suffered three years ago. Perhaps the Angel of Death, about whom Devin had just been thinking, was now beckoning him? But that worrisome feeling vanished as quickly as it had appeared and Devin turned in the darkness, squinting to see if he could make out who had spoken those words; to determine if this person was someone known to him or just some other anonymous old man who had also given up on sleep. Indeed, he recognized the Philadelphian Morrison…Chester Morrison was the man's full name, Devin recalled from his foggy, sleep-deprived memory. In his determination to exit the sleeping tent as quietly as he could without waking Seamus, Devin McAteer hadn't even noticed that Morrison's cot must have also been empty.

As his eyes became acclimated to the darkness, he could make out Morrison's features and dress. The man was impeccably attired, even at 3:25 or 3:30 in the morning, whatever time it now was. Whereas Devin had simply pulled his suspenders onto his shoulders and left the tent without his tie or jacket, this Morrison fellow looked as if he had just exited a meeting at one of those fancy bank buildings that no doubt existed in downtown Philadelphia, just as they also stood in Devin's Pittsburgh.

Devin eyed this Chester Morrison as the two men began walking towards each other. Devin and Seamus had spent perhaps ten minutes talking alone with Morrison after arriving at their tent the previous afternoon until others assigned to their tent began arriving, and the discussion evolved into a larger one. They had of course exchanged information about where they had been on those fateful days exactly fifty years earlier. Devin and Seamus had told Chester about their presence at the siege of Vicksburg with the 45th Pennsylvania, while Morrison had looked around the tent as if he could see right through the fabric exterior, as if he were surveying the vast scenery of fields and woods outside, and told the cousins about his presence on these very grounds with his comrades of the 69th Pennsylvania. The discussion had then shifted to their respective hometowns. Devin and Seamus had told Morrison about being from Pittsburgh – though Seamus had resided up in Luzerne County to the northeast for many years – while Chester had related being from the grand city of Philadelphia.

The conversation had then of course swung to the mention of each man's chosen profession. Devin, the laborer at Andrew Carnegie's steel mills, following a decade in the Reconstruction-era Army after the war had ended; and Seamus, the coal miner. Chester Morrison had simply told the cousins that he had worked, indeed still worked, at Baldwin Locomotive in Philadelphia since shortly after the war, and then changed the subject to the scorching heat of the day. Both Devin and Seamus could tell, though, that this man's work at Baldwin had nothing to do with toiling in the yards or being a machinist and assembling those locomotive engines with his own two hands, or transporting the company's completed locomotive engines to the many railroads around the country. This Chester Morrison was clearly a high-muck-a-muck at the locomotive manufacturer; definitely not a laborer and not even a mid-level manager, but rather someone who ran the company and probably conversed and did business with the old Scotsman Carnegie or maybe even that devil Frick who had so brutally brought the Pinkerton agents and their weapons to the Homestead Strike back in '92.

The McAteer cousins had each taken notice, however – and discussed it between themselves later that evening while strolling around the encampment grounds – that this man Morrison, despite so obviously being a high-muck-a-muck, did not seem to carry himself with the self-important haughtiness one might expect from a robber baron. He seemed to be more like Colonel Schoonmaker of the Pennsylvania & Lake Erie Railroad, appointed by Governor Tener to be the Chairman of this magnificent gathering but who could be seen wandering around the encampment grounds throughout the previous day, conversing easily with dozens of veterans…gray as well as blue.

The men closed within a few feet of each other as Devin McAteer answered Chester Morrison's question by replying:

"Not a wink."

* * *

Unlike Devin McAteer, Chester Morrison had managed a bit of restless sleep until he himself had decided, only half an hour earlier, to slip outside to wait out the final couple hours until daylight, safe from falling back into the endless terror of the dreamworld. Chester was reminded of another night a little more than one year earlier, after his son Jonathan had handed him the *Philadelphia Evening Telegraph's* editorial announcement of the forthcoming "Gettysburg Celebration." Just as he had suffered a series of excruciating nightmares of ferocious battle on that night more than a year ago, so too had he slid back in time fifty years to once again suffer one dream after another filled with cannon fire and the hail of Minie balls and bayonet-bearing hand-to-hand combat with gray-clad rebels. In Chester's imagination that night, the two days of battle endured by the 69th Pennsylvania blended together so in any particular dream sequence he wasn't quite sure if he was fighting to hold Cemetery Ridge on the 2nd of July, or facing the futile, heroic ferocity of Pickett's Charge a day later. All he was certain of was that for several hours until he awoke, he did little in any of his dreams but spend every single second fighting for his very life.

As this Pittsburgh man McAteer halted a few paces away, Chester Morrison quickly time-traveled in his mind back fifty years. The 69th Pennsylvania wasn't yet at Gettysburg in the early morning hours of July 1, 1863, but rather still in Maryland, just south of the Pennsylvania state line. Nobody knew, of course, how ferocious the coming battle on the grounds near Gettysburg would be, but almost every one of the Irish Volunteers of the 69th Pennsylvania was aware that a clash with the Rebels was inevitable.

Chester could not help but recall how, during their march north from Taneytown, Maryland that first afternoon of July, they could hear the artillery from the first day of battle and knew that the hell of war awaited…perhaps not this very day since they were still en route towards the direction of the distant sounds of battle, but their fates had been most certainly been sealed.

He suddenly and almost violently shook these thoughts and visions from his head as Devin McAteer replied to Chester's earlier question about not being able to sleep. He had just endured hours of conjured, relived battle in the theater of his mind, and no doubt would be forced by his imagination to endure this same unpleasantness again and again while here at Gettysburg. For now, though, he would simply engage in conversation with this Pittsburgh man

McAteer, who had spent years toiling in Carnegie's and Frick's mills.

God help this man's soul, Chester Morrison thought to himself. The employment practices of those Pittsburgh titans had largely been so distasteful to Chester Morrison during the '80s and '90s in particular that Chester had gone out of his way to take Baldwin Locomotive in the opposite direction with regards to the treatment of their workers. Still, this McAteer had obviously survived his years working in the steel mills, not only with his life but also with all of his limbs attached and, apparently, only the stiffness of old age rather than a crippling injury and the resultant severe limp or dragging lifeless leg that no doubt so many of McAteers fellow workers had succumbed to over the years.

"What say we walk over to the big mess tent and see if they have any coffee?" Chester suggested, to which Devin McAteer simply nodded. Each man looked around, trying to gain his bearings in the darkness on these strange grounds, and once Devin McAteer was fairly certain he knew which direction they should head, he simply began walking that way, figuring that this high-muck-a-muck could follow a mere mill worker for a change.

* * *

Halfway to the mess tent, Chester Morrison and Devin McAteer passed Philip Roberdeau walking in the opposite direction, back towards the sleeping tents in the area occupied by the Louisiana delegation. Neither man knew Philip Roberdeau by this point, so a quick, wordless, gentlemanly tip of the hat by Chester Morrison and a simultaneous nod on the part of Devin McAteer was met in response by a simple returned nod by the man from New Orleans as all three passed without breaking stride.

Like Chester Morrison – and hundreds of other men, both blue and gray, that first night of June 30th and into the following early morning hours of July 1st – Philip Roberdeau had been able to manage only a small bit of sleep. What little rest he had been able to muster had been mostly dreamless; at least Philip thought so, since he couldn't recall any details or even wispy, gauzy fragments of dreams when he had decided sometime around 2:00 in the morning to stroll about the encampment grounds.

His mind kept insisting that he would turn the corner on one of these newly constructed temporary streets or avenues on the encampment grounds and walk squarely into General Longstreet. Whether it would the man himself, somehow in flesh and blood despite having passed nine years ago, or his ghostly apparition, Philip wasn't quite sure; but there was no question he could feel "Old Pete's" presence as the moments ticked down towards the 50th anniversary of the commencement of those terrible days of battle.

Philip recalled how, at the 25th anniversary commemoration back in '88, he and the old General had stumbled upon one another in the dining room and shared reminisces of not only Gettysburg but also how, more than eleven years later, their fates crossed paths again during the Battle of Liberty Place in Louisiana. Both had been among the militia captured by the Crescent City White League as part of an uprising against the Reconstruction state government of Louisiana, and both had been rescued by Federal – Yankee – troops a few days later.

What Philip did not know at this moment, though he would soon find out, was that one of the two men he had just passed and to whom he had nodded a polite, detached greeting under the starry southern Pennsylvania nighttime sky had been one of his rescuers nearly forty years earlier.

* * *

Also sleepless this night was John K. Tener, the Governor of Pennsylvania. Unlike Chester Morrison and Devin McAteer and Philip Roberdeau and so many others, though, Governor Tener's sleeplessness was the result of red-hot rage of the present day, rather than terrifying recollections from fifty years earlier or wistful remembrances of so many years gone by. Tener, in fact, was still three and a half weeks shy of being born when the Battle of Gettysburg had commenced on that long-ago July 1st. Between his age and the fact that he lived the first ten years of his life in County Tyrone, Ireland, Tener knew nothing of the Battle of Gettysburg until his family crossed the ocean to America a year after his father's death.

Tener's fury was once again with Lindley Garrison, the Secretary of War. Only days earlier, the Governor had moved heaven, earth, and even a little bit of hell to overcome the idiocy of the War Secretary who had insisted – at the very last minute, in a surprise attack worthy of the Rebels at Shiloh during the war – on refusing to allocate adequate federal funds above and beyond what had previously been promised for the initial estimate of 40,000 veterans. Work on the encampment grounds had ceased until Tener's forceful actions had catalyzed the Pennsylvania Assembly to pass a bill to procure enough additional funds to care for as many as 15,000 additional veterans to meet the now-expected attendance of some

55,000 in total, and around-the-clock work began again on the 28th.

Alas, it had been too little, too late.

All through the day and the evening hours, reports came to Governor Tener that hundreds of veterans, most of them from his state of Pennsylvania and many of those from or near his home base in Pittsburgh, had been unable to secure sleeping accommodations at the encampment grounds. Tener immediately mustered his forces to do whatever they could to find more tents or some way to care for these old men, but many of them simply gave up after wandering the encampment grounds for hours. Hundreds dropped their heads en masse in defeat and headed back to the Gettysburg train depot to catch trains back home.

Worse, even when some tents were eventually secured and hastily erected for veterans from other states, they still lacked cots and blankets. Some of those old men from the other states elected to remain and sleep on the ground, but many more decided to depart in frustrated defeat as their Pennsylvania comrades had.

A reporter from the *Pittsburgh Press* with whom Governor Tener was on friendly terms came to Tener's temporary office after midnight and warned the Governor that despite doing his best to squelch the news, the *Press* would, in its afternoon edition for July 1st, report the heart-breaking news of so many Western Pennsylvania veterans being turned away and those men giving up to return to Pittsburgh. At first, Governor Tener thought about calling in whatever favors he could to halt this news from being reported, but then he calculated that the tragedy of it all reflected poorly not on himself nor the Gettysburg Reunion Commission (at least he hoped not), but rather on the Secretary of War and Woodrow Wilson's Democratic administration. Let the stories run, Tener decided, and let the nation and the world learn how the Department of War so callously treated so many of those who had once served so gallantly on its behalf.

Also after midnight, Army Lieutenant Colonel A.E. Bradley, under whose care the Army had now placed the medical facilities that Samuel Chambers had so magnificently organized, came to Tener's office to report that a veteran from Almond, New York named Otto L. Stamm had suddenly dropped dead around 10:30 the previous evening while futilely searching the encampment grounds for a place to sleep. The old man had been 75 years of age, and Tener was informed that Mr. Stamm had been severely wounded at the Battle of Roanoke Island in early 1862 and after recuperating for close to two years, re-volunteered and fought in several more battles even though he suffered so much pain from his earlier wounds. He had been captured by the Confederates at Drury's Bluff in May of 1864 and survived the notorious Andersonville Prison for six months until being transferred to St. Anthony Prison, from which he escaped in the winter of '65. Despite his return to the Union Army, after the war he was only able to work occasional jobs over the years because of his wounds and subsisted mostly on a war disability pension.

Colonel Bradley reported this to Tener as having been tearfully related by Mr. Stamm's close friend, one Charles Barber of New York in whose arms Stamm had actually died; it had seemed as if this Barber fellow wanted his friend's legacy known so his spirit might still be in attendance at this Great Reunion, despite having passed away on the grounds shortly before it had begun. Tener listened silently, his fury rising at each fact conveyed by

Bradley, and when the Army man had finished Tener stood from behind his desk, drew himself up to his full height, and raged through clenched teeth:

"You tell your good-for-nothing boss Garrison to come see me *immediately* after he gets here, and if he doesn't I will personally make him the sorriest Secretary of War this nation has ever seen!"

Bradley watched and listened to the six foot, four inch tall Tener – the former Major League baseball pitcher who no doubt had had his share of dustups with umpires and other players back in the previous century when baseball was populated by many of dubious character and combative nature – and only nodded, thankful not only that he wasn't Lindley Garrison but also that Tener had elected to save his true fury for the Secretary of War whose political maneuvering had triggered the shortage of accommodations.

*   *   *

In Louisa May Sterling's dream, the details vividly recalled when she would shortly awake, she was again at that West Point social in early March of 1902. Her date was again Ulysses S. Grant III and yet again, as in real life, she was standing between young Grant and his classmate and rival Douglas MacArthur, listening to the two of them jab at each other, back and forth, about their respective class standings in the West Point Class of '03 and their famous patriarchs. In the dream, as had happened in real life, Louisa looked across the room to where she knew Cadet Terrence Sterling would be standing and gazing at his future wife, captivated by her beauty and her very presence.

In this dream, though, Cadet Terrence Sterling was standing next to Doctor Samuel Chambers, and *both* the boyish cadet and the thirtyish doctor from Philadelphia were looking back at her with that very same look. Even in the dream Louisa could feel herself flush and immediately become enveloped by unsettling confusion and uncertainty.

Chapter 16

Governor John K. Tener's anger and disappointment aside, today would be a glorious day.

The official ceremonies of Veterans' Day would begin in the Great Tent at precisely 2:00 in the afternoon. For two hours the gathered masses would hear a series of addresses from Colonel Schoonmaker and Governor Tener; the Secretary of War; and the Commanders-in-Chief of both the Grand Army of the Republic and the United Confederate Veterans. The Chaplains-in-Chief of these same two organizations would each offer prayers amongst the speakers, with the GAR's Lovejoy being afforded the privilege of the opening prayer while the UCV's Hamill closing the day's ceremonies shortly before 4:00 P.M.

Until 2:00 arrived, the veterans would continue to mingle among themselves and the increasing crowds of onlookers who had come from all over Pennsylvania and nearby states – indeed, some others from very far away – to bear witness to this occasion. Many smaller reunions would occur during the morning hours, similar to the one for Buford's and Wheeler's cavalries in the Big Tent that Johnny and Edgar Sullivan had attended the previous day. The 6th Pennsylvania would gather, as would the 10th New York Cavalry and the 188th Pennsylvania and the 10th Michigan, and many others. The United Prisoners of War would come together, as would the Army and Navy Medal of Honor Legion.

All of the old men, whether gathered for a meeting of an old unit or simply mingling about the encampment grounds – the bystanders as well – would do their best to fight off the heat and humidity that was expected to be every bit as oppressive this day as the day before.

* * *

"You awake?"

Edgar Sullivan briefly contemplated the prospect of not answering his brother's question, but dismissed that notion as foolish. He was awake; the morning sun was mustering its strength and Edgar reckoned the hour was past seven in the morning by now. What was the use of lazing in this sleeping tent, on this cot, for much longer? He had, in fact, been awake for close to two hours by now, even as his brother Johnny had still been noisily snoring in the cot directly across from his. At one point around 5:30 or so Johnny had let out a snorting gasp in his sleep, a sound so sharp that Edgar had leaned forward to peer at his brother and make sure Johnny wasn't choking to death in his sleep. Clyde Hodges, the former Southerner who had ridden with the Sullivans all the way from the Tucson train depot, had also been startled and had similarly risen to peer at the younger Sullivan. Edgar and Clyde Hodges had looked at each other and though no words were exchanged during that early morning hour, at least this time Edgar's stare wasn't one filled with the combined bitterness and disdain of both long-ago battle and advancing years.

"Yeah, I'm awake," Edgar said. "Been awake for near two hours while you was over there snorin' away."

Johnny Sullivan contemplated what his brother had said.

"Then why didn't you wake me?"

Edgar sat up in his cot, swung his legs over the side, and paused in the sitting position as he willed his aging body's strength to gather before attempting to stand.

"Why would I?" he replied, looking over at his brother. "It was still plenty dark outside and I don't think the kitchen tent was open that early for breakfast. I figured we both had a busy day yesterday and you could use the sleep. Just wish I coulda had more of it myself."

"Well, I'm sure it's open now," Johnny replied, referring to the closest kitchen tent, "and I'm mighty hungry. What say we head over there and grab some chow?"

Edgar shrugged and then nodded his wordless agreement. He still didn't feel quite up to attempting to stand. The brothers had, in fact, walked so much around the encampment grounds and through the Buford's Cavalry gathering in the Big Tent yesterday that by Edgar's figuring, they had covered more ground in that one afternoon than they typically covered in an entire week, maybe even longer, back in Tucson. The typical day back in Arizona had very little movement once the brothers had settled into the daily card game at the Windsor Hotel. At one time long ago both Johnny and Edgar would walk there almost every day from their respective homes – each about a mile and a half away from the hotel – but for the past couple of years Edgar would drive his Tin Lizzie there each morning and back home each afternoon (Johnny still walked more days than not), which meant that very little walking for more than a couple dozen steps at a time could be found anywhere in the older brother's daily repertoire.

Yesterday, though, had been reminiscent of those long-ago Tombstone days when the brothers would cover ten, maybe fifteen miles each day walking about the town for one reason or another. Sometimes the reason was lawman work, assisting the Earps, and other times it would be just moseying from one establishment to another for various reasons, paying visits or taking care of some business matter or another. Today, indeed since late the previous evening, both brothers were feeling the effects of attempting to reprise those long-ago, more mobile days.

In the Great Tent, the brothers had come across five other veterans of the 8th Illinois whom they recalled from long-ago days. Surprisingly, Edgar had turned out to have a better memory for these old faces and names than his younger brother, and by the time an hour had passed after that Army Lieutenant Patton had directed them towards the first of the men with whom they renewed acquaintances, Edgar Sullivan was in the most pleasant, almost cheery mood that his brother could recall covering the past...well, a great many years. The elder brother seemed transformed and reenergized by the conversations, one after another, with the other veterans of Company E in the 8th Illinois; renewed acquaintances as well as a few newly-formed ones.

Among the group of men that spent much of the afternoon in each other's company, only Edgar and Johnny had ventured as far from Illinois as Arizona after the war, though one of the other men they had once known – Amos Forsyth, who had ridden with the Sullivans from Fair Oaks through Antietam and Gettysburg and all the way to Monocacy – had eventually settled in Pittsburgh, and did a fair bit of business down in Virginia after Reconstruction had concluded. The other four had all remained in their parts of Illinois, and were particularly interested in hearing the Sullivans describe the frontier days way out in Arizona Territory. Others from Buford's Cavalry, and even a few of Wheeler's old Rebels, circulated in and out of the growing circle that had formed around the Sullivans by mid-afternoon. Even that Army Lieutenant Patton had, at one point, halted his purposeful West Point strides about the Great Tent when he passed nearby the group and heard Edgar Sullivan mention the name "Wyatt Earp."

By the time that event had concluded, Edgar was dog-tired. Usually by this point in a typical afternoon he would be snoozing away in an arm chair in the Windsor's lobby, the remnants of his third or fourth Old Overholt either clasped in his hand on his lap or settled alongside on an end table. The resulting aches from this unusually active day wouldn't be fully felt for another couple of hours until the brothers were strolling about the encampment grounds shortly after dark, but after returning to the Arizona delegation's sleeping tent Edgar immediately fell into a deep sleep for the next three hours.

Now, however, the daylight morning hours of the First of July had arrived and both brothers were ready for a good, solid breakfast to start their day. Edgar finally felt he had mustered enough strength to stand and after slowly rising from his cot (and wincing for the entire five full seconds it took him to assume a standing position), he reached for his mess kit as Johnny did the same.

The intense sunshine hit the Sullivans as they exited their tent, and for a moment both felt as if they were back in the blazing desert heat of Arizona. This Gettysburg heat, however, was far more humid than what they had grown accustomed to, even at 7:00 in the morning. Johnny Sullivan felt the beads of sweat instantly break out on his forehead underneath his hat brim and on his neck underneath his shirt collar, and knew that before long he would be enveloped in the same stale stickiness that he had endured all of yesterday. He looked over at Edgar as the two began to walk towards the kitchen tent and for the first time this day reprised his frequent complaint of a day earlier.

"I forgot how damned sticky it is most everywhere else in the middle of summer except the desert. Give me our heat any old day, this is insufferable!"

Edgar chuckled.

"Well look who's complaining again," he said good-naturedly. "You gonna tell me once more that I'm spoilin' the whole thing with my surly attitude or whatever words you been using?"

Johnny allowed himself a small smile.

"Yeah, I s'pose you been in a good mood," he conceded. "But keep in mind that so far we ain't done much too talking to any Rebs, just a little bit here and there in groups. Let's see how good a mood you're in after you come face to face with one of them, just you and him or maybe just the two of us and a couple of them, and you ain't in a big group like we was yesterday with only a few of them outnumbered by old Yankees."

Edgar Sullivan just shrugged as the two kept walking, joining a growing crowd of men headed for breakfast. Some wore blue; others gray; many simply wore suits, though some of those non-uniformed men wore either a Union or Confederate hat or cap. The Arizona delegation's single sleeping tent was among those that housed other smaller state delegations and in turn all of those were closest to most of the Southern State delegations...Virginia's in particular. Attendees were told during their registration that they were particularly encouraged to mingle with those from other states and, especially, from the other side of the war; and so many of the heartier, more lively veterans ventured a bit farther than the closest kitchen to see what acquaintances might be made from other states, north and south alike.

As the Sullivans joined the line at the kitchen tent, they fell in line behind a stooped man who appeared to be by himself. This man looked to be much older than the brothers – easily in his eighties – and he wore a baggy dark suit of clothes but his gray cavalry hat indicated which side of the war he had been on. As the brothers halted, the man slowly turned around.

"Howdy," he nodded a greeting.

"Howdy," each of the Sullivans replied almost – but not quite – in unison.

"Hot mornin' already, huh?" Johnny Sullivan made idle conversation, stating the obvious.

The old Rebel looked back at them for a moment before replying.

"Not as bad as yesterday, at least for me," he answered. "I wound up collapsing and spent the night in the field hospital."

Both of the Sullivans were taken aback. Like almost every other veteran present they had heard the spreading tales of many of their comrades taken sick from the heat, but had yet to run across someone who had actually fallen ill. During the entire time in the Great Tent, despite the stifling heat that insisted on penetrating inside, they hadn't noticed any of the men from either Buford's or Wheeler's forces succumbing and needing attention.

"Yeah? What happened?" Edgar Sullivan asked this man, who proceeded to give a brief summary of having passed out on the encampment grounds and his rescue by the pretty nurse and the doctor.

"They just let me out about half an hour ago," the man – Angus Findlay, he told the Sullivans that's what his name was – said. Then his face took on a mischievous look.

"They gave me breakfast in the field hospital but by golly that was a couple of hours ago, so I figure why not come over here and have another breakfast while they're feeding us for free?"

"Yeah, I guess," Johnny Sullivan nodded. You couldn't argue with the old Rebel's logic; why not get as much free food as possible while here?

"So you're cavalry," Johnny continued, his eyes rising slightly to eye Angus Findlay's hat.

"I was," came the reply, "a very long time ago."

"You here at Gettysburg?" the "were" as in "were you here" was implicit in Johnny's follow-up question.

The man dropped his eyes for a moment, as if mustering the strength for a reply to this direct inquiry.

"Yes I was," he nodded as he looked back at Johnny first and then at Edgar. The breakfast line was shuffling forward so Angus Findlay turned back towards the front to take a few steps in that direction, and then turned back towards the brothers.

"So how 'bout you boys?" Angus Findlay continued. "You don't sound like Virginians or southerners," he noted with a light chuckle, "so I'm guessin' you're Union, right?"

"Yes sir, we were," Johnny replied. "We was cavalry also."

"That right?" Angus peered at the men as if he had just encountered a couple of long-lost distant cousins.

"We rode with Buford; 8th Illinois," Edgar said.

"Buford, huh? Then you were there when the whole thing started."

"That we were," Edgar nodded. "Company E, in fact."

He hesitated for a moment, as if unsure whether he should really say what he was about to utter. He looked over at his brother who, Angus Findlay noted, appeared to give a slight impatient nod back, as in "oh, go ahead already; it's about time you said it to somebody."

"I was the one who pointed out the Rebs – I mean, Harry Heth's men who were marching down the road towards Cashtown," Edgar continued. "I made note of that to Sergeant Shafer who then called Lieutenant Jones and after he spotted what I seen, he took that shot and that's when it all started."

Angus Findlay absorbed what he had just heard, and a wry smile came to his face.

"So you were *very* early to the party, huh?" He cackled. The story of how the Battle of Gettysburg had been triggered – Lieutenant Marcellus Jones of Buford's 8th Illinois, Company E aiming at Harry Heth's men marching at a distance after one of his pickets had earlier taken notice, and then taking what was supposed to be a warning shot with a carbine borrowed from a Sergeant named Levi Shafer – had circulated for years. A monument had been erected back in '86 proclaiming the tale to the world. A few others in Buford's Cavalry, particularly one fellow in the 9th New York, had made similar claims but most agreed that the single shot by this Lieutenant Jones had set the whole battle in motion. And now here was this fellow, this Edgar Sullivan whom Findlay had just met, adding the final important piece to the jigsaw puzzle.

Angus looked over at the man's brother, as if seeking confirmation that this Edgar Sullivan fellow wasn't just some fibber, trying to inflate his own legacy as his days wound down. Still, even before Johnny Sullivan nodded – what my brother says is the God's honest truth, the nod and the accompanying look on Johnny's face said – Angus Findlay knew that Edgar was telling the truth. This wasn't some teller of tall tales, making himself out to have played some important role in history that in actuality he didn't deserve. The man was reserved; his eyes bloodshot, no doubt from too much whiskey over the years; and he seemed to be all business, carrying the mighty weight of deeds past. No; what this man had just claimed was fact, plain and simple.

"Sounds like we're all gathered here today then because of you, is that right?" But the moment those words passed through Angus Findlay's lips he instantly regretted having spoke them, immediately embarrassed at his clumsy attempt at levity. He could see Edgar Sullivan visibly wince.

"I'm sorry, I didn't mean that," Angus began croaking an apology. "I meant…"

Edgar Sullivan simply held up his right hand.

"That's all right," he nodded. "I know what you meant. Yeah, I guess you could say that but truth be told, if I hadn't spotted those Rebs someone else would have in another moment or two. And even if Lieutenant Jones hadn't taken that shot, someone else would have. We all knew the fight was coming one way or another."

"So how 'bout you?" Johnny Sullivan changed the subject and asked after all three had shuffled forward a bit more in the breakfast line, now just barely outside the kitchen tent's door flap. "What unit did you ride with?"

Now it was Angus Findlay's turn to personify history.

"I rode with Stuart's Cavalry, so we were a little bit later to the party here then you fellows were," he replied, referring to the still-controversial delayed arrival on the second of July, halfway through the three days of battle, of Major General J.E.B. Stuart and his cavalry.

"Yeah? What unit in Stuart's?"

Angus shook his head.

"I rode with Stuart," he answered. "I was his *aide-de-camp*."

Now it was the Sullivans' turn to absorb what they were hearing.

"J.E.B. Stuart?" Edgar's eyes narrowed.

Angus Findlay just nodded.

"Well I'll be," Edgar replied. He looked over at his brother. "Like us riding with Wyatt and Doc, huh?"

At mention of the names "Wyatt" and "Doc" Angus Findlay's ears perked up.

"You boys said you're from Illinois?" he asked the brothers.

"We was from Illinois during the war," Johnny replied, "but afterwards we went out to Arizona Territory."

"So you rode with Wyatt Earp and Doc Holliday," Angus Findlay offered after hearing "Arizona" to confirm what he had inferred from Edgar Sullivan's words a moment earlier.

"Yeah, we did," this time it was Edgar who replied. "Ain't that funny; I guess all of us here had our brushes with history back in the old days."

"I suppose so," Angus Findlay replied, and as he did Johnny Sullivan noticed that the hunched-over old man seemed to be a bit less stooped and was standing just a little bit taller than he had been only a few minutes earlier.

Chapter 17

6:45 A.M.

Louisa May Sterling's gaze caught that of Samuel Chambers barely more than two minutes after entering the field hospital, and he appeared to have been searching for her presence every bit as much as she was for his. At least that's the way it seemed because for the nearly thirty seconds between the time she had spotted him before he noticed her, he was looking all around the large bustling ward in a purposeful manner.

Stop it, she had told herself an instant before their eyes locked; he's a doctor so he must be looking for a nurse or an orderly or a Boy Scout to assist him with some hospital matter or another; nothing more.

But when their eyes met, Louisa was as certain as she had been that long-ago evening about Cadet Terrence Sterling that this shared look came bestowed with far more than casual eye contact. For an instant she wasn't sure how to react but after a tight smile came to Doctor Chambers' face, Louisa did likewise before turning away to search out the head nurse of the ward and receive her orders for the morning.

Louisa had told herself time and again during her two-mile walk early that morning from her small house to the encampment grounds that once she set foot inside the field hospital she needed to put the remembrances of having made this same journey, in the other direction, the night before accompanied by Doctor Chambers out of her mind.

Not just the recollection of what they had discussed – their shared Philadelphia backgrounds; their renowned physician fathers knowing each other; and what they had shared with each other about their personal lives – but more importantly, the sensations that had begun stirring in Louisa even before she arrived at her home.

Louisa spent a fair bit of her journey conversing with her son Randall, who despite his own shortened sleep was as eager as he had been the past two days to arrive at the encampment grounds and commence with his Boy Scout duties of the day. During the morning hours Randall would be circulating about the encampment accompanied by two or three older Scouts and helping with anything and everything that they were asked to do. Once noon arrived, though, he would be among the Boy Scouts assigned to escort old veterans from the Pennsylvania delegation to the Great Tent in preparation for the opening ceremonies. Randall would then remain in the Great Tent for the full two hours of speeches assisting the veterans with moving to and fro as necessary, and would be privileged to see and listen to Governor Tener and the other speakers in person. Louisa already had a sense that this Jubilee would be an historic event, recalled for years to come, and was pleased that her eight-year old son was here to see this occasion in person. If he were blessed with a long life – unlike his poor father – then perhaps even near the end of this century he would still be alive and retelling the tale of assisting all these old Yankee and Confederate veterans of that long-ago terrible war between the states.

But when Louisa May Sterling wasn't conversing with her son, she not only obsessively recalled every minute detail she could about strolling alongside and talking with Doctor Samuel Chambers, but she found herself wistfully fantasizing that the hour hadn't been so late when they had arrived at her house and, instead of quickly bidding each other a good night, he had lingered there for an hour or two after she had put Randall to bed. The theater of her mind began to show a moving picture, one accompanied by sound as well, of Louisa and Samuel seated in two wicker chairs abreast of each other, sipping iced lemonade to cool themselves after the excruciating heat of the day and the long walk home. Their conversation proceeded in this imagined show, veering into even more personal matters. After two more hours passed, she watched Doctor Chamber rise from his chair, walk two quick paces to where the picture show's Louisa May Sterling was seated, and hold out his right hand to her as if he were indicating that he was desirous of...

Stop it! Louisa's sensibilities came to life and put a screeching halt to these images and sounds and sensations in her mind. My Lord, she wasn't a hussy who would forego the proprieties of courting and entertain the notion of...well, *that* with a man she had just met! Leave alone the fact that she was a widow and a mother, only a woman of questionable morals would walk home with a man she had just met, entertain him on the front porch of her house, and then proceed to shamelessly embark on *any* sort of intimacies that very same night! Louisa had been raised by her parents – her mother in particular – to *always* be aware of the proper way to do something, and what her imagination was insisting on conveying to her as she daydreamed away was most definitely not the proper way to act with any man!

Still, a corner of that same mind insisted on reminding Louisa that in two days she would be thirty years old, and whereas she may have given up on any ideas of finding a new husband (to her parents' dismay, of course) perhaps Divine Providence had different ideas. Her shameful fantasies (or at least the Overture of such imaginings) aside, last night's stroll and the discoveries that she and Samuel Chambers had made about each other may well be part of some Grand Design, and maybe it behooved her to pay attention and not dismiss any notions out of hand, no matter how farfetched they might seem.

* * *

Nearly half an hour passed once her shift began before she found herself in the proximity of, and in conversation with, Doctor Samuel Chambers. He approached her just as she was turning away from a hospital bed containing a Confederate veteran who, like so many others, had been admitted a day earlier after collapsing. This man was now fully recovered after spending a night in the hospital ward and Louisa was preparing to recommend his discharge.

"Good morning, Nurse Sterling," she heard the doctor's voice even before she finished turning around and noticing him.

"Good morning, Doctor Chambers," Louisa replied, again forcing a tight, uneasy smile onto her face.

"You remember Mister Findlay from last night? The eighty five-year old Virginian we helped out on the grounds and were talking to later on?"

"Of course, Doctor," Louisa nodded. For a moment she was wondering why he had felt the need to amplify the details of Mister Findlay, but then she realized that hundreds of men had been admitted and treated, and it was only natural for Doctor Chambers to make sure Louisa knew which one of them he was referring to.

Then the thought suddenly came to her.

"Did he..." she asked with trepidation, fearing she was about the hear the worst. The very old man had recovered somewhat before she and Doctor Chambers had left for the night, but then again...

"Oh no," Samuel said very quickly. "He's fine; I'm sorry, I didn't mean to alarm you."

Louisa felt herself breath a deep sigh of relief as Doctor Chambers continued.

"I was just going to tell you that Mister Findlay was doing very well when he was discharged this morning and I'm sure he's out on the encampment grounds. I'm particularly glad since he is the oldest patient I've personally treated thus far, and it's fortunate that he recovered so quickly given his age."

Louisa nodded.

Samuel Chambers looked about the hospital ward, and Louisa's gaze followed his.

"Most of those still remaining should be discharged within the hour," he said, "which will be timely for us because I fear we will need all of these beds and perhaps more for new patients today who will also succumb to the heat."

Chambers looked around the ward again, and began walking away from the bedside where they were standing, Louisa following alongside, towards one of the doctors' writing stations against the far wall.

"They found another man dead in his tent last night," Samuel said solemnly. "A Mister Rigsby of Wisconsin. That's four dead so far."

Louisa looked over at him as they continued walking.

"Four?" At the time they had departed the field hospital the previous night the fatality count had stood at two.

Chambers proceeded to tell her of the sorrowful death of Otto Stamm of New York, the man whose collapse and sudden passing while futilely searching for a place to sleep had so infuriated Governor Tener when he had been informed by Colonel Bradley. Chambers and Bradley had conferred early this morning about all medical matters on the encampment grounds and the Army man warned Samuel that should he encounter the Governor this morning he should be prepared for Tener's rage. Not necessarily at Samuel himself, but still…

"That's terrible," Louisa shook her head after Samuel finished his short narrative of Stamm's death.

They reached the doctors' writing station and Louisa paused for a moment before preparing to continue walking on.

"Is your son here again today?" Samuel asked.

Louisa quickly related Randall's obligations of the day.

"Ah, I envy him being able to attend the ceremonies in the Great Tent," Samuel said when she had finished. "I believe I shall be here in the hospital ward the entire day, as you will be."

Louisa thought she saw a look of contemplation, maybe even cunning, quickly come to the doctor's face before vanishing in a flash.

"Perhaps late this afternoon young Randall could relate to you, and to me as well, what he remembers of hearing our Governor and Colonel Schoonmaker and the others say during their speeches this afternoon. I know I would be very appreciative of him doing so."

Louisa fought off a smile that, at the same time, might convey both a leap of the heart as well as embarrassed uneasiness.

"I will ask him to do that, Doctor," she instead replied in tones as even and dispassionate as she could muster.

"And perhaps," Samuel Chambers continued, "you might join me around noon if I can sit for a few moments in the kitchen to enjoy a quick lunch if the affairs of the field hospital will allow me to do so."

This time Louisa May Sterling was helpless against the smile that came to her face, and equally helpless against the words that spilled from her lips.

"I would like that, Doctor Chambers," she nodded, hoping at the same time that her eyes were not betraying the confused swell of emotions now engulfing her thoughts.

Chapter 18

7:15 A.M.

"Pop?"

Chester Morrison looked up at the sound of his son's voice. He had been engrossed in conversation with the five other Pennsylvanians seated at the breakfast table outside the kitchen. Chester and Devin McAteer had been in each other's company for nearly four hours now, since encountering each other in the darkness outside their sleeping tent and then heading over to the main Mess Tent in search of coffee. The two men had been joined by Devin's cousin, the coal miner Seamus McAteer, sometime around 5:30 and then three others from their sleeping tent had joined Morrison and the McAteers as they headed off to one of the kitchen tents for a hearty breakfast.

Chester had been engrossed in the McAteers' tale of slipping away from Pittsburgh and hopping a railroad train to Harrisburg to volunteer for the 45th Pennsylvania, and had been shocked into silence when Devin quietly told of the horrific explosion at the Allegheny Arsenal only weeks later that had claimed the lives of two of his sisters and almost certainly would have cost Devin his life if he had still been working in the Arsenal's main laboratory. Earlier, before being joined by Seamus, Devin's tales of Reconstruction-era Louisiana as a member of the occupying United States Army had captured Chester's attention. Chester Morrison had certainly lived an interesting life himself, rubbing shoulders and doing business with Morgan and Guggenheim and Vanderbilt and Astor, not to mention men such as Carnegie and Frick who had furnished this man McAteer with his livelihood for so many years after finally leaving the Army back in '75. In those too-rare quiet moments, Chester could recall so many evenings spent at the Union League in Philadelphia, or on occasion at the counterpart in New York City when Baldwin Locomotive business called him up there. Chester Morrison's life since the end of the war had not been tranquil by any stretch of the imagination but it had been mostly comfortable. His worries for most of the past forty years or so had been focused almost exclusively on ensuring that Baldwin Locomotive could navigate its way through the Panics of 1893 and 1907 and continue to thrive in the brave new world of 20th century American commerce.

These two men, however – as well as the three other Pennsylvanians who joined them to share breakfast this first morning of July, 1913 – likely had seen and experienced even more in their lives than Chester had. None of the other five had gathered wealth and possessions that came anywhere near to what Chester Morrison had acquired during that time frame, but – and surely this was but an old man's wistful, jumbled thinking – he found himself sorrowful in a way that during his life he had never experienced being part of the Reconstruction Army or knowing what it was like to work shift after shift in a Luzerne County coal mine. He found himself wondering what it might have been like to operate a simple dry goods shop in a Pittsburgh neighborhood, day after day, as one of these other men – the Pole Wyzghra, a veteran of the 11th Pennsylvania and who had also been here at Gettysburg – had for the past fifty years.

Just before hearing his son's voice, Chester Morrison acknowledged that wistful, even nonsensical imaginings aside, that he was indeed fortunate to have lived the life he had – the loss of his beloved Sadie notwithstanding – rather than the much tougher lives these men had endured.

Chester tore himself away from his meandering thoughts and looked up at his son.

"Hello, Jonathan," he answered his son's greeting.

Jonathan Morrison quickly took in the scene of his father gathered with the five other veterans, sharing coffee after all had finished their breakfasts. He had been terribly concerned about his father's well-being throughout the night and even though he had slept, Jonathan had also suffered terrible dreams. In at least two of them, his motor car journey from Gettysburg back to Philadelphia had not been with his father sitting alongside Jonathan in the front seat of the Pierce-Arrow, singing *Abie Sings an Irish Song* or some other ditty of the day, but instead accompanying his father's body back for burial. Jonathan had left the Hotel Gettysburg shortly after waking for good around 6:30 this morning and hurried over to the encampment grounds to check on his father. Coming upon Chester Morrison apparently engrossed in some other old man's story, seemingly in full health and vigor, was a tremendous relief to Jonathan.

"Have you been awake long?" Jonathan asked his father who, before answering, looked over at Devin McAteer.

"Well, yes I have," he replied to his son's question. "I actually didn't sleep much last night. Mister McAteer here" – he nodded towards Devin – "and I encountered each other sometime around 3:30 this morning out on the grounds, and we've been engaged in discussion ever since."

Chester noticed the alarmed look suddenly appear his son's face upon hearing that his father had been awake for almost four hours now, even though it was still relatively early in the morning. For his part, Jonathan's confidence in his father's well-being evaporated in an instant in light of what his father had just disclosed.

"I'm fine," Chester reassured his son. "A bit weary but I'm sure as the day proceeds I will feel as if I had had a full night's sleep."

"Did you sleep at all before then?" Jonathan pressed, and noticed the shadow quickly cross his father's face as the elder Morrison quietly replied "A little." Jonathan was about to ask his father if, once again, disturbing nightmares of terrifying days at Gettysburg long ago had prematurely forced him out of the world of dreams into the safety of the starry nighttime sky. Jonathan knew the answer to his question, though; at least he was almost certain of what his father's answer would be, so he let the moment pass without inquiring. He would keep a close eye on his father throughout the day, though; that much was certain.

"Allow me to introduce my son Jonathan," Chester Morrison said to the gathering of men before proceeding to introduce each of them by name, home, profession, and wartime affiliation to his son. The two McAteers, and Karol Wyzghra, the shopkeeper from Pittsburgh. Also Lawrence Armstrong from nearby Carlisle, today another shopkeeper but who, as a member of the 33rd Pennsylvania Volunteer Militia, had helped defend that city against the cavalry of J.E.B. Stuart himself during the all-but-forgotten Battle of Carlisle fifty years ago today, on July 1st...the same day that the Battle of Gettysburg began. And finally Edward Reed of Erie, a physician who had fought at Gettysburg as a member of the 145th Pennsylvania.

Pleasantries were exchanged among Jonathan Morrison and these men, and Seamus McAteer – who had been sitting to the left of Chester Morrison – shifted to his left closer to his cousin to make room for Jonathan Morrison, who proceeded to join the group. Lawrence Armstrong had just begun telling the group the tale of the Battle of Carlisle so he backtracked to describing how Stuart's cavalry arrived on the first of July. Then, after getting to Stuart beginning to lay siege to Carlisle with only the Pennsylvania militia defending the town, Armstrong cackled:

"We found out later that old J.E.B. Stuart thought we were regular Army of the Potomac, not just state militia, so he just halted outside the town and sent in Fitzhugh Lee to tell us to surrender rather than just go ahead and attack us. Old Baldy Smith" – all of the gathered men knew of Union Major General "Baldy" Smith and, on the other side, Robert E. Lee's nephew General Fitzhugh Lee, so no amplification on their names was necessary – "...refused, and so Stuart began bombarding us..."

Armstrong's tale continued as he told of the great surprise to one and all holding down the fort, so to speak, in Carlisle when Stuart's men set fire to the Carlisle Barracks before abruptly departing. Surprised at Stuart's withdrawal, the men quickly learned of the heavy fighting underway over in Gettysburg, which explained their unanticipated reprieve from the Confederate cavalry.

For the next hour the men took turns telling one tale after another about the war, the immediate aftermath, the years leading up to the turn of the century, and the passing time since then the 1900s began that coincided with their own sunset years. The day grew hotter and as a quarter past the hour of eight came and went, all were perspiring freely but none seemed to care. Jonathan Morrison simply sat and listened, finding himself enraptured by the tales these contemporaries of his father were sharing. Laborers, a physician, shopkeepers, and his father the industrialist: for the moment all were equal.

"Well, if it isn't Chester Morrison!" A brief pause. "And Jonathan Morrison also!"

The commanding voice came from behind the side of the table where Jonathan and his father were seated, and the conversation halted at once. Even as Jonathan was turning around he knew whose voice it was that he had heard, but it was his father who responded first.

"Well, James Schoonmaker, as I live and breathe! Or given the occasion, should I address you as *Colonel* Schoonmaker?"

"Ah, Chester," came the reply from the Pennsylvania Commission's Chairman himself as Chester Morrison – Jonathan also – rose in greeting. "Or should I address you as '*Colonel* Morrison' as well? And how are you on this very hot morning?" Schoonmaker wiped the perspiration from his brow as he spoke, but a new beaded layer of moisture reappeared almost instantly.

"I'm well, thank you James," Chester Morrison added before looking back at the McAteers, Lawrence Armstrong of Carlisle, and the others. All of them – save the physician Reed from Erie – seemed both awestruck and terribly uneasy at the sudden appearance of the illustrious Schoonmaker: Medal of Honor winner and Pittsburgh industrial tycoon. Of course it made sense, Devin McAteer thought to himself, that this newfound acquaintance Morrison knew Schoonmaker from the railroad business; no doubt Morrison's Baldwin Locomotive supplied engines to Schoonmaker's Pennsylvania & Lake Erie Railroad. Devin instantly felt the camaraderie of the past hour for all these men with Chester, and more than five hours for himself, evaporate as he watched the easy exchange between Morrison – his son as well – and the eminent James Martinus Schoonmaker. Three high-muck-a-mucks conversing among themselves, the lesser classes suddenly forgotten.

But to Devin McAteer's surprise – and a touch of shame – Chester Morrison turned back towards the table and, looking over his shoulder at Schoonmaker, said:

"James, may I introduce you to several of our Pennsylvania comrades in arms?"

Indeed, Morrison began his introductions with Devin McAteer, taking nearly a full minute to describe Devin's participation in the siege and conquest of Vicksburg during the war, his time spent in the Reconstruction-era Army, and his time in Carnegie's mills. Devin leaned forward to shake hands with Schoonmaker, who – Devin could almost swear – seemed to look back at the steel mill man from Pittsburgh with a touch of admiration.

The introductions proceeded to Seamus McAteer, and then the physician Reed, and then the shopkeepers Armstrong and Wyzghra. Schoonmaker warmly shook hands with each man in turn as he was introduced, and then finally he turned back to Chester Morrison and said:

"I've been making the final preparations for my opening address at this afternoon's ceremonies but I could use a pause. May I join all of you for a cup of coffee?"

With that, Colonel James Schoonmaker, the Chairman of the Pennsylvania Commission for the Fiftieth Anniversary of the Battle of Gettysburg; winner of the Medal of Honor for his heroics in '64 at the Third Battle of Winchester; Chairman of the Pennsylvania & Lake Erie Railroad; and Mellon Bank board member sat down at the picnic table this morning of July the first, 1913, and proceeded to spend the next hour sharing stories with not only his long-time business comrade Chester Morrison, but also all of these other Pennsylvanians of lesser renown who long ago had gone through much the same in the heat of battle and the hell of war as these high-muck-a-mucks had.

Chapter 19

11:30 A.M.

Ned Tomlinson hobbled towards his sleeping tent, and for the final twenty yards wondered if he had enough strength to make it that far. His wife Mabel's words of concern and warning from months ago when he had brought up attending this Great Reunion echoed in his head: "But you're not well enough to travel all the way up to Pennsylvania and live in a tent for three or four days!"

The Devil with three or four days, Ned Tomlinson thought to himself as he planted his crutches and paused, still ten yards away from the tent's door. He was having tremendous difficulty surviving this very first day!

He had arrived at the train depot via the Western Maryland Railroad just after 7:00 P.M. the previous evening and two hours later was settled in this sleeping tent that was, at the moment, taunting poor Ned Tomlinson. The mirage in the desert; the refuge from the deadly heat…could this man make it that far and if he did, was that sanctuary even real?

None of the other men in his sleeping tent was known to Ned, so he had risen even before dawn this morning and set out amongst the other tents that housed the Virginia delegation in search of familiar faces. He had found more than a few, even beyond those of his UCV comrades who had made the journey from Norfolk alongside Ned on the railroad. But the effort had been exhausting, Ned realized too late, and after five hours he was feeling as weak and ill as he had when his crippling wound during Pickett's Charge left him prone on the battlefield here; the wound that would require the Union Army surgeon to remove Ned's left leg before they sent him off to the Yankee prison at Fort Delaware.

Mustering his remaining strength he swung his crutches again and then again and again, covering the final ten yards to the tent's entrance and then another three or four yards to his cot. He almost missed the cot as he collapsed in exhaustion but fortunately caught himself with his left arm – always the stronger one of his two, no doubt from compensating for the missing leg on that side of his body – and pulled himself onto the bedding.

Nobody else was in the sleeping tent, and Ned Tomlinson laid on his back, sweating profusely, and simply stared upwards through terribly blurred vision at the tent's ceiling.

*   *   *

Philip Roberdeau sat by himself at a table outside the kitchen tent closest to the Louisiana delegation's area within the encampment grounds. He had been present on the grounds for more than 24 hours now, and he had yet to encounter a single soul known to him. The Louisiana delegation only consisted of one hundred and twenty five Confederate veterans in all, and about half of them were from New Orleans as Philip was. Still, not a single one of those men was one whom Philip had either served with during the war or whom he had encountered in some manner in the years since.

All throughout the latter part of the morning, Philip wandered about the encampment grounds in search of a familiar face among those from the other Southern delegations, but his efforts were futile. Plenty of the other former Confederates were happy enough to nod or speak a short greeting to Philip as he passed, just as so many of the Yankees were. A tip of a hat or a wordless nod; "howdy" or "howdy there" or even a slightly stiffer "hello" might be exchanged; and once in a while a comment about the weather would follow: "Howdy there, it sure is a hot one already, huh?" But not a single greeting thus far went beyond those detached exchanges, and Philip increasingly wondered why he had bothered making the trip. He just as easily could have remained comfortably seated in the parlor of his New Orleans home, reading about this gathering in the *Times-Picayune*.

He rose and began to stroll aimlessly through the grounds, eventually continuing into the fringes of the Virginia delegation's many tents. Not surprising given Virginia's proximity to Pennsylvania – and the Borough of Gettysburg in particular – Virginia had the largest number of Southern veterans present; more than 3,000 ex-Confederates. Philip had yet to make his way into the area occupied by the Virginians; perhaps someone here may be familiar, or at least interested in sharing more than a detached word or two in passing.

Philip Roberdeau would never be sure what forces urged him to belay a left turn at that one street intersection among the sleeping tents and instead continue walking abruptly forward, nor would he ever be sure why his ears seemed especially attuned when, as he walked by one of the tents thirty yards past that intersection, the very faint, muffled sounds he heard made him stop; pause for a moment; and then enter the tent to investigate the origins of what he heard.

Whatever the reasons had been – whether they were Divine Intervention or a matter of loneliness-driven curiosity, or simply happenstance – Philip slowly entered the sleeping tent from which those sounds had originated. His eyes took a moment to adjust from the intense late morning sunlight to the duskier inside of the tent, but even before his vision had fully adapted he could make out the prone figure of an old man on a cot against the far side of the tent. The man was panting – that was the sound Philip had heard, he realized – and clearly was in distress.

"Are you alright?" Philip asked the man as he hurried over, knowing both that the answer was "no" and that the man likely wouldn't even be able to utter that simple syllable. As he reached the cot, Philip noticed that the man was staring directly upwards but his eyes seemed to be unfocused, as if he were staring beyond the ceiling of the tent into the very Heaven above them.

Instantly, Philip Roberdeau spun and hurried outside the tent as quickly as his seventy-three years allowed him to do and called for help.

*   *   *

Just as Philip Roberdeau would never be certain why he had taken this particular path through the Virginia delegation's portion of the encampment grounds this morning, neither would Devin McAteer be certain why he was even in the midst of the Rebel tents of the Virginians. The gathering of Pennsylvanians that had come to include James Schoonmaker himself had broken up a short while ago and his cousin Seamus told Devin that he wished to rest for a spell to gather his strength for the upcoming opening ceremonies of the Jubilee in the Great Tent. Devin should have felt the same way, given his lack of sleep the previous night, but he felt surprisingly refreshed and decided to stroll about the grounds for a bit before lunch and then the afternoon ceremonies.

His mind had been engaged in woolgathering as he ambled about the grounds, and at any given moment Devin wasn't quite sure where he was, let alone why he was there. Even when confronted with the panicked persona of Philip Roberdeau doing his best to string together a coherent plea for assistance, Devin McAteer had no idea he was now among the sleeping tents of the Virginia delegation.

Still, there they were: Devin McAteer and Philip Roberdeau, the latter finally successful in communicating to this Yankee that a man was struggling for his life inside the tent nearest them. Devin hurriedly followed Roberdeau inside and, upon surveying the condition of Ned Tomlinson, said:

"We need to find ambulance medics to render this man first aid and then transport him to a field hospital or aid station. Come on, help me with him."

And so the two elderly men, one of them past the age of seventy and the other closing in on that mark, leaned down to the cot where poor Ned Tomlinson lay as the old Virginian's very life slowly seeped away in light of the terrible heat. With a deep breath from Devin McAteer – and another from Philip Roberdeau – the two men hoisted this stranger into a sitting position and then swiftly pulled him to what passed for a standing position. Between Ned Tomlinson having only one leg and his condition, he could do little more than dangle helplessly between the two Samaritans as they wasted no time shuffling Ned towards the tent door and out onto the street in front of the tent that ran through the Virginia portion of the encampment grounds.

Just as Providence placed these two men in the proximity of Ned Tomlinson's tent as his life began to slip away, so too did Providence cause two Army corpsmen to follow the exact same path that Devin McAteer had taken only a moment earlier. One of the corpsmen was gazing about the area, taking in the magnificent scene of tent after tent, but the other immediately noticed Devin and Philip doing their best to carry Ned Tomlinson. He elbowed his fellow medic and they both rushed forward to take Ned Tomlinson from the old men. Placing him gently on the ground, one of the corpsmen began tending to Tomlinson while the other rushed to the closest aid station that fortunately was only seventy yards away. He returned with two more corpsmen and a stretcher, and together the four men quickly hoisted Ned onto the stretcher and rushed off with him back towards the aid station.

The rescue effort happened so quickly that both Devin and Philip found themselves standing on the boardwalk of the makeshift street gape-mouthed, wondering if indeed the entire event may have been but a shared dream since they were now alone. After a few moments Philip Roberdeau realized he didn't even know this man's name or his home state. He could tell from the few words uttered by this stranger that the man was definitely Yankee, but that was all.

"Thank you for assisting me," Philip held out his right hand towards Devin. "My name is Philip Roberdeau, from Louisiana."

"Devin McAteer, from here in Pennsylvania," came the reply along with the handshake. "Though from over in Pittsburgh."

"Mister McAteer," Philip acknowledged with a slight nod while maintaining the clasp of hands and then simultaneously tipping his hat with his left hand as he slightly nodded; a Southern gentleman's gesture.

"I hope and pray that man will regain his health," Philip continued. "I believe we stumbled upon him just in time."

"I agree," Devin nodded.

The two men remained standing on the boardwalk street in front of Ned Tomlinson's tent, but both had run out of things to say for this meeting of strangers. The hour was now closing in on noon, and Philip realized that lunch was now being served at the various field kitchens scattered about the encampment grounds.

"Would you care to join me for lunch, Mister McAteer?" He nodded towards the kitchen that stood some seventy yards distant and the growing crowd of Virginians.

"That is, if you don't mind eating amongst a crowd of old Confederates instead of the safety of your Yankee brethren," Philip added.

Devin paused for a moment, instantly uneasy at the thought offered by this Louisianan, but the apprehension passed as quickly as it had appeared.

"I s'pose so," Devin replied and the two men set off towards the field kitchen, where they joined the growing line of men.

"I would bet that fifty years ago this very scene would have made your heart stop?" Philip said with a small chortle. "Just you and an entire crowd of Rebs here on the field at Gettysburg?"

"Ain't that the truth," Devin chuckled, then added:

"Of course, I wasn't at Gettysburg back then, I was with Grant's Army of the Tennessee down at Vicksburg those very same days…"

Devin abruptly cut off his own words as he realized what he was saying. Here he was, telling this man from Louisiana that fifty years earlier – in fact, fifty years ago this very day – he was besieging that vaunted Southern city not far from where this stranger lived. In fact, depending on what part of Louisiana this man hailed from, it might be as close as only a hundred miles. Devin immediately felt very uneasy about having blurted out his role in the siege of Vicksburg.

Philip Roberdeau sensed the cause of this man's abrupt silence.

"So it appears that I was up here in your neck of the woods fifty years ago and you were down in mine," Philip offered. "I am from New Orleans so Vicksburg is some two hundred and thirty miles away from my home, and I believe that your Pittsburgh is about the same distance from here in Gettysburg?"

Devin nodded.

"Something like that," he replied, relieved that his anxiety had been for naught. Upon hearing this Roberdeau fellow mention "New Orleans" he almost mentioned that indeed he had spent the entire decade following the war in and around New Orleans as part of the Union Army's occupying force during Reconstruction, but caught himself. *That* revelation might not be received so evenly by this newfound acquaintance as Devin's wartime placement outside of Vicksburg.

The two men were mostly silent as they slowly shuffled forward in line towards the opening to the kitchen tent; the same scene that was being repeated all about the encampment grounds and would be repeated at all meals for the next few days during the Jubilee. Devin's mess kit, still unwashed from the morning's breakfast but at least on his person, would have to suffice for him while Philip would have to rely on the availability of a spare once inside the tent; or perhaps a last-minute request to borrow one from another veteran just finishing his lunch, after which Philip would have to seek out the man and return it.

The latter option – a borrowed mess kit – was what Philip wound up handing to the Army cook and which the sergeant handed back filled with roasted chicken, macaroni, and canned corn. Devin's mess kit was likewise filled, and the two men headed outside the kitchen in search of seats. They found an unoccupied table and sat, expecting to be joined at any minute by several of the Virginians milling around, also in search of seatings for their lunches.

The two men began sharing tidbits of information about themselves. Philip related how he had been a West Pointer when war broke out and how he had left the Military Academy alongside the famed P. G. T. Beauregard to join up with the newly formed Confederate Army of the Potomac, and after finishing that tale Philip looked around and said:

"I don't believe I have previously mentioned that I was here back in '88 for the 25th anniversary commemoration of the battle, did I?"

Devin shook his head as he buttered the bread roll that had been placed on his tin plate.

"There were not nearly as many Union and Confederates on the grounds that time," Philip continued. "Maybe 300 Southerners in all, and perhaps five or six times that many Northerners."

Philip looked around again.

"But not nearly as many as are on the grounds this time," he repeated, his voice even more pensive than only a moment earlier.

He looked across the table at Devin McAteer.

"Of course a few of our Southern generals were in attendance that first time and their presence lent an air of substance to that gathering, considering it had only been a quarter of a century since our side had warred with yours. This time, though, I understand only General Law will be here since I believe he is the only one of our generals still alive, though I've not recognized him."

"Well, from our side I hear ol' Dan Sickles of New York is here," Devin replied. "Don't know about anybody else."

A wistful smile came to Philip Roberdeau's face at the mention of Sickles' name.

"I was in his company here back in '88, in a manner of speaking. Sickles, I mean. The General came upon our General Longstreet and the two men greeted each other as if they were long-lost brothers rather than long-ago adversaries. There was even an article in the *New York Times* about that meeting that I've saved all these years."

At the mention of the name "Longstreet" Devin lightly smiled.

"I happened to meet General Longstreet years ago just as you met Sickles," he began before realizing that relating the story of how he had once met – indeed, rescued –

General Longstreet would necessitate him sharing with this newfound acquaintance that he had once been part of the Union Army occupying this man's state of Louisiana and hometown of New Orleans. Still, Devin felt compelled to continue.

"Long ago after the war had concluded I remained in the Army and was in fact dispatched to your Louisiana." Devin avoided mentioning "Reconstruction," certain that word was still hated by Southerners, one and all.

"Back in '74," Devin continued, "I was there when the Crescent City White League shot the General and held him prisoner for several days when he was with your State Militia, and I was among those who rescued General Longstreet from them as we restored order…"

Devin abruptly stopped speaking as he observed the shocked look that had suddenly appeared on Philip Roberdeau's face. This man must have been part of the dreaded White League, Devin suddenly thought to himself; an enemy from even after the war had concluded! Why else would he have such a stunned look upon his face in response to Devin's words?

"Do you happen to recall if, when you rescued General Longstreet, he was alone as a prisoner?" Philip Roberdeau asked after he had regained his composure.

"No," Devin replied after a moment's hesitation as he concentrated to recall that long-forgotten detail from nearly forty years earlier, but – still nervous about this man Roberdeau's facial reaction to Devin's tale – not taking time to wonder about the origins of the question. "I believe that several other State Militia men had been captured along with the General, and we rescued all of them safely."

Philip Roberdeau slowly shook his head as scenes from decades earlier suddenly began playing before him, as vividly realistic as when they had occurred so many years earlier.

"I was one of those other men whom you freed along with General Longstreet," he quietly informed his long-ago rescuer.

Chapter 20

1:00 P.M.

Governor John K. Tener was standing to the right of the large stage in the Great Tent, from which he and the other dignitaries would deliver their addresses this day. For a few moments he had finally been able to forget about his fury with the Secretary of War in light of those hundreds of veterans no longer being in attendance at this celebration due to having no place to sleep. There had, in fact, been no sightings at all of Secretary of War Lindley Garrison despite the time being but one hour before the opening words that Colonel Schoonmaker would offer at precisely 2:00. Perhaps the Secretary had decided not to attend after all in light of the problems, or maybe he was hiding out elsewhere on the encampment grounds, waiting for the final possible moment to make his appearance here in the Great Tent…and hopefully sidestepping the Governor's rage that Garrison most certainly knew of.

Tener was gazing over his handwritten speech, doing his best to immerse himself in the cadence he had tried for when he had written and rewritten these words over the past few days when he heard:

"Governor Tener, I presume?"

Tener looked up from his notes and then down at the shorter man addressing him. This man was flanked by two heavily perspiring men wearing suits as well as an Army sergeant and an Army captain. Though he had never previously met this man, Governor Tener knew who he was.

"Secretary Garrison," Tener replied stiffly through clenched teeth as he felt his eyes narrow in disdain, still shaking hands with this man as a matter of common courtesy. "I would like a word with you."

The Secretary of War seemed to have anticipated this request because he let out a small chuckle.

"Why of course, Governor," he replied but made no motions to step away from his entourage nor to turn and tell those men to leave he and the Governor alone. When Tener realized that Garrison would not be making any efforts to talk privately, he decided that these other four men, civilian and soldier alike, could simply stand by and witness the exchange that was about to begin.

"As I'm sure you have heard," Tener began, "hundreds of these veterans are no longer amongst us on the encampment grounds because they had no place to sleep last night. We were short hundreds of tents and cots, and despite all of our efforts" – Tener almost said "my efforts" but decided on the spot to depersonalize his anger as much as he could – "we were unable to secure additional tents until well into the night, and even then we were still short hundreds of cots. This was a totally unacceptable turn of events after all of the machinations we were forced to endure last week in light of your surprise telegram and what had to be accomplished to overcome your unwillingness to provide adequate funds. I can assure you, Mister Secretary, that had we not been forced to halt construction on the encampment while we waited for the additional funds we needed, this unpleasantness would *not* have occurred!"

Lindley Garrison looked around at the two civilians and two soldiers accompanying him, and then back at Governor Tener. He paused for another brief moment before looking the Governor squarely in the eyes and replying in flat tones:

"I will make sure to relate your displeasure to the President of the United States, Governor Tener."

With those dismissive words, the Secretary of War and his entourage turned and walked away from the Governor of Pennsylvania, leaving John K. Tener to summon all of his will to resist chasing after this insolent politician and kicking a healthy amount of the dirt of the Great Tent's floor all over the Secretary's suit of clothes, much as Tener would have done during his baseball playing days to an umpire who had contemptuously turned and walked away in this manner.

Chapter 21

1:30 P.M.

Louisa May Sterling's stomach continued to rumble at a regular cadence, as it had for nearly the past two hours as she made her rounds among the beds in the field hospital's ward. For the past hour she had been tempted to ask the head nurse if she could slip away for five minutes to the small eating area in the back of the hospital building and quickly partake of a lunchtime meal to squelch the rumblings of her empty stomach. Yet every time Louisa felt that her hunger had become so acute it was time to make this request, she halted before doing so in hopes that Doctor Chambers would appear by her side and honor his earlier request that they eat their afternoon meals together.

Finally, half past the hour of one having arrived, Louisa had given up hope of Samuel making an appearance and just as she finished checking on a seventy-six year old man from Rhode Island who seemed to be on the mend, she turned around and did indeed come face to face with Samuel Chambers.

"I apologize for the delay in seeking you out," he began, "and I fear you have already had your lunch, have you not?"

Louisa shook her head.

"I have not," she quickly replied. She wanted to add "I've been waiting for you, in fact" but of course wouldn't dare utter such a bold sentiment.

Samuel looked around for a brief moment and satisfied that no other doctor nor any of the nurses were trying to catch his attention, he said to Louisa,

"I think the situation here is calm and stable enough for us to step away for a lunchtime meal, if you would still care to do so."

Louisa nodded, fighting to keep the smile of relief from breaking out on her face.

"Of course," was her reply.

They walked to the back room that had been set aside as an eating area, and where a small serving line had been established for the hospital's medical staff. Mess kits identical to the ones that had been distributed to the veterans were available to the staff for their meals, and Samuel reached for one that he handed to Louisa and then took another for himself.

Though a dozen doctors, nurses, and ward attendees were scattered among the seating tables in the room, Louisa and Samuel were the only two in the serving line. He nodded and extended his left hand in a gesture of "please, ladies first" and then watched as the Army cook assigned to the field hospital and who was also manning the serving line began to place the afternoon's selection on Louisa's mess kit plate. Samuel watched a boiled egg be served followed by a small helping of roast turkey and a bread roll, and also a small sliver of cherry pie for dessert. As he stepped forward to receive his meal, Samuel Chambers couldn't help but be engulfed in the sensation that this very scene had been played out before...or if not the exact scene, one very similar to it. Though his eyes were watching a boiled egg and roast turkey and the rest of the meal being placed on his mess kit in this windowless room in the back of a field hospital, Samuel's mind was insisting that the scene was instead playing out somewhere outdoors; perhaps in the midst of a picnic.

A very odd sensation, Samuel thought to himself as he brought himself back to the here and now once the slice of cherry pie had been plopped onto his mess kit plate. *I feel not only as if I've lived this moment before, but indeed that this same woman was with me as well. Perhaps some fragment of a forgotten dream, one involving a picnic with a woman, is insisting on being recalled and acknowledged?*

As they walked towards the only unoccupied table in the kitchen, Samuel forced from his thoughts this unsettling sensation of replaying a prior event. What was important, he told himself, was the here and now; a chance for ten or fifteen minutes of conversation with this woman who, only one night earlier, had enraptured him and had dominated his thoughts during dream after dream last night and during his waking hours throughout this entire morning and early afternoon. Several times Samuel had to force his thoughts back to hospital matters as he bustled about the field hospital's various ward rooms; almost every idle moment when he wasn't observing a patient he found his thoughts slipping away to a remembered moment of dialogue from the previous night's walk accompanying Louisa and her son, or some imagined moment of conversation with her that had yet to happen. Samuel had never felt this way about any woman, even his former fiancé from medical school days before that engagement had ended.

The first five minutes of conversation were about the morning's events in the field hospital. Just as Samuel had predicted, the hundreds of beds vacated by the previous day's victims of the terrible heat had quickly been filled by newcomers who had been overcome by this day's temperatures that were every bit as oppressive as yesterday's. Many of the newly admitted cases were "routine" – that was, there was little concern about their prospects for recovery now that they were under care – but at least two dozen were of grave concern.

"I would say the most severe of all is this man Tomlinson from Norfolk, Virginia," Samuel pondered. "He was rushed in by four Army corpsmen less than two hours ago and though he has stabilized, I must say I fear for his recovery."

A somber look came to Louisa Sterling's face. She had been a nurse for a long while, and had certainly seen her share of death. But there was something particularly heartbreaking about the prospect of one of these old Civil War veterans coming to the Gettysburg in his sunset years and not leaving alive. Perhaps some of them, the veterans of that terrible battle here even more so than others who had fought elsewhere those same days, wished to depart this world in this manner; Louisa had entertained that prospect as well. Still, the very idea that a Gettysburg veteran – Northerner or Southerner – would survive not only the horrors of that battle and the rest of the war, and then all the years since then and whatever hardships he surely had faced, only to pass away on that same field of battle fifty years later in the midst of comrade and enemy alike, was one that saddened Louisa terribly.

"Have you any word from your son Randall yet this morning?" Samuel's words brought Louisa back to the present from her sorrow-tinged musings. As she began to reply Louisa felt certain that Doctor Chambers had purposefully used her son's first name in his question, his intention being to establish a more personal bond of sorts.

"Not so far," Louisa shook her head, answering after she had swallowed a delicate bite of the boiled egg and ensuring that she didn't answer this man's question with her mouth still holding even the smallest bit of food.

"I believe that now he is solidly immersed in escorting the veteran guests to available seats as the ceremonies should be getting underway soon, should they not?"

Samuel withdrew his pocket watch and noted the time as now being fifteen minutes before the hour of two o'clock.

"In another quarter hour," he nodded as he replaced his watch and looked back at Louisa. "As I believe I mentioned this morning, I envy him being able to hear Colonel Schoonmaker and Governor Tener and Secretary Garrison and the others this afternoon. I hear that the speeches will be recorded on a Edison wax cylinder recorder device and perhaps one day we will be able to listen to the actual sounds of what those gentlemen said. But your son will have the privilege for the rest of his life to recall the actual sights and sounds of this monumental day. And to think tomorrow he will be able to hear the recitation of the Gettysburg Address during Military Day ceremonies as well. In fact, even as I'm speaking those words I'm imagining that Edison's invention had been available fifty years ago and recorded the actual voice of President Lincoln delivering that address! How magnificent!"

Louisa only half-heard the final sentences of Doctor Chambers' reflections as she finished the final two bites of her boiled egg before turning her attention to the roast turkey. Her thoughts were still focused on several words he had spoken earlier in his musings; specifically, speaking about the wax cylinder recording of the ceremonies that were about to get underway, "perhaps one day we will be able to listen to the actual sounds…"

Louisa's mind insisted on inserting the word "together" in its own wax cylinder replay into her thoughts of what Samuel Chambers said. And so Louisa May Sterling helplessly "listened" to the ethereal voice of this man saying, several times in succession:

"Perhaps one day we will *together* be able to listen to the actual sounds…"

Chapter 22

1:45 P.M.

The spirit of forgiving past grievances most certainly had descended on the men of the Blue and Gray alike as the minutes ticked down to the start of the Veterans' Day ceremonies. Otherwise, the jostling of Yankees and Confederates as they filed into the Great Tent may well have triggered harsh words or worse between former enemies. However, other than some occasional grumbling when brushed or accidentally shoved, the old combatants from both sides patiently moved forward in extremely close quarters with one another towards the various door openings until, once inside the Great Tent, they could fan out in search of the limited number of seats.

Thirteen thousand individual chairs had been placed throughout the Great Tent, which of course meant that with more than *fifty* thousand Yankees and Confederates and then tens of thousands of spectators present, many of the veterans and spectators alike would be forced to stand for the two hours of ceremonies held today, and likewise for the ceremonies and speeches during each of the next three days. Not every single soul at the encampment grounds would be present in the Great Tent this afternoon or during the following days' ceremonies, but most would at least try to be in attendance. Given the mid-afternoon heat even under the shade of the Great Tent, being seated for two hours rather than standing was a coveted reward and once inside the Great Tent, great urgency was observed in most of the veterans as they anxiously did their best to secure a chair before all were occupied. Fortunately, most of the spectators were genteel enough to not even attempt the act of securing chairs for themselves, instead leaving those chairs – and even most of the standing locations with the best vantage points for viewing the stage – for the old veterans.

With ten minutes left before the opening remarks by Colonel Schoonmaker, all chairs had been occupied. Those veterans still filing in were told of this and directed by the Boy Scouts and other guides to various portions of the Great Tent where standing room still remained. It was feared that even the standing room might not be adequate, but those remaining on their feet would simply have to crowd together as closely as possible in hopes that anyone who wished to observe and hear the speeches of this historic day would be able to do so.

Anticipating the limited seating, Edgar and Johnny Sullivan had arrived nearly half an hour earlier and easily found chairs squarely in front of the stage, some twenty rows back. They were accompanied by their new-found acquaintance and fellow former cavalryman, Colonel Angus Findlay of Virginia. In the hours since the Sullivans had met Angus in the breakfast line and the men learned of their respective pasts, they had settled into a sort of camaraderie. Angus Findlay had been particularly curious about the events at the very earliest stages of the Battle of Gettysburg – indeed, the events even before the battle had begun – and both Edgar and Johnny Sullivan found themselves surprisingly eager to share the tale of the arrival of Buford's Cavalry at Gettysburg on the thirtieth of June, a date on which Angus had been with J.E.B. Stuart fighting in Hanover, Pennsylvania on his way up to Carlisle before turning south again on the second of July to join the fight at Gettysburg.

Meanwhile, as the Sullivans had already related to Angus Findlay, the shooting in Gettysburg had already gotten underway but nobody knew for certain at the time if this would be just another minor skirmish between the Yankees and the Rebels, many of which had been taking place for weeks all over northern Maryland and southern Pennsylvania, or if this encounter might shape up to be a major battle. Few outside the most senior Generals on both sides had any idea that the next three days would come to be recorded in the annals of history alongside Shiloh, Antietam, Chickamauga, and Spotsylvania Courthouse.

As he listened to the separate tales told by each of the Sullivan brothers throughout the morning, Angus Findlay painted a picture in his mind of what had taken place on the Union side that very first day, particularly as the Union's John Reynolds and the Confederates' Richard Ewell arrived and the forces of both sides engaged en masse. And all the while, J.E.B. Stuart's forces had been on their roundabout journey, skirmishing through much of south-central Pennsylvania until turning back to join the fight at Gettysburg on the second of July.

Ironically, by that time most of Buford's Cavalry had been ordered with withdraw down to Maryland, meaning that these men – the Sullivan brothers and Angus Findlay – had never had occasion to face off against one another during the Battle of Gettysburg.

"I supposed we did fight against one another at Brandy Station, though," Angus Findlay said thoughtfully as talk of their respective roles at Gettysburg began to falter about an hour before the opening ceremonies were to begin. "I survived Brandy Station without a scratch; how about you boys?"

Alan Simon

"Same with us," Edgar Sullivan replied after a moment's hesitation, this Virginian's words conjuring up his ponderings during the train ride from Arizona to Gettysburg of the prospect of coming face to face with a former enemy who might very well have killed or wounded him. In his conversation with his brother about that matter he had surmised coming face to face with one of Harry Heth's men from that first day of battle here. That particular situation had not occurred – yet – but here he was, talking away with J.E.B. Stuart's *aide-de-camp* who, three weeks before Gettysburg, had engaged Union General Alfred Pleasonton's Cavalry Corps that included Buford's Cavalry and thus the 8th Illinois. The number of casualties at Brandy Station had paled in comparison to the three days of Gettysburg, of course; 1,400 on both sides versus the fifty thousand, give or take, at Gettysburg. Still Brandy Station turned out to be the apex of cavalry-versus-cavalry during the war, and arguably the first time during the entire war that Northern cavalry had matched up well against their gallant Southern opponents.

So quite possibly, despite the Sullivan brothers and Angus Findlay having survived Brandy Station unscathed, Findlay and one of these Illinois men may well have crossed sabers during the heat of that battle in an attempt to mortally wound the other, and the deeds had simply been left uncompleted.

Edgar Sullivan contemplated that prospect for the next hour and finally concluded that if perhaps that had been the case, then his brother Johnny had indeed been correct all along: it hadn't been personal and that's what this occasion was all about anyway, for the Yankees and the Rebels who were still alive to put all of that long-ago unpleasantness behind them once and for all.

*   *   *

Seated not far from the Sullivan brothers and Angus Findlay were Devin and Seamus McAteer, accompanied by Philip Roberdeau, Chester Morrison, and Lawrence Armstrong of Carlisle. The Sullivans and Findlay did not know the McAteers or Roberdeau or the other men with them, at least not yet. If Edgar or Johnny Sullivan happened to gaze about and notice Devin or Seamus McAteer, there would be no sense of recognition, not even the knowledge about which side of the war any of them had been on. And the same was true for Devin and Seamus, and the others with them as well.

For their part, Devin and Philip were still talking animatedly…to the annoyance of Seamus McAteer. All morning long, Seamus tried to understand why his own demeanor had turned so irritable. He finally concluded that unfair as it might be, the new friendships that his cousin Devin had made had put Seamus into a foul mood.

For months, Devin had been extremely reluctant to commit to attending this grand reunion of Blue and Gray. Not until the middle of May, and three more exchanges of posted letters with Devin after those of mid-March, would Devin finally agree to attend the commemoration. And even then, for the next month, there were hints that Devin might indeed change his mind. In early June Seamus had walked down the street to one of the houses in Pittston that was fortunate enough to be equipped with a Bell System telephone, and he placed a long-distance call all the way to Pittsburgh to Kerwin McAteer's house – where a telephone had been in place for nearly five years – to speak over the wires with Devin. A neighbor listening to this conversation on the shared party line would have found it humorous; for the ten whole minutes the two McAteers spoke to each other, the phrase "What did you say?" had been uttered by one or the other of the cousins more than twenty times. Between two old men hard of hearing and the crackling static of the Bell System's long-distance lines – especially on a humid day – neither of the McAteer cousins could easily understand what the other was saying or asking. But by the end of that conversation, Seamus was confident that his cousin would not fail him and would indeed be coming to Gettysburg only weeks later.

But here they were, and the reluctant, reticent Devin McAteer had already befriended a Philadelphia high-muck-a-muck from Baldwin Locomotive, an act which had put him in direct and affable conversation with James Schoonmaker himself! And this very same morning, he had come across this Roberdeau of New Orleans who was sitting with them this very moment, about to listen to the aforementioned James Schoonmaker utter the opening words of this Jubilee. And of all things, they discovered that Devin had rescued not only the famed General James Longstreet but also this very same Louisianan back in '74!

Why was he so agitated at these occurrences? Seamus McAteer couldn't quire put his finger on the reason, but there was no doubt that his mood had definitely darkened throughout the morning.

For his part, Philip Roberdeau was still in a shock of sorts at the discovery that this old Pittsburgh man had been among the Federal troops who had freed him during the Battle of Liberty Place. He was flooded with memories of those days as a prisoner of the Crescent City White League as well as discussing that event with Pete Longstreet himself a decade and a half later here at Gettysburg back in '88…maybe even on this very same spot! Philip couldn't recall given that the layout of the encampment for the 25th anniversary gathering was certainly different than the current one, but wouldn't that be something!

All of Philip's somber reticence about coming to this commemoration that he had felt for months before departing from New Orleans, and which had also consumed him since his arrival, had disappeared. There was a reason he had come in contact with this man Devin McAteer; of that Philip was certain. Of all the tens of thousands of men in attendance at this encampment; indeed, in the midst of the Virginia Delegation where neither Philip nor Devin should even have been this morning, the two of them had come together quite by accident to assist that poor old man gasping for help in that tent. Philip's faith in the Almighty had certainly been tested over the years, but he was certain Divine Providence had indeed caused these two men to meet.

At the recollection – again – of the incredible circumstances under which he came to meet Devin McAteer, Philip wondered if that old man was still with them or if he had passed. He wondered if there might be a way later this afternoon, after these ceremonies had concluded, if he could find out any information from the field hospital. Without the man's name or even a good idea of what he looked like he doubted his chances, but still he thought he might make an effort anyway.

*   *   *

"This is the man Tomlinson whom I mentioned," Samuel Chambers said to Louisa May Sterling.

They arrived together at Ned Tomlinson's bedside as the ward's clock showed the time as three minutes before the hour of two o'clock. Their lunchtime meal and conversation now completed, and with definite plans to meet again in the late afternoon or early evening to hear Randall Sterling's report of the ceremonies that were about to get underway, it was time to resume their care of the ward's patients.

As Louisa prepared a thermometer Samuel picked up the chart board that was hanging from the bottom of the man's hospital cot and read the updated remarks written there by one of the other nurses only ten minutes earlier. This man Tomlinson from Norfolk, Virginia – his identification tag had been located in his coat's inner pocket, so at least the staff knew the name and state of their patient – had yet to regain consciousness, and his temperature at last reading was still hovering above one hundred and three degrees. The reading Louisa was about to take would likely be little changed, but convention called for her to perform this act while Doctor Chambers proceeded to examine the man with his stethoscope.

Two minutes later, with the latest readings of both temperature and heartbeat recorded on the chart, Samuel paused to look thoughtfully at the man for a few moments. Louisa noticed a quick, almost imperceptible shaking of Doctor Chambers' head as he looked down at the bed, his lips pursed. She felt her heart sink, certain that the physician was wordlessly indicating that he had little hope for the man's survival.

Samuel looked up and tilted his head upwards and to the left, indicating that he wished to have a word with Louisa away from the man's bedside. She replaced the chart board on the foot of his bed and followed Samuel a dozen steps away towards the center of the room, away from any patient beds.

To her surprise, his sentiment was the opposite of what she had expected.

"It defies logic for me to say these words, given Tomlinson's readings and current condition, but I somehow feel that he will make a full recovery. I can't explain why I feel this way other than to say that it seems these men are all under God's watch at the moment. We've had so few deaths despite this terrible heat and how frail so many of them are; I can think of no other explanation."

He paused for a moment, wondering why he would have just shared such a non-medical sentiment with a nurse. But of course, he realized, this woman was far from just a nurse; she had transcended that role during the past twenty-four hours.

"Still," Samuel continued, "God's watch or not, we must do our utmost for the care of these men and right now, Mister Tomlinson in particular. I will speak to the head nurse in a moment and ask her to assign you exclusively to his care so you will be able to remain mostly at his bedside, save perhaps an emergency situation elsewhere. Would that be alright with you?"

"Of course," Louisa replied without hesitation. She had come into contact with so many doctors since she had taken up nursing as a profession following the loss of her dear Terrence. Some of those physicians had borne a detached, purely clinical demeanor while others seemed to take a special interest in their patients. Still, she had never had such a sentiment shared with her by a doctor as the one that Samuel Chambers had just conveyed. Whether it was because of some special quality of his, or the circumstances of this healing reunion of old enemies – or

some swiftly growing bond between her and this man –
Louisa felt privileged that he had shared these thoughts
with her and had enlisted her in a special cause, of sorts, to
do everything possible to bring this man Ned Tomlinson
back to health.

Chapter 23

2:00 P.M.

The booming voice burst forth from the speaking stage at precisely 2:00 P.M.

"Comrades of the Blue; Comrades of the Gray; Your Excellency, Governor Tener; our honored guest, Secretary of War Garrison; Ladies and Gentlemen! The honor falls to me, as Chairman of the Pennsylvania State Commission, of presiding at the opening ceremonies of a celebration unparalleled in the history of the world; an occasion on which the survivors of two might armies, locked in deadly conflict for three consecutive days, fought a battle in which the mortality was greater than in any other recorded in history, before or since that memorable event, fighting for a principle as God gave them to see the right..."

With these words, Colonel James Schoonmaker began the opening ceremonies of Veterans' Day and the Great Reunion at Gettysburg was now officially underway. Fifty years ago at this moment many of these old men in the audience were locked in mortal combat with one another, or soon were about to be. During the two hours that this day's opening ceremonies would take, those same two hours fifty years earlier would see the rapid escalation of the Battle of Gettysburg to the eventual all-out warfare that would hallmark those days for all time. Names from both sides that were already famed, or that would be, were already engaged in the battle: Ewell, Reynolds, Buford, Early, Hill, Lee, Hancock, Pettigrew. Thousands of these men seated or standing this day in the Great Tent that had been erected on that old battlefield had served under these Generals during attack and counterattack during these same two hours fifty years ago at Gettysburg. Now, though, they sat side by side, peacefully, as they listened to one of their own – the Medal of Honor winner Schoonmaker – open the official ceremonies.

"...to assemble here in sight of yonder beautiful cemetery," Schoonmaker continued, "where peacefully sleep thousands of our beloved comrades who fell on this memorable battlefield, while we are permitted to join in this glorious Reunion..."

Schoonmaker went on to note, in his short introductory remarks, how in the country's most recent war – now more than a decade in the past, though – former Union and Confederate Generals had joined together in unity under one flag to defeat the Spanish, signifying that at least from a military perspective the nation was one again. And now, forty-eight years after the cessation of hostilities between the North and the South, the final healing had begun.

"Chaplain-in-Chief Lovejoy of the Grand Army of the Republic," Colonel Schoonmaker introduced the G.A.R.'s Reverend Doctor George E. Lovejoy as he concluded his opening speech, "who, as a private in the Twenty-second Massachusetts Infantry, fought all through the Battle of Gettysburg, will now invoke the Divine blessing."

With those words James Schoonmaker yielded the podium to Chaplain Lovejoy as most of the thirteen thousand seated veterans – all those who were able to stand, other than the infirm and the very weary – rose to join the tens of thousands of others already standing in the Great Tent.

Lovejoy's opening prayer lasted close to five minutes, and many of the veterans who had risen found themselves in need of retaking their seats before the Chaplain had concluded. No one looked askance at any of these old men who sat down even as Chaplain Lovejoy spoke. Finally the Chaplain concluded and as James Schoonmaker again began to speak, the rest of the men who had previously secured a chair resumed their seats as well.

Colonel Schoonmaker, well aware of the controversy and animosity between the next speaker – Secretary of War Garrison – and Schoonmaker's friend Governor Tener, pushed aside his own personal distaste with the Secretary's actions surrounding appropriations that had led to the premature departure of so many Pennsylvanians and others. His duty was to introduce Secretary of War Garrison, but instead of lauding the man personally Schoonmaker confined his remarks to the War Department's role in general. After all, Garrison had only been in his lofty position for mere months, dating back only to the beginning of Woodrow Wilson's new administration this past March. Much of the War Department's role in this Great Reunion had occurred long before Lindley Garrison assumed his role after being appointed by the new President.

Thus, it wasn't until the final sentence of his introduction that James Schoonmaker mentioned Garrison by name, and he made sure to precede that mention with words that on the surface sounded like praise for the man but to those in the know, were no less than under-the-breath criticism:

"When the recent change in the administration of affairs in the War Department was made, we were concerned lest a different policy would follow," Schoonmaker said following his praise of the Taft Administration's partnership with the Pennsylvania Commission as plans for the encampment took shape over several years, "but with a quick conception of the situation, its incoming Secretary added new life and encouragement to all engaged in our big preliminary work by his prompt response to all requests made by his subordinates, for which I now beg to personally thank him, and have no greater pleasure than in presenting to you our new War Minister, who will welcome you on behalf of our Nation, the Honorable Lindley M. Garrison."

As Schoonmaker yielded the podium to Garrison, he could detect a flash of anger in the Secretary of War's eyes in response to the Colonel's words. Schoonmaker's observation that Garrison had indeed provided a "prompt response to all requests made by his subordinates" was an accurate one; the Secretary's answer, however, had often been a resounding and occasionally dismissive "no." Even the Secretary of War's designation in early June, only weeks before the opening of the encampment grounds, of Lieutenant Colonel Bradley of the Medical Corps as the Chief Surgeon of the Camp, essentially placing Bradley in charge of all medical matters above Doctor Samuel Chambers and even Pennsylvania's Commissioner of Health – Doctor Samuel Dixon – had seemed to largely be an assertion of power and authority by Garrison. Fortunately Bradley had proved to be a capable administrator and thus far had worked well in cooperation with Chambers, but that fact did little to diminish the complications Garrison had caused since assuming his new office in March.

While tens of thousands of veterans of that long-ago war, and tens of thousands of spectators, didn't need to be aware of these facts, James Schoonmaker could not resist including his "complement" in his words with full knowledge that Garrison himself, Governor Tener, and others on the Commission and in the War Department would know with absolute certainty the message being delivered in Schoonmaker's words. After all, if one were to look at the accomplishments of the likes of James Schoonmaker (or John K. Tener) versus those of Lindley Garrison, one could come to no other conclusion that the words spoken by the Pittsburgh industrialist and Medal of Honor winner carried far more weight than any spoken by the Wilson crony with his roots in New Jersey and Philadelphia.

For his part, Lindley Garrison followed his glare at Colonel Schoonmaker with a quick reminder to himself that at this very moment, he was before the eyes of the nation and the world for the first time as the Secretary of War. He quickly suppressed his own anger as he began to speak:

"In the name of the Nation I bid you welcome. In the name of a whole people of a united country, I bid you twice welcome. In the name of its people who recognize the high import of this fraternal gathering, you are thrice welcome."

Garrison cleared his throat then continued.

"Once again is Gettysburg the center of the world's attention. Once again does this field tremble under the tread of a mighty host – not now in fear, however, but in joy. The field of enmity has become the field of amity. You have trodden under your feet the bitter weeds of hate and anger, and in their places have sprung up the pure flowers of friendship, and love."

Governor Tener turned his head slightly to the right and caught the eye of James Schoonmaker. Their shared look conveyed that they both felt the same: Secretary of War Lindley Garrison may have proven persnickety rather than caring and empathetic in matters of appropriations related to this Great Reunion, but his speech was starting off as a magnificent one. A raised eyebrow from Tener to Schoonmaker – "let's hear what else he has to say" the facial gesture communicated – and then both men turned back to listen to Garrison continue.

The Secretary of War proceeded to note that fifty years ago today had marked the beginning of that epic struggle, taking care to note that "equal met equal" and that the name "Gettysburg" would forever be associated with valor and heroics.

"Four months afterwards," he continued, "the field of Gettysburg inspired in the great mind and heart of Abraham Lincoln the most wonderful prose poem ever written. Its music literally rang around the world and sang in the hearts of men, and will continue to sing in the blood of the sons of men until Time itself shall be no more."

Garrison, ever the politician, followed his praise of the valor of the men gathered before him with a surprising detour into the political and historical buildup to the Civil War.

"And then the time for the inevitable arrived. Those who honestly believed that the United States was a voluntary association of independent sovereign states, met in irrepressible conflict with those who honestly believed that the United States was an indissolvable union of otherwise independent states. Each side, with all the earnestness of those whose hearts, minds, and consciences are committed to an ideal, sought to mold the Government to their respective views. There was no earthly tribunal before which this great issue could be tried and determined. The arbitrament of arms alone remained."

As Garrison's speech wound down, and John K. Tener began to prepare his mind for his own speech, the

Pennsylvania Governor was forced to admit to himself that Garrison's oratory was of the first order. Tener looked out at the field of faces before the stage, and most were enraptured by Garrison's words. I may not care for the man or how he conducts his office's affairs, Tener thought, but his words have truly captured the sentiment of this day and this event. Now let us see how I shall do.

After Garrison concluded his speech by paraphrasing Lincoln – "And so the picture will go forth to the Nation, and it will rejoice with you, and the whole world will realize that not only has the government of the people, by the people, and for the people not perished from the earth, but that it will not ever perish!" – he turned and nodded politely to both James Schoonmaker and Governor Tener and made his way back to his seat on the stage amidst the polite applause from the audience. Schoonmaker was already standing and walking to the podium to introduce the next speaker, the Governor of Pennsylvania.

"The Pennsylvania State Commission was indeed fortunate in having as its directing spirit our host on this occasion. From the hour on which he buckled on his armor as the Chief Magistrate of the great Commonwealth of Pennsylvania, at a time with the work of the Commission, because of its magnitude, seemed beyond the limit of human agency to successfully combat, until the moment of triumph in its completed task, his one endeavor was to aid in every way in his power."

Schoonmaker had been determined to lavish as much praise on his friend and colleague as he had withheld from the Secretary of War. His motivations weren't merely partisan ones, though; Tener had indeed been the driving force behind this event since he had assumed office in '11, and Schoonmaker wanted the Governor's magnificent contributions to be noted by one and all present this day.

Still, Schoonmaker couldn't resist one more slap at the War Department's political machinations of the past weeks and what the cost had been.

"His counseling was invaluable – his words of encouragement gave new heart to the workers – his appeal to the Legislative body of his State, that everything possible be done for the comfort, safety and happiness of the old veterans while our guests – that the amount of funds necessary to secure same was not to be considered, as nothing was too good for the old veterans, whose big body is not large enough to hold within itself his bigger heart, overflowing with consideration for his fellowman – the one man more beloved in this great Commonwealth over which he presides than any other within its borders. I now propose a standing vote of welcome to our host, the Honorable John K. Tener, Governor of Pennsylvania!"

With those words from James Schoonmaker a mighty roar rang forth from the thousands of Pennsylvania veterans present in the Great Tent as those who were able rose to their feet and clapped their hands in appreciation of the Governor and Colonel Schoonmaker's words about the man. They were quickly joined by nearly every other veteran present, Union and Confederate alike, and the ovation was joined by those already standing. Nearly a full minute passed before the rumble died down and the veterans began to take their seats again. In the meantime, Governor Tener maintained a stoic look on his face yet felt an overwhelming sense of pride at not only the ovation he was being offered by these gallant soldiers of yesteryear, but also by James Schoonmaker's words. No doubt Schoonmaker had fallen to the desire to tweak the Secretary of War's nose just once more, but there had been a genuine appreciation in what the industrial tycoon and former war hero related to his fellow veterans. For the rest of his life, John K. Tener would always remember this moment along with several others that would shortly follow.

Finally, the Great Tent had quieted enough for Tener to begin speaking.

"Mister Chairman, Veterans, Ladies and Gentlemen: As Governor of the Commonwealth of Pennsylvania and speaking for her people, I extend a welcome to the soldiers and sailors, both the Blue and Gray survivors of the great hosts of brave men who, fifty years ago, wrote upon the pages of the world's martial history the enduring fame and glory of the American soldier.

"We gather today on the greatest battlefield of the Civil War and of the World; not to commemorate a victory, but rather to emphasize the spirit of national brotherhood and national unity, which, in the years since the close of that War, has enabled this Republic to move forward and upward, until today she leads the nations of the earth in all that makes for the advancement and uplift of the human race."

Tener paused to swallow before continuing with the words he had toiled over for weeks, struggling to be able to put forth exactly how he felt about this event and the years of work leading up to this day.

"We meet on this occasion to participate in a ceremony that stands unmatched in all recorded time; for nowhere in history have men who opposed each other in mighty battle thus come together in peaceful reunion fifty years thereafter, all content with the result of the struggle and grateful that in defeat or victory, there left no stain upon American manhood, and no question as to the bravery or devotion to duty of the American soldier."

As the Governor continued speaking, Colonel Schoonmaker looked outwards from the stage towards the sea of faces before them. Some of these old men were showing the weariness of their advanced years combined with the stifling heat, and they sat slumped with their eyes closed; hopefully asleep, Schoonmaker thought to himself, rather than suffering from illness. But other than the scattered slumberers, nearly everyone else was enraptured by Governor Tener's words even more than they had seemed while listening to Lindley Garrison. Leaving aside the political dueling over appropriations, Schoonmaker was convinced of one thing: both Garrison and Tener were magnificent in their respective efforts to capture the aura of the occasion in words.

"After the lapse of half a century, the wounds are healed; and true, 'no wound did ever heal but by degrees.' The bitterness is gone, past differences are now settled, and hand in hand, the foes of other days stroll in soldierly companionship through the vales and over the hills of this great battlefield, and as they wander far and near, no hostile gun will break the summer stillness of the peaceful scene."

Tener blew out a breath before concluding his speech.

"The great heart of the whole people of Pennsylvania goes out to you as honored guests of the Nation and State. Our sincerest desire is for your greatest enjoyment while here, and our fondest wish is that when you return to your homes, you may recall, in most pleasing memory, the scenes and incidents of this day and time when heroes in Blue and heroes in Gray joined hearts and hands, guaranteeing for all time the protection of our Country's Flag and the preservation of the Nation's institutions."

The conclusion of the Governor's speech was met with a reprise of the many Pennsylvania veterans rising to their feet, cheering and clapping, closely followed by their comrades from the other Northern and Southern states. Another full minute went by before Colonel Schoonmaker was able to continue with his introduction of the Commander-in-Chief of the Grand Army of the Republic, who had the next speaking slot. In the meantime, as the clapping and cheers continued to ring, Schoonmaker leaned forward to the Governor and said, loudly enough for Tener to hear over the ruckus,

"Well done, John."

John K. Tener finally allowed himself a small smile.

"Thank you, James," he said to his friend.

All the while, one hundred and fifty five newspapermen from cities across the nation and from many other countries furiously scribbled what they could recall from Governor Tener's oration, as they had during the other speeches thus far. Many also recorded their observations about the sentiments inside the Great Tent this first afternoon of July, 1913; in particular, the harmonious spirit of collegiality among former enemies who sat side by side to listen to the speakers' observations about this event; that long-ago battle here on the grounds; the Civil War in its entirety; and the years of healing since the end of the war that were culminating on this very spot, on this very day.

Colonel Schoonmaker moved to introduce the G.A.R.'s Alfred DeBeers, who – despite the boisterous show of appreciation for Governor Tener that had just concluded – asked for "every person present who loved the Union and its flag" to rise and offer three more cheers for Tener and, as a whole, the Commonwealth of Pennsylvania for being such gracious and competent hosts. And again the cheers and applause burst forth before the audience quieted.

The Grand Army of the Republic's commander from Bridgeport, Connecticut proceeded to offer his thoughts on behalf of the Union veterans of the G.A.R., and was followed by his United Confederate Veterans counterpart, Bennett Young.

General Young, aware that many in the audience were growing weary, preceded his prepared remarks with a surprising request, especially given the location and circumstances of this gathering:

"Comrades, I can give you something that no one else in the world can give you, and, in recognition of the splendid hospitality of this great Commonwealth, extended from the Governor, we propose to give him the Rebel Yell!"

In response to those words, the thousands of Confederates in the Great Tent did exactly as requested: they let out a mighty reprise of their Rebel Yell, directed in honor of Governor Tener. More than a few Union veterans in the tent felt instantaneous shivers at the first notes of that sound in remembrance of days past, though James Schoonmaker leaned over to Governor Tener, seated to the Colonel's left, and said: "Well, John, imagine that you had been born twenty years earlier and we were fifty years in the past; *this* sound would have brought you face to face with the specter of Death himself!"

The Tent eventually quieted and as Young finally began to speak, out in the audience Chester Morrison leaned over to Seamus McAteer and said:

"I know Mister Young quite well, in his capacity as the President of the Louisville Southern Railroad; he has purchased locomotive engines from Baldwin Locomotive in the past. You do know the story about Lieutenant Young, his rank at that time, during the war, don't you?"

Seamus McAteer, at first mystified that this important man Morrison felt compelled to speak one-on-one with the Luzerne County coal miner, shook his head.

"He was the Rebel lieutenant who invaded Saint Albans, Vermont in late '64 coming down from Canada, and they robbed three banks up there. Even though they claimed the town in the name of the Confederacy, all that happened was that they burned down a woodshed and made their way back to Canada with a fortune! Two hundred thousand dollars!"

Seamus McAteer had never heard this story; in fact he had thought that the skirmishes throughout South-Central Pennsylvania– Hanover, Carlisle, York, Wrightsville – leading up to all-out battle at Gettysburg was as far north as the fighting had ever been during the war. Though, he supposed, a Rebel lieutenant and his men committing bank robbery way up in Vermont may not quite qualify as armed conflict between the Union and the Confederacy. Still, what this man Morrison had just told him was both interesting and surprising, and he still found himself wondering why the Philadelphian had felt compelled this moment to share the tale with Seamus.

General Young proceeded with his remarks that followed the G.A.R.'s DeBeers. More than any other speaker thus far this morning, Young brought those in the audience back to the Battle of Gettysburg itself:

"Turning our vision backward half a century, we behold on this spot one of the most sanguinary battles of the ages. We can see the hosts marshaled under the Stars and Bars and under the Stars and Stripes. We can again hear the rattle of musketry, the booming of cannon, the bursting of shells, the shouts of charging legions; and we can see the hills and slopes and valleys about Gettysburg stained with the blood of gallant men, and amidst the fields of growing grain, in the thickets on the hillside, and on the crests of those heights the dead bodies of thousands who were true to truth as they saw it. These dead gave their lives as a sacrifice for principles that appealed to them as the most important among really great political doctrines. Grim determination, undaunted courage, and noblest patriotic impulses filled the souls of the warring armies, who were aligned about this quiet and secluded village to try out the issues that the exigencies of war had imposed upon them and to meet the emergencies that conflict of opinion had forced them to adjust by appeal to the court of last resort."

Thousands of the old veterans who had begun to grow weary as the ceremonies moved forward in their second hour – the Rebel Yell of a few minutes earlier notwithstanding – were suddenly alert, and many leaned forward in their chairs, spellbound as the U.C.V. Commander-in-Chief continued:

"The terrors of this battle defy the brush of the artist or the words of oratory. Only those who participated in the struggle can conceive what horrors hovered about this spot, now forever historic in the world's annals. A few of the men who fought here fifty years ago are with us today. More than eight of every ten men on both sides are now sleeping the sleep of death. Some of the rifles that did execution then are here, but the men who bore the arms are well nigh all gone. Some of the cannon, that thundered then are here; but the cannoneers who loaded, trained, and fired them have, most of them, passed from human scenes and have gone to be with the immortals. Some of the banners that on the days of the battle guided those who fought, now torn and tattered, are still held aloft."

Sobs could be heard coming from many of those in the audience as General Young transported the men back in time to those three days of bitter conflict, while also reminding them of their own mortality with his words.

"Then we looked on war with complacency. The lessons so greatly magnified in this valley and on these mountain tops on those baleful days will never be forgotten, though succeeding generations turn from its tragic and distressing scenes with horror. Time is not only a great vindicator, but it is also a great pacificator. Those who fought then now meet as friends. They grasp each other's hands; they look kindly face to face. War's animosities are forgotten; the noise of battle is hushed. Peace waves its wand over these bloodstained hills and cries out to war: 'Be still.'"

Young's speech was by far the longest in duration this first day of the Great Reunion. He reviewed much of the history of the war as well as healing and reparations since its end, including care for the graves of the war's dead. He made mention that he himself had delivered one of the first speeches that paid tribute to those who slept in Confederate graves north of the Ohio River, near Columbus, Ohio and Camp Chase, noting that someone had written over the entrance to the cemetery the words "They were all Americans."

Young concluded his speech and was greeted with an ovation from the audience much like that given to Governor Tener. A short final prayer was offered by the U.C.V.'s Chaplain-in-Chief Reverend Doctor Hamill, and as the Army band struck up the notes of "America" the great audience began to slowly file out of the Great Tent sharply at 4:00 P.M. Fifty years ago, many of these men were face to face with mortal combat; now their primary enemy was the mid-afternoon blazing sun as they stepped outside, as well as the soaring temperatures.

Thousands of conversations among veteran and spectator alike ensued as the attendees departed. The near-universal sentiment was that despite the growing discomfort throughout the ceremonies caused by the heat of the day encroaching into the Great Tent, and – for those unable to secure a chair – the necessity of standing in place for two hours, the event they had just witnessed had been an historic one. As both Colonel Schoonmaker and Governor Tener had remarked, the world had never before borne witness to a gathering of this magnitude by former enemies, especially fifty years after many of them had met in combat on this very spot. Of all the Blue-Gray reunions over the past quarter century, this one was already by far the grandest of all...and three whole days still remained!

Tomorrow's ceremonies would be similar to today's, and include a recitation of the Gettysburg Address by the son of one of the physicians who had attended to President Lincoln following his mortal wound. Other speeches would be from one soldier each of the North and South, as well as the Lieutenant Governor of Rhode Island. At some point the veterans and spectators might grow weary of speech after speech...but today, July the first, 1913, was not that day.

Chapter 24

6:30 P.M.

Thousands of the old veterans used the hours immediately following the conclusion of the Veterans' Day ceremonies to make their way back to their sleeping tents and rest for a spell in the midst of the worst of the late afternoon heat and humidity, while others milled about the encampment grounds, trading stories or playing cards with old acquaintances or newfound ones.

Chester Morrison and the McAteer cousins all made their way back to their sleeping tent in the midst of the Pennsylvania delegation with the intention of being among the former group, and all three quickly fell asleep soon after arriving at their tent. Jonathan Morrison had accompanied his father and these men back to their tent after miraculously locating them among the throngs of the crowd, not two minutes after the three men had stepped out into the bright sunshine. The men shared tales of their impressions of the ceremonies they had just witnessed, and all agreed the two hours had been among the grandest spent thus far in each man's life, even for the much younger Jonathan Morrison.

Philip Roberdeau departed the company of his new acquaintance Devin McAteer to make his way back to his own sleeping tent within the Louisianans' area of the grounds, with plans to make his way to the Pennsylvania delegation portion sometime around 6:30 to join these men for supper at one of the field kitchens by the Pennsylvanians. Likewise, the Sullivan brothers and Angus Findlay departed towards their respective portions of the grounds with similar plans to meet back near the Great Tent, after which they would wander to whichever field kitchen seemed less crowded as they strolled about the encampment.

On his way to his sleeping tent, though, Philip Roberdeau recalled his earlier concern for the Virginian he had helped save. Though tired and in severe need of a rest, Philip instead walked a quarter mile to the main field hospital in hopes of learning whatever information about this man's condition might be available.

He found and then entered the field hospital and was struck by the dozens of beds laid out in the first of the patient wards into which he had walked, each one filled with an old veteran. He quickly took in the scene. Most seemed to be resting comfortably and likely out of danger, but for a moment Philip was overcome by sadness at the thought that each and every one of these men had missed what he and thousands of others had just witnessed. Philip wished that the ceremonies were like a moving picture – with sound, though – and these men would be able to view the occasion at some later point after full recovery. As it was, the afternoon's speeches and ceremony were now instantly as much a part of the past as the battle itself on these grounds fifty years ago was, never to be replayed again.

Philip shook away this melancholy thought and searched for a doctor or nurse from whom he might be able to learn the information he sought. After a moment of searching about the ward with his eyes, he spotted a young woman wearing a white dress with a white cap placed upon her head. He walked over to her, feeling the stiffness of the day in his legs with every step.

"Pardon me, ma'am," he said as he reached the woman, removing his hat before speaking, "I was wondering if I might be able to learn the condition of a man who was brought in here in the late morning hours, shortly before noon." Philip proceeded to describe what he could recall about Ned Tomlinson as well as the circumstances of having discovered him in poor condition in the sleeping tent, and the Army orderlies coming to hurry the man to the hospital.

"We have several patients who fit the description you have related," the nurse said when Philip finished. She nodded towards the doorway to her left, about fifteen yards, leading to another patient ward.

"Each of those men is in that ward," she said to Philip Roberdeau. "You are welcome to inquire of one of the nurses in there to see if you can locate your friend."

Philip was about to correct the nurse – the man was not Philip's friend, but simply someone he had stumbled across in the midst of struggling for life – but halted. That detail was unimportant and besides, even if the man was not a friend, he was still a comrade in much the same way that all of these other men here were. Philip still was enveloped by some of his uneasiness about being from an era that had passed and thus was out of place here in the modern day of nineteen hundred and thirteen, but his conversations with Devin McAteer and the Pennsylvanian's cousin and acquaintances throughout the afternoon had done wonders for his disposition.

"Much obliged," Philip nodded to the nurse with a small bow, and turned to walk towards the doorway she had indicated. He passed through the portal and in an instant could tell that many of the men in this slightly smaller ward seemed to be in poorer condition than those in the room from which he had just come.

His eyes lit on a bed against the far wall, a bed with a nurse sitting in a chair close by, and at a distance the patient lying there looked much like the man from earlier today. But then again, Philip thought to himself, don't we all at this point in our lives? Still, he walked in that direction and as Philip got closer he could see that indeed, this was the man from the tent.

The nurse, sensing the newcomer's presence, looked up from the papers on which she was writing when Philip was still twenty feet away, and watched him carefully as he walked to within a few paces away from the bed and then halted.

"Howdy, ma'am," he nodded when his failing eyes detected that the nurse was now looking at him. "I would like to inquire as to the condition of this here man, to see if he is regaining his health."

The nurse – who happened to be Louisa May Sterling – looked quickly at Ned Tomlinson prone in his bed, a slight grimace of discomfort still on his face as it had been for the past several hours, and then back at the newcomer.

"Your friend is doing a bit better this afternoon," Louisa chose her words carefully. Ned Tomlinson was indeed farther from death than he had been a day before or during the night, but by no means was he totally well. Doctor Chambers may have expressed his faith earlier this afternoon in the likelihood of Mister Tomlinson's recovery, but at the moment he was still a very ill old man.

"He definitely has not fully recovered," Louisa decided to share a somewhat more candid assessment with this newcomer, "but he is most certainly better off than he was yesterday."

Louisa looked down at Ned and then back at Philip Roberdeau.

"Your friend cannot speak right now, I'm afraid, and he does need his rest; but would you like to sit with him for a while?" she asked.

Just as with the previous nurse from five minutes earlier, this nurse's usage of the phrase "your friend" made Philip want to correct her misperception…and this time he did just that.

"Big your pardon, ma'am, but the man here isn't 'zactly a friend. In fact, I don't even know his name. I came across him in his tent yesterday when he was in a bad way and helped find the medics to bring him in here."

Louisa nodded, the picture now clearer for her.

"I see," she said. "Well, it is very fortunate that you found him when you did because I fear he would not have lasted more than another five or ten minutes without the immediate medical attention he received when he was brought in here."

Even as she spoke of Ned Tomlinson, Louisa's thoughts wandered in a different direction as her mind began showing her omniscient scenes of she and Doctor Chambers out on the encampment grounds, tending to Angus Findlay the previous evening. My Lord! Was that less than 24 hours ago? How was that possible? It seemed to Louisa that a week or more had passed since Angus Findlay had collapsed just as she had walked past him, just before she called for assistance from a passing doctor who had turned out to be Samuel Chambers.

So much has happened since that moment, she thought to herself before she realized that she had finished relating her opinion of the timeliness of Ned Tomlinson's rescue to this man...whose name, she just realized, she did not know.

"This is Mister Ned Tomlinson from Norfolk, Virginia," she said as she looked back at Ned. "And you would be?"

The man's answer came with a polite nod and slight bow.

"I am Philip Roberdeau from New Orleans, Louisiana," he said.

Louisa slightly nodded in return.

"Mister Roberdeau," she said. "Again, I do want to commend you on your timeliness in coming across Mister Tomlinson because otherwise I fear we would not be having this conversation at the moment."

Philip nodded in understanding.

"I s'pose I should leave him to rest," Philip said. "I just wanted to check and see how he was."

"Well, Mister Roberdeau, please feel free to stop by tomorrow or even later tonight if you would like. I have been personally assigned to the care of Mister Tomlinson and while I am in the hospital, his condition is my primary concern. So you won't need to introduce yourself or explain your story again, unless you come late this evening after I've left."

"I understand, ma'am," Philip replied with another slight nod before he took one more look at the sleeping Ned Tomlinson and then turned to leave the hospital. Louisa watched him depart the interior room into the larger outside ward.

*   *   *

Fresh from their late afternoon rests, tens of thousands of old veterans began to converge on the many kitchen tents that had been scattered throughout the encampment grounds. The phenomenon that had begun during the lunchtime meals served on this first day of July – the intermingling of Virginian and Pennsylvanian; Louisianan and New Yorker; Rebel and Yankee – continued into the evening meal. Men sought out not only their own long-lost comrades from the war but acquaintances newly formed over the past several days; and for the most part, a man's status as former comrade or former enemy mattered not the least bit when it came to asking if he wanted to share a bite of supper.

Devin McAteer, for example, was joined at a table outside one of the many kitchens within the Pennsylvania delegation's area of the encampment grounds by not only his cousin Seamus but his two new-found acquaintances; one Union and one Confederate. Chester Morrison and Philip Roberdeau had been introduced to one another earlier when the men all found their seats before the afternoon's formal ceremonies in the Great Tent, and Chester had marveled at the tale of Devin McAteer having been one of the soldiers who had rescued this man Roberdeau along with General Longstreet nearly a decade after the war had ended.

Those men were joined for supper by Lawrence Armstrong, the volunteer militiaman from Carlisle, and Doctor Edward Reed of Erie. Some of their other acquaintances from earlier in the day – including Karol

Wyzghra, the Pittsburgh shopkeeper – had sought out other companionship for the evening meal.

But sitting at the adjoining table to this particular contingent was one that contained Johnny and Edgar Sullivan along with the man with whom they had become friendly, Angus Findlay. The old cavalrymen had agreed to "reform the ranks" (as Angus Findlay had cackled as he made the suggestion; apparently not only in good spirits but fully recovered from his own scare the previous day), and as fate would have it the group they had fallen in with had a few Pennsylvanians who suggested this particular kitchen as their meeting place.

Initially the conversations at the two tables were separate from one another, but just about the time the stragglers in each group were getting around to the slice of apple pie and scoop of ice cream that had been placed on each man's mess kit, Angus Findlay heard this from the adjoining table, the words spoken by Lawrence Armstrong:

"I sat up when that General Young from the UCV mentioned J.E.B. Stuart along with all those other Confederate Generals. I ain't never seen none of the others nor been in a fight against any of their boys, but all these years I been telling my own boys and my grandsons how I helped hold off J.E.B. Stuart himself just before Gettysburg."

Just as he finished speaking, out of the corner of his vision Lawrence Armstrong caught the penetrating glance coming from the next table. He slowly turned his head in that direction and saw the very old Confederate cavalry officer – one who appeared older than anyone else around him – staring back directly at Armstrong.

Armstrong was just about to ask the man to state his business – he didn't much like the glare he was getting from this man – when the man spoke up first.

"Sir? Did you mention J.E.B. Stuart?"

Lawrence Armstrong hesitated for a moment before answering, wondering just what sin he had committed in the eyes and ears of this old Reb.

"Yes I did," he replied with a touch of hesitation in his voice…but still forcing volume into his voice so the old man at the next table might actually be able to hear him. He added nothing else, waiting to see what this man would say – or do – next.

"And where, pray tell, did you encounter General Stuart?" was the man's next question.

Oh great, Lawrence Armstrong thought to himself. This is headed in an unfortunate direction. Still, he felt compelled to answer.

"At Carlisle on July the first," was the answer. "I was with the forces defending the Barracks when General Stuart's men came up and bombarded the town before headin' down to Gettysburg to join the fight here."

Lawrence felt a knot in his stomach as he watched the old Reb ease himself up from his seat and, once steady on his feet, begin to walk to the adjoining table where Lawrence was seated. He looked over at Chester Morrison, whose eyes wordlessly conveyed the message of "stay calm; let's see what this man wants, maybe it's nothing."

It took Angus Findlay nearly fifteen full seconds to make it to the next picnic table – he was feeling a touch weaker as this day went on and the terrible heat only now beginning to dissipate – and as he did he reached out with his right hand just as he arrived behind where Lawrence Armstrong was seated.

At first, Lawrence was at a loss for explaining this man's actions. He seemed to be wanting to shake hands, but that couldn't be it…or could it?

The man's right hand remained outstretched so Lawrence Armstrong reached up hesitatingly, enveloped it with his own, and sure enough the old man pumped their clasped hands up and down several times.

Sensing the confusion on Lawrence Armstrong's face, Angus Findlay explained.

"I was General Stuart's *aide-de-camp* during the campaign," he said, looking back at the Sullivan brothers as he spoke; almost as if he felt the need to reconfirm for Johnny and Edgar what he had told them earlier in the day in the breakfast line.

"I was with General Stuart at Carlisle, of course, and in fact when General Fitzhugh Lee came in under the white flag to ask for your General Smith's surrender of the town and Barracks, I was the one who quickly fashioned that white flag to take with him; out of fabric in my saddlebag and a small tree branch. General Lee came back to me after General Smith's refusal cursin' a blue streak" – Colonel Findlay smiled and cackled again at the memory of the usually proper nephew of Robert E. Lee swearing like a common infantryman – "and then saying to me, 'Go tell General Stuart to bombard the town.' And that's what I did."

Lawrence Armstrong's hand was still clasped with that of Angus Findlay and at the old cavalry Colonel's words, he relaxed a bit, no longer worried that he was about to get pummeled by an old fool's cane in response to some long-ago grievance.

"Sir," Lawrence responded as their grasps finally loosened and their right hands separated, "it's a pleasure and an honor to make your acquaintance, even though the way you tell it, you personally asked General Stuart at the request of your 'other' General Lee to bombard me for several hours." Lawrence's tone contained just the right touch of lightheartedness – or at least he hoped so – that Angus would not take offense at the words.

"Another amazing coincidence," Chester Morrison spoke up, looking over at both Devin McAteer and Philip Roberdeau as he spoke. "These two men here" – he nodded at them – "happened to be in proximity to one another long after the war ended, in '74, and way down in New Orleans…and they just discovered that fact this very morning. And now here are the two of you who happened to share a bit of history up in Carlisle."

"Well," Angus said to this distinguished Yankee whom he hadn't yet been introduced to, "it ain't nothin' like these boys here." He looked back at the Sullivan brothers – Edgar in particular – and then back at those gathered around the adjoining table where he now stood as he briefly told the tale *he* had learned this very morning of Edgar Sullivan being in the company of the men from Buford's Cavalry who fired the first shot of the battle.

As soon as Angus finished his short narrative Chester Morrison introduced himself by name to Angus and, leaning over, to those who were seated at Angus' table. Men from both tables began exchanging names and states and professions and the units in which they had served during the war, and within two minutes even more acquaintances had been made.

As they all resumed their meals, two conversations now one and transcending the two tables, nearly every one of the men seated there felt that this first day of the Jubilee was indeed a glorious one and the ones that followed would be hard-pressed to top today.

The only man who seemed immune to the spirit of the occasion – despite introducing himself to the others with forced pleasantness – was Seamus McAteer.

Chapter 25

7:15 P.M.

The scene was an almost identical reprise of the one from earlier in the day, in the field hospital's back room that had been set up as a dining area for the Jubilee's medical staff. A handful of other nurses were finishing their supper meals as Louisa May Sterling entered the room. Her eyes scanned the room for the sight of Doctor Samuel Chambers, and even as she looked in vain for him she chastised herself for having done so. *You're acting like a school girl, Louisa May! You're not at a social dance at Yale or West Point, searching for whatever dashing young man has your fancy at the moment. You're a mother – and a widow – of almost thirty years of age, and you're acting foolishly!*

Just as Louisa had almost convinced herself to push aside these foolish impulses, she heard the voice from behind her:

"I was afraid that I was too late, that you had already enjoyed your supper. Or am I mistaken; have you already eaten?"

Louisa turned to face Samuel, doing her best to prevent a warm smile of gratitude and relief caused by the sound of his voice from betraying her emotions.

"No, Doctor Chambers," she said, allowing a small smile to come to her lips, "I've not eaten yet." But no further words; let the man, *this* man, make the overture.

"Well then," Samuel said, and Louisa could swear that the doctor was struggling just as mightily as she was to keep his emotions off of his face, "shall we dine together one more time for this day?"

"I'd like that," Louisa felt the words come to her lips but she was powerless to halt them and change them into a more benign, dispassionate utterance. Samuel Chambers' reaction was a simple nod, however, and an awkward moment between the two was apparently avoided as he turned towards the serving line but courteously motioned Louisa to precede him.

The meal placed on Samuel's mess kit, as well as the one onto Louisa's, was a reprise of what each had been served for lunch earlier in the day: boiled egg, a small helping of roast turkey, and a bread roll accompanied by a small sliver of cherry pie for dessert. Both Samuel and Louisa were nearly ravenous, however, and neither would be complaining about the lack of variety of the food made available to the Reunion's medical staff. They took their mess kits to a nearby table and sat down. Each of them ate nearly half of the food on the mess kit before another word was spoken.

They began to converse about various medical cases, and Louisa told Samuel about the visit by the Louisianan Philip Roberdeau to the bedside of Ned Tomlinson. The Norfolk man had improved a touch more even since Roberdeau's visit, and though Tomlinson was not up to speaking as of yet he appeared alert to his surroundings and condition. Both physician and nurse were now of the opinion that if the Virginian could survive this upcoming night, his prospects were very good for a full recovery from his collapse and having approached the specter of death.

Eventually there were no more medical matters to discuss, and the conversation between the two turned to the events of the afternoon. Word had filtered into the medical facility of the grand speeches by Governor Tener and Secretary Garrison and the others, and Louisa was anxiously awaiting the appearance of her son Randall and the inevitable rapid-fire retelling of what the boy had seen and heard that afternoon in the Great Tent while performing his scouting duties.

Samuel leaned back, wishing he had a cigar in his possession...or even better, a snifter of Hennessey. His duty day was coming to a close, and he was already silently scheming to find an excuse to accompany Louisa May Sterling and her son on the two-mile walk this evening back to the northern part of Gettysburg. He was all but certain the nurse would welcome his companionship on the journey, but did not want to appear too forward, as if but a single day after meeting her he was already setting about to court her. Samuel could tell that first and foremost she was a devoted mother to her young son and still mourned for her deceased husband; so quite possibly any sort of courtship was an impossibility.

Still, all through this entire day, despite the crushing workload in the encampment's field hospital and the rapid, nearly frantic pace at which Samuel moved from one medical or administrative matter to another, there had been this pervasive presence of Louisa May Sterling – her appearance, the sound of her voice, her skill as a nurse; indeed her very essence – in the back of Samuel's mind.

"I must say I am very much in awe of this entire occasion," Samuel said, still wishing for the taste of Hennessey or a cigar. "I've been around veterans of that war for most of my life but the sheer magnitude of so many of them gathered in this one place is just..."

He paused for several seconds before continuing.

"I can't even come up with the words, and usually I am not at a loss for the proper expression of how I feel. But the very presence of these tens of thousands of men from that war coming together is something that is deeply moving to me, even more so than I would have imagined."

Louisa allowed herself a small smile at the doctor's words.

"I know how you feel," she said. "In fact the very first memory I have of anything at all was my fifth birthday and my father taking me to the parade through Germantown to celebrate the 25th anniversary of the victory at Gettysburg. I only remember the tiniest fragment of that day but I recall sitting on top of my father's shoulders as I watched the Union Army veterans march down the main thoroughfare in front of the war memorial at Market Square. There were hundreds of those men not just from Germantown but from all over Philadelphia, and I remember that at the time they looked so old..."

Noticing the calculating look suddenly appear on Samuel Chambers' face Louisa halted mid-sentence. She immediately knew what the man's sharp mind was trying to determine, and was just beginning to silently chastise herself for what she had just uttered when Doctor Chambers spoke.

"Your fifth birthday, you say?"

Louisa hesitated, wishing so much she could take back that last shared recollection. She simply nodded in response, though.

"That day was actually *on* your fifth birthday?" Doctor Chambers persisted.

Another silent nod.

"Then that means…" his voice trailed off as Louisa reluctantly nodded in acknowledgment of what she knew Samuel Chambers had just discovered.

He decided to finish expressing his discovery.

"Your thirtieth birthday is in two days, then," he said.

Yet another silent nod, this time with more than a hint of sweet sadness radiating from her own face.

*   *   *

For months now Louisa had forced away any consideration of her upcoming thirtieth birthday whenever they suddenly insisted on worming their way into her conscious thoughts. Why in the world would that day be cause for any sort of celebration? Her beloved Terrence was gone, buried for nearly four years now up in Carlisle. Any sort of milestone birthday celebration without Terrence Sterling would be empty; a travesty.

Her life was now comprised of her son and her work, in that order. She had anticipated having a quiet moment of birthday commemoration with Randall, perhaps after their respective obligations two days hence had been completed and this Grand Reunion would be one day away from its conclusion. Maybe a small cake late in the evening when they made their way back home; but that would be it.

Louisa had gone out of her way not to share any information about her upcoming birthday with any of the other nurses with whom she had been working for months now in preparation for this gathering. She had feared that they would want to make a big affair of that milestone day since many of them had worked together for months now and they would all be gathered in one or another of the encampment's medical facilities. The last thing Louisa wanted was to be surrounded by smiling nurses congratulating her on this occasion and then to suddenly burst into tears, overcome with tremendous sorrow that Terrence had not lived to share this day with her.

But now, Louisa contemplated as she looked across the table at Samuel Chambers, she had slipped and in sharing a recollection from her childhood that at first seemingly had no connection with her milestone day of July the third, 1913, this sharp-witted doctor had immediately made the connecting calculations and deduced the fact that Louisa had tried so hard to hide.

For his part, Samuel was about to utter something along the lines of "we must have a celebration among the medical staff of this occasion" but caught himself. He was indeed as sharp-witted as Louisa presumed. In the flash of a second he *knew* what Louisa was thinking – how she felt – about her birthday two days from now. He looked back at Louisa May Sterling, his eyes locking with hers, and his look conveyed without the necessity of words that he understood how she felt.

"We should get back to the patients," Louisa said abruptly.

"I suppose so," Samuel nodded. As they both rose, though, he was determined that in some manner that he did not yet know of, he *would* help make Louisa May Sterling's thirtieth birthday a memorable one...and would do so in a way that did not cause her too much sorrow in recollection of her departed husband.

They were both walking back to the medical ward, Samuel's mind contemplating ideas that just might be suitable for two days from now, when Louisa turned to him and said:

"I do not mean to impose on you, but I would be most grateful if you would accompany Randall and me home again tonight on our long walk as you did last night."

She paused before continuing.

"If doing so meets with your schedule, that is," Louisa added. "Though you may need to remain here tonight longer than me and if so, then I understand."

Doctor Samuel Chambers was nearly at a loss for words.

"Of course," he finally said. "I would be most honored to accompany you."

Chapter 26

9:45 P.M.

The activities of the day had taken their toll on the old men, though for most of them physical exhaustion was overshadowed by the emotional, once-in-a-lifetime significance of the day each had just experienced. Even for those who had been at the encampment since it had opened two days earlier, this particular day had truly been a remarkable one, far surpassing those that had preceded it. The same milling around and strolls underneath the blazing sun had occurred today as they had during the preceding days, but the official ceremonies in the Great Tent that most had witnessed had given July the first of 1913 special meaning that would remain a centerpiece of most everyone's thoughts for the rest of their lives. Listening to the speeches from Governor Tener and the Secretary of War, and those magnificent words of the UCV's Bennett Young – "Peace waves its wand over these bloodstained hills and cries out to war: 'Be still.'" – still echoed through the thoughts of many of these men as their day came to an end.

A witness to history who might have been walking about the encampment grounds on this evening of July 1st, 1913, would have seen many gatherings of three or five or eight men, a fair number of them Blue and Gray combined, seated outside many of the sleeping tents underneath the now-darkened skies that had begun to slowly fill with stars. Some groups were engaged in friendly card games, while other clusters of men such as the one in which Edgar and Johnny Sullivan were ensconced gathered around someone softly playing a harmonica, bringing back memories of similar encampment scenes from during the war. Or, for the Sullivan brothers, invoking long-dormant memories resurfaced of their old friend Wyatt Earp playing the harmonica down in Tombstone before the unpleasantness in that town began; the Marshall surrounded by his brothers and others (including the Sullivans) under a star-filled sky not unlike the very one over their heads at this moment.

Other men such as the McAteers, Chester Morrison, Philip Roberdeau, and thousands more were already inside their sleeping tents for the night. Some were already snoring away, exhausted from the day's pace. Others – such as Devin McAteer and Chester Morrison – sat on the edges of their cots and continued conversations with tent-mates that had begun earlier in the day, or began new ones. Some of those conversations were naturally about the war, but most of these men had already done their share of talking about the clashes at Gettysburg or Vicksburg or Appomattox Courthouse; enough with reliving those horrors, they had talked plenty to exorcise decades-old demons of terror and were finally ready to lay their vivid memories of battles long since concluded to rest for all eternity. So they resumed discussions of their life's work after the war and their families and places they had visited over the years, or how they intended to spend whatever remaining time on this earth that God might grant them.

Still others did their best to recollect and share specific phrases spoken earlier this very day by Colonel Schoonmaker or Governor Tener or one of the other speakers in the Great Tent, and all agreed that the ceremony had been magnificent; one not to be have been missed and which the world would remember for all eternity as, to quote Colonel Schoonmaker, "a celebration unparalleled in the history of the world." How could such an occasion be forgotten? All agreed that would be impossible!

Newspapers had begun showing up at the encampment grounds, even afternoon papers from other Pennsylvania cities such as Pittsburgh and Philadelphia that had been shipped to Gettysburg to give veterans from those places a taste of what the folk back home were saying and writing about this Great Reunion. Many satisfied themselves with the local *Gettysburg Times*, and one of the men in their tent, an Altoona man named Owens, saw an advertisement on the first page of the *Times* for the newly released motion picture called *The Battle of Gettysburg* that was showing over at the Walter's Theatre, obviously timed for this reunion and the attention of the entire borough of Gettysburg on that long-ago battle.

"What say we all go over to town and see this motion picture? The advertisement says that it's 'an intense drama' and 'it's like never seen before.'" Those had been the man Owens' words, tongue in cheek of course, reading directly from the advertisement and even Chester Morrison – with his recurring nightmares about the second and third days with the 69th Pennsylvania here at Gettysburg – let out a nervous chuckle along with most of the others occupying the tent. Not a single one of these men felt the need for one of these new motion pictures to entertain them with "an intense drama" about the Battle of Gettysburg, that was for certain!

A copy of that afternoon's *Pittsburgh Press* had made its way into the tent occupied by the McAteers and Chester Morrison and the others, and Devin was granted first access to the out-of-town newspaper since he was the only

Pittsburgher in the tent. He found his heart heavy with sorrow as he read the two front page stories that detailed what most already knew by now: that hundreds of veterans, many of them from Pennsylvania, had sorrowfully departed the Jubilee the previous night and that day due to the lack of accommodations. The headlines for the two stories – "HUNDREDS OF VETERANS WERE WITHOUT SHELTER" and "VETERANS, UNCARED FOR, RETURN HOME" – were sad enough, but reading the final paragraph of the second story, specifically about veterans from Allegheny County, made Devin McAteer's blood boil:

> "The old soldiers today expressed themselves as being disgusted. They said they walked many miles through the different camp grounds and were refused even a bite to eat, and when they asked for a place to sleep they were laughed at. One of the veterans said conditions now at Gettysburg are not a whole lot better than they were at the time of the great battle."

Devin set the *Press* aside, not wanting to read any further about this stain on what had otherwise been a magnificent day – a magnificent occasion – in the whole. He said a silent prayer that the sleeping situation had already resolved itself, and that no more old men who had made such a difficult journey would be forced to depart prematurely and with – seemingly – such a lack of regard and caring for them.

*   *   *

Halfway between the encampment grounds and his home, young Randall Sterling finally ran out of tales to tell his mother and this nice Doctor Chambers about what he had witnessed this afternoon. The sea of old men in blue and gray uniforms, or wearing suit coats, all crowding into the Great Tent; the speeches by Colonel Schoonmaker and Governor Tener, and the other men; the solemn, often far-away looks that would appear on so many of these old men's faces as they listened spellbound to the words that were spoken; and the camaraderie shown by former enemies to one another throughout the day…all were part of the meandering narrative that the excited Boy Scout related to the two adults as the three of them walked.

As the boy was winding down his chronicle of the day's occurrences, Samuel Chambers marveled to himself at the way he surprisingly felt this moment. One might have thought that given the chance to accompany Louisa May Sterling again this night on her long walk home – at her invitation, nonetheless! – the insistence of her young son to dominate the conversation for nearly a full half hour could be nothing but an annoyance; essentially stealing valuable time from Samuel that he could have otherwise used to get to know more about this captivating woman and to better position himself for courting her after this gathering had concluded…if she would agree to him doing so, of course. Time was a precious commodity; almost as much for Samuel Chambers in this personal matter as it was for more than 50,000 old men as each one's scarce number of remaining days slowly dwindled. Samuel had joyfully and fortuitously been able to seize not one but two occasions this very day in which he had been alone with Louisa, sharing a meal and conversing. This invitation to accompany her home again this evening had initially seemed to be a very clear signal that she felt something for Samuel, and likewise was aware of the finite amount of time the two of them might be granted to begin to explore…well, something.

Samuel hadn't given much thought to Louisa's son as he finished up his doctoring for the day – even after she had specifically mentioned Randall when she had asked Samuel if he would accompany her this evening – but ever since the boy had excitedly run into the field hospital's outer corridor, his day's obligations now concluded just as his mother's and Samuel's were, he had monopolized the conversation with his narrative.

Yet…despite what Samuel might have earlier thought of as an annoyance or hindrance or obstacle, he found himself feeling…he wasn't quite sure; comfortable perhaps? At peace? Content? Whatever the proper word or phrase might be, Samuel Chambers felt "right" about walking along with Louisa May Sterling and young Randall Sterling.

Almost as if the three of them were a family.

He silently chastised himself for allowing himself to feel this way, or for allowing himself to hope that this stroll was anything but a chivalrous accompaniment of a woman and her son that was necessitated by the long workdays of the occasion at hand. Louisa May Sterling was obviously still in mourning for her husband, even though nearly four years had gone by since his death. She had made a life with her son, apparently not in need of quickly finding a new husband as so many young widows were wont to do…and as Samuel knew, those young widows who didn't remarry soon after losing a husband very often never did.

Nascent stirrings of romantic feeling aside, Samuel felt foolish for allowing this odd sense of "family-centered contentment" or whatever it might be to creep into his thoughts as he walked along, listening to Randall Sterling wind down his tales of the day. Still though…

As the boy finished what would become his last story, that of helping two veterans – one Yankee and one Rebel – weave their way out of the Great Tent onto the encampment grounds, and the incredibly warm handshake followed by a quick embrace between the two old men as they parted company, Samuel Chambers could feel the gears of his brain slowly whirl to life as his brain went to work trying to figure out how to make this July 3rd – Louisa May Sterling's thirtieth birthday, two days hence – an occasion on which he could find out once and for all if there might be a future with this woman who had captivated his waking and sleeping thoughts.

July 2, 1913
Military Day

"If the gentle and strong spirit of Lincoln could today revisit the field of Gettysburg he would see there a fulfillment of all his visions."

- *The Atlanta Constitution*, July 2, 1913

———

"Mister Chairman: I want to say to this great audience that I am glad to be here. The first time I was here I was not glad; the next time I came, I was."

- From the address by Confederate Sergeant John C. Scarborough of North Carolina, Gettysburg, July 2, 1913

———

"As we stand upon this hallowed ground, where every footprint marks an act of sacrifice; as we lift our gaze to these surrounding monuments, raised to the memory of heroic deeds; as we recall Lincoln's words, that seem to come as a message from the celestial county, pregnant with the spirit of this solemn place, we should be unworthy of the heritage of fame, here left us, if we failed once again to highly resolve that 'these dead shall not have died in vain.'"

- Rhode Island Lieutenant Governor Roswell B. Burchard, Gettysburg, July 2, 1913

Chapter 27

Portland, Maine
7:15 A.M.

The young man from the *Portland Evening Express and Daily Advertiser* stood nervously as he watched Joshua Lawrence Chamberlain's weary eyes read through the advance copy of the editorial for this evening's edition of the newspaper. The newspaper's publisher wouldn't dream of printing an editorial about the former Governor without sending a runner to General Chamberlain's house bearing an advance typewritten copy for the General's approval. Or, should the General desire changes to the words, the young man was fully prepared to dutifully record each and every one of Joshua Chamberlain's requested modifications.

Fifty Years Ago Today

One would be hard-pressed to find a Maine boy or man who is unable to relate the victorious valor of the 20th Maine that occurred at Little Round Top on the second day of the Battle of Gettysburg. Despite the heroics of then-Colonel Joshua Lawrence Chamberlain and his men having occurred two and a half score ago, the tale of winning the day at Little Round Top has vividly persisted throughout Maine all these years since, as if those events had occurred mere days before any retelling.

Our beloved General and former Governor was most recently at Gettysburg a mere six and a half weeks ago for the Fourth and Final General Conference of illustrious leaders among our veterans in preparation for the grand reunion taking place this very moment on the field at Gettysburg. Now, more than fifty thousand veterans of both the Blue and the Gray have come together once again to commemorate the fiftieth anniversary of that momentous, tide-turning battle.

Alas, General Chamberlain is not among those aging men who have made the pilgrimage to that hallowed ground for an event described by Colonel James Schoonmaker, the Pennsylvania Commission's Chairman and another Medal of Honor recipient (as is our General Chamberlain, of course), as "a celebration unparalleled in the history of the world." General Chamberlain is a private man and certainly not one to bemoan the pains and ailments that he has endured for many decades as a result of his many wounds during the War. No doubt, though, the General would be at Gettysburg if at all possible for what is both a solemn gathering as well as a jubilee.

Joshua Lawrence Chamberlain paused in his reading. He was – as described in the editorial's text – a private man, and he felt a touch of pique at the editorial writer having made reference to his inability to journey to Gettysburg for this grand commemoration, despite having made the exact same trip less than two months earlier.

That gathering in mid-May had been his personal farewell to Gettysburg; the General had recognized that melancholy reality even before arriving to confer with his fellow veterans who comprised the distinguished membership of the General Conference. During the two days he remained in Gettysburg, Joshua Lawrence Chamberlain had several times taken leave from meetings and other events to privately wander about the hallowed grounds. More than once he found himself gazing at Little Round Top and was tempted to try to make one last visit to that hill where his own march to fame had begun that terrible day fifty years earlier. He wished that he would be able to stand on that ground, looking downward as he had on July 2nd, 1863, and find himself surrendering to his Mind's Eye as comrades and enemies alike slowly materialized.

Of course, General Chamberlain had no desire to relive the loss of so many of his own men, nor his Confederate adversaries who likewise lost their lives or who were wounded that day. Still, they had all been young then...some younger, even much younger, than others but mostly boys and young men with a sprinkling of middle-aged men on both sides. Those who had been there that day, Yankee and Rebel alike, and who were still alive by the middle of May, 1913 were of course half a century older now. But one last time, standing in that spot and having the memories of brave young warriors from both sides come to life around him...

Alas, it was not to be. The fabled war hero, professor, and governor would have to settle for leaving his memories of Little Round Top behind forever in the distance. And on that recent afternoon of May 17th, as Joshua Chamberlain boarded the train to depart Gettysburg, he had paused and turned around for what he knew would be his final look at that battlefield of long ago. Now, in this year of 1913, all was calm and peaceful, unlike how the land had been a half century earlier after two days, then three, of battle. Perhaps it was best that this would be the way Joshua Lawrence Chamberlain, General and Medal of Honor winner, would last gaze upon the panoramic vision of that small Pennsylvania town and its surrounding countryside and hills, recalling this particular vista whenever he would think of that consecrated place for however many more days he had left on this earth.

Joshua Chamberlain's mind eased its way back to this present day and his eyes, now clear of conjured images from both weeks earlier as well as fifty years ago, resumed scanning the remaining two paragraphs of the editorial. He saw nothing objectionable; the words and the tone were praiseworthy not only of the man himself but of the 20th Maine as a whole, and Chamberlain found himself nodding as he absorbed the laudatory tributes to the men who had once served under him.

He turned to hand the sheet of paper back to the newspaper's runner who had stood by anxiously the entire time, half-expecting to find himself on the receiving end of the wrath of this legendary man. The General detected the young man's outward relief as the document was exchanged.

"How old are you, sir?" Joshua Chamberlain asked the young man.

Thrown off by being called "sir" by Maine's most famous man – a common courtesy and politeness of speech, of course, but still one totally unexpected by this inconsequential newspaper runner given whose presence he was in – the young man finally croaked out:

"I'm eighteen years old, General…I mean Governor…"

Joshua Chamberlain allowed himself a small smile, hopefully putting the nervous youngster – who was now freely perspiring – at ease.

"You realize that if this were fifty years earlier, you and I might be standing side by side as we are this very moment, but instead we would be doing so on that hilltop near Gettysburg, waiting for the next charge from General Law's men…"

His voice trailed off, his mind threatening to wander back in time once again. The young man's voice broke the spell, though.

"What was that like, General?" The newspaper runner couldn't believe he had uttered those words even as they were still being spoken. Was he actually daring to ask General Joshua Lawrence Chamberlain for a personal description of the defense of Little Round Top?

The General lowered his head slightly, a sad smile coming to his lips as he did. As he raised his head back up, his tired, now-misty eyes found those of his temporary companion.

"What is your name, sir?" Chamberlain asked the young man, thinking that thus far he had failed to make that inquiry.

"Dalton…James Dalton, General." The young man had indeed properly introduced himself upon his arrival at the General's house, but he was not about to call Joshua Chamberlain's attention to the old warrior's failing memory.

"Well, James Dalton," Joshua Lawrence Chamberlain gestured towards the richly patterned Louis XVI sofa that rested just behind where the young man stood, "please have a seat and I will describe that day to you as best as I can recall, considering that it was fifty years ago."

Stunned, the newspaper runner – young James Dalton, age 18 – could only silently comply with the General's command. He was due back at the offices of the *Portland Evening Express and Daily Advertiser* very soon with the editorial copy – and perhaps the General's edits, though of course there would be none, he now knew – but there was no way he would decline this unexpected treasure of an opportunity. He knew this aging, ill man would only have so much time and energy and it wouldn't be long before James Dalton would be on his way. But if Providence were to somehow bestow the former governor with the strength to converse throughout this entire day with young Mister Dalton, and if doing so were to cost James his job at the newspaper, he would not lament that outcome for a second. This unexpected gift, whether it lasted ten minutes or ten hours, was one he would remember and cherish for the rest of his life.

And so, even though General Joshua Lawrence Chamberlain was unable to journey to Gettysburg for the occasion of the Great Reunion, he would – on this morning of July 2nd, 1913 – bring a tiny bit of the Great Reunion to his own home in Portland, Maine.

Chapter 28

7:45 A.M.

Almost the entire small group of men whom fate had brought together during the previous evening's supper were now gathered together once again, this time for this morning's serving of breakfast. The McAteer cousins; the Sullivan brothers; Angus Findlay; Philip Roberdeau; and Lawrence Armstrong of Carlisle filled seven of the eight seats at one of the tables, again within the area set aside for the Pennsylvania delegation and not far from where they had all joined together the previous night.

Missing from the group this morning of July the second, though, was Chester Morrison. More than two hours earlier, amidst the receding peaceful blackness of the Pennsylvania countryside, he had begun his journey to the Hotel Gettysburg to breakfast with Jonathan, reversing what father and son had done a day earlier when Jonathan had ventured out to the encampment grounds to locate his father.

The journey between the encampment grounds and the hotel in the center of town was approximately two miles; a difficult trek for a man nearing 70 years of age. The oppressive heat of the previous day was gone but would soon be back, so at least the temperatures were on Chester Morrison's side, albeit only temporarily. Nevertheless, Jonathan would be driving his Pierce-Arrow back to the encampment grounds for the afternoon's speeches in the

Great Tent, meaning that the older man would only have to make the journey on foot into town, not back.

Matters of age and weather aside, Chester Morrison felt an overpowering need to embark on the two-mile walk. His nightmares last night had been the worst yet, no doubt because it was this very date, mere hours from now though of course fifty years removed, that he had first tasted – and survived – vicious combat on Cemetery Ridge. The distant past was as alive as ever in the nighttime images that continued to haunt Chester Morrison's sleep, and once again he had given up on a restful night after several hours of both remembered and conjured battle. No doubt this coming night would be much the same with the remembrances of Pickett's Charge awaiting him the next day. How much more could an old man endure? Chester Morrison hoped that when he finally departed the encampment grounds sometime on the Fourth of July after listening to President Wilson's speech that he would forever leave behind these nightmares of war and death.

After strolling leisurely and reflectively about the blackened encampment grounds for a long while to pass the time until a reasonable hour, Chester finally decided it was time to begin his walk to the hotel. As he made the journey into town, the first light of dawn that was becoming all too familiar to him peeking up from the east, Chester Morrison once again questioned if his decision to attend this Great Reunion had been a wise one. The oppressive heat; the lack of sleep and with what little sleep he could muster, one nightmare after another; was it worth it?

But then Chester Morrison thought of the men he had met during this gathering and who would soon presumably be gathering together this morning for their own breakfast. For a brief second he felt a twinge of regret that he would be breakfasting with his son rather than those other men, all of them total strangers until so very recently. Perhaps he should have insisted that Jonathan instead have come to the encampment grounds, as he had the previous day. This way Chester would have been able to share a meal with both his son and his newfound comrades at the same time.

As quickly as that flicker of a thought came to Chester Morrison, though, it just as hastily evaporated. Chester was feeling guilty for how little time he was spending with his son thus far on this entire adventure. Jonathan had eagerly agreed to accompany his father from their home in Philadelphia, both to keep an eye on his father as well as to ease his own mind while his father was away; but he was doing so at the cost of his own obligations to Baldwin Locomotive for an entire week. One would expect that Chester Morrison's senior-most lieutenant would be responsible for the company's fates and fortunes during the President's absence to attend the jubilee, but that individual was none other than Jonathan Morrison himself. Chester could detect the stress his son was bearing being out of touch with what was happening at the company's offices back in Philadelphia. True, a telegram from Philadelphia might eventually find him in Gettysburg, but perhaps many hours after it had been sent…and possibly too late and too distant for Jonathan to take the actions he might have been able to do if he were sitting in either his own office or his father's. Both men had agreed to this arrangement, however, under the premise that it would be best for all if Jonathan Morrison kept a close eye on his father.

But now, not even halfway into the events of the encampment, Chester had befriended not one or two other individuals, but perhaps ten or eleven men in total. And not just fellow Union Army veterans, either; several former

Confederates as well! Not a single one of those men could approach the stature and wealth that Chester Morrison had achieved in years since the end of the war, and in days past and under ordinary circumstances the locomotive company president would have had little in common with any of them…not out of haughtiness or a sense of superiority but merely as an immutable consequence of their relative stations in life.

Embracing the Great Reunion's spirit of reconciliation and brotherhood, however, Chester Morrison found himself thinking fondly of the brothers from Arizona and the cousins from the far corners of his own state of Pennsylvania; the Louisianan Roberdeau and the old cavalryman Findlay from Virginia; that Armstrong fellow from nearby Carlisle; and several other men with whom he had shared food, conversation, and remembrances since his arrival.

Chester Morrison found himself again feeling remorseful that he had thus far spent so little time with his own son since their arrival. And even what little time he and Jonathan had spent together hadn't been alone but rather in the company of some or all of those other men. And so, Chester Morrison was determined that he would breakfast with his son – and only his son – at the Hotel Gettysburg this morning of July 2nd before journeying back to the encampment grounds for the afternoon's ceremonies that he would listen to, as well as the memories of that long-ago afternoon on Cemetery Ridge that would no doubt be patiently awaiting his return.

And perhaps he would return to the hotel this evening in Jonathan's motor car, after the afternoon's events in the Great Tent had concluded, to share this evening's supper as well with his son…just the two of them.

*   *   *

"I'm goin' back for more," Johnny Sullivan declared as he rose slowly, stiffly, from the bench, grimacing all the while as he spoke and moved. "Anybody goin' with me?"

The question was asked in general but was specifically directed at his older brother Edgar, who had grown sullen again this morning. In fact, Johnny thought, his brother's demeanor was about as inhospitably surly as it had been during the train ride out here from Arizona. What had happened to ruin his brother's good mood of the previous day?

"I'll go with you," Devin McAteer volunteered, casting a sideways glance at his cousin Seamus, seated to his right, as he rose even more stiffly than Johnny Sullivan had only seconds earlier, wincing the entire time. These two men were hardly the only ones out of more than 50,000 that felt the effects of their age, and most of the others at the table not only took notice of the near-identical difficulties of their two comrades they also could feel their own twinges and aches even as they remained seated.

Devin trailed closely behind the younger Sullivan brother, and when they got out of earshot of the men at the table, said:

"I think the same thing that's eating my cousin is doin' the same to your brother."

Johnny Sullivan paused a beat but kept striding ahead as he looked back over his left shoulder to Devin.

"Yeah, whatever that is, and beats me to hell what it might be."

Devin shuffled quickly forward so he was astride the other man as Johnny Sullivan continued.

"Of course, my brother was bein' disagreeable way back when we boarded the train in Tucson and then all the way from Phoenix out to here. In fact, he's a surly one most of the time, anyway."

He looked over to the kitchen tent they were fast approaching, noticing that the line wasn't too long, and then back at Devin before continuing.

"Your cousin like that usually?"

"No sir," came the reply, but then Devin thought for a moment.

"At least I don't think so," he continued. "I haven't seen him for a while now since we live so far apart but he was always a pleasant one to be around."

He chuckled, then went on.

"In fact, even during the war and especially the siege of Vicksburg you woulda thought he was on some sort of adventure or somethin'. He would spend hours each day sitting and reading his books that he brought with him, and the only time he would get irritated was when we had to go fight and that interrupted whatever book he was reading at the moment."

Devin paused to reflect on Johnny Sullivan's question. Exactly what had gotten into his cousin Seamus? The coal miner had been pleasant enough when the two cousins had encountered each other upon Devin's arrival, and throughout that entire day of June the thirtieth they had spent hour upon hour catching up on each other's lives as well as seeking out old comrades. It wasn't until last evening's supper that Devin first noticed Seamus begin to grow sullen; right about the time that the two tables of old warriors joined together as one when the cavalryman Findlay and that fellow Armstrong from Carlisle realized their connections. The spirit of camaraderie had quickly fallen over all of those veterans as they came together, but Devin now recalled having glanced at his cousin after a particularly amusing anecdote from the old Colonel Findlay and noticing Seamus with his eyes downcast, staring gloomily at the table. His attention had then been called back to a retort from the Carlisle man Armstrong and he hadn't given his cousin's demeanor much more thought. Seamus had been quieter than usual as they made their way back to their sleeping tent, but Devin had become engaged in a discussion with Chester Morrison and when he happened to look over at Seamus' cot, his cousin was fast asleep.

Johnny Sullivan, on the other hand, had taken notice of Edgar being in such good spirits yesterday, even before encountering Angus Findlay in the breakfast tent line and then sharing their stories. Johnny had expected Edgar's pleasant disposition to diminish somewhat as the day wore on but to the younger Sullivan's surprise, that wasn't what happened at all. Up until the moment the Sullivan brothers limped back to the Arizona delegation's sleeping tent, Edgar had been as jovial and congenial as Johnny Sullivan could remember in a long while.

This morning of July the second, though, might as well have been the morning of June the twenty-fifth when Edgar had snarled at Clyde Hodges, the lone Confederate veteran in the Arizona delegation, at the Tucson train depot before the journey from Arizona had even begun. Just as Devin McAteer was trying to figure out what had gotten into his cousin Seamus, so too was Johnny Sullivan asking himself the same question about his older brother.

Lawrence Armstrong was the first man at the table to notice Angus Findlay suddenly shove his right hand inside of his suit jacket and clutch at his chest, a look of shocked dismay coming to the old Virginian's face at the same time. Armstrong was quickly rising as Devin McAteer and Johnny Sullivan were approaching the table, headed back from the kitchen tent. The two men noticed Armstrong's sudden movements but they also followed his gaze to Angus Findlay, whose back was turned towards the walking men, and even from behind they could detect that Angus Findlay was suffering from some sort of distress. They both hurried to the table, setting down their mess kits on either side of Findlay. Devin's mind immediately travelled back to the prior day when he had assisted with the immediate care of Ned Tomlinson – no doubt Philip Roberdeau, now aware of Angus Findlay's distress, was thinking much the same – and he fully expected to be immediately searching for an Army corpsman to aid Angus. All at the table were aware of Colonel Findlay's tale of collapsing two days prior and his night spent in the field hospital, and they expected that a second occurrence of that ailment was just beginning.

"My railroad ticket!" were the words emitted by Angus Findlay, though, when he could speak. Since all at the table were of the mind that the 85-year old man was suffering from immediate physical distress, his pained utterance didn't register with anyone.

"My railroad ticket!" Angus repeated. "I've lost my railroad ticket!"

He looked, panic-stricken to his left at the anxious face of Devin McAteer, and then to the right, taking in the worried looks of both Philip Roberdeau and Johnny Sullivan.

Finally beginning to understand, Johnny Sullivan asked the old Confederate cavalryman:

"You sure 'bout that? It ain't back in your tent, maybe?"

"No!" Angus Findlay's head shook quickly back and forth, left to right and back again and again, his eyes now wide open and conveying alarm and fear.

"I've been keeping it in my suitcoat pocket for safe keeping, and now I've lost it!"

Worried that Angus Findlay's sheer panic might actually serve to bring on the physical attack the others had originally thought he was suffering, they all immediately tried to calm the old man.

"It probably fell out onto your cot…"

"Somebody probably found it and they'll get it to you…"

"Even if you did lose it I'm sure they will give you another one…"

*   *   *

As it turned out, Angus Findlay's railroad ticket back to Virginia was indeed lost, and he was hardly the only old veteran suffering such a calamity. With the early morning hours of July the second, 1913 came the realization that close to two hundred of the old men at the encampment grounds had managed to lose their return railroad tickets back home. Word of the situation reached Governor John K. Tener by mid-morning, who didn't hesitate to act.

*   *   *

"Would you please inform Colonel Beitler to see me immediately," the Governor informed one of his aides sometime around 9:00 that morning. The aide went scurrying off to locate Lewis Beitler, the Commission's Secretary who was one of James Schoonmaker's top aides for this Great Reunion. The Philadelphian Beitler was quickly found and within twenty minutes was seated in Governor Tener's temporary office at the encampment grounds.

"Please make arrangements for replacement tickets at the Commission's expense for anyone who has lost theirs," Tener directed Beitler, who simply nodded in agreement. Thus far approximately 125 of the veterans had reported they were in need of a replacement ticket; no doubt more would come forward throughout this day and those that would come, and in his mind Beitler was calculating the estimated cost even as the Governor was speaking and he himself was nodding. This would take the total for all of the railroad transportation costs up to more than $140,000, Beitler figured. Still, if the number of replacement tickets could be kept to around 200 or 250, this would not present a significant problem. Besides, he thought to himself, I'm the Secretary of the Commission, not the Treasurer; Samuel Todd would be the one to address any shortfalls.

At the direction of the Governor, Lewis Beitler immediately contacted the Presidents of two railroads – the Western Maryland, and also the Philadelphia & Reading – and informed them that some number of replacement tickets would be needed. The logistics would be simple: all a veteran needed to do was present his credentials that he was carrying around with him at all times as a result of registration, and a return ticket would be issued; it would be as simple as that for the veterans. The railroads would keep a good accounting of these additional tickets issued and present those figures to the Commission, which would promptly reimburse the railroads for their troubles.

Well aware that so many of the old men who found themselves in this predicament weren't anywhere near as methodical or calm as those involved in resolving the problem, Beitler also immediately set out to publish word of this resolution for one and all at the encampment grounds. Bills were quickly printed and tacked far and wide across the encampment grounds, and veterans were encouraged to spread the word to their former comrades and former enemies alike that should someone have found himself in this predicament, he need not worry any further.

Shortly before noon, the news reached Angus Findlay as he lay distraught on his cot in his sleeping tent. Philip Roberdeau, in fact, was the one who sought out the Virginian to make sure that he was aware that his dilemma had been resolved.

Roberdeau could see the relief instantly spread across Angus Findlay's face as the old man breathed a heavy sigh.

"Would you like me to accompany you to the train depot to secure your replacement ticket?" Philip asked. "I would be honored to do so."

Angus Findlay smiled.

"I appreciate that, young man," Angus replied, a touch of ease making its way into his tones for the first time in several hours. "I think I'll wait until later; perhaps even tomorrow. It appears that the railroad companies will issue tickets upon request so there doesn't appear to be any rush."

Philip Roberdeau nodded.

"I agree," he replied. He reached inside his jacket and extracted his pocket watch.

"It's getting close to noon," he remarked. "I believe I should like to eat again before the two o'clock festivities in the Great Tent. Would you care to accompany me?"

Angus thought for a moment. He wasn't particularly hungry, but if he didn't eat now then he likely wouldn't eat before tonight's supper. Perhaps a light bite...

"Certainly," he said as he began to slowly rise from his cot. Philip Roberdeau, observing the difficulty the old man was enduring to get to his feet, hesitated for a moment but then did reach over to help Angus finish getting up.

Unlike this morning's breakfast and the previous night's supper, these two Confederates did not invade Union territory at the encampment grounds, electing instead to stay within the Virginia delegation's area for the midday meal. What was turning into the Great Reunion's staple of roasted chicken, macaroni, and canned corn found its way onto the mess kit of each man before they walked outside into the stifling heat that again was threatening the 100 degree mark. There had been no additional word of fatalities among the veterans, from the heat or otherwise, but both men had no doubt that dozens or perhaps even hundreds had been taken to the field hospitals, just as Angus Findlay had been two days earlier, and also that man Tomlinson whom Philip had assisted. As Philip thought about Ned Tomlinson for the first time this day, he felt guilty for not having recalled that man's plight thus far today. He resolved to visit the field hospital again this afternoon after the day's ceremonies had concluded, just as he had yesterday. Philip hoped and prayed that Tomlinson was well…hopefully recovering but if not, at least not in a worsened state.

"So you were here back in '88?" Angus Findlay asked after the two men had taken seats and began to enjoy their meal, even though Angus mostly picked at his own food.

"I was," Philip replied, nodding. He related the same story to Angus Findlay that he had to Devin McAteer a day earlier about being in the company of General Longstreet.

"Ah, General Longstreet," Angus sighed. "The man certainly bore more than his fair share of ill will for the better part of his life…"

His voice trailed off as Philip Roberdeau looked across the table, nodding.

"That he did, sir," Philip agreed, his eyes taking on that distant cast as he spoke. For forty years, from soon after the Battle of Gettysburg until "Old Pete's" death in '04, the General had personified the defeat of the Confederacy in the eyes of so many who blamed him for the failure of Pickett's Charge. If only Longstreet hadn't ordered the charge…if only he had argued more forcefully with General Lee to call off the charge…if only the charge had happened earlier in the morning…If only Longstreet had better prepared his men…

"Just as General Stuart has as well," Angus' words interrupted Philip's distant thoughts.

"Of course," Findlay added, "General Stuart did not live to suffer the blame; not long, anyway," referring to J.E.B. Stuart's death in battle less than a year after Gettysburg.

"However," Philip Roberdeau offered, "I gather that as the General's *aide-de-camp* you have heard plenty of that criticism yourself in the intervening years. Am I correct?"

"You are correct, sir," was Findlay's reply after a lengthy, pained pause, his own eyes now taking on that distant stare that only moments earlier had been on Philip's face.

"Yet here we are; you and I," Philip said quietly, almost as if he were speaking to himself. "General Stuart is gone; General Longstreet is gone; all but one of those men who led our side at Gettysburg is gone. The same for the Yankees as well; almost all gone."

He started to bring his fork to his mouth but laid it down onto his plate.

"Yet here we are; you and I," Philip repeated. "The great men are gone, and possibly those from our side are up in Heaven or perhaps down in Hell arguing with one another about who was at fault for losing Gettysburg, or what might have been done differently to stop Sherman and save Atlanta, or what our Confederacy would certainly have done differently and better if Stonewall Jackson hadn't been mortally wounded in battle and had still been leading our men. Even now in Virginia and Alabama and South Carolina, men are having those same arguments that they have been engaging in for fifty years. And on the other side, even as victors, their arguments are about the decisions and performance of General McClellan and General Burnside and, right here, General Sickles. No doubt those disputes will continue until the last one of those quarreling men has breathed his last breath, and then their sons and grandsons will take up those same arguments."

Philip looked to his left, then to his right, then back at Angus.

"Yet here we are; not just you and I, but all of us gathered here. Am I correct that not once since arriving have you encountered a vicious disagreement over what General Longstreet or General Stuart should have done differently to have avoided our fate? I've certainly not heard such utterances."

Philip waited for a nod of acknowledgement from Angus before continuing.

"Perhaps sitting around the fires at night some of the boys might get to speculating about different actions and different outcomes, but I daresay that such speculations will almost certainly be resigned and contemplative, and not carry the vehemence that you have heard about your General Stuart, and I have personally heard said to General Longstreet's face when we were with the Louisiana militia after the war."

This time Philip did scoop up a helping of canned corn with his fork and brought it to his mouth. He chewed slowly, thoughtfully, before continuing.

"I think the Yankees – I mean, the Pennsylvania Commission – had the right idea with this reunion. Almost every one of us here bore the burden of the fighting during that war, and no doubt hundreds or even thousands of those who are here today were responsible for killing hundreds or even thousands of brothers and sons and fathers and close friends of former enemies who are likewise here. Yet we seem to have put the animosity aside, perhaps once and for all. And not only animosity for our enemy, but animosity among ourselves."

Philip looked across the table at Angus Findlay.

"Do my words make any sense?"

Angus nodded.

"They do," he affirmed. "I myself was very uneasy about attending this event for the very reasons you mention; afraid of not only being confronted with acrimony about General Stuart, but perhaps even being attacked by someone feeling that way who wasn't in his right mind anymore. Yet after two days, I feel as if I could stay here forever, if that were possible."

Philip nodded again in agreement as he reached for a glass of iced water, painfully aware of the oppressive heat and humidity.

"I do as well, sir," he replied.

Chapter 29

1:15 P.M.

The crack of thunder reverberated through the field hospital, and the bullets of rain steadily sprayed against the windows. Even inside the building the heavy winds could be heard. The morning's cruel heat was suddenly gone, replaced by this sudden early afternoon thunderstorm. Those who dared to venture outside the field hospital came back inside to report that this storm would likely pass as quickly as it had appeared, and the afternoon's festivities in the Great Tent would almost certainly begin as planned.

Not that any of the nurses, doctors, or patients in this particular field hospital would be venturing anywhere near the Great Tent, for that matter. Many of the current roster of patients in the building had been in the Great Tent yesterday for the opening day's ceremonies before later being overcome by the heat or some non-weather-related ailment, and hopefully many of them would be discharged from the hospital later this afternoon or this evening in time for tomorrow's Governors' Day speeches. But for this day, for Military Day, they were destined to remain in their hospital beds – or at least in the hospital wards – under the watchful eyes of the nurses and doctors.

Louisa May Sterling jolted at this latest thunder burst just as she was beginning to take Ned Tomlinson's pulse. The poor man was still extremely weak, but he had stabilized since last night. He would certainly be going nowhere today; Louisa knew that without even needing to hear those directions from Samuel Chambers or any other physician. Perhaps tomorrow though, if he could somehow rally...

Louisa was determined to keep her distance from Samuel Chambers this day. The doctor was taken with her; that much she now knew for a certainty. Of course Louisa found herself attracted to Samuel; she had never been one to lie to herself and so that fact was without question. But after last night's dream...

In that dream United States Army First Lieutenant Terrence Sterling II was again of this world, accompanying his wife Louisa and their son Randall to the Carlisle Barracks Officer's Club for a celebratory dinner to mark Louisa's thirtieth birthday. Gathered at the table where three seats were vacant, awaiting the Sterlings' arrival, were Governor Tener; President Wilson; President Lincoln, curiously enough; and two long-bearded Generals – one Union, the other Confederate, each in their respective dress uniforms – who were unknown to Louisa. Louisa had looked over at Terrence and thanked him for arranging such a magnificent gathering of prominent individuals, all in celebration of her milestone birthday. This time, unlike in most of her dreams that featured her late husband, Terrence's voice sounded just as it had when he was alive as he replied: "Anything for you, my lovely Louisa; you know I wouldn't miss your thirtieth birthday for anything in the world."

Louisa recalled nothing of the dream after Terrence's words, though she was keenly aware when she jolted awake that she had indeed continued to conjure images in the theater of her mind. She was also firmly of the belief that somewhere in – well, some sort of Heaven that was now Terrence Sterling's home for eternity – he was watching over her, and the thought of having things progress any further with Samuel Chambers than mere companionship would be partaking in behavior that was patently disloyal to her husband.

This would stop now; Louisa told herself this morning, time and again, as she and Randall walked the two miles from their home to the encampment grounds. Randall was already off preparing for this afternoon's speeches in the Great Tent. As he had done yesterday, he would again be escorting veterans from the Pennsylvania delegation to open seats. Hopefully the thunderstorms would cease soon, Louisa fretted; the thought of the young boy – not to mention all of those old men – underneath this ferocious rainfall worried her terribly.

"How is Mister Tomlinson today?" the voice whose tones she had come to recognize instantaneously interrupted her thoughts.

Louisa looked over at Doctor Samuel Chambers.

"He is slightly improved, doctor," she said, lowering her voice as she spoke to a volume that she hoped could not be overhead by Ned Tomlinson, "but I'm still very concerned about his well-being." She quickly recited various vital signs from her just-concluded examination of the patient, and Samuel absorbed what she related to him.

He nodded slightly away from Ned's hospital bed, indicating that he wanted Louisa to accompany him out of earshot of Tomlinson.

"I agree with your assessment based on what you have related to me," Samuel said when they were a few feet further away. "You will continue to keep a close eye on him throughout the day?"

"Of course, doctor," came her reply. Her second use of the "doctor" formality was not lost on Samuel. Come to think of it, he realized, in the brief moments they had been conferring about Ned Tomlinson, Louisa had been surrounded by a barrier-like aura; almost as if she did not want to converse with Samuel about anything at all, hospital matters or otherwise.

Samuel was perplexed, but decided now was not the time to pursue the matter. He had rounds to make and administrative tasks to accomplish. Louisa May Sterling wasn't going anywhere; Samuel knew that for a fact, considering that he had ensured that even as doctors and nurses rotated among the various field hospitals here at the encampment grounds, Louisa would remain right here, in this facility.

Right where Samuel was.

Chapter 30

2:00 P.M.

As precisely as a day earlier, the Military Day ceremonies began at exactly 2:00 in the afternoon. That morning, the Great Tent had been the site of the Indiana Reunion Commission's gathering, an event that lasted until 1:00…at which time the venue was quickly prepared for the much larger gathering scheduled to begin only one hour later. The wind whipped the fabric of the Great Tent to and fro and the rain battered against the tarp as those preparations were made, but in the spirit of the many old survivors gathered here on this occasion the Tent showed no signs of surrendering to the elements.

By 1:30 the rain had faded to a light sprinkle that most thought would stop any minute now, and the wind had evacuated the encampment grounds just as soldiers from both sides had departed following battle fifty years earlier. The temperatures now hovered around 80 degrees; for how much longer no one was certain, but even a brief reprieve from the dangerous heat and humidity was most welcome. Veterans from all corners of the grounds began shuffling towards the Great Tent, many assisted by Boy Scouts such as young Randall Sterling.

Many hundreds of the veterans who had been in the encampment grounds the prior day had decided to depart prematurely, apparently satiated by the momentous speeches that first afternoon and the magnitude of that first day's ceremonies as well as the many smaller-scale events so many of them had attended a day earlier on the thirtieth of June, shortly after the grounds had opened. Still many hundreds of other veterans had arrived in Gettysburg last night and even into this morning; latecomers perhaps, but nonetheless enthused about belatedly joining in the commemoration. The mix of veterans in the Great Tent this Military Day afternoon might be slightly different than that of the prior day, but for the most part many of those who would attend this day had also heard Colonel Schoonmaker, Governor Tener, and the other speakers that first day. Their expectations for grandeur this Wednesday afternoon would surely be high given the magnificent speeches they had witnessed on Tuesday.

The roster of Military Day speakers was far less illustrious than that of Veteran's Day. Today would be more of the voice of the common soldier preceding the recitation of the Gettysburg Address, though the Union's "common soldier" representative was indeed a Major General. The South would, however, be represented by Sergeant John Scarborough of North Carolina...certainly a common soldier of the war, representative of so many of his comrades and former enemies gathered here this afternoon.

Into the Great Tent they poured by the thousands, the throngs as orderly as they had been a day prior. Chester Morrison had returned from town before the noon hour just as the rains began, and had retired to his sleeping tent for a short rest while Jonathan sought shelter in one of the nearby kitchen tents. By 1:45 Chester – accompanied by both Devin McAteer and a still-sullen Seamus McAteer – had rendezvoused with the Sullivan brothers, Philip Roberdeau, Angus Findlay, Lawrence Armstrong, and four other Pennsylvanians who had once been comrades of the McAteers in the 45th Pennsylvania. A small group of three Boy Scouts (including Randall Sterling) approached the group and offered to escort them to seats; an offer eagerly accepted by the men, one and all.

Given that the beginning of the ceremonies was fast approaching, no cluster of a dozen contiguous seats could be located. Eight of the men were guided in one direction by two of the Boy Scouts, while the other Scout indicated that four of the men should follow him to another section of chairs not too far away. Devin McAteer, ensconced in the larger group, was surprised when his cousin Seamus abruptly and wordlessly turned to follow the lone Boy Scout to the separate seating section. Joining Seamus were Lawrence Armstrong and two of the four veterans of the 45th Pennsylvania, both of them from Northeastern Pennsylvania and comrades of Seamus' from the Luzerne County G.A.R. Devin was about to call after his cousin to ask Seamus to perhaps trade places with one of the men in the larger group, but Seamus was quickly out of earshot amidst the din in the Great Tent. Devin caught the eye of Johnny Sullivan – who had observed this curious occurrence – and shrugged before continuing to follow the Boy Scouts to the seats they had eyed for this particular group of old soldiers.

*   *   *

His opening words brought forth a rich, knowing laugh from nearly every veteran seated in the Great Tent this afternoon; and from the spectators as well.

"Mister Chairman," Sergeant John C. Scarborough of North Carolina began, "I want to say to this great audience that I am glad to be here. The first time I was here I was not glad; the next time I came, I was."

"That about says it all, I expect," the Louisianan Philip Roberdeau said to the Pennsylvanian Chester Morrison, raising his voice enough to be heard over the laughter that surrounded them. Devin McAteer, seated on the other side of Chester, added alongside his own chuckling:

"I'll say."

Sergeant Scarborough proceeded to relate a plain language, almost folksy narrative of the events of North Carolina's anguished secession from the Union; the West Point-trained Southerners who resigned their United States Army commissions and took up the military leadership of the Confederacy (Philip Roberdeau felt the eyes of many of those nearby upon himself as Scarborough spoke those words, and Philip's thoughts drifted back in time to that long steamship journey in the company of General Beauregard); and even his own personal thoughts and beliefs he now publicly called into question.

"One night after the close of the war I woke up and thought about all I had been doing and thinking. I had learned to hate folks, which was wicked. I had learned to hate folks along sectional lines and that was unpatriotic."

Even as Sergeant Scarborough continued speaking, a great many of the old veterans gathered here this afternoon of the second of July, 1913 immediately began looking into their own thoughts and feelings during the war, immediately afterwards, and in the years since. Many of them, just as Sergeant Scarborough had confessed, had learned to hate one another not only because they had been wartime antagonists on the same battlefield – locked in a lengthy, frantic struggle for life itself as much as a fight for victory – but just as much because of the "sectional lines" the North Carolinian mentioned. Long after the war was concluded, men now seated in this Great Tent might have looked at some other man likewise present and, without knowing anything about him, have hated him merely because he was from the other side of the sectional lines that had once existed...even though by then they were both citizens of the same nation.

Yet so little animosity was present here on the field at Gettysburg these days. This North Carolina man, once a sergeant and now that state's Superintendent of Public Schools, could stand in front of thousands of former combatants, North and South alike, and talk as plainly as day about prominent North Carolina politicians of the day who originally intended to remain with the Union until learning that President Lincoln had called upon that very state to provide troops to force South Carolina back into the Union, and the anguished decision those men had made at that point to likewise leave the Union and join the Confederacy. He could state how he had once hated the overwhelming majority of men seated in this Great Tent – the Union veterans – without ever having known a single one of them.

Yet, as Sergeant Scarborough proclaimed not only on behalf of himself but also as a self-appointed proxy for his former comrades and antagonists alike, those days were now in the past forever. For some, healing had come soon after the end of the war; while for others, sometime during the decades that followed. And perhaps for others, it wasn't until this Great Reunion in the present day that forgiveness and compassion finally took hold, casting in stone how they would now feel about the war and their former enemies for the remaining time each of those men had left upon this earth. But regardless of when each man here had come to embrace the soothing peace of that forgiveness, they were all now truly brothers.

* * *

"When that great President, the friend of the whole country, was assassinated," Colonel Cowan said, referring of course to Abraham Lincoln, "the first surgeon to reach his side was Dr. John Wells Bulkley, who remained with him to the end. His son, Mr. Barry Bulkley, will read Lincoln's Gettysburg Cemetery Dedication address at this time."

Upon the conclusion of those words Barry Bulkley came to the podium and began reciting Abraham Lincoln's famous Gettysburg Address. Each man present, save for the inevitable few whose age and general health had brought forth an afternoon nap despite the clamor surrounding them, sat enraptured as Lincoln's words of dedication and determination washed over them. Even the former Confederates, so many of whom had personally suffered defeat on this very ground mere months before Lincoln arrived to speak those words on that blustery November afternoon, could find no malice in the memories stirred by the recitation of those very words. The thoughts of nearly every man present who had engaged at the Battle of Gettysburg travelled to their brethren who had given that last full measure of devotion for whichever cause had brought them to this place and, ultimately, their death. Even those veterans who had fought elsewhere – men such as Devin and Seamus McAteer – were remembering former comrades who had done likewise on so many other battlefields.

As the hour of three o'clock and the halfway point of the day's formal ceremonies approached, many of the men seated in the Great Tent were becoming restless. Yesterday had been such an awe-inspiring occasion with the speeches by so many luminaries. Today's speeches were no less inspiring, despite being delivered by men of lesser stature than a day earlier. Still, many a man felt as if he had remained seated from the conclusion of yesterday's ceremonies straight through to this very moment, and his aching bones and joints groaned in agreement.

The thunderclaps, spectacular lightning, and renewed downpours that burst forth just after the introduction of the final speaker, Rhode Island Lieutenant Governor Roswell Burchard, were so intense that the Commission was forced to halt the ceremonies for half an hour. The attendees took advantage of this pause in the ceremonies to rise and stretch their legs, wandering about the Great Tent a bit to get the blood flowing and the joints unstiffened.

Devin McAteer looked around to see where his cousin might be, and after a moment or two spotted Seamus about twenty yards away. He began walking in that direction and after only a few steps, keeping his focus on Seamus the entire way, he saw his cousin look in Devin's direction and catch his eye. Devin was shocked, then, to see Seamus quickly glance away and begin shuffling in the opposite direction, away from Devin. Determined, Devin quickened his pace, nudging his way through one small cluster of old men after another, until he knew he was within earshot of his cousin.

"Seamus!" he called out, sharply.

Seamus McAteer had no choice but to break off his escape and slowly turn in the direction from which he had heard his name being called.

Devin had apparently decided enough was enough.

"What has gotten into you?" he demanded when he arrived within a few feet of where Seamus had halted.

"Ever since last night," Devin continued, "you have been acting as if all the sorrows of the world have come down upon your shoulders at once. I must say, your demeanor has been most unkind!"

Devin noticed his cousin's eyes narrow as he awaited Seamus' explanation.

"Why don't you go back to your new friends," Seamus replied, resignation dripping from his every syllable.

Suddenly, it was all clear to Devin. His own thoughts traveled back to the previous March when he was still wavering over whether or not to attend this gathering, despite Seamus' fervent pleas by way of the United States mail service. He recalled his cousin's pleading letter, relating how Seamus had made the effort to consult with officials of the Luzerne County Grand Army of the Republic to gather immutable confirmation that Devin was indeed welcome at the Gettysburg Reunion, despite not having fought on the field there. Seamus had been the one so actively engaged with his fellow veterans; the one who had attended the Pennsylvania G.A.R. encampment that had ended just before this Great Reunion began; and for whom memories of that long ago war and its warriors had been such an integral part of his life in all the years since.

For Devin, however, from the moment he finally left Army service as Reconstruction neared its conclusion, everything about the war had been neatly placed in a box in Devin's mind and that box had been sealed shut. For nearly forty years, while Seamus attended G.A.R. meetings and other commemorations, Devin had proceeded with his life as if he had instead been living in some other country during the first half of the 1860s rather than fighting under the flags of the Union Army. He rarely spoke of the war; he had not joined the G.A.R. or any other veteran's organization; he never attended any sort of commemorative gathering or ceremony; indeed, except for two occasions he had never even paused to bear witness to a parade of old veterans for Decoration Day or any other civic holiday.

That must be it, Devin told himself as he stood opposite his cousin. Devin thought back to two days earlier, when the cousins had greeted one another soon after their arrival. For the first few hours, from the half hour spent waiting in the registration line to their first stroll about the grounds, Seamus had seemed to have taken a calling to ensure that his cousin felt included in the events going on around them. Devin had only slightly taken note of that at the time, but now recollections came rushing back, forming a picture in his mind of exactly what Seamus seemed to have been doing. Even when the reached their assigned sleeping tent and met Chester Morrison for the first time, Seamus had taken the lead in engaging the Philadelphia high-muck-a-muck in dialogue, going out of his way to steer the conversation towards Devin at every opportunity.

It must have taken Seamus by surprise, then, when Devin and Chester turned out to take a shine to one another even when Seamus wasn't around. And the discovery of Devin's years-earlier encounter with Philip Roberdeau, which – along with their joint rescue of the Norfolk man Tomlinson – spurred yet another burgeoning friendship without any need for Seamus to become involved, seemed to have settled his cousin into a foul mood.

The announcement coming from the stage that the ceremonies would soon resume (the newest storm departed as quickly as it had appeared) meant that Devin would have no time to discuss his revelation with his cousin and, hopefully, straighten out matters.

"I would like to talk to you when this ceremony has concluded," Devin said firmly.

Not receiving any reply from his cousin, he remained planted in place, refusing to move, until Seamus finally nodded his agreement as he lowered his eyes.

Chapter 31

5:45 P.M.

"Nurse Sterling?"

Louisa turned at the sound of her name, knowing with all certainty even before her eyes fell on the person addressing her that it had been Samuel Chambers.

"Yes, doctor?" Louisa had managed to not share this afternoon's midday meal with Samuel, and the two had barely crossed paths this day. Samuel, in fact, had been absent from this hospital for the past half hour, and Louisa was about to learn why.

Samuel slightly tilted his head to the left, indicating that he wished Louisa to move further away from the bed in which Ned Tomlinson rested. The Norfolk man's condition had changed very little throughout this entire day thus far, though at least it hadn't worsened. Philip Roberdeau had indeed visited Ned after the conclusion of this afternoon's speeches in the Great Tent, and had just departed the field hospital five minutes earlier, unhappily worried about the fate of his fellow former Confederate.

When doctor and nurse were out of earshot of Ned Tomlinson, Samuel said, in lowered tones:

"We have another fatality among our veterans." Samuel's eyes bore the grief of having received this news as well as being obligated to share this information.

Louisa's lips tightened for a brief instant and was about to reply when Samuel continued.

"The poor man succumbed suddenly in town at the Hotel Gettysburg this afternoon, not long ago," he related. "I just received word from Colonel Bradley," he added, referring to the Army's Chief Surgeon at the encampment grounds.

"No physician in town could be summoned before the man expired, unfortunately," he continued, "nor has one been located to examine this man. Colonel Bradley has asked me to take an Army ambulance motor car into town to bring him back to the hospital here so we can attempt to determine what ailment caused his death."

"I understand," Louisa replied, wondering if Samuel was going to ask her…

"I would like you to accompany me to the Hotel Gettysburg to retrieve this man's body," Samuel said, as if reading Louisa's very thoughts.

Louisa was all but certain that Samuel's request for *her* to accompany him was far from random. Yet she could see no alternative but to agree. Within ten minutes after their short conversation had concluded, they were seated side by side in the back seat of an Army ambulance vehicle that was driven by one Army corpsman – a corporal – with another corpsman, this one a sergeant, occupying the other front seat. Louisa recalled Samuel's admission prior to that first journey from the field hospital to her house that he did not know how to drive; that explained why they were accompanied by the two Army men, which secretly gladdened Louisa. There would be no interrogation from Samuel during the short ride into town as to Louisa's indifferent demeanor today as compared to yesterday, as there might have been if just the two of them had been in the vehicle.

"His name is – was – Landis Travis," Samuel said to Louisa as the Army driver eased his way through a congestion of veterans milling about, slowly making their way to one kitchen tent or another to receive their supper meals. "His identification credentials were on his person. I believe he was from Westmoor, up in the northeastern part of our state, if my memory holds true from what Colonel Bradley told me."

He paused for a moment before continuing.

"It is unknown why he was at the Hotel Gettysburg this afternoon, and not at the encampment grounds. I fear we may never find the answer to that question since no one at the Hotel Gettysburg has claimed familiarity with this man or would admit to accompanying him into town this afternoon. Perhaps he felt in need of a journey following our rainfall earlier this afternoon, and was lulled into a false sense of well-being by the cooler temperatures we had, which of course have since passed."

In fact, in the aftermath of the two thunderstorms, not only had the temperatures shot back up well above the ninety degree mark but the humidity was now even worse than it had been the prior two days, if that was indeed even possible.

"I'm saddened for him as I am for the other men who have passed away here," Louisa replied. She wanted to add – but didn't for fear of the opposite becoming true – that still thus far the number of deaths was far below what any of them would have expected, especially given the harshness of the temperatures and humidity.

The ambulance soon arrived in front of the Hotel Gettysburg. A number of men, several of whom were most certainly veterans here for the reunion, were lazing about in front of the establishment. The others looked to be local businessmen and perhaps a spectator or two who had come to Gettysburg for the commemoration. Samuel, Louisa, and the two Army corpsmen eased their way through the crowd into the hotel, where they were met by the manager, who directed them into a small room off of the dining area.

There they saw the body of Landis Travis. The man's remains rested there on one of the hotel's sofas that had been extracted from the lobby and brought into this room. As they approached the body, neither Samuel nor Louisa noticed anything that immediately caused them to assign a particular cause to his death. He looked peaceful, as if his passing had been just one more event in his life…albeit the final one.

Samuel proceeded with a rapid examination of Mister Travis' remains, assisted by Louisa, while the corpsmen and the hotel manager observed at a respectful distance. The examination was concluded within three minutes and as Samuel had expected, further scrutiny of Landis Travis' remains would be required back at the field hospital.

Suddenly every person in this side room – save for the deceased Landis Travis – heard a loud commotion coming from the hotel's dining area. Initially the sounds were those of overturning chairs, and perhaps even a dining table or two, but that clamor was soon followed by loud yelling…and then several screams. The hotel manager leading the way, all of those in the side room (again, except for the departed Mister Travis) hurried into the dining room and encountered a wild-eyed man of around thirty, perhaps forty years of age brandishing a knife. Some of the diners were attempting to close in on the man – no doubt to attempt to disarm him – while many more were fleeing in the opposite direction, away from this terrible scene.

Louisa Sterling was helpless against clasping her left hand against her mouth to choke off an anguished cry as she saw the man's blade strike home against the chest of one of the rushing men, and seconds later inflicting a slash on another man's arm. Several men – including a state policeman in uniform – were already lying on the ground, obviously in severe pain, as the melee continued.

Both Louisa and Samuel – standing side by side – were suddenly aware of the two Army corpsmen rushing past them, one on either side of the doctor and the nurse, apparently intent on confronting and disarming the knife-wielding man. One of the soldiers – the sergeant – lunged at the man first and initially it appeared he had sidestepped a wicked swipe of the man's knife, but then the knife sliced the Army man's shoulder as the assailant brought his weapon back around. The sergeant immediately grabbed for his shoulder with the hand of his other arm as the other soldier likewise lunged at the assailant, but that second Army man ended up empty-handed when the attacker dodged to his left and then fled into the hotel lobby. Samuel and Louisa could hear yelling and screaming coming from the hotel lobby and each wondered if the man was fleeing out of the hotel or if he might be attacking others there, as he had done in the dining area.

Catching the assailant would have to be the responsibility of the local police and perhaps the Army. Samuel and Louisa had more immediate concerns – caring for the victims of that man's attack – and immediately went to work. They quickly surveyed the victims lying on the dining area's floor, and their practiced eyes also took in at least two men still standing who were grasping their shoulders or arms, apparently also having suffered the blade of that man's knife.

Samuel determined which of the prone men needed to be treated first and he was just about to inform Louisa when he saw her take a couple of steps forward and quickly kneel down near that same man's chest. Samuel immediately followed, intent on what he needed to do medically but still with a small part of his mind praising and admiring Louisa for her excellent medical instincts.

The two of them examined this first victim, who was beginning to bleed profusely from a wound in his left breast. Samuel ripped the man's suit jacket open, popping several buttons as he did, and then did likewise to the man's vest and then his shirt. The skin of his chest now exposed, both Samuel and Louisa could see the extent of the knife wound. It was bad, but – presuming the man reached a hospital soon – most likely not fatal. Samuel looked around, hoping to see a rush of local Gettysburg physicians and nurses coming to assist, but none had arrived yet. Hopefully soon, he prayed. Their aid was desperately needed!

Louisa had already jumped up to grab a tablecloth from a nearby dining table. She selected an unsoiled sector of the linen and pressed that section against the man's wound, forcing as much pressure as she could down onto the man's chest.

"I've got this one," she looked over and said to Samuel, indicating that he was free to move onto another one of the knifed men. He simply nodded and shifted about four feet to his right, kneeling in front of another man. Just then Samuel could hear the clamor of what he knew were Gettysburg doctors and nurses rushing into the room, and he felt himself breathe a sigh of thanks now that assistance was here.

Hospital corpsmen quickly followed bearing stretchers, and as the most serious of the victims were stabilized each was quickly loaded onto stretchers and then carried out to an ambulance vehicle for transportation to the local hospital. Samuel was about to walk over to one of the victims leaning against the wall, a man holding his sliced right shoulder and bearing a painful grimace on his face, when he heard his name called out:

"Samuel Chambers!"

Samuel turned in the direction from which the sound of his name had come. If Samuel and this other man had been standing in a different establishment – the Union League in downtown Philadelphia in particular – he no doubt would have immediately recognized the man addressing him. As it was, Samuel knew the man's face and voice to be familiar, but given the chaotic circumstances all around he couldn't immediately assign a name to this gentleman.

Fortunately, by the time the other man reached Samuel, recognition had arrived.

"Jonathan Morrison!" Samuel proclaimed.

Samuel and Jonathan were acquainted from not only the Union League but also other exclusive establishments and clubs in the city of Philadelphia. Samuel's father Edwin Chambers was likewise acquainted with Jonathan's father Chester, as one might expect from their relative stations among the Philadelphia elite…though the two were more acquaintances than fast friends.

"My father has been stabbed," Jonathan exclaimed when he had taken several more steps towards where Samuel was standing. "In the lobby area, as that man with the knife was hurrying past outside the hotel."

Samuel took a quick look at the wounded man leaning against the dining room's wall whom he had originally intended to treat next. Fortunately one of the newly arrived local Gettysburg physicians was only a few feet away, surveying the room but not currently engaged in treating anyone else. Samuel quickly asked the doctor if he would examine and treat the man with the right shoulder wound so he could depart to the lobby to look after Jonathan Morrison's father, and the local doctor immediately agreed.

Samuel swiftly followed Jonathan Morrison out into the hotel lobby. That potion of the hotel was so crowded now in the aftermath of the commotion that not only Doctor Chambers but Jonathan as well had difficulty locating Chester Morrison amidst the heavy crowd. It took perhaps thirty seconds for Jonathan to spot his father, half-slumped on a different wing chair than the one in which Jonathan had left him moments earlier to seek medical help for the sudden wound.

"Pop?" Jonathan anxiously inquired after the two men forced their way through the crowd to where Chester Morrison was seated.

"Pop?" Jonathan asked again a few seconds later after not receiving a response, his forced calm demeanor now threatening to dissolve into panic.

This time, in response to hearing his name, Chester Morrison turned to his right where his son stood and where Samuel was urgently reaching into his black leather doctor's medical bag.

"It looks like I ended up being wounded at Gettysburg after all," was what Chester told his son, irony dripping from his words.

Initially, Jonathan didn't fully comprehend the meaning of what his father had declared, but then the sardonic meaning of Chester's statement came to him.

"I guess you did, Pop," Jonathan let out a sigh. "Look who I found, Pop; Samuel Chambers. From the Union League? Doctor Chambers? He will take good care of you."

"Ah, Doctor Chambers," Chester responded upon recognizing the physician's name even before identifying the face of the man standing next to his son. "And how is your father Edwin? I've not seen him for a while, I believe."

"He is fine, sir; thank you for asking," Samuel responded even as he was completing his search in his bag for the suturing materials he would need. As his fingers located the small folding case with the suturing needles, he looked up at Chester.

"How does your arm feel, Mister Morrison?" he inquired, his eyes traveling from Chester's face down to where his left hand pressed a now-crimson monogrammed handkerchief against his right bicep.

"It's very painful of course, but at the same time also beginning to feel a touch numb," Chester answered.

Samuel nodded. He was just about to send Jonathan Morrison back into the dining area to search for any available nurse to come assist him when, as if once again responding to his unspoken thoughts, Louisa Sterling appeared at his side.

"Ah, Nurse Sterling," Samuel exclaimed. "You have appeared just in time."

Samuel wordlessly handed his physician's bag to Louisa. He felt no need to inform her of his wishes; she would know exactly what the doctor expected. She peered into the bag and located another small case, this one containing a collection of glass syringes and injection needles as well as a tiny vial of anesthesia. As Louisa busied herself preparing the injection that would precede Doctor Chamber's suturing work, she heard Samuel's voice address the patient.

"Mister Morrison, this nurse assisting me is the daughter of Doctor Randolph Talbot of Germantown, whom I believe   you   know."

Even suffering the pain of his wound, Chester Morrison seemed to light up at Samuel's words.

"Why Louisa May Talbot! Can that possibly be you?"

At the first utterance Louisa had heard in a long while of her full maiden name, she looked up from beginning to prepare the injection at the patient, this man Chester Morrison. He didn't seem familiar to her, but then again he obviously knew her, perhaps from long ago when she had been a young girl.

"I am, sir," she replied with a tight smile, before admitting: "I apologize, though, for not recognizing you."

"Oh, that's perfectly all right," Chester Morrison replied. "I remember you as a very little girl at your father's knee, and the last time I saw you was at your wedding nearly ten years ago…" Chester abruptly stopped speaking, apparently remembering all of a sudden that Louisa's beloved Terrence was no longer of this world.

Louisa smiled sympathetically at the older man. No doubt he felt terrible for having stumbled into mentioning Louisa's tragic loss.

"It's all right, sir," she added and then changed the subject. "Soon after I administer this anesthetic injection Doctor Chambers will be able to suture your injured arm."

Samuel watched Louisa give Samuel the local injection and when she had completed the task he turned to Jonathan Morrison.

"Does anyone know what precipitated this madness?"

"I do not," Jonathan replied. "My father and I had just entered the hotel to enjoy supper here. I had driven out to the encampment grounds to retrieve him and after our meal we planned to drive back to the grounds for whatever festivities might be occurring this evening. Suddenly that man came rushing out of the dining area with his knife blade slashing back and forth, and unfortunately we were in his path, with my father in front. I tried to lunge in front of my father...or maybe push him to one side. To be honest, I'm not exactly certain what specific evasive action I attempted since the whole affair happened so quickly."

A young man, perhaps twenty-five years of age, had been standing nearby and had heard both Samuel Chambers' question and Jonathan Morrison's answer. When Jonathan finished speaking, the young man interjected.

"I apologize for my interruption, sirs" – and then, after noticing Louisa Sterling, added "and ma'am" – "but I happened to overhear the doctor's question and I was in the dining room when the disturbance erupted. The man with the knife was dining with several other companions and I believe they had consumed a great deal of spirits with their meal. They began discussing President Lincoln, no doubt due to the Jubilee that is underway, and speaking the most unpleasant words about Mister Lincoln. All of the nearby diners could overhear them and most looked at them with disgust but just turned back to their meals."

When Chester Morrison grunted, no doubt because of a surge of pain despite the anesthetic that was beginning to take hold, the young man paused in his story. Chester, though, looked at the speaker and said:

"Please continue, young man, for I would like to understand exactly why I ended up with this wound."

"Well sir, the man with the knife – though we did not know he had a knife just then – yelled out the most vile name one could imagine about Mister Lincoln. I believe the dining room manager was heading over to their table to ask those men to leave, when an older gentleman wearing a Union Army uniform, no doubt a veteran of the war, jumped to his feet and hurried over to their table. He almost stumbled twice on his way because he was so excited and angry. He began berating them and I believe he might have actually thrown a tumbler at them in response to their outrages, and that is when all of the men seated at that table stood up and one suddenly brandished that knife. Other men in the dining room hurried over there, as did I, because we were fearful that the veteran was about to be stabbed, and in fact that is when those men did begin their attack. Not just the man with the knife either, but the other men began pushing and punching those who came to the aid of the veteran. A state police constable was dining in the room and he surged into the melee. He actually pushed me to the side just as the attacker lunched forward with his knife and that was how he was stabbed."

The young man, who had been calm during his retelling of the incident, now began shaking...no doubt due to the belated recognition that he himself might have been one of the men stabbed if the constable hadn't pushed him away a split-second earlier.

"Are you alright, sir?" Samuel Chambers asked the young man. He was awarded several tentative nods of the young man's head in a wordless response.

"Nurse Sterling, would you please see to our young friend here?" Samuel directed.

"Of course, doctor," Louisa replied as she gently laid her left hand on the young man's right forearm. She could feel the intense shivering even through his suit jacket.

"What is your name?" she softly asked.

"Martin," came the reply after several seconds in which the young man seemed to be mustering his strength to verbalize a response. "Martin Franklin."

"Are you from here in Gettysburg, Mister Franklin?" Louisa was doing what she could to calm the man through simple discussion.

"No-o," he shook his head, his voice quivering a touch in his response. "I am from Philadelphia. I came here as a spectator for the Reunion and am staying here at the hotel."

"Well, sir," Louisa said, forcing amiability into her voice, "you are in good company then. All of the men here are from Philadelphia, and I am originally from nearby Germantown. You are among kindred spirits!"

With the brief exchange about Philadelphia, Martin Franklin's anxiety seemed to instantly dissipate, at least somewhat.

"This discussion of Philadelphia just made me realize something very curious," Martin Franklin offered. "One would have thought from the discourse coming forth from those men that they were devout Confederates and southerners, and I believe two of them did sound as if they were from Virginia or perhaps another southern state. But the man with the knife who shouted those vile words about President Lincoln clearly did *not* have a southern accent. In fact, his voice sounded distinctly as if he came from Philadelphia!"

Martin looked at Samuel Chambers, then at Jonathan Morrison and Chester Morrison, then over at Louisa Sterling, searching their faces as if one of them might have an explanation for this curiosity. In fact, an explanation would be forthcoming in the next day's edition of *The Gettysburg Times* when the newspaper reported that the man arrested on the sidewalk just outside the Hotel Gettysburg had indeed been identified as a Philadelphia man who claimed to be the son of a Confederate General from Virginia.

For now, though, Samuel Chambers was focused on addressing Chester Morrison's injuries rather than solving the mystery of the assailant's accent, where that man was from, or what had caused events to turn so violent. Satisfied that enough time had passed to begin his handiwork, Samuel turned his attention to Chester. He inserted the needle into the upper portion of Chester's right bicep just where the deep slice began on the top – drawing a fresh grimace from Chester Morrison as he did – and expertly began suturing the wound. He completed his task in less than ten minutes. All the while he worked, Samuel calculated the true severity of the wound and the possibility of infection. As soon as he completed his suturing, Samuel turned to Louisa, who had been assisting the entire time.

"Please find our Army corpsman, the one who wasn't hurt – the corporal, I believe – if you are able."

Louisa nodded and turned to go back into the dining area but just then, as if summoned by Providence, the uninjured Army corpsman hurried over to Samuel.

"Doctor?"

"Ah, Corporal," Samuel said, "I was just sending Nurse Sterling to look for you."

"Sergeant Bownes got stitched up in the dining room by one of the local doctors," the corpsman said, referring to his fellow Army corpsman who had been stabbed in the melee, "but that doctor told me to tell you that we should get him back to the field hospital at the encampment grounds."

"I agree," Samuel said immediately, "and in fact my patient here – Mister Chester Morrison – needs to go there as well. Is our ambulance car still here?"

"It is," the corporal nodded.

"Then if Sergeant Bownes is able to walk under his own power can you please bring him to the ambulance car, and I will bring along Mister Morrison and his son; then you shall quickly drive all of us back to the field hospital."

The corporal quickly did an about face and hurried back into the dining room as Samuel turned to Louisa.

"With all of the people needing to go back to the field hospital, I believe there won't be room for you – or for our original patient, the deceased Mister Travis – but I have an idea. You should stay here and see if you can assist any further and after we have everything all settled in the hospital, I shall gather your son Randall and have our corporal drive him right back here to where you are, and then you shall be very close to your home and not have to suffer the long walk this evening. Would that be agreeable?"

Louisa thought for a moment. Even as part of her mind calculated the comings and goings of herself and her son according to the doctor's plan, another part of her mind was inexplicably saddened somewhat by what Samuel had just proposed.

"It would," she replied. "But Doctor Chambers, are you sure you won't need my assistance back at the field hospital?"

Samuel shook his head.

"We will be fine," he answered as he turned away from Louisa to Jonathan Morrison, deciding he should confirm the plan he had just devised.

"You will be riding with us back to the encampment grounds?"

"Of course," Jonathan replied without hesitation. There was no way he would let his wounded father leave his sight until he was absolutely certain that the older man was fully out of danger.

"It's settled then," Samuel said. He turned back to Louisa Sterling one last time this evening.

"Nurse Sterling, thank you so much for you assistance this evening. I must say your performance here was admirable, especially under such unforeseen circumstances. I daresay that if this were fifty years ago and we were in this very place, treating wounded soldiers fresh from battle, your performance as a battlefield nurse would be admirable."

With those words of praise, Samuel left Louisa's side and accompanied Chester and Jonathan Morrison out the front door where they would shortly rendezvous with the Army corporal and his wounded sergeant. A brief drive back to the field hospital would follow, leaving Louisa May Sterling behind, deep in confusing, despondent thought.

Chapter 32

9:00 P.M.

"We've got the Johnnies this time!"

The cry rang out from one of the Union veterans amidst the ranks of old men huffing their way along Seminary Ridge into the ranks of the Confederates awaiting them.

"All right, boys, come on, we're all ready for you!" came the retort.

Had this scene been occurring fifty years earlier, one would naturally have expected to witness a titanic, bloody clash once the Union men reached their objective and the two opposing forces encountered each other. In this year of 1913, however, when the old men finally came together, brotherhood wound reign as it had through this entire encampment...other than the brawl several hours ago in town, though in that case the assailant had not been one of these old veterans at all.

Indeed, this particular maneuver that the Union "Army" was undertaking in their "attack" on Seminary Ridge was one that had not actually occurred fifty years earlier. This operation wasn't a reprise of Little Round Top or Peach Orchard or East Cemetery Hill – or Pickett's Charge against Cemetery Ridge – and thus no single man present this evening would be reliving an actual engagement in which he had fought, and which he had survived, during the war. To the casual observer, what transpired on the night of July the second, 1913, might appear as if several hundred old men had decided to "play war" just as several hundred young boys might do.

Among the Union veterans marching on Seminary Ridge this evening were Devin and Seamus McAteer. As Devin had demanded, the two cousins spoke following the conclusion of this afternoon's ceremonies in the Great Tent. When Seamus refused to tell his cousin why he had been so gloomy since the previous night, Devin offered his own opinion. Seamus' downcast eyes and shameful face were all the confirmation Devin had needed.

A mumbled apology by Seamus McAteer followed, and for Devin that was enough…at least for the time being, pending Seamus' demeanor the rest of this evening. And indeed, during supper Seamus was much more personable than he had been the previous night, perhaps because Devin requested that the two of them dine alone this evening rather than as part of the larger ensemble that had come together. Neither man knew of the injuries that had befallen Chester Morrison in town at the same time that the McAteers suppered together; it wouldn't be until they returned to their tent from this particular endeavor at Seminary Ridge at close to 10:30 that night and saw that Chester Morrison's cot was empty that they realized something might be amiss. In fact it was Seamus McAteer, not Devin, who thought to check the field hospital. After discovering Chester Morrison there with his son Jonathan resting in a nearby chair, Seamus left Devin at Chester's side and hurried back to the sleeping tents. As fast as his advanced years would permit, Seamus scurried among the many states' delegation areas to round up Philip Roberdeau, Angus Findlay, Lawrence Armstrong, the Sullivan brothers, and several other Pennsylvania veterans of Chester's old Philadelphia Brigade known to Seamus to inform them about what had befallen Chester Morrison earlier this evening.

A late night gathering ensued at Chester Morrison's bedside. As fate would have it, the bed Chester Morrison had been taken to upon his arrival at the field hospital was a single row over from the one occupied by Ned Tomlinson. Tomlinson was sleeping deeply, apparently undisturbed by the large group of men milling about so close to his bed. Philip located the night nurse and inquired about Tomlinson's condition. Upon hearing the words "slightly improved" Philip nodded and turned his attention back to the ensuing discussion at Chester's bedside.

Chester was, in fact, reprising his "being wounded at Gettysburg after all" line he had offered in the lobby of the Hotel Gettysburg, and was rewarded with chuckles from one and all who were present. Even Philip, the only man present who actually had been wounded during the Battle of Gettysburg, found himself laughing lightly at Chester's wry observation.

With the time nearing 11:30, the night nurse informed the men that they would be required to leave the field hospital. None of the men objected, given the late hour and how tired each one was from the day's occurrences. Tomorrow would be another event-filled day, and each was more than ready for a night's rest.

As the men said goodnight to Chester Morrison in turn, one of the Philadelphia Brigade men named Horace Barnett – a member of the 72nd Pennsylvania – asked Chester:

"Will you be well enough to be discharged tomorrow and then participate in the ceremonies at Bloody Angle?"

Chester looked quizzically at the man in response, not comprehending the question. Sensing Chester's confusion – no doubt due to lack of information – Barnett continued.

"The survivors of Pickett's Division will march on the stone wall at the Angle, where a number of us from the Philadelphia Brigade will greet them."

Chester's eyes widened at Horace Barnett's description, as did the eyes of every other man present…even those who, like Devin and Seamus McAteer, had been engaged elsewhere and had not fought at Gettysburg.

What Horace Barnett seemed to be enigmatically describing was a reenactment of the terrible tragedy of Pickett's Charge.

Chapter 33

11:30 P.M.

Louisa's dream was almost an reprise of the previous night's dream.

Almost.

Louisa was again walking into the Carlisle Army Barracks Officers' Club for a celebration of her thirtieth birthday. Governor Tener was again seated at the table awaiting her arrival, as was President Wilson and – again – President Lincoln. Also present again were the two unidentified Civil War generals, one North and the other South.

In this dream, however, Louisa was entering the dining room alone rather than accompanied by her husband Terrence and her son Randall as she had been in the dream of the previous night. In fact, both Terrence and Randall could be found seated side by side at the table along with the illustrious dignitaries. Still, Louisa noticed two empty chairs at the table, to the other side of Randall from where Terrence sat, as she approached. One of those seats she knew was for her.

"When will Doctor Chambers be arriving?" her son Randall anxiously asked her as she approached the table.

In her dream, Louisa looked directly at Terrence in response to their son's words.

Terrence just looked back at Louisa, smiled sadly, but said nothing.

Alan Simon

July 3, 1913
Civic Day/ Governors' Day

"Rather let us remember that this could happen only in America; that no where else upon the habitable globe could men, who fifty years ago had engaged in stormy conflict, meet and clasp hands as brethren under the same flag."

- Vice President Thomas R. Marshall, July 3, 1913

Chapter 34

7:00 A.M.

Three times during their walk from the town of Gettysburg to the encampment grounds, Randall Sterling was forced to repeat a question he had asked his mother after waiting many seconds but receiving no response at all from her. Randall noticed that she seemed particularly distracted – deep in thought, perhaps – this morning. Randall had wished his mother a happy birthday upon waking, though at the tender age of eight he wasn't aware of any sort of milestone attached to this particular birthday of Louisa May Sterling. To Randall, it was just another birthday without his father there to help his mother celebrate, as the past several had been.

Still, Randall Sterling was an eight-year old boy not typically given to melancholy thoughts, and he was still in the midst of the greatest adventure of his young life. The previous night had seen Randall delivered to the Hotel Gettysburg in an actual Army ambulance car, driven by an actual Army corpsman…yet another exhilarating aspect to this incredible escapade. But in doing so Randall had missed the opportunity of the long walk home from the grounds to relate to his mother – and to Doctor Chambers – all that had occurred in the Great Tent that afternoon. And so Randall was attempting to do just that this very morning, but his mother's thoughts seemed to be elsewhere.

For her part, Louisa May Sterling was likewise giving little thought to her milestone birthday itself. She had allowed herself a brief, private display of tears early this morning before Randall awoke; not because of her new age, of course, but because her beloved Terrence was not there to celebrate the occasion with her. As she contemplated the previous night's dream, however, and in particular how that dream contrasted with the one from the night before, her tears quickly dried as she wrestled with the meaning of her competing and conflicting nocturnal visions.

Terrence Sterling had been the most glorious part of her life, and she would be bound to him forever even though he no longer was of this earth. But were her bonds with Terrence such that she would never feel affection or even love for another man? In last night's dream Terrence's sad, resigned smile as he sat at that Officers' Club dining table, accompanied by those conjured dignitaries, listening to his son ask Louisa when Samuel Chambers would be arriving…certainly those images and words were of Louisa's own mind, but were they some sort of ethereal message to her as well? She had, exactly as she had intended, spent very little time in the company of Samuel the prior day, and what brief time they had been together had been spent at the Hotel Gettysburg briefly examining the departed Mister Travis and then frantically addressing the unexpected stabbing wounds. There had been no noonday meals or suppers, or encounters of any other kind.

But if yesterday's fleeting encounters with Doctor Chambers had indeed been what Louisa had told herself earlier in the day that she truly desired (excepting the poor deceased veteran and the wounds suffered during the melee, of course), why then did she feel so empty today?

Alan Simon

* * *

Louisa's confused soul-searching and self-reflection immediately ceased seconds after she walked into the ward where Ned Tomlinson was housed shortly before 8:00 that morning. To her astonishment, the man was no longer prone and unconscious; instead he was sitting on the side of his bed, hunched over, yet fully awake and talking!

"Mister Tomlinson!" Louisa couldn't help but blurt out. "You're awake!"

Ned Tomlinson slowly raised his head until he made eye contact with Nurse Sterling.

"I am," he replied, letting out a sigh as he spoke. "The other nurse who was here when I woke up told me that I been layin' in this bed since a couple of fellas found me in my tent out there on the grounds."

"That is correct," Louisa replied. "In fact, one of those men – I believe his name is Roberdeau – has visited you several times since he and another gentleman found you and then summoned the Army corpsmen to bring you to the hospital. That man has been very concerned about your well-being."

Ned Tomlinson seemed surprised by this information. Was this Roberdeau fellow someone he knew? He searched his memory but couldn't recall anyone by that name, and in fact that name sounded as if it belonged to someone from Louisiana. Maybe the man – this Louisianan, probably – was someone known to him from long ago in the Yankee prison camp at Fort Delaware.

At that moment, Samuel Chambers strolled into the ward, looking downward the entire time at a set of notes another nurse had scribbled about a different patient. His study of those papers was interrupted by an excited cry from a familiar voice.

"Doctor Chambers! Look! Mister Tomlinson!" Louisa had no concern for hospital decorum at the moment; *this* was an occasion to be celebrated, far more so than the mere changing of a calendar date with regards to herself.

For a moment Samuel was speechless. He had just arrived at the hospital himself after an especially long night, remaining at the encampment grounds until 1:30 A.M. and then receiving a motor car ride back to his room at the Pennsylvania College. Bleary-eyed and weary this morning, seeing Ned Tomlinson sitting upright on the side of his bed sent a jolt of energy through the doctor.

He looked over at Louisa Sterling, who was unable to suppress a broad smile of gratitude; perhaps even a smile of victory over suffering and death in the case of Ned Tomlinson of Norfolk, Virginia.

And Doctor Samuel Chambers was equally unable to suppress an even bigger smile at the sight of this lovely nurse's elation.

*　*　*

After Doctor Chambers and Nurse Sterling thoroughly examined Ned Tomlinson, they departed his bedside. As they walked out of earshot of Ned and anyone else in the ward, Samuel turned to Louisa, pausing his steps as he did which likewise caused Louisa Sterling to halt.

"I understand that you have very strong emotions about this day," Samuel began, "but I would be remiss if I didn't briefly extend my best wishes to you today on this occasion of your birthday."

Louisa dropped her head but a smile instantly came to her face as she did. She then raised her head to gaze upon Samuel Chambers, but the smile on her face did not fade.

"Thank you so very much," Louisa replied. "Coming upon Mister Tomlinson nearly recovered is a wonderful birthday present, and I am in a much better frame of mind than I was yesterday…"

Louisa's voice trailed off. Both doctor and nurse stood side by side, their eyes locked, and both seemingly wanting to say something in particular…with neither apparently having the resolve to utter whatever words were queued up.

The voice of another nurse, this one assigned to the hospital by the Red Cross, interrupted.

"Doctor Chambers! Doctor Phillips requested that I locate you and bring you to him for a consultation about a patient."

Samuel hesitated for a second or two after hearing these words, not wanting to disengage from the unspoken connection with Louisa. Finally, reluctantly, wordlessly, he nodded at Nurse Sterling and followed the Red Cross nurse out of this ward to another.

Louisa watched him depart, realizing that just as with herself, Samuel Chambers had departed with important words unspoken. Perhaps later this day Samuel and Louisa would have the opportunity to tell the other what it was that each one wanted to share.

Perhaps.

*   *   *

"So I understand you have been here in the field hospital since the first day of the encampment," Chester Morrison said to Ned Tomlinson. "In fact, I've become quite acquainted with Mister Roberdeau of Louisiana who was one of your rescuers."

So far, Ned Tomlinson's conversations since regaining consciousness had been with two fellow former Confederates who occupied beds near his. But this Yankee's words, particularly the mention again of that fellow Roberdeau, caught his attention."

"That right?" Ned replied. "You mean to tell me you and a Johnny Reb from Louisiana are acquainted?"

The question caught Chester off-guard. The spirit of Blue-Gray brotherhood that had enveloped this entire affair – save for last night's commotion at the hotel in town – had come over Chester by this point, and the idea of anything peculiar about new acquaintances forming across those "sectional lines" about which Sergeant Scarborough had spoken yesterday now seemed perfectly ordinary. But this man Tomlinson had missed out on nearly two full days and nights in which most remaining simmering animosities were buried and old men from both sides made a lasting peace with others in the face of their own mortality.

"We are indeed, sir," Chester made sure to use proper cordialities as he addressed the Norfolk man. "In fact, it was Mister Roberdeau and one of my fellow Pennsylvanians, Mister Devin McAteer of Pittsburgh, who together found you and summoned the Army corpsmen who brought you to this hospital."

This was the first Ned Tomlinson was hearing that a Yankee had played a role in his rescue from certain death.

"You sure 'bout that?" Ned's eyes narrowed as he asked that question.

"Oh, I am quite certain, sir," Chester replied. "Mister McAteer and I have become acquainted as well, and I must say he feels a great sense of pride at assisting Mister Roberdeau in your rescue."

"Well I'll be," Ned said, shaking his head slightly. He hadn't exactly expected a reprise of the Civil War itself here at Gettysburg in this year of 1913, but he had journeyed here largely because of reasons of solidarity with the rapidly fading ranks of his Confederate brothers in arms. He hadn't given much thought at all to the Yankees who would be here; he had just assumed that other than official ceremonies in the Great Tent the Southerners would keep to themselves and the Yankees would do likewise.

His eyes traveled to Chester Morrison's bandaged upper right arm.

"What happened to you?" Ned Tomlinson asked the Philadelphia man.

"Ah," Chester answered. "I believe you have not heard about the incident last night at the Hotel Gettysburg."

"Nah," Ned Tomlinson shook his head. Chester proceeded to relate an abridged version of what that young Philadelphia man had told them about what precipitated the brawl and how he happened to be wounded.

As if reading Chester Morrison's mind for the words that were about to be uttered, Ned interrupted.

"Wounded at Gettysburg, huh?"

Chester chuckled in response.

"I was just going to speak those exact same words," he replied. "I have uttered that phrase several times since suffering that wound, and all who hear it have appreciated the rich irony."

Chester then added:

"Including your rescuer Mister Roberdeau, I should add; and he was wounded here on the field fifty years ago."

"That right?" Ned Tomlinson thought about the appropriateness of his Louisiana rescuer having suffered a wound in this place, as he himself had.

"How about that Yankee…what did you say his name was again?" he asked.

"Devin McAteer," Chester replied.

"McAteer," Ned repeated. "Was he wounded here?"

Chester shook his head.

"Mister McAteer was otherwise engaged those days, down at Vicksburg," was Chester Morrison's answer.

"I see," Ned nodded, then peered intensely at Chester.

"And how about you?" he probed.

"I was here," Chester replied, a bit hesitantly, his eyes involuntarily traveling to the empty space where Ned Tomlinson's left leg should have been. "But I was fortunate enough to spare being wounded during that encounter."

After a few seconds, Ned replied.

"Wish I could say the same. I lost my leg here on the final day, and then spent the rest of the war in a Yankee prison."

Before Chester could ask Tomlinson the question that the mention of "the final day" of course brought to mind, Ned took the conversation in that direction.

"So what regiment were you with here?" was the Virginian's question.

"I was with the 69th Pennsylvania," Chester replied, knowing full well what his answer would mean to Ned.

"I see," was Ned's reply. "Then you were on the other side of our assault on Cemetery Ridge this very afternoon, fifty years ago."

"I was," was Chester's hesitant reply.

Silence came over the two men as they contemplated their respective roles – their respective horrors – in the course of the doomed charge of more than 12,000 Confederates that afternoon of July 3, 1863, that ever since had borne the name of General Pickett.

Chester finally broke the awkward silence.

"No doubt because of your condition these past days, you have not heard that this afternoon men from your Pickett's Division will reenact a portion of your heroic march and be greeted by a number of men from my Philadelphia Brigade. I myself just heard about this event only last night."

Chester's words took a few seconds to register with Tomlinson.

"You mean they're going to recreate Pickett's Charge?" was Ned's skeptical question. Who in the world who had survived that bloody carnage – from *either* side – would want to reenact that terror?

"Apparently so," Chester replied.

Ned thought for a moment.

"You goin' to participate?" he asked Chester.

"Oh no," was Chester's immediate reply.

"Why not?" Ned Tomlinson challenged. "Your side won the day."

Chester Morrison thought for a moment about Ned's words. He could see how, from a Confederate's point of view, an Army of the Potomac veteran such as Chester Morrison might not have the same terrible memories of that afternoon as a man who had lost his leg in that encounter and then found himself locked away in a Union Army war prisoner camp for nearly two more years. Yet Chester's memories of that afternoon were every bit as horrific; his experience just had a more favorable outcome than Ned Tomlinson's, that's all.

"You know," Ned offered after a short silence, "the more I think about it, the more I believe I would like to go participate in that maneuver. I been stuck in this hospital for nearly the entire encampment and I ain't seen or done nothin' yet, and then it's all over tomorrow. Maybe if I go march for a spell with my fellow Confederates, I'll feel that this journey hasn't been a wasted one."

At that moment, one of the hospital nurses – not Louisa Sterling – happened to wander close to Ned Tomlinson's bed. Upon hearing the Virginian's words, she peered at Ned with a shocked look on her face.

"Mister Tomlinson! I'm afraid you are not going to be participating in any sort of march, or anything of the kind!

You've barely regained consciousness, and I'm certain that you will be required to remain present in this field hospital at least through the end of tonight!"

The nurse turned and headed towards the doorway adjoining this hospital ward with the next. Ned Tomlinson didn't deliberately wait until the nurse was out of earshot, but the moment or two it took him to absorb what she had said had the same effect.

"We'll see 'bout that," was Ned Tomlinson's quiet reply, as much to himself as it was in absentia to the now-departed nurse.

Or to Chester Morrison, who himself was now deep in thought.

Chapter 35

10:15 A.M.

"Mind if I join you?"

Angus Findlay's voice interrupted Edgar Sullivan's wandering, gloomy thoughts. The Virginia cavalryman was carrying a tin cup filled with piping hot coffee. Edgar, for his part, had his own nearly full tin cup of coffee resting on the table in front of him, though his had cooled considerably since he sat down more than fifteen minutes earlier.

"Sure," was Edgar's non-committal reply. He was in no mood for company or discussion of any type, but to refuse the old man's request would be a distasteful thing to do.

Angus eased himself onto the bench on the other side of the table from Edgar, wincing as he lowered his body.

"Is your brother nearby?" Angus asked after he had finished taking a seat.

"Nah," was Edgar's short answer this time without lifting his eyes from gazing at the tabletop.

After several moments of silence, Angus offered:

"I sense that you have a great weight on your mind, and I'd be most honored to hear your troubles and see if I might be of some assistance."

This time Edgar looked up, sharply. He was about to tell the old Rebel to mind his own damn business but as his eyes fell on Angus, his mind flashed back to their conversation in the breakfast line two days earlier, and the camaraderie they had all felt – Johnny Sullivan as well – as that conversation had ensued. The old cavalryman doesn't mean anything by his prying, Edgar Sullivan told himself.

"It ain't nothin'," was Edgar's flat reply rather than a sharp-tongued, unpleasant retort.

Angus took a sip of his coffee and, still holding the tin cup, looked back at Edgar.

"The past several days have been very confusing ones to me, I must say. I feel this wonderful kinship with so many former allies and even former enemies I've met – such as you and your brother – and after nearly fifty years, I feel I can finally put that war and its aftermath behind me for the rest of my days. I'm more at peace with all that transpired than I have ever been, or ever hoped to be."

The tin cup becoming heavy, he lowered it to the table before continuing.

"Yet at the same time, I'm more aware of my mortality than I have ever been. I fell ill and collapsed on the very day of my arrival, and quite possibly might have been among the casualties of this second engagement at Gettysburg. Even after my recovery, I feel the aches and pains of age more than ever. Tending my tobacco back home in Virginia is an increased strain with every passing year, but I only have a small patch these days and I am able to care for the plants with only mild aches for the most part. Yet here I've spent two days walking and walking since I was released from the field hospital, and I have the pains to show for it."

Angus Findlay took another sip of his coffee, then locked eyes with his Yankee companion.

"I feel *old*, Mister Sullivan," he said to Edgar. "Ever since I lost my beloved Charlotte I've felt alone and I thought I felt old as well. But now I know what feeling *old* really is, and to tell you the honest truth, I don't like it one bit."

"I reckon that's what's got me feelin' so low," Edgar finally replied, nodding as he did. "Back home in Arizona I don't get out much, and it don't put much strain on an old man's body to play cards and drink Old Overholt down at the local hotel most days. But like you said, ever since I been here I've been walking all over the place, then sitting to listen to those speeches, then getting up and walking all over the place again. I'm feeling pains in places I didn't even know existed on me."

Edgar looked down for a moment, then continued.

"But I think what's got to me is that what I've been doin' – all this walking here and there – is pretty much the same thing I did for years. Back in Tombstone Johnny and me would sometimes do fifteen miles a day on foot, and then we'd be on our horses for maybe a week or two, off doing somethin' or the other. I mighta gotten a bit achy, but nothin' like I'm feelin' now. I think you said it exactly: I feel *old*, and I don't like the feeling one damned bit neither."

Angus sighed.

"Well, Mister Sullivan, I believe all we can do is accept the fact that we are in our advanced years and we are no longer young men. Doing what we've been doing for several days now *will* make us feel as we do, but instead of becoming upset by it, I think the best we can do is get through it, rest up, and then do it again. I can say for my part that after losing my dear Charlotte a decade ago, very little has been pleasing to me. I will say to you, for your ears only, that many an afternoon I stood outside near my small tobacco patch and wondered if the Good Lord would be kind enough to take me that day; and when dusk came and I had been denied my wish, I would slowly walk back to my lonely house and wonder if the next day would perhaps be the one."

"My Katie passed nearly fifteen years ago, and many a day I felt exactly as you just described," Edgar said. "I'd be sittin' in a chair at the Windsor Hotel in Tucson after playing cards for a spell and having a few Old Overholts, and I'd fall asleep and dream that the Good Lord had come to take me home to be with my wife, just like you said. Then I'd wake up and still be there, and I'd be…"

His voice trailed off, but there was no need for him to complete his sentence or his thoughts. Angus Findlay knew exactly how Edgar Sullivan felt.

"My advice to you, young fella," Angus said, reaching across the table to pat the back of Edgar's right hand in a friendly gesture, "is to embrace whatever time you have left. I know it sounds like I'm preachin' what I don't practice, but I can say with all sincerity that this gathering has been just the right medicine for me. I may be alone back on my small tobacco farm but I know when the Good Lord does decide to call me home, all of the boys who are here, and all of those who have already left, will be my brothers waiting for me wherever the Good Lord wants to send me. It don't matter if those boys wore gray or blue; we've all made it this far, fifty years later, and I believe we've all come together for a purpose that is only partly of this world."

Angus Findlay sighed before finishing his thought.

"I may be an old man in *this* life, but I feel like I've been reborn."

Chapter 36

11:30 A.M.

The special train carrying Vice President Marshall; Speaker of the House Champ Clark of Missouri; and a host of other Congressional representatives had left Washington, D.C. promptly at 8:00 that morning and was due into the Gettysburg Depot precisely at noon. Governor John K. Tener was seated at his desk, preparing to leave his office at the Pennsylvania College when a brief knock on his door was followed by the entrance of James Schoonmaker.

"A word, John?" Colonel Schoonmaker said.

"Of course, James," was the Governor's reply.

"You have heard, no doubt, about the incident in town yesterday evening? At the Hotel Gettysburg?"

"I have," the Governor replied. "Is there further grievous news?"

Schoonmaker shook his head.

"None, fortunately," he answered. "All of the men who were stabbed will fully recover, including those who were injured the most severely. I had worried that this affair might cause animosities among those at the encampment grounds, from either side, but thus far we've barely even had a quarrelling word. And what little malice exists is directed towards the weather once again rather than other men."

Schoonmaker paused before continuing.

"You do know that the single veteran among the wounded was Chester Morrison of Baldwin Locomotive?"

Governor Tener nodded his head.

"I had heard that news," he affirmed. "I know Mister Morrison is a business associate of your and I had occasion to meet with him several times during my campaign for Governor. I thanked him for his support in that part of our Commonwealth. How is he faring?"

"I visited him in the field hospital here on the grounds earlier this morning," Schoonmaker replied. "He is doing well, and may be discharged from the hospital today. His son Jonathan was in attendance at the hospital as well, looking after his father."

Governor Tener nodded again. Jonathan Morrison was someone to keep an eye on as a political and business ally, hopefully following in the footsteps of his father.

"On the subject of the field hospital," Schoonmaker added, "they are preparing for a new influx of patients with the temperatures back up but the doctors there seem to be less worried about their ability to treat all of the incoming veterans they might receive than they have been since the encampment opened."

The cooling effect from the previous day's thunderstorms would not be reprised this day, unfortunately: a fact now known to all the men in charge of the encampment as well as the hospital staffs. The temperatures would not be as dangerous as they had been on the opening day, but neither would they be as agreeable as they had been yesterday afternoon. The rotation of patients into and out of the various field hospitals would indeed continue, though at a slightly slower pace than any of the previous days of the gathering. The reduced number of men requiring medical attention was due in part to a large number of veterans having already departed the grounds…as many as one-third of the attendees by some estimations. Still, all field hospital doctors and nurses were busy caring for new patients as well as existing ones, and discharging men back to the encampment only when prudent to do so.

"I'm sure that Doctor Dixon, Doctor Chambers, and Colonel Bradley will keep me apprised of the activities of the various hospitals," the Governor said.

"And what news of our President?" Colonel Schoonmaker changed the subject of conversation, knowing full well what type of response his question would bring.

"Woodrow still intends to arrive mere moments before his speech, and depart seconds after he has concluded," Governor Tener answered derisively, taking great care to refer to the President by his first name…as he himself had so often addressed his former neighboring Governor in venues such as the Union League.

"Shall I be expecting a dust-up when our President arrives, then?" James Schoonmaker said lightheartedly, knowing full well that if his friend Governor Tener could control his temper in the presence of the Secretary of War, after all of that unpleasantness, he could certainly respect the office of the Presidency for what it appeared would be less than one hour!

With a grunt, John K. Tener pulled himself up to his full height of six feet, four inches.

"Let us go greet our Vice President," was all he said in reply.

Chapter 37

12:30 P.M.

Once again, the afternoon's ceremonies would begin precisely at 2:00 and once again, every seat inside the Great Tent was expected to be filled. Today, however, far less standing space would be required because of so many veterans having already departed. Even more veterans who remained in the encampment grounds had decided to not attend this afternoon's procession of speeches and instead join other smaller, unofficial gatherings around the grounds.

And many veterans and spectators alike would instead attend the reenactment of Pickett's Charge scheduled to also begin at precisely 2:00 this very afternoon, fifty years to the very hour of when the original event had taken place.

Devin and Seamus McAteer were drinking coffee (ironically at the exact same table where Edgar Sullivan and Angus Findlay had spoken that morning, though of course neither of the McAteer cousins knew that), with Seamus doing his best to make amends for his previous moodiness. As much as the cousins would have liked to listen to Vice President Marshall's speech, they intended to watch the reenactment of Pickett's Charge that would soon take place and were pausing from this day's activities before walking to that portion of the grounds.

Edgar Sullivan was slowly walking alone about the encampment grounds, mulling over Angus Findlay's words. The old Virginia cavalryman had put matters in perspective for the old Arizona lawman and for that, Edgar was grateful. What he might be able to do with this knowledge, though, was another matter. He checked his pocket watch and saw that he still had time to spare before he needed to begin walking to the area where the reenactment would occur.

Johnny Sullivan, for his part, was accompanying Philip Roberdeau and Angus Findlay to the Gettysburg train depot to secure Angus' replacement railroad ticket, intending to accomplish the deed and then return in time for the reenactment. A modest-length line had already formed at the Gettysburg railroad depot where representatives from the *Philadelphia & Reading* and also the *Western Maryland* were complying with Governor Tener's directive to issue replacement railroad tickets to veterans who had lost theirs. The three men – Angus Findlay, Johnny Sullivan, and Philip Roberdeau – had been fortunate enough to procure a motor car ride to the station rather than be forced to walk under the brutal noontime sun. Several Army regulars had organized a shuttle service of automobiles for veterans leaving the encampment as well as those who, like Angus, needed to secure their replacement railroad tickets.

"I had a conversation with your brother Edgar earlier this morning," Angus said to Johnny Sullivan as they waited in the *Western Maryland* ticket line, slowly shuffling forward.

"Yeah?" Johnny said after a moment's pause. "What about?"

"I came upon him sitting alone at one of the tables when I walked by, and I asked to join him. He's a somber man, your brother…"

"Ain't that right," Johnny Sullivan interrupted. "I have to say I regret pesterin' him to come here. He really didn't want to, but I thought it might be a good thing for him to come here. All he does is sit and play cards and drink rye all day. Hell, all *I* do is sit and play cards and drink rye all day, but at least I ain't as surly as he is."

Johnny looked over at Philip Roberdeau, then back at Angus Findlay before continuing.

"What I don't understand is how two days ago he was all of a sudden in a good mood for the entire day, and then yesterday morning he turned right back into his usual unpleasant self."

"I hope I'm not breaking any confidences," Angus answered, "but he confided in me that he is in great discomfort from all of the walking he has been doing here. But more than the physical discomfort is the exact same affliction I myself feel when suffering that same discomfort: I must face that I'm no longer a young man, able to endure those physical trials with relative ease, and my days are rapidly coming to a close."

Johnny Sullivan's face immediately took on a look of skepticism.

"I don't see my brother thinkin' that deep," he retorted.

"Ah, that's just it," Angus countered. "Until our conversation he has not thought of that at all. He *feels* it, just as I do, and just as you also do, I'm sure."

Angus looked over at Philip Roberdeau.

"And I'm sure Mister Roberdeau feels the same as well; am I correct?"

Philip thought for a moment.

"I suppose you're correct," he nodded. Thoughts and memories raced by at lightning speed in Philip's head. Back home in the French Quarter, with each passing Mardi Gras, Philip felt further and further removed from the joyous Carnival celebration. He would watch the revelries all around his house but for the past fifteen years or so in particular, Philip felt like a stranger to the festivities that he had grown up with and had embraced all through his adult years after the war had concluded. Of particular joy had been parading through the streets of the Quarter on Fat Tuesday back in '66, right in front of Union Army occupation troops.

A thought came to Philip: was Devin McAteer perhaps among those occupation troops that day? He would have to ask Mister McAteer when he next saw him.

Philip's thoughts snapped back to the present day.

"I agree with Mister Findlay," Philip said to Johnny Sullivan. "Until this very moment I will say that I had not put a firm grasp around the gloom I so often feel these days, and that lack of comprehension has been every bit as bothersome as the gloom itself. But listening to Mister Findlay's words, I daresay he is correct. I feel old and that sensation is an unwelcome one. I can no longer do so many tasks I was able to accomplish easily in my younger years, and those that I can still undertake are far more arduous than they ever were."

Philip looked over at Johnny Sullivan.

"How about you, Mister Sullivan?" he asked.

Johnny let out a deep sigh.

"I s'pose so," he agreed. "My brother might be the ornery one and I ain't as aged as him, but I feel old too. We used to walk all over Tombstone, miles each day, and then ride for weeks…"

"That's exactly what your brother said," Angus Findlay interrupted. "He made mention of your exploits in Arizona Territory and how doing far less than that here at the encampment pains him so much. You feel it as well, I'm sure."

"I do," Johnny nodded, then retorted: "But I ain't gloomy all the time like he is."

"All I can say, Mister Sullivan," Angus offered, "is that perhaps my conversation with him has given him a new perspective and a new insight into the matter. I wouldn't expect miracles, but perhaps going forward…"

Angus' sentence was interrupted by the ticket master's cry of "Next!" and upon realizing that the three men had finally arrived at the front of the line, Angus turned away from his two comrades to request his ticket home.

*   *   *

"Nurse? May I have a word?"

The ward nurse, upon hearing Chester Morrison's request, paused and turned towards the man's hospital bed.

"Yes, Mister Morrison? How are you feeling?"

"I am feeling just fine," Chester replied.

"You know that I was a member of the 69th Pennsylvania within the Philadelphia Brigade, I assume."

The nurse immediately knew where this conversation was going.

"I do indeed, Mister Morrison. And I am sure that you would very much like to watch your comrades this afternoon. However..."

Chester interrupted.

"Oh no; that's not quite correct. I want to *join* my comrades of the Philadelphia Brigade this afternoon..."

"I'm sorry, Mister Morrison," the nurse retorted. "That is out of the question. The doctor will likely discharge you later this afternoon, however..."

Once again Chester's interruption came immediately after the nurse's usage of the word "however" as if he had precisely timed his rebuttal to interdict whatever rationale she was about to offer.

"And Mister Tomlinson here would very much like to join his comrades of Pickett's Division when they set out this afternoon," Chester added.

"Absolutely not!" the nurse's eyes flew wide open. "That is even more out of the question that your request for yourself! I'm sorry, but both of you men will remain here!"

"What seems to be the commotion?" Samuel Chambers said, walking over to the area from which he had heard the nurse's voice grow increasingly louder.

"Mister Morrison seems to feel that he is well enough to join the afternoon ceremonies at the stone wall; Mister Tomlinson as well," the nurse indignantly informed Doctor Chambers. "I told them in no uncertain terms that was an impossibility!"

"Thank you, nurse. I will handle this matter. Would you be so kind as to assist Nurse Sterling in the adjoining ward?"

"Of course, doctor," the nurse replied, thankful to be relieved from this particular disagreement.

After the nurse had exited through the doorway, Samuel turned to Chester Morrison.

"How are you feeling at this moment, Mister Morrison?" he asked.

"I feel fine," came the answer.

Samuel wasn't one for imprecise generalities.

"In particular, how does your right arm feel?"

Chester paused for a moment, wondering exactly how he should reply.

"It is painful," he finally admitted. "There is a persistent dull ache across the entire area and periodically I feel sharp, shooting pains."

Taking notice of the look of contemplation on Samuel's face, Chester added:

"But other than my upper right arm, I feel perfectly fine."

Samuel reached for the nurse's chart hanging from the bottom of Samuel's hospital bed, and scanned the most recent writings from less than half an hour ago. All of Chester Morrison's vital signs seemed in order. Still...

"I must say, Mister Morrison, that I would be remiss as a physician if I released you from the hospital at this moment. While it is true that you are out of immediate danger, the most prudent course of action is to maintain observation for at least the rest of this day and night."

"Doctor Chambers," Chester said quietly, "I do appreciate your obligations as a physician. I must say, though, that this is a very special circumstance. I shall never again have the opportunity to join my comrades to commemorate what we endured that day, and to honor those who were not as fortunate as I to come through unharmed. I know that as a medical man you have a different perspective, and I beg of you not to share this sentiment with my son Jonathan, but if I were to fall this very afternoon while standing at the stone wall amidst this reenactment and commemoration, I would leave this world in peace, without any regrets for having participated."

Doctor Chambers sighed. The Philadelphia man's request presented a significant quandary for Samuel. The man's well-being and very life were in Samuel's hands, for one thing. For another, the death toll at this encampment had been extraordinarily, miraculously low thus far. Quite possibly Chester Morrison might have been added last night to the roster of veterans who had passed if the knife wound had been a thrust to the chest rather than a slice of the old man's bicep. If Samuel acquiesced to Chester's request, was he tempting fate by putting Chester in a position where might be vulnerable and wind up succumbing anyway?

Still, the old man's heartfelt request was one Samuel couldn't entirely ignore. After fifty years, and in the twilight of his own life, shouldn't a man have the right to make such a decision for himself and control his own destiny?

*   *   *

Just before 1:00 that afternoon, the nurse who had fielded and then immediately denied Chester Morrison's request for discharge reentered that ward for the first time since Samuel had sent her in another direction. She halted abruptly when she gazed upon the empty hospital bed that had most recently been occupied by Chester Morrison.

She had barely recovered from that shock when she realized that Ned Tomlinson's bed was likewise unoccupied.

Chapter 38

2:15 P.M.

Many of the more than twelve thousand men who began their march into history fifty years – and fifteen minutes – ago never made it past the Emmitsburg Road on that long-ago afternoon, due to Yankee artillery and rifle fire. Today, most of the one hundred and twenty survivors of Pickett's Division participating in this commemoration ceremony would begin their advance at Emmitsburg Road, slowly marching towards the stone wall at The Angle.

Some of the Confederates, though, would instead await their comrades approximately one hundred feet on the Confederate side of the stone wall, at which point they would form their ranks and march as one to meet their Yankee counterparts. The handful of men who would be making the abbreviated march were men of very advanced years and ill health, or other men who had lost a leg and required crutches to walk.

Men such as Ned Tomlinson.

The Rebs would march under the watchful eye of thousands of other veterans and spectators, and awaiting them underneath the scorching afternoon sun would be one hundred and eighty survivors of the Philadelphia Brigade. Among those men was Chester Morrison. Like most of his comrades on his side of the stone wall, he gazed across at the dozen or so Johnny Rebs only slightly more than thirty yards away. If this were fifty years ago, he couldn't help but thinking, they wouldn't be just standing there in the tall grass that came almost to their waists, half of them looking back at their Confederate comrades slowly approaching their position, the other half gazing in the other direction at their former enemies. Instead, those Confederates would be shrieking their blood-curdling Rebel Yell as they relentlessly pressed on towards The Angle. Rifles would be firing; sabers would be brandished; men would be falling on both sides...

Chester shook the unwelcome images from his head. Today was July the third of 1913, not that same date in long-ago 1863. No matter what had been occurring fifty years ago this very minute, those events were in the past forever. These once formidable enemies, bravely rushing forward into the face of Yankee fire, were now just more tired old men, the same as Chester himself.

Chester caught the eye of the Virginian Tomlinson. The man had been so insistent that he be discharged from the field hospital to be able to participate in this ceremony! Even though he was not making the march from the Emmitsburg Road and instead was a mere one hundred feet away, Chester still felt that this reenactment might indeed turn out to be the man's final act on this earth. Samuel Chambers had been far more reticent about discharging Tomlinson than he had Chester, but in the end when Chester joined the Virginian in pleading the man's case, Samuel had simply surrendered.

Ned Tomlinson was, in fact, entertaining very similar thoughts to those of the Yankee Morrison. Ned was not a gambling man – his Mabel was a church-going woman and in her mind gambling was a sin against The Lord – but if he were forced to lay a bet as to whether he survived this afternoon's ceremony, he would be hard-pressed to choose which outcome he favored with his wager.

Still, if God deemed that he would fall here a second time and this one would be for all eternity, Ned Tomlinson would depart this earth at peace with his decision.

*   *   *

"Here they come!" Seamus McAteer was the one whose cry caused the heads of those standing near him to pivot down towards the Emmitsburg Road. Indeed, more than one hundred Rebels – some wearing their old uniforms, others wearing their best suits – were slowly making their way through the tall grass. Many of them were waving their service caps, straw hats, or fedoras – whatever they happened to be wearing – back and forth in greeting to fellow Rebels waiting near the stone wall; Yankees on the other side of the wall; and spectators alike, while others kept their hats firmly placed on their heads. Still others carried their head coverings at their sides as they marched along.

"Oh my Lord!" Philip Roberdeau heard himself mutter. Philip's Louisiana Tigers had seen action mostly on the second day at Gettysburg, and while he eventually became aware of Pickett's Charge and its terrible outcome during the sullen march south from Pennsylvania, for fifty years the specter of that bloody march had been an abstract one to Philip. Now, even though the reenactment was being undertaken by a mere handful of old men, Philip Roberdeau was helpless against his mind conjuring up the entire panorama of the actual event itself; thus his reaction.

"We were riding on the other side of the Union lines," Angus Findlay said to nobody in particular. His thoughts had likewise traversed time and he could almost swear that he was astride his horse at this very minute, galloping back and forth across the field with communiqués among J.E.B. Stuart, Wade Hampton, Fitzhugh Lee, and others as they clashed with Custer's cavalrymen. All of those men were here this very moment gazing with intense interest upon this event; of that Angus Findlay was certain, even though of course none of those men was alive in this year of 1913.

Johnny Sullivan looked over at his brother, who was standing between Johnny and Angus Findlay. Edgar was keenly watching the Rebel advance, circa 1913, and not a scowl was anywhere to be seen upon the older Sullivan's face. At that moment Edgar happened to look across Angus and caught the eye of his brother.

"Never seen nothin' like it," Edgar said, then clarified:

"I mean this here march; today. A bunch of old Johnny Rebs makin' their way through the tall grass…"

Edgar abruptly stopped speaking, then after a moment's pause looked away from his brother up towards the stone wall, where the Philadelphia Brigade men stood and waited.

"Look at them too," Edgar said as he turned back towards Johnny. "I wonder how many of them are thinkin' that if this were fifty years ago they would be reloading as fast as lightnin' and shooting down on those Rebs. But now, they're just standing there and waiting…"

This time his voice trailed off as he left his sentence unfinished, but Johnny Sullivan didn't need to hear a conclusion to either of Edgar's observations. He could read his brother's thoughts as clearly as if they were spelled out on a large telegram pasted to Edgar's forehead. The elder Sullivan felt cheated in a way that he was unable to participate in this magnificent event and instead was relegated to being a bystander. Nearly every one of those three hundred men, Yankee and Rebel alike, suffered the same pains and ailments – or worse – that had colored

Edgar Sullivan's mood in recent years and (with the exception of one day) his time here at the Jubilee. Yet whether marching or standing, those men were right this very moment stoically recreating that seminal event of fifty years ago, leaving behind their complaints for a little while at least. Edgar was in awe of their collective resilience as they remembered the past and honored – sanctified – today's survivors as well as the memory of so many dead from both sides who had taken part in Pickett's Charge.

*   *   *

The Confederates marching the distance from the Emmitsburg Road met up with their waiting comrades one hundred yards distant from the stone wall, but then a curious event occurred. The occasion called for the Pickett's Division men to halt at that point, form their ranks, and then proceed to precisely march en masse towards the stone wall at Bloody Angle where formal greetings, speeches, exchanges of flags, and other ceremonial events would take place.

Instead, the instant that those marching the full distance joined up with the remainder of the surviving Rebels, they began moving at the double-quick – or as close to the double-quick as any individual man's age and condition would allow – towards the stone wall and the awaiting Philadelphia Brigade veterans. Many of the Confederates were now indeed shrieking the Rebel Yell as they ran. Spectators gasped at this sight, and newspapermen from United Press and papers all around the country quickly began scribbling what they were witnessing. On the other side of the stone wall, more than a few Yankees were taken aback by the sight of the rushing Johnny Rebs, yet every Union man stood his ground and watched intently.

The one hundred feet distance was quickly covered and the first two Confederates who reached the wall did so with the broadest grins on their faces as they extended their right arms towards their former enemies on the other side. Two men from Chester Morrison's 69th Pennsylvania were the first to react to the Pickett Division men, and they responded by likewise reaching across the stone wall to clasp an oncoming hand.

But that wasn't enough for the Pickett's Division men, nor would it be satisfactory for the Philadelphia Brigade men. One of the Confederates awkwardly leaned forward over the wall, immediately striking memories in more than a few of the Philadelphia Brigade survivors and the veterans among the spectators of the brief breach of the stone wall by General Armistead's men…perhaps fifty years ago this very minute! Some could swear that they could actually see a specter of the Confederate general Armistead, his hat planted on top of his raised sword, present on this earth again and once more rallying and leading his men at the double-quick as South collided with North at Bloody Angle.

Another Confederate leaned across the wall in an attempt to embrace one of the Yankees, and at that point most of the Union men abandoned the their scripted actions just as their Southern counterparts had. Those Philadelphia Brigade men nimble enough to climb over the stone wall at that very spot did just that, while others hurried to one side or the other, looking for a spot low enough for them to likewise cross over and come face to face with their former enemies.

A bustle of back-slapping and hugs commenced, with cries of glee intermixed with sobbing from many of the men from both sides. They wept for their lost comrades; whether on this field fifty years earlier, or at some other point during the Battle of Gettysburg, or at a different time during the war; or for that matter in the years since the end of the war. Tears flowed in memory of those who had not been granted the days of their lives to be here at this moment. They wept for survivors as well; those who had struggled with the mental and physical scars of war all these years, haunted by what they had witnessed and in many cases, what they had been forced to do in battle.

And they wept for themselves; for their lost youth and their own agonies, and what might have turned out so very differently in their own lives if it hadn't been for that terrible war.

*   *   *

"Hello again, Yank," Ned Tomlinson wheezed as Chester Morrison approached him. Even the hundred feet of walking had taken a great deal out of Ned Tomlinson; with his single leg he had done his best to keep up with his comrades marching at the double-quick, but Ned and several others had quickly fallen behind the majority of their fellow rebels.

"Are you alright, Mister Tomlinson?" Chester asked, his voice unable to mask his great concern for Ned's welfare.

Ned Tomlinson paused for a moment before answering, doing so at least in part to catch his breath.

"Well, I didn't lose a leg this time," he said, adding: "And I made it a lot farther than I did back in '63."

"That you did," Chester acknowledged, still concerned about the Norfolk man's health despite Ned's attempt at levity…if indeed that's what it was, given that Tomlinson made no attempt to smile.

"Would you like me to summon Doctor Chambers to examine you?" Chester said, his eyes quickly scanning the crowd of spectators to where he had noticed Samuel standing earlier next to Louisa Sterling.

Tomlinson shook his head.

"Not now," he replied. "I'm just winded, I believe. If Doctor Chambers comes over I'm certain he will require me to remove myself from the ranks and I will be unable to continue participating."

Chester nodded.

"I understand," he answered, still wrestling with whether or not Mister Tomlinson's very life was once again in peril as it had been when Mister McAteer and Mister Roberdeau had helped rescue him. Finally, Chester decided to let things be; the Virginian had made it clear that if the specter of Death himself appeared to summon the Norfolk man on this day and from this spot, Ned would quietly accede without complaint.

"I would like to congratulate you, then," Chester said, "on arriving at the stone wall with your comrades." He reached across to give Ned Tomlinson a gentle slap on the back with his uninjured left arm, but instead the Virginian leaned forward, initially balancing on his crutch but then dropping the crutch and falling into Chester, his arms extending as he did. At first Chester thought that the man had just abruptly died at that very moment in his arms, but then he heard Ned Tomlinson begin to sob as he too, like so many former comrades and former enemies alike, wept for all that had been lost as a result of that wretched yet glorious event that had been unfolding fifty years earlier.

*   *   *

Eventually the Confederate and Union ranks were reformed on their respective sides of the stone wall, and the unexpectedly delayed scripted ceremonies commenced. Photographers recorded a dozen or so of the men in gray standing rigidly at attention on one side of the wall as representatives for their comrades, each one reaching across the wall to clasp hands with a likewise precisely standing man in blue who correspondingly represented the remainder of the Philadelphia Brigade survivors formed here today. Chester Morrison was one of those men in blue in the photographs – though like several others, his uniform was in fact a dark business suit with his Union Army hat on top of his head – and because of his injured right arm, his image was captured with Chester using his left hand to clasp the right one of the man in gray directly across from him: Ned Tomlinson.

Congressman Hampton Moore of Philadelphia – who, as it happens, was a close friend of Chester Morrison's – then climbed on top of the stone wall with Yankees to one side and Rebels to the other and proceeded to read the speech he had labored over for more than a month now. Spectators strained to hear the congressman's speech – a difficult endeavor given the outdoor venue – yet those close enough to the stone wall heard Moore proclaim:

"...And while you have come from the South and the North bearing the tattered colors that once distinguished you as enemies, wearing the Blue and the Gray as you gallantly wore them through the tumult of battle, you meet again here at the Bloody Angle, the very zenith of the mighty current of the war, not as furious, fighting champions of State or Section, but as messengers of peace; as men and brothers…"

The congressman continued his exultations of the men from both sides and their respective causes, and then proclaimed:

"Fifty years ago to this very hour it was the duty of Pennsylvania, of the Philadelphia Brigade, to resist at this stone wall the highest tide of Lee's invasion, the memorable charge of the dashing Pickett. It was the most terrific hand-to-hand encounter of the war, a titanic test of human courage. Unionist or Confederate, the honor of this day rests with those who stood on either side, rests with those who fought and passed unscathed, with those who carry yet the wounds they then sustained, with the memory of those, your comrades, who sacrificed their lives upon this field."

The congressman continued on with the many additional paragraphs of his speech – as congressmen will inevitably do – as quiet weeping began once again among the survivors on both sides of the wall.

Chapter 39

8:30 P.M.

"Mother?"

The second utterance of "Mother" snapped Louisa Sterling back to the present moment. Her thoughts had partially been travelling through time, back to happier birthdays celebrated alongside Terrence. But her thoughts had also been partially in the present day…just not the present location, nor the reality of the moment. Louisa had been in town, at the Hotel Gettysburg – now fully back to normalcy after yesterday's melee – and commemorating her thirtieth birthday alone with Samuel Chambers. They were sharing a delectable feast; one far more elegant than the staple mid-day meal and supper of each of the past few days at the encampment grounds, and almost always within the field hospital. All pretenses and reservations had been set aside, and Louisa was captivated by the conjured overtures of interest and affection coming forth from Samuel as their eyes locked…

Louisa willed herself back to the present moment; to reality rather than fantasy.

"Yes, Randall?"

"Mother," the boy said again, hesitating just a touch this time to indicate that he was about to ask his mother for permission to do something that ordinarily she wouldn't approve, "may I watch the fireworks with the Boy Scouts? Several of the Scouts have asked me if I would join them to watch the fireworks, and I really would like to watch the fireworks with them…"

Randall continued repeating his request in various forms for another thirty seconds or so until he apparently ran out of breath. Louisa then replied:

"Of course you may," she answered. "But the moment the fireworks are over I want you to meet me back right on this very spot. Is that understood?"

"Yes!" Her son's excitement could in no way be masked. Here was young Randall Sterling, a young boy not even nine years old yet, with permission from his mother to watch the magnificent fireworks exhibition in the company of dozens of older Boy Scouts as if he were just another one of their group! The fireworks were expected to last nearly two full hours, and what a glorious two hours they would now be!

Randall ran off to share the good news with two slightly older Boy Scouts standing about twenty yards away. Louisa smiled sadly at the sight. On the one hand, she was thrilled that her son was having the time of his life at this Jubilee, and for the first time since poor Terrence had passed the boy seemed genuinely happy. On the other hand, though, Randall's departure meant that she was destined to watch the fireworks exhibition alone…if she even chose to watch it. Now, Louisa thought about perhaps waiting until the expected 9:00 start time and observing the first five or ten minutes of the show, and then heading home. But then she remembered that she had just directed Randall to meet her on this very spot upon the conclusion of the show, which meant that walking home was not an option for Louisa. Perhaps she should head over to the field hospital after the beginning of the fireworks, see if anybody needed any assistance, and then return here later.

Louisa was still wrestling with what to do when she heard his voice, as if summoned by her thinking about the field hospital.

"Nurse Sterling?"

Louisa looked up at the sound of her name – her formal, professional name – and was helpless against the warm smile that came to her face.

"Doctor Chambers," she replied, her voice as sweet as if she were again a young Vassar girl and one of those long-ago Yalies with whom she was infatuated had suddenly appeared to express his undying love for Louisa.

"Where is your son Randall?" Samuel asked.

"He has gone to join his Boy Scout friends to watch the fireworks exhibition," Louisa answered. She made no attempt to hide her mixed feelings about this turn of events.

"In that case," Samuel said without a moment's hesitation, "may I join you to watch the fireworks? Or are you expecting other company, perhaps?"

"No!" Louisa blurted out, a thousand thoughts racing through her head even as that single syllable burst forth. Then, suddenly realizing that her "no" could have been the answer to *either* Samuel's first question or his second, she quickly added before Samuel could react:

"I mean, no I am not expecting any other company; and yes, I would appreciate you joining me to watch the exhibition."

Just as with Louisa, a myriad of thoughts had raced through Samuel's mind at the sound of that single "No!" utterance. To his credit, Samuel had initially presumed that Louisa had been answering his second question but before she clarified her response his thoughts had shifted to perhaps she had indeed blurted out that she was declining his self-invitation to join her. Instantly relieved as Louisa cleared up any confusions, Samuel nodded.

"Then may I sit?" he inquired.

"Of course," Louisa said, scooting over slightly to her right to make room for Samuel on the small picnic blanket she had brought with her and laid out on the grass in the middle of the field. Fifty years ago at this very moment, the three days of vicious, deadly battle at Gettysburg was now concluded but the spot on which Louisa and Samuel sat – approximately halfway between Seminary Ridge and Cemetery Ridge – had no doubt been littered with dead and wounded.

The picnic blanket was actually on the smallish side, but that was because it had originally been meant for Louisa and Randall, with just enough room for a slightly built woman and an eight-year old boy. Samuel, well aware of Louisa's sensitivities about this day and not wanting to appear as if he were a man without proper graces, hugged the left side of the blanket and actually was sitting partially on the grass to allow enough space between their two bodies.

Samuel and Louisa spent the next couple minutes catching up on hospital matters but the discussion quickly shifted to the Pickett's Charge reenactment each had attended earlier this afternoon. Doctor and nurse alike had kept a close eye on both Ned Tomlinson and Chester Morrison throughout the entire ceremony, and there was a moment when the two men came together in front of the stone wall that both Samuel and Louisa were certain that they would need to rush forward to aid Mister Tomlinson. Yet the Norfolk man had proved more resilient than either of them could have imagined, and while he was winded and spent – and indeed, at this very moment, was again back in the field hospital, resting – he had made it through the entire ceremony and was in relatively good health, all things considered. Hopefully he would be discharged in the early morning hours to be able to hear President Wilson speak, and then would soon be on his way home to Norfolk.

A single tremendous detonation exploded through the nighttime Gettysburg sky, but no other sound or sight followed.

"The signal gun," Samuel explained, noticing the puzzled look on Louisa's face when she didn't see any fireworks immediately follow the cannon shot. Samuel had learned from Pennsylvania's Doctor Dixon a few hours earlier how the fireworks display would occur. The signal gun was planned for precisely 8:45, and with military precision it occurred nearly to the second. Following fifteen minutes of last-minute preparation, a series of dynamite guns and mortars – weapons that no doubt would cause more than a few veterans in attendance to break out in shivers – would launch their salvos at 9:00, after which nearly two hours of glorious fireworks would take place.

Samuel quickly explained this sequencing to Louisa, who seemed satisfied with the doctor's explanation. But with fifteen more minutes until 9:00, and with hospital matters and the Pickett's Charge reenactment and Mister Tomlinson's condition having already been covered, what was left for the two of them to discuss until the fireworks began?

"Louisa," Samuel suddenly said, willing his eyes to meet hers even though every instinct in his body told him to avert his gaze.

Struck by the rare usage of her first name, Louisa paused for a long moment before responding. She almost replied "Yes, doctor?" before catching herself; she was all but certain that such formalities, so necessary in the field hospital or yesterday amidst the chaos at the Hotel Gettysburg, would be most unwelcome at this very moment.

"Yes?"

Samuel seemed to have changed what he was going to say or ask on the spot; or he was incredibly nervous about what his words would be, Louisa wasn't sure which.

"How do you feel at this moment about…"

His voice trailed off.

"My birthday?" Louisa decided to finish his question…at least in part.

"Yes," Samuel replied, but he seemed to want to continue the question with words that were difficult to express. So Louisa decided to do so for him.

"And the fact that my husband is no longer alive to celebrate this occasion with me?"

Samuel was struck speechless by Louisa's directness, and he found himself stammering.

"Uh…yes…I was wondering…uh…"

Louisa smiled softly, sadly at Samuel.

"I mentioned this morning in the field hospital that I was feeling much better than I had been yesterday. I miss Terrence; I hope you don't mind me saying that…"

"I don't," Samuel interrupted.

"I understand completely," he added.

Louisa nodded.

"I miss Terrence," she repeated, "and I especially miss him today."

She contemplated her next words carefully before speaking.

"However, even though I feel that in some ways his spirit is with me at the moment and always will be, I do not believe that his intention is that I should remain saddened and lonely…"

Louisa's voice trailed off. Earlier, in her thoughts, the words she wanted to speak to Samuel Chambers had seemed so natural. She wanted to indicate that it was acceptable for Samuel to begin courting her…if indeed he desired to do so, which Louisa was all but certain he did.

But now, sitting side by side with this man, she couldn't bring herself to utter those words. She was a woman of thirty years of age! She was no longer a young Vassar girl not yet turned twenty, flitting among the directed affections of Yalies and West Pointers, coyly waiting for so many of those young men, one after another, to express their attractions to young Louisa. Why was Louisa unable to just put a simple, straightforward sentiment into words?

Suddenly Louisa noticed a darkened, rectangular shape to the other side of Samuel.

"What is that shape over there?" she indicated, grateful for the opportunity to ease away from her futile efforts to express what she felt.

Samuel looked briefly in the direction that Louisa had indicated and then back at her.

"I brought a picnic basket in case you might be hungry while watching the fireworks," he answered, smiling lightly as he did. Samuel turned back towards the basket and after shifting a bit more to his left to make additional room between himself and Louisa, he began unpacking boiled eggs, roast turkey and bread, cherry pie – and a covered jar of iced lemonade – and placing the food onto the blanket.

"That's very kind of you, Samuel," Louisa smiled as she watched the bounty take shape, item by item, in front of her. "I very much enjoy picnics."

Samuel hesitated briefly before responding.

"Then I hope this is the first one of many that we shall enjoy together," he said just as the first boom from the dynamite guns shattered the stillness of the night, soon followed by the glorious fireworks exhibition above Little Round Top that lit up the nighttime Gettysburg sky.

July 4, 1913
National Day

"But the hardship endured has not been in vain. Of the spirit shown at the first Gettysburg by both sides the whole nation feels a pride mixed with a regret over the fearful division of the country that was the occasion of battle. For the spirit shown on both sides at the second Gettysburg there can only be unmixed rejoicing."

- *The Indianapolis News,* July 4, 1913

Chapter 40

11:00 A.M.

Precisely at eleven o'clock, as scheduled, the special Western Maryland train carrying the President of the United States arrived at the Gettysburg train depot. Governor John K. Tener, Colonel James Schoonmaker, and several other dignitaries were on the platform to greet the train…as were as a number of Pennsylvania state policemen temporarily assigned to see to the President's well-being.

"Mister President," Governor Tener said as President Wilson stepped off of the train car's steps onto the depot's platform.

"John; it is good to see you again," Wilson replied, a broad smile already on his face as he extended his right hand towards Tener, flash bulbs popping all around the two men. Quite possibly the pleasantries on the part of the President were for show; displayed mostly for the newspapermen and photographers who had already closely surrounded the two men. Perhaps once the two men were in one of the three motor cars that would take the President's party and those greeting them over to the encampment grounds, the smile would disappear and aloofness would overtake the atmosphere inside the vehicle. But for now, the pictures would record – and the newspaper reports would indicate – that the former

Governor of New Jersey was warmly greeted by his former colleague amidst pleasantries and reminisces.

A motorcade of three automobiles swiftly proceeded to the encampment grounds. The state police had cleared the route of all traffic, but hundreds of people lined the borough's main road, waving to the President in his motor car as he passed through Gettysburg. The vehicles soon arrived at the encampment grounds, and the President strolled among many of the veterans on his way to the Great Tent, the foot procession led by a cadre of state police and Army men.

Wilson was almost to the Great Tent when he passed through a cluster of old men wearing Confederate gray. He couldn't help himself.

"Are there any Virginia men among you here?" he shouted out, paying homage to the state of his birth.

A great roar went up among the men in gray; within that particular group, more than half of the men were indeed from the President's home state. Wilson smiled broadly as he scanned the cheering faces, then decided to move among the men, shake hands, and exchange a word or two. He had just been elected President a mere eight months earlier and inaugurated even more recently, but it wasn't too early to begin campaigning for 1916 and to remind Virginians that even though Woodrow Wilson was more associated with New Jersey these days, he was originally one of them.

"What is your name, sir?" Wilson asked one man after another as he slowly made his way towards the Great Tent. None of the names he received in response meant anything to him, though he made sure to recite each man's name back to him to convey familiarity: "I am most glad you have come here for this occasion, Mister Harrison" or

"Mister Allbaugh, I am honored to count you among my fellow Virginians."

"What is your name, sir?" the President, now only steps away from the entrance to the Great Tent, repeated for perhaps the thirtieth time.

"Angus Findlay," came the reply. Wilson was just about to begin yet another perfunctory response when he paused. The name sounded familiar.

"Mister Findlay, were you by some chance a politician in our state?"

"I was," Angus Findlay replied after a brief hesitation.

"During Reconstruction," he added. The word "Reconstruction" no longer carried the revulsion it once did; thus none of the Virginians standing close enough to Mister Findlay to hear his reply recoiled at the word, as they once might have done.

"I remember," Wilson nodded. "My family had moved to South Carolina where my father was a professor at the Columbia Theological Seminary, and I recall him discussing several times that of all the states in the Confederacy, our home state of Virginia had been the single one to keep the scalawags and carpetbaggers mostly at bay during Reconstruction. And I also recall him mentioning you by name as one of the men who stood fast to accomplish that deed."

Angus was struck by the President of the United States actually having some familiarity with his own long-ago deeds.

"Well, it was a long time ago," Angus replied.

"Indeed it was," Wilson nodded. "Well, Mister Findlay, I am most honored to count you as among my fellow Virginians."

With those words, the President turned away from the ranks of the Confederate veterans towards the opening into the Great Tent. At that moment a loud explosion shook the sky, courtesy of twenty-one United States Army field artillery cannons. Even the President startled for a second at the sound before continuing his strides into the Great Tent.

He quickly mounted the stage and took his seat – for only a few seconds, though – as Governor Tener declared:

"Veterans of the Blue and Veterans of the Gray, I have the honor to present the President of the United States."

With that one-sentence introduction, John K. Tener yielded to Woodrow Wilson for the first address by any President of the United States since Abraham Lincoln.

"Friends and fellow citizens," Wilson began, "I need not tell you what the Battle of Gettysburg meant. These gallant men in Blue and Gray sit all about us here. Many of them met upon this ground in grim and deadly struggle. Upon these famous fields and hillsides their comrades died about them."

Wilson proceeded to weave his way through a sometimes meandering monologue that sometimes spoke of that long-ago war and the men who had fought it, and at other points in his speech he addressed present day America; while at still other times, Wilson spoke of past and future together as one continuum.

"These venerable men crowding here to this famous field have set us a great example of devotion and utter sacrifice," the President intoned. "They were willing to die that the people might live. But their task is done. Their day is turned into evening. They look to us to perfect what they established. Their work is handed unto us, to be done in another way but not in another spirit. Our day is not over; it is upon us in full tide."

In the audience Angus Findlay – his mind still partly on the curious coincidence outside the Great Tent of President Wilson recognizing his name – sat between his fellow Virginian Ned Tomlinson on one side and the Pennsylvanian Chester Morrison on the other. Morrison's son Jonathan was on Chester's other side, and within that cluster of men inside the Great Tent on Independence Day, 1913 could be found Edgar and Johnny Sullivan; Devin and Seamus McAteer; Philip Roberdeau; and the Carlisle man Lawrence Armstrong.

To a man – even Jonathan Morrison – tears began to well and sobs were quietly choked back – as the President uttered these words near the end of his speech:

"Whom do I command? The ghostly hosts who fought upon these battlefields long ago and are gone? These gallant gentlemen stricken in years whose fighting days are over, their glory won?"

*   *   *

As precisely as Woodrow Wilson arrived in Gettysburg at 11:00 on the morning of this Independence Day, so too would he depart Gettysburg exactly at noon, being on the grounds of the borough of Gettysburg and the encampment site for exactly one hour. Even more Army artillery guns than had marked his arrival – forty-eight this time, one for each state of the Union including the recently admitted New Mexico and Arizona territories – launched their ammunition to mark the President's departure from the encampment grounds.

"Wonderful speech, Mister President," Governor Tener said to Wilson when the two men entered one of the motor cars that would comprise the motorcade back to the Gettysburg train depot with a planned arrival at the station a quarter hour before noon.

The truth was that John K. Tener had thought the President's speech to be an uneven one, especially when compared to the addresses of that first magnificent day of the Jubilee, as well as those of the second day. Wilson had sprinkled a few poignant gems amidst his words – particularly when he spoke several times of the gallantry of the old veterans gathered before him and that of their departed comrades – but a healthy portion of the President's speech seemed to meander through Wilson's own puzzlements about the fortunes and directions of the nation he now led. Tener had actually felt some discomfort when the President had uttered a self-deprecating declaration that "I have been chosen the leader of the Nation. I cannot justify the choice by any qualities of my own, but so it has come about and here I stand." Fortunately for the President, his superb "Whom do I command…" segment immediately followed, and the President's self-effacing remarks were quickly forgotten by almost everyone present.

Indeed, the following day the *Baltimore American* took Wilson to task, indicating in that paper's editorial that "President Wilson appears to have ignored the challenge sent him by the immortal speech of Lincoln upon the field of Gettysburg. Despite the predictions that he would use the occasion to produce a masterpiece that would gem literature he was content to address his audience in the words of simple and obvious intent, being much more concerned to lay emphasis upon the general good will of the Nation and its magnificent unity than to lift up new standards of service, to set forth slogans of conquest, to phrase the philosophies of the present in aphorisms of brilliance."

For the moment, however, President Woodrow Wilson could only accept Governor Tener's congratulatory words on their face value.

"Thank you, John," Wilson replied to the Governor's overture, even as Tener was still comparing Wilson's speech as a whole with those of Bennett Young, that Sergeant Scarborough of North Carolina – even Tener's nemesis, Secretary of War Garrison – and so many others.

And – John K. Tener couldn't help himself – he contrasted the President's speech with the Governor's own address three days earlier; and being as unbiased and true in spirit as possible, he thought his own words as a whole to have been more in keeping with the spirit of the occasion than those of his former neighboring Governor.

The President's railroad car was in the process of being reattached to a different train, this one headed for Wilson's summer home in New Hampshire, when the automobile arrived at the train depot. The Jubilee's closing ceremonies were to follow precisely at noon as soon as Governor Tener returned to the encampment grounds, so he proceeded to rapidly take his leave from the President. Wilson seemed to show no concern for Governor Tener's presence – or lack thereof – and proceeded to busy himself for his final fifteen minutes at Gettysburg with a small stack of papers removed from his railroad car by an aide and handed to the President on the platform for review.

During the short drive back to the encampment grounds, Governor Tener found himself overcome by emotion. It was all almost over! More than four years of planning that had begun with Tener's predecessor, Governor Stuart, had come to fruition to bring forth the most glorious, most solemn celebration of healing anyone could have imagined. More than fifty thousand blue and gray veterans had made the pilgrimage to this hallowed ground. Despite the terrible and oppressive temperatures, almost every single one of those men had come through unscathed. And now, the hour had arrived; the Great Reunion was nearly concluded!

For the first time during the entire Jubilee, Governor Tener found himself doing what so many of these old veterans and spectators had done at some point during the celebration…many of them more than once.

He quietly wept.

* * *

By the time the motor car had arrived back at the grounds, John K. Tener had composed himself. He had the closing of the encampment to preside over, and the planned ceremonies were solemn enough that Tener needed to be in full control of his emotions to be able to lead the event without breaking down in front of the tens of thousands of veterans still remaining in camp.

The Governor would be at the encampment grounds with many of the dignitaries, but others – including most of the Pennsylvania Commission members – would participate from the Pennsylvania College campus as well as the nearby Seminary. Each delegation's actions would only last for less than ten minutes, so minimal scripting and hardly any rehearsal had been required.

At noon, just as Tener was departing the automobile that had carried him back to the grounds, the church bells of Gettysburg began tolling, and somewhere out of sight at the encampment grounds – though not too distant – a single bugler began to play. The Governor quickly joined the rest of the encampment's closing ceremony delegation and all the men, military and civilian alike, came to attention. Then the colors were slowly lowered by two Army men to half-staff, where they remained as thousands of veterans of that long-ago war likewise came to attention.

Somewhere in the distance a cannon boomed, and then another, and then another. The invisible bombardments, distant enough to be faint of sound, contrasted with those of the previous night that had preceded or accompanied the glorious fireworks exhibit. This afternoon's bombardments were not part of a magnificent celebration; they were instead emblematic of a solemn memorial.

For five full minutes, all present who were able to do so remained silently at attention in homage to Gettysburg's dead; to the war's dead. Periodically another cannon would boom its tribute amidst the silence, adding to the solemnity of the occasion. To no one's surprise, tears were again present on many faces amidst the crowd – and even in the eyes of many of the dignitaries at the encampment grounds and also at the other locations – and few made any effort to suppress their sobs that for five long minutes were the only sounds heard other than the periodic boom of both homage and memory coming forth from one more cannon.

And then, in an instant, the Great Reunion at Gettysburg in the year of 1913 – the occasion that John K. Tener himself had lauded as a ceremony standing unmatched in all recorded time – had slipped into history forever.

*   *   *

"I s'pose we will get goin' now," Johnny Sullivan quietly said. For the moment, he was as gloomy – perhaps even more so – than his older brother had been on so many recent occasions.

Not one to be outdone on the scale of melancholy, Edgar Sullivan responded with a subdued:

"Yeah, I s'pose so."

Johnny's remark hadn't actually been addressed to his brother, but rather to the small crowd of men gathered outside the Pennsylvania delegation tent that had been the home for Chester Morrison and the McAteer cousins. The Sullivan brothers had already gathered up their belongings and were reluctantly saying their goodbyes. Three of the other Arizonans from that state's delegation would be accompanying them on the journey west; two of the others had already departed, and three more would remain for another day or two since the encampment grounds wouldn't formally close until July the sixth.

None of the other men present seemed to want to be the first to acknowledge the initial departures from this ad hoc group that had slowly come together during the Jubilee. To a man, each felt as if by conceding the Sullivans' imminent departure, the magic of this event that had enveloped and rejuvenated so many thousands of old veterans would begin to evaporate and before long they would once again be not honored, valiant surviving warriors but rather tired old men whose best days were long in the past.

Finally Philip Roberdeau broke the awkward silence, stepping forward to embrace Edgar Sullivan first and then Johnny, saying as he reluctantly released the younger Sullivan:

"I am honored to have met both of you and to have shared this occasion in your company. I wish you Godspeed on your journey back to Arizona, and I hope that one day we will have occasion to come together again."

Johnny Sullivan could only manage a sad nod of his head, his eyes downcast, while Edgar Sullivan choked out a single word: "Yeah." The silence now broken, one by one the other men present – Seamus McAteer, Chester Morrison and then his son Jonathan, Ned Tomlinson, Lawrence Armstrong, Angus Findlay, and finally Devin McAteer – said their goodbyes to each of the Sullivan brothers. Somehow, each of the men present – the Sullivans as well as their former comrades and former enemies – managed to avoid tears and sobs as the farewells were said. Perhaps that was because Philip Roberdeau's hopeful words – "I hope that one day we will have occasion to come together again" – had planted in the mind of each man that indeed on some other occasion these veterans of the war might again come together for some sort of commemoration.

Each man present knew, though, that even if such an occasion were to come to fruition, in no way could it possibly come close to the majesty of the just-concluded event.

*　*　*

Next to depart after the Sullivans were Chester Morrison and his son Jonathan. Jonathan said his goodbyes first to the veterans, and then tactfully took his leave...ostensibly to retrieve his Pierce-Arrow but actually to give his father the old man's desired privacy as he said his own farewells.

The past night had been the first in more than a week that had been void of nightmares for Chester Morrison. The railroad man was certain the reason was because of his participation in the Pickett's Charge ceremony the previous day. Haunting memory and also menacing fantasy had been exorcised – perhaps for all time – by standing fast at the stone wall at Bloody Angle and greeting men who fifty years earlier would have done their best to kill Chester had they encountered him at that very place. His curious wound at the Hotel Gettysburg two days earlier aside, the Great Reunion at Gettysburg had been everything Chester hoped it could possibly be. In fact, Chester thought to himself – and not for the first time – that the slash of the knife that turned out to be only a minor wound may have also contributed in some way to Chester's being able to set aside those horrific nightmares. All these years Chester had felt that it was only a small touch of luck that had allowed him to escape both the second and third days' clashes without even a flesh wound, and should there have been a fourth day of the Battle of Gettysburg, he almost certainly wouldn't have come through that next encounter unscathed. Now, though, he had actually engaged in an additional encounter at Gettysburg – albeit in the most peculiar manner one might have imagined – and while he did indeed suffer his fated wound, he had come through the ordeal with surprising little damage to body and actually stronger of soul.

Chester looked at Ned Tomlinson, standing next to Angus Findlay. He felt a kinship of spirit with the tough old survivor from Norfolk who had not only survived his ordeal fifty years ago, but also came through his brush with death at the same location here in the present day. Chester couldn't help but feel that fate had placed him in the lobby of the Hotel Gettysburg at the precise moment to be on the receiving end of that slashing blade; then to be placed in the field hospital bed adjoining Ned Tomlinson's; then to be present when the Norfolk man finally regained consciousness; and then finally to be able to persuade Samuel Chambers that not only should Chester be released in time to participate in Pickett's Charge commemoration, so should Ned Tomlinson. The reenactment of Pickett's Charge had not only been cathartic for the Yankee Morrison, but also for the Confederate Tomlinson.

*   *   *

Lawrence Armstrong's son had come from Carlisle to drive his father the short distance back home, and Armstrong was the next man to depart, soon followed by Angus Findlay and Ned Tomlinson. Mister Armstrong, recalling the discussion several nights earlier of the Battle of Carlisle that had caught Angus Findlay's ear and had served to bring this group together, said to Angus when they said their farewells to each other:

"You are more than welcome to visit Carlisle once again, sir, and this time you will not be required to bombard and set fire to our town upon your departure."

Chuckles were offered by those still present in response to Armstrong's witticism that – one and all agreed – would have been an unthinkable utterance only a week earlier.

Since both Findlay and Tomlinson were traveling into Virginia, they had made arrangements the previous day to travel together as far as Petersburg. At that location they would depart for their respective homes; but until then the two Confederates who had each fallen but had rallied to survive the second engagement at Gettysburg would keep each other company.

Findlay and Tomlinson said their goodbyes to the remaining men. Ned Tomlinson, when it was his turn, dropped his crutch to bear-hug Philip Roberdeau. Nearly a half minute passed before Ned could summon the words:

"I thank you for saving my life, Mister Roberdeau."

Tears coming to his eyes, Philip could only nod as he held the embrace. Another full minute passed before the two men reluctantly broke the embrace, though Philip was cognizant enough to keep his hands on Ned and help maintain one-legged man's standing position, given that Tomlinson's crutch was prone on the ground. Philip continued to shuffle to his right and into the void stepped Devin McAteer, who immediately was on the receiving end of another bear-hug clinch from Ned Tomlinson.

"You too, Yank," Ned said. "I thank you also for saving my life."

Standing ten feet away, listening to the one-legged Norfolk man embrace and express his gratitude to Devin, Seamus McAteer felt an instant twinge of jealousy for the bond those two men shared. That sentiment had surprisingly and unfortunately hallmarked a good portion of Seamus' time at the Jubilee, but this time Seamus was aware enough of the ugly sentiment to immediately will it away. So what if some Virginian who had never previously met Devin might forever be in Seamus' cousin's debt for helping to save his life? The important point was that indeed, Devin had helped Philip Roberdeau save Mister Tomlinson's life, and the fact that the Virginian was standing here today expressing his gratitude was a living testimonial to Devin's good deed.

Eventually Devin and Ned released their embraces upon each other, and Seamus stepped into the void created as Devin eased his way to his right, still clasping Ned as Philip Roberdeau had done a little while earlier. Seamus extended his right hand for a goodbye handshake with this Virginian he barely knew and had personally said little to, but Ned Tomlinson was having none of that. He leaned forward, just as he had with Philip and Devin, tightly embraced Seamus, and said:

"And thank you, Yank, for insistin' that your cousin come to this gatherin'. If you hadn't, I might not be here today because he wouldn't have been around to help our Louisiana friend rescue me. So I thank you as well…"

Ned Tomlinson couldn't resist adding the word one more time.

"…Yank."

* * *

The McAteer cousins had already decided that Independence Day would not be the date of their departure from the encampment grounds. The tents and field kitchens would remain open for another two days (and though nobody knew so at the time, more than a few of the old veterans dawdled for another three days until July the ninth when the grounds were finally vacated by the last of the old men), and both Devin and Seamus had already decided to remain…as did Philip Roberdeau.

Devin, upon hearing from Philip that the Louisianan was in no particular hurry to board a train back to New Orleans, asked Seamus if he would be agreeable to Philip remaining in their company for another few days. To Devin's pleasant surprise, Seamus seemed to brighten at the prospect; almost as if being given another couple of days to make up for his earlier moodiness was just the thing to cleanse his conscience. And so for the next two days, the McAteer cousins and Philip Roberdeau shared meals, exchanged stories (many of them retold for the third or fourth time by now), and continued to cement the bonds of healing between the remnants of the Civil War-era United States and their former enemies in the Confederacy.

And when the sixth day of July had almost passed, as the three men prepared to depart, Seamus abruptly suggested to his cousin that perhaps Devin would like to first accompany Seamus to Pittston for a brief spell to continue their own personal reunion. Helen would be most pleased to see her husband's cousin for the first time in a long while. Devin was just about to accept Seamus' offer – pending Noreen McAteer's permission for her husband Devin to delay his homecoming, of course – when to Devin's surprise, Seamus turned to Philip Roberdeau and asked:

"If you are not in a hurry to return to New Orleans, Mister Roberdeau, perhaps you would also like to travel north with us and visit my humble home, and enjoy your time in Pennsylvania for a short while longer."

Philip looked over at Devin, who seemed both struck by and grateful for the offer his cousin had just extended, before looking back at Seamus McAteer and nodding.

*   *   *

The field hospitals formally closed on July the sixth, but many of the doctors and nurses remained behind to treat the final small population of patients until those men were either well enough for discharge or could be transferred to the care of the local Gettysburg hospitals. Of course among the remaining staff were Samuel Chambers and Louisa May Sterling.

Samuel and Louisa shared each meal, every day. They did their best to cross paths dozens of times each day in the field hospital. As the days wound down and the numbers of souls remaining on the grounds dwindled, and as free time became a precious gift that could now be enjoyed, they would leave the field hospital for a stroll around the encampment grounds, or perhaps a lengthier, leisurely walk up to the town of Gettysburg.

On the night of July the fifth, matters at the field hospital quite under control, Louisa agreed to accompany Samuel to supper at the Hotel Gettysburg. Randall was in the care of a neighbor for the evening, so the meal and the occasion could proceed at an unhurried pace.

Samuel appeared on Louisa's front porch at a quarter before eight that evening to call on her. The two had taken their leave from each other several hours earlier to allow Louisa time to go home and bathe, and for Samuel to do likewise in the hallway washroom several doors down from his room at the Pennsylvania college.

The moment that Louisa opened her front door in response to Samuel's knock, he realized that he had never seen this woman wearing anything other than her nurse's uniform. Tonight, though, she was dressed in a cream-colored, lacey dress that was clinched with a silk ribbon of the same color high on her waist. Samuel found himself unable to prevent his eyes from slowly traversing the full length of Louisa's garb, from the sheer material that covered her ankles and shoes to the top portion of the dress that fully concealed her bosom but still left a wonderful vision of her delicate skin uncovered.

My Lord, Samuel thought to himself; she's beautiful!

The meal at the Hotel Gettysburg was delectable. The hotel manager, recognizing Samuel and in gratitude for his service the evening of the stabbing incident, refused any payment from the doctor as he ensured that Samuel and Louisa were attended to by his two finest waiters.

Three hours passed, and by 11:15 that evening Samuel and Louisa were the only guests still dawdling in the dining room. They eventually rose from their table, their meals now at least partially settled, and began the stroll back to Louisa's house. Upon arriving back at her house and then climbing the five stairs up to her front porch, Samuel's mind was on a delicious stolen kiss – thus far, their first and only – that had taken place an hour into the fireworks exhibition two nights earlier, underneath the glorious color-filled sky. He was still contemplating when exactly the proper time would be, in the here and now, to attempt to kiss her once again when Louisa said:

"I'm not quite ready for this wonderful evening to end. If you are not in a hurry to return to the Pennsylvania College, would you like to sit here on the porch for a little while longer and continue talking? I can bring out two glasses of iced lemonade."

Samuel smiled warmly.

"I would like that very much," he said. "I hope you don't find this too forward of a remark, but I would be most happy if this wonderful time with you were to continue forever."

Louisa didn't verbally respond to Samuel's words before entering her house to retrieve the promised refreshments, but the warm, loving smile on her face conveyed to Samuel the exact answer he would have most hoped for.

Epilogue

Present Day

Pittsburgh, Pennsylvania
November 19, 2013
12:00 Noon

The very old man shuffled into the common area of the nursing home. He had a television set in his room, but these days he spent so much of his time by himself in that private room, just thinking or perhaps listening to his programs he could longer see beyond opaque milky images because of his nearly failed eyes. Every so often, on occasions such as this very moment, he was consumed by an overwhelming need to be out among others rather than sequestered.

He was by far the oldest resident of this nursing home in one of the central neighborhoods of Pittsburgh, his adopted city for more than seventy years now, since just after the beginning of the Second World War. He had moved to that industrial city to work in a war plant and do his part for the nation's war effort against Germany and Japan. He had been close to forty years in age then; too old to be drafted by the Army but not too old to volunteer, which indeed he had tried to do back home in Gettysburg. Alas, a variety of physical ailments combined to classify him as 4-F for military service despite the nation being in such desperate straits in those dark days of early '42.

He had worked in two different war plants during those years. The first one had been up on Mount Washington, making army boots and shoes, and then in late '43 he had begun working at an armaments plant over in Wilkinsburg, only three blocks from the nursing home where he now lived and would, he acknowledged, die before too much more time passed. He had lived in this particular nursing home for nearly twenty years now, outlasting not only every one of the residents who had been here when he had first come long ago in 1990 but almost all of the staff of that time as well. Nobody would have expected the man to still be alive in 2013, three months past his 109th birthday…but alive he was!

Three other older men (none lengthier in years than ninety, though) were in the common area, watching one of those cable news broadcasts they had been showing for several decades now. The very old man still missed watching Murrow and Cronkite and Swayze and Huntley on those long-ago nightly network news broadcasts but had resigned himself that those programs and everything surrounding them − his black and white television set warming up; the product commercials that looking back now were so incredibly amateurish; the stature that came with those newsmen and the words they conveyed; all of it − were as much a part of a bygone era as he himself was.

"Did you see this program about the Gettysburg Address?" one of the three residents loudly asked, knowing both that the very old man was now almost as deaf as he was blind and that he was originally from Gettysburg. The very old man could not recall this other man's name; nor, actually, the names of the other two either. Or for the most part, the names of most every other resident in the nursing home. He still had his faculties; he was painfully aware of his surroundings and the events of both the nursing home and what he could glean about the world at large from the television news. He had just lost almost all of his abilities to retain names, but he had learned not to let this little matter bother him.

"What about it?" the very old man asked in return as he reached an open seat on the sofa and eased himself onto the cushions, using his walker for support as he always did these days. Failing vision notwithstanding, he had learned every possible path around this nursing home over the years and had no fear of attempting to lower himself onto what he thought might be a sofa but was in fact nothing but air.

"Today is the one hundred and fiftieth anniversary of the Gettysburg Address," one of the other men chimed in. "November the nineteenth, eighteen hundred and sixty three; that's when Abraham Lincoln himself made that speech. I remember they made us memorize that date back in primary school."

The third man, known by nearly everyone in the nursing home to be quick-witted and somewhat of a jokester, leaned over to elbow the second man as he said:

"Maybe Randall here was actually alive to hear ol' Abe Lincoln himself deliver the Gettysburg Address; you think so?"

The second man chuckled, while the first man nervously looked over at Randall Sterling. Would someone closing in on one hundred and ten years old see the humor in what had just been uttered? The truth was that Randall Sterling hadn't missed the delivery of the Gettysburg Address by all that much; only slightly more than forty years. Or as ol' Abe Lincoln himself might have put it, "two score and one year ago…"

To the first man's relief, Randall Sterling showed no sign of irritation at the "joke." For a brief moment that first man thought that perhaps Mister Sterling had not even heard the utterance due to his nearly failed hearing, but that misconception was quickly corrected when Randall Sterling said:

"No, I'm not quite old enough to have been at Gettysburg to hear Lincoln deliver that speech. But I was there one hundred years ago, back in nineteen hundred and thirteen, when all of those old veterans came to Gettysburg. And on July the second of that year I was in the Great Tent when the son of the doctor who had tended to Lincoln after he was shot spoke the Gettysburg Address to the audience of tens of thousands of those old Rebels and Yankees sitting there that day. I don't remember that feller's name who gave the speech all these years later but I can tell you all those old Confederates and Yanks just sat there listening to that man recite that speech, and many of them were so moved they began weeping."

The other three men all leaned forward at Mister Sterling's words, each one of them to a man surprised by the sudden vigor in Randall's voice that had heretofore been unheard by any of them.

"I was with the Boy Scouts and we were escorting those old soldiers all around the grounds for days. My Lord, it was so blazing hot the first couple of those days! I can still feel the heat and all those old fellers were walking around in their old war uniforms or full suits of clothes, and everyone was so afraid that they would be dropping over like flies…"

The other three old men just sat there listening, enraptured, as Randall Sterling went on for several more minutes about his recollections from a century earlier. The old man may have been closing in on one hundred and ten years of age, and he couldn't recall a person's name these days to save his life, but the clarity and precision of his recollections from just over a century earlier grew sharper with each sentence. None of the other three had ever even heard of the Great Reunion, and each was astonished to learn that more than fifty thousand old Confederate and Union soldiers had come together on the fiftieth anniversary of the Battle of Gettysburg for that most remarkable event.

"They say that one of those old soldiers was one hundred and twelve years old; even older than I am now!" Randall Sterling cackled. "But most of them were in their seventies, I would say."

"My father had been an Army man and died of the typhoid a couple of years earlier," he suddenly said, "and my mother was a nurse right there in Gettysburg. During the Jubilee she met a doctor from Philadelphia and before too long he began courting her and they ended up getting married."

Suddenly Randall Sterling's gauzy eyes still managed to take on a far-away look as if gazing across a century of time; not just at memories of the Great Reunion in July of 1913, but at the memory of his long-departed father who he had barely known; his mother who, after losing her first husband, had devoted her life to raising her young fatherless son; and also the memory of how his mother had been granted a second chance at happiness when she met and then later married Doctor Samuel Chambers.

The very old man had last thought about his mother early this past summer, back on July the third, on what would have been her 130th birthday if she were somehow still alive. Despite his failing memory, Randall Sterling would never forget his mother's birthdate – the same date as the climactic third day of the Battle of Gettysburg, and also the same date as that fireworks exhibit above Little Round Top during the Great Reunion fifty years later –

just as he would never forget the woman herself. Now, though, as he shared his dredged-up memories of the Great Reunion – the occasion on which her mother and Doctor Chambers had met – it almost seemed as if Louisa May Talbot Sterling Chambers were still present in some ethereal manner alongside her only son.

Randall Sterling knew with certainty that before too much more time passed he would be joining his mother – his father and Doctor Chambers as well – in whatever lay beyond this world. For now, though, he was still earthbound. He had lived well past his allotted number of days and was certainly on borrowed time.

"I know you can't see it clearly," one of the other men in the room gently but loudly said to Randall, "but there's a man dressed like Abe Lincoln on the television reciting the Gettysburg Address."

Suddenly the slight murmuring of a man's voice on the television set became clearer and understandable to Randall Sterling, and he knew that one of those other men in the room had graciously turned up the volume on the television set.

"…The brave men, living and dead, who struggled here, have consecrated it, far above our poor power to add or detract…"

With those words that Randall could now hear clearly – or as clearly as someone 109 years old and nearly deaf might hear – his thoughts took flight, instantly traversing some 200 miles of southwestern Pennsylvania villages and farmland and coming to rest in that small borough just north of the Maryland state line. Not unexpectedly, Randall Sterling's thoughts negotiated time as well as space.

In his Mind's Eye, faces Randall hadn't seen in more than a century or even thought of in many decades were now suddenly materializing...faces with stories for which Randall could frustratingly only recall a fragment or two here and there. The railroad man from Philadelphia; the two brothers from Arizona who had once been Union cavalrymen and later Wild West lawmen; another set of brothers – no, cousins, Randall somehow recalled; where were these vivid, long-forgotten memories coming from? – from different parts of Pennsylvania; another old cavalryman, this one a Rebel from Virginia who had ridden during the war with some famous Confederate general whose name Randall could no longer recall; another Virginia man who had lost a leg at Gettysburg and who had taken ill at the Reunion, but who had recovered in time to commemorate that tragic, futile charge named after some other Rebel general whose name Randall couldn't bring to memory; a man from Louisiana who had regaled Randall and several other Boy Scouts one afternoon with his tales of having been a cadet at West Point just before the war began and then his riverboat ride back to the South and the new, burgeoning Confederacy...

These men, and perhaps a dozen others, were suddenly as alive to Randall as if calendar and clock had instantly been turned back one hundred years. No doubt before too much time passed their faces would all fade back into the recesses of Randall Sterling's memory, perhaps never to be recalled again. But for the moment it was the early days of July, 1913, not November of 2013. Those long-ago warriors were the old men, while Randall Sterling was once again a very young boy who hadn't yet celebrated his ninth birthday...a young boy who still terribly missed his father, but who was gladdened to see his mother unexpectedly be granted a second chance at love and happiness with a man who became a wonderful second husband to her and a wonderful second father to Randall.

Alan Simon

Author's Afterword to
Gettysburg, 1913: The Complete Novel of the Great Reunion

Want to learn more about the real-life Great Reunion?
Visit http://gettysburg1913.wordpress.com/

The Idea for the Book

I was working at my "day job" – consulting – in Harrisburg, Pennsylvania long ago in mid-2001 when late one afternoon, my workday concluded, I paid a visit to the National Civil War Museum. I had been a history enthusiast since childhood, visiting historic locations in or near my hometown of Pittsburgh such as Fort Pitt and Fort Ligonier many times over, and our summer family vacations often were to historic locations such as Williamsburg, Jamestown…and Gettysburg.

Doing my best to make it through the museum before they closed, I wandered into a room that featured photographs, film clips, and artifacts from an occasion I had never previously known about: The Great Reunion at Gettysburg that was held in 1913 on the 50th anniversary of the battle.

Unfortunately, the doors to the museum were soon closing, so I was only able to make a quick tour of that particular room that hallmarked that great event as well as another a quarter century later, in 1938. Still, of everything I had viewed during my short visit that afternoon, the idea of old foes coming together at Gettysburg half a century later on such a momentous occasion touched me deeply.

I left the National Civil War Museum that day with the first inklings of an idea for a novel set during that long-ago reunion back in 1913, and a sequel with many of the same characters set 25 years later.

"Extras" – visit alansimonbooks.com for much more about Gettysburg, 1913: The Great Reunion

- Would you like to learn more about the historical background of the Great Reunion…including the many different names used to describe the gathering at Gettysburg in July of 1913?

- John K. Tener, the real-life Governor of Pennsylvania during the Great Reunion, is featured as a character in the novel. Learn more about this accomplished political figure and former businessman who was also a former major league baseball player and, beginning even while he was still Governor, the President of the National League.

- It is true that hundreds of veterans who arrived on June 30th had no place to sleep that night, and that many of them chose to depart that very night so soon after arriving. Learn more about this sad, almost-never-reported aspect of the Great Reunion.

- Was Douglas MacArthur actually a West Point classmate and rival of Ulysses S. Grant's grandson?

- On the subject of (later) famous generals making cameo appearances in Part I, George Patton's attendance at the reunion of Buford's cavalry on June 30th, 1913 (attended in our tale by the Sullivan brothers) not only actually occurred, it was documented in the middle of an article in the July 1st, 1913 evening edition of *The Pittsburgh Press* on Page 4, which is how I came to learn of this historical tidbit when Patton's name jumped out at me:

> "Lieut. George S. Patton, United States Army, was in charge of Troop A, Fifteenth cavalry, commanded by Captain Eltinge, yesterday when they marched with pealing bugles through the town and out by the Emmitsburg rd. to the big assembly tent where Buford cavalry survivors held their reception. Lieut. Patton went to the Olympic games last year, and scored higher than any other foreigner in the modern pentathlon being fourth in the contest, the first three men being Swedes. He is designee of the new cavalry saber, and was for a time an aide to Gen. Leonard Wood, chief of staff, U.S.A."

> (The above excerpt is exactly as was printed, including an apparent error: "designee" instead of "designer.")

> Learn more about George Patton's real-life attendance at the Great Reunion.

- Why were so Medals of Honor for actions during the Civil War awarded during the 1890s…more than a quarter of a century later?

- Did you know that a number of books about The Battle of Gettysburg were written by those who actually fought in the battle, and many are still available in print and eBook form today?

- Did you spot the literary "Easter Egg" in the following paragraph from Chapter 2?

During the War both of the Sullivans had served in General John Buford's famed division in the 8th Regiment Illinois Cavalry; not just at Gettysburg but also earlier at Antietam and Fredericksburg. It had been that Illinois connection that put them into the confidence of the Earps even before they moved down to Tombstone. Up in Prescott in 1878 they began regularly playing cards with Virgil Earp, the town's constable and a veteran of the 83rd Illinois Infantry during the War, and the war veterans from the same home state took a shine to one another. Both Sullivans began assisting Earp with escorting stagecoaches and other lawman matters, and a year later when Virgil headed down to Tombstone to join his brothers Wyatt and James in that silver boomtown, the Sullivans weren't far behind.

- In an early chapter in our tale, Doctor Samuel Chambers is seated in a chair in the Union League building in downtown Philadelphia, contemplating the prospect of Gettysburg's summer heat and its effect on the old veterans who will be attending the Great Reunion. Later, Chester Morrison contemplates visiting Union Leagues in Philadelphia and New York after the war. What exactly is a "Union League" and where might you still find one even today?

- Our fictional Edgar Sullivan is placed alongside other real-life cavalrymen from the 8th Illinois,

Company E...the very men who, according to lore, were present when the very first shot of the Battle of Gettysburg was fired. Learn more about the historical background of Lieutenant Marcellus Jones (the soldier who claimed to have fired the first shot) and Sergeant Levi Shafer (the soldier whose carbine was loaned to Lieutenant Jones)...as well as other competing claims for having fired the first shot of the Battle of Gettysburg.

- A puzzle that I, your author, have yet to fully solve is the attendance during the opening ceremonies of the Great Reunion from 2:00 – 4:00 PM on July 1, 1913. Consider that: 1) more than 50,000 veterans and nearly as many spectators attended the Great Reunion, and 2) the opening ceremonies were held in the Great Tent, but 3) according to the official Pennsylvania proceedings the Great Tent contained approximately 13,000 chairs...a great number of seats, but nowhere near enough to have seated every one of veterans and spectators at the same time! How, then, does that all calculate together? Learn what I think happened...

- John K. Tener, Pennsylvania's real-life Governor and a character in the novel, received several standing ovations (and a Rebel Yell, also!) during the opening ceremonies of the Great Reunion on July 1, 1913. Did this in fact happen?

You can also learn about:

- The awe-inspiring reenactment of Pickett's Charge fifty years later to the hour

- The real-life stabbing incident at the Hotel Gettysburg on the evening of July 2, 1913 that was precipitated by – just as portrayed in our story – a "vile name" directed at Abraham Lincoln by a Philadelphia man who, upon his arrest, claimed to be the son of a Confederate General

- General Joshua Lawrence Chamberlain's inability to attend the Great Reunion, even though he had been in Gettysburg for the Reunion's final preparations only six weeks earlier

- The fireworks exhibition lasting nearly two hours on the evening of July 3, 1913

- The curiously brief visit to Gettysburg (only one hour!) by President Woodrow Wilson on Independence Day for the climactic speech of the Great Reunion

Each of these stories, woven into our tale and interleaved with the actions of both real-life and fictional characters, is worth exploring further.

Made in the USA
Columbia, SC
11 February 2019